Welcome
to
Thebes

BOOKS BY GLENDON SWARTHOUT:

Willow Run
They Came to Cordura
Where the Boys Are
Welcome to Thebes

GLENDON SWARTHOUT

Random House · New York

WELCOME
TO
THEBES

First Printing

Fiction is stranger than truth. Except for persons identified by their true names, the village, its people, and the events in which the purposes of this novel engage them, are fictional; and any correspondence between them and reality is wholly coincidental.

Grateful acknowledgment is made for the following material: "Poem XXIII" from A Shropshire Lad, authorized edition, from Complete Poems by A. E. Housman, Copyright © 1959, by Holt, Rinehart and Winston, Inc., reprinted by permission of the publisher and the Society of Authors, London; and several lines from "The House of Christmas" by G. K. Chesterton, from Collected Poems of G. K. Chesterton, Copyright, 1932, by Dodd, Mead and Company, Inc., reprinted by permission of Miss D. E. Collins and Burns & Oates, Ltd., and the publisher.

Design by Tracey Penton

in memory of
Lila Esther Swarthout
1893   1957

STROPHE : 1938

STROPHE : 1937

STROPHE : 1954

STROPHE : 1944

STROPHE : 1939

STROPHE : 1937

STROPHE : 1934

ANTISTROPHE : 1954

Harlan Murninghan

Charles Baird

Charles Reason

William Vandevelde

Oram Kropf

STROPHE : 1938

Thebes; not of antiquity but of Michigan; 1938 and long long autumn; in a certain night's sharp chamber judgment of frost upon tree; at last the leaves are fallen; then do men their duty to the tree-crop, rite singular to towns, to which only fathers and sons may be initiate: leaf-burning. October is peninsular here, as is the land, locked in by great fresh-water lakes. Like blue almoners, glacial and wise, these hoard the summer's heat and pay it out to autumn's need and bid the winter wait upon their benefaction. Thus gold and slow, drops urged from an earlier season's grape, the days take one another's stead in splendor. Finally a night of knife, irrevocable and white. Wind follows. At last the leaves are fallen. In the morning shirt-sleeved fathers shaven new and prescient step out on porches to appraise the dia-mond air and later, breakfasting, observe it a fine day to burn the leaves. That afternoon, unpent of school, their sons move through the sunslants and with rakes impose first order on chaotic lawns. Redoubts are built and from them small boys explode with cries and dogs with barking, how-itzered into joy. Sound tatters the black limbs above, maple, elm, infrequent oak, trees bereaved, and clings along the ledges of the air. There is no dusk. Day smokes out sud-denly. From brick and frame and stucco houses lamps flash a heliography of welcome to lads stomping in leaf-eared. Homing fathers find the windrows high and taking other rakes assist their elder sons in darkness rustling and an-ticipative. Not until each lawn is harvest-walled is supper called. Impatient meal, for those of the family male taste mystery and leave the table unappeased to merge again with night in corduroy and hunting canvas, the men hatted, youths bareheaded, standing then at curbs disguised to one another by the dark until their neighbors too are ready. How each home shall have its burning falls within the jurisdiction of the heart; a young man, being young, would fire the battlements of leaves at both ends; having less of time to tend hence more regard to consecrate it well his father, whose wish will yet be law a little while, prefers to set the blaze at one end only, that the hour may be assured, his testament to his son made perfect. Now as though with timing set by generations past the match is struck. Now are the streets of Thebes true streets of fire. Mounds flame across the River Button, halving the village north to south; east and west they range along the banks of Michigan's broadest stream, the Ionian, which circumscribes it on the south. Now is Thebes, underhilled from the world by the marriage of these valleys, one grid of brilliant, tonguing light and choked with smoke, oak-acrid, elm-sweet, maple-nostriled, which heaves its way aloft in columns to support the cold-starred cornice of the night. And all the art of burning leaves is this: to satiate the fire's hunger; to let it roar along the barrow's skin and following upon its wake thrust in the tines and turn, unleashing smoke, exposing strata of new fuel; this do again and again, more deeply, until what had been long October's catafalque is glowing ruin. Of many arcane legacies smalltownsmen have to leave their sons it is but one: the churning of ice cream by hand; how to fit the first and index fingers along seams to throw a curve; bewitchment of a bluegill limit from a lake's chasm in drouth; how to gentle a country girl when she has first come in to high school from the farm; how to prime the carburetor of a Ford ensepulchered in rust; with thumbs and broad grass-blade and puckered lips, creation of a whistle. So stand they, then, while small boys drowse at panes upstairs, while wives and mothers watch, doing dishes, their heads and shoulders oracular in kitchen light; so stand men by their beacons in the Theban streets and teach their sons to tine and turn the votive leaves, looking not into their faces but seeking out a hope through glare and murk, entreating with each thrust of rake, speaking not, but through a ritual silence saying:

My son, on this altar offer I my life to you. Accept it, as from my father's hand before me mine was taken. Formed

4

of minor clay, deeds near the blood, a balanced weather, fulfillments humble as sleep, days which grow beloved in their likeness, it is a good life. Do not go, stay with me in Thebes, live my life again. Then, although I pass away to ash, like smoke upon the air you breathe I shall remain. Stay, O my son, I beg you, stay and let us burn the leaves together every year; stay, and in your time keep you communion with your son; stay, and what we are will never die.

—Come with me, L.V. said.—Downtown. I have something to show you. As remarkable as the sound of his voice, level and soft over the inhalation of the flames, was his order, given on what seemed impulse, and his son stood with rake at half-thrust.—Let them smolder.

Sewell put his rake on the curb.

—Always lay a rake tine-down.

Sewell turned the rake and fell into cadence with his father, a quick count, for he was a short-legged man, yet measured and inexorable, and together they moved along the fiery street and through the tunneled smoke. It was only before the labyrinthine stucco Baird home that ceremony became circus. By nature and repute theatrical, Renis Baird had directed that his sons, Morse and Harris, rake all their leaves into one vast pyramid; boys, all three, they ran about its base delightedly and pointed upward where the cone, volcanic, spewing flame and periling a maple's branches, callioped the neighborhood's attention. To his friends Sewell spoke and to their father L.V. nodded. Not stopping gave Sewell added cause to wonder at their errand, to note the urgency implicit in their pace. Unalterable of purpose, shy of mien and gesture, calendar in the management of ends and means, in appearance combining that serenity and reserve a man of his profession studies, these were characteristic of his father; haste seldom; improvisation never. His look at you lasted. He listened to you as does a cave. His smile was an accretion. They swung abruptly onto Ionian Avenue, both main street and state highway, unique in that its center block consisted of a bridge under which was dammed the River Button, so that the stores, anchored by hidden piles, seemed to rest like boats on water. Except for through-town traffic, rare and haltless, Ionian Avenue was hushed. Two clusters of cars were angle-parked, moths drawn to the marquee of the Attic Theatre and the pulsatile windows of The Live and Let Live, a tavern whose hundred-year-old name was now elided to The Let Live. Opposite father and son winged Oram Kropf returning home from being read to; hunched, swift, he aimed himself, his white cane alate, swinging, reminding one of some early flying contraption antic to prove its scorn of earth. When they reached the building, two-storied and brick, L.V. had ready his key and unlocking the door preceded Sewell through darkness. As though it knew his hip the gate opened, the small lamp upon his desk winked on almost by itself, and there appeared, dimly, the floor of the State Bank of Thebes: two oaken customers' tables upon the black and white parquetry; three glassed-in tellers' cages; and at the front, under the high window with its State of Michigan seal and behind a spindled rail waist-high and gated, the office, carpeted in green, chaired in leather, decorated on one wall by a lithograph of the wharves of Detroit in 1836 alive with paddle-wheeled steamers freighting, so the caption annotated, a thousand emigrants daily from York State. The desk, too, was of oak, bounded on the far side by that day's issue of the *Chicago Journal of Commerce,* folded meticulously, and on the near side by the name plate black on bronze: L.V. Smith, Vice-President and Cashier. Motioning his son to follow, L.V. passed through the cages to the vault's steel door, paused briefly to twirl the combination lock, eased its weight ajar, unlocked the fire door, snapped on the bulb over the separate iron safe which held the cash and the bank's own bond assets. Of tin and lock-fronted, the antiquated safe-deposit boxes were shelved in wooden racks open at both ends. L.V. slid out one of the largest of these and led the way through a hall to the Directors' Room where, turning on yet another light, he placed the box on the long table, sat down, removed his hat and with a nod indicated the chair opposite.

—Only a damn fool, he said after Sewell was seated and waiting, looks for a boy when he has a man for a son, or a near-man. It struck me just tonight, while we were burning leaves, that you're eighteen and will be done with high school next June. Therefore it's time you knew where you stand and what you can do.

He unbuttoned his fishing jacket and lifted the thin silver chain across his vest. His habit was to hang his suit coat after work, brushing it fastidiously, and spend the evening in his vest; his shirt was clean daily, but he would change it for a fresh if going out, whether to a meeting of the Town Council or of the School Board or merely to the Creel & Cartridge. He wore dark suits of serge or worsted, somber ties minute-patterned, and pointed shoes buffed every morning on the basement steps. He was a man conscious of lint. At one end of the chain was a small key which, leaning forward, he attempted to place in the lock of the safe-deposit box. He could not. His hand quavered. Sewell was astonished. More than emotion was betrayed. To relieve the embarrassment of both, L.V. rose, drew the window shades, and taking his chair, recalled out of no context: —I came here as Teller in 1913, I wore armbands and an eyeshade. Do you know what I was paid? Fifty dollars a month. I couldn't be married for three years and then we couldn't afford you for another five. In 1924 they made me Cashier and gave me twenty-eight hundred. Do you have any idea what I get now?

Sewell shook his head.

—Four thousand.

He tried the key again and this time, his hand no longer impotent, opened the box. Laying back the lid he spread out upon the table sheaf after rubber-banded sheaf of documents ornately printed and designed, the paper stiff and flecked with color as is currency. When the box was emptied he touched arithmetically each sheaf. —These are stock certificates. They're worth at today's market $162,000.

7

—Whose are they?

—They're mine.

They listened to a clock's slow counting. With thought's irrelevance it occurred to Sewell, as it seldom did to anyone, that his father, despite his lack of height, was handsome: the brick solidity of his shoulders; the clear brown eyes, steadfast but boyish now with pride and younger, probably, for the moment than his own; finally the small mustache fitted precisely to the firm mouth and hair red-brown, unmortgaged as yet by gray, combed tight and parted in the center so that the whole portrait was already, at forty-nine, old-fashioned and impregnable.

—You're surprised. I am myself, constantly, to be worth more than any man in town except Murninghan and Baird, and maybe Claude Reichert. But I had twice this ten years ago, when we bought the house, on paper at least. The crash took it all, and I've been another ten pulling myself up by my ears. This is why I could give you a car last year. It means also that you may go to college anywhere you want. Have you thought about schools?

—Just about Ann Arbor.

—Fine. You'll be close to home and we can see you often. What will you take?

—I don't know. Probably business, depending on what I decide to do afterward.

—Have you ever considered living in Thebes after school, permanently?

—I guess I've always wanted to, really. But what would I do? Morse and Harris have everything figured out, their whole future.

—And you can't. I thought as much. L.V. folded his arms, resting gracefully his chin on his right hand. —That's another reason why I brought you down here tonight. Money makes the mare go, and when you graduate you can buy into any business in town except two. There's ample on this table and by then there'll be more. You might also come into the bank and in time succeed me. It's a good life and damned interesting. The three most important organs of a

8

man's body are his mind, his penis, and his pocketbook. People wonder why I never take a vacation, well, I would rather sit at that desk out front than be in Wall Street. As a boy, I remember when my father would bring me with him in the wagon to Big Rapids and I would sit on the curb imagining which of the men there I would like to be. I watched the banker behind his window. I watched the expressions on the faces of people going in and coming out of the bank. You saw through the skull into the brain. And for producing those expressions they paid him, the banker. He drove the finest automobile in Big Rapids, a Pope-Tribune. I had an easy choice.

From one who accepted confidences as readily as he was offered, yet who never yielded them, it was as prolonged a discourse, and as intimate, as Sewell could recall; not more incredible was it, however, than the evening's central revelation. He throttled his excitement while the safe-deposit box was refilled, the lid closed, the lock keyed; then the words split from his lips:

—All that money!

—Yes, his father said, with each assent striking the box a light blow, yes, yes, yes. I'll tell you something else, how I began keeping company with Catherine and what happened. To have one year at Ferris I worked too as a field hand after high school to put aside the hundred dollars for tuition. Room was two dollars a week, which I earned tending furnaces. Professor Hogg, your grandfather, he died when you were two, was a kind of genius at rapid calculation. He taught Mental Arithmetic and was quite famous. He wore a stovepipe hat in class. He would dash off long columns of figures on the blackboard to see who could total them fastest in his head. I was his prize student that year and eventually he invited me to his home for dinner. I had never met a girl like Catherine. There was to be a square dance at the Firemen's Hall and I asked her. Except for that meal at the Hoggs' I'd been living for a week on a bushel of apples someone let me have for a quarter. This was the winter of 1912. I borrowed a suit and we went to

9

the dance. I thought there would be refreshments, but you had to buy them and I had no money. In the middle of a set I fainted from hunger. Naturally I couldn't tell anyone what the matter was. I walked her home and when we reached her front steps I fainted again. This time I had to tell her why. She took me into the house and fed me. It was the most terrible night of my life. A boy from a stump farm, though I was twenty-one then, to escort a young lady, a real lady, to a social affair and then to take charity from her in the form of food. Food!

His chair cried out at the indignity as he pushed it from beneath him. Safe-deposit box under his arm, L.V. left the Directors' Room, placed it in its wooden pigeonhole, clanged shut and locked the vault, and quick-stepping through the tellers' cages to his desk, switched off the lamp. At the street door so sudden was his halt that Sewell, coming after, blinded by the loss of light, shouldered into him and recoiled in alarm. A moment passed in breathing. Then there grew visible the short and hatted outline, there issued words delayed by ascent to the ceiling of the State Bank of Thebes and acoustic whisper downward. Waiting for them Sewell felt a thing on its first occasion work deep within him, a force, a presence troubling and devisive: his heredity. It was as though himself older, cryptic, addressed himself younger:

—To get a son you gamble your genes, L.V. said. Win or lose, you stay in the game for life. I never believed he deserves everything his father can amass merely because he is the son. Why should he win all in one hand of showdown dealt on a dark night?

Next himself younger, bitter and sardonic, addressed himself older:

—I suppose your hero for years, L.V. said, you and your friends, the one you looked up to and aped, was Johnny Scripter. After tonight you may understand it's better to be left something more substantial than a joke no one laughs at. A story as pointless as a pinch of dried owl dung. Oh, yes, and a motorcycle.

Then the reverse, himself older, wise with love, prayerful and generous, to himself younger:

—If you must have more from the world than a small town offers, I will help you try for it, L.V. said. But what you would have here as my son, using what I can give and someday leave, representing what I represent, is more than I can express. Here you would always know who you are. If you want all this, it is yours.

Self to self at last, both young, made diffident by their monologue, eagerly after caesura:

—Let's go home and burn the leaves.

The dying streets were hushed with smoke. Father and son walked side by side with eyes half veiled against the haze; rather than seeing they sensed along the curbs mourners muffled in gloom and tending still the blackened pyres of long October. A block from home they heard the song.

A contralto voice rang out above them, the notes rich and of such energy as to rip the smoke, to carry across the entire neighborhood, the mad phrases turning to shrieks inside them: "You're my little true lover/ You're my little boy blue/ But I'm your old Auntie, darling/ And I cannot marry you."

—My God, it's your mother!

Frantically they broke into a run as the singer spurred them with a patriotic air: "And while the glorious battle raged/ It lightened freedom's will/ For, boy, the God of freedom bless'd/ The Sword of Bunker Hill."

White, larger than those surrounding it, a scrolled and filigreed veranda adjunct along one side and halfway across its front, the house crowned a corner knoll. Two majestic oaks, lightning-sawn and warped by old winds, guarded it. Running faster than either had known he could, by one street lamp's effluence they could glimpse what both feared: the high spectral figure, familiar yet risen disembodied out of smoke. Catherine Smith stood upon the flat roof of the veranda. She wore a nightgown. Her hair was down. Hands clasped formally at her waist she sang, the repertoire of her throat varying as she tried her range against the town's incredulous ears, her tones pure now with an almost angel serenity: "Flee as a bird to your mountain/ Thou who art weary of sin/ Go to the clear-flowing fountain/ Where you may wash and be clean."

Lungs like bellows they reached the house and fell for support on the clapboard until L.V. could gasp instructions. —Go up and bring her in. My God, I've been afraid of something like this. Do it slowly, be kind to her. If I go up she may throw herself off the roof. I'll get Charles Reason over here on the phone. Go on!

Sewell entered the house. Cautiously, fighting the need to run again and choke off by brute means the awful music which shamed him, he made his way to the front hall. Sight of her grand piano, mute and reproachful in a corner of the living room, transfixed him; he remembered; the gift of his father ten years ago, she had refused to play it; she had not performed in public for three; yet often in the afternoons, coming home from school, he sensed a concert interrupted, for chords died away in drape folds, secret harmony lingered everywhere; the memory made grief of horror. He doubled into tears. He mounted the stairs as Catherine Smith resumed her first demented ballad: " 'Tis grand to be going to school, dear/ 'Tis fine to be dress'd in blue/ But I'm your old Auntie, darling/ And I cannot marry you."

He rushed into her room. Sobbing through the open window he begged her to come in. Her song ceased. She obeyed at once and accepted his help across the sill where with suspicious warmth she took him briefly in her arms.

—Darling Sewell, don't cry. Did you like to hear me sing again? I haven't seen you cry since you were such a little boy.

Awkwardly, for she was taller than he, he helped her sit upon the bed. He found himself on his knees before her. He heard downstairs his father's desperate telephoning. Smiling, tender, with stemlike fingers she winged the tears from his cheeks. He was startled by the gray paths in her long hair, hidden heretofore by coils and tortoise combs mathematically arranged. Until this night, when she was undone, taken by the mind's surprise, by what other feminine chicaneries had been maintained that grace which was innocent, that comeliness unartful, that cool illusion which gave the lie to forty-six?

—I can't bear to see you unhappy, dear. Did you know your father cried the first time we ever went out together? It was the year he attended Ferris. He was Father's, your grandfather's, best student, and he took me to a dance. I had few beaux, I was considered too intelligent and father too formidable. Have you burned all the leaves, dear? Lucian was so poor, so pitifully poor. He'd been existing on apples, and at the dance he fainted from lack of nourishment. He was too proud to tell me why. Except for her loquacity, her metastasies, Catherine Smith gave no other sign of dispossession. She was composed, serious, the carriage of her head regal; and kneeling before her Sewell wondered as he always had that so delicate a shell could house the manifold machinery of life: so fragile was the bone of her shoulder that it resembled the cross-stave of a kite, so slender her throat that no more precarious a vessel for a voice of such power could be conceived; she had no bosom. —I do wish Carrie Murninghan might have heard me tonight, she must think my voice is gone. Why, dear, I've been practicing for years, here alone in the house while you were at school. Do you remember what I did to his new car? It seems to me I used a chisel, yes that was it, a chisel, and it was very, very difficult for me, the Lord's labor, I worked at it nearly all night. And bringing me home Lucian fainted again. This time he told me, he was simply hungry. I took him into the kitchen and gave him broth. That old song, Sewell, the one called "Auntie," you'd never remember but I used to sing you to sleep with it when you were a baby. Chicken broth it was, and Lucian was literally starving, and he ate and cried at the same time, he was so shy and ashamed. I presume he never forgot it. But darling, there was absolutely no truth in what my father, Professor Hogg, once said, not to me of course, but to my uncle. It was while Lucian was working in the

13

bank here to save enough so we could be married. We had to wait three years, you know, and I worked too, in Big Rapids, in the office of a furniture manufacturer. Everyone thought it quite daring and suffragette of me to work, but I was an excellent typist and bookkeeper, I graduated from Ferris in both. Your grandfather was very eccentric, I must admit, perhaps that's why I've always tried to be genteel and unassuming. He wore a stovepipe hat in his classes. I overheard him say to my uncle that Lucian, after we were married, might have to make his sexual appointments with me two weeks in advance, by mail, and on business stationery—

—Catherine, dear, Charles Reason has stopped by, her husband said. —He'd like to talk to you.

—Charles, how pleasant!

As, smiling, she extended her hand to the doctor, L.V. took Sewell into the hall and closed the door behind them. —You'd better go and stay at the Baird's.

On the day following there was not one who had not attended by reportage Catherine Smith's recital, who was not apprised that upon Charles Reason's recommendation she had been taken in the night to a private home near Battle Creek, not one in all of Thebes.

14

STROPHE : 1937

Petitioning with his tongue he parted soft, girl-sculptured lips until anodic contact; with his tongue he tempted hers to dance. (—Holy cow, can she French-kiss!) Lovely were the waters of her mouth. Society with her breathing made jubilant the muscles in his back, his shoulders. In her silence, heavy-lashed, in her impassivity he sensed triumph to be; the change of late had made him sure of her at last. He had looked in vain for the toss of head and foal-curl of smile and nostril; the awkward, winning abandon of arms and legs was gone. Closely he had watched, every animal thirst alert to what impended; more than a season's girlish turning, the alteration in her was character-wide, identity-deep. It was as though the hero's daughter had been overnight reborn the offspring of the village idiot. Unnerved not so much by bereavement as by the riding away forever, as it were, of her champion, vulnerable emotionally she must be now to any assault, he intuited, surrender she must, not to a boy but to circumstance. Testing, importunate, he clasped the coltish length of her thighs, inducing friction to the hem of her cheap cotton shorts, and she did not demur; lifted to her halter and the barrier of those breasts which, at games of post office, had been the first to rob his hand of innocence, and she did not say no. She was sixteen, his age; she was in the tenth grade, his also. (—One of these days she'll break down and put out and I want to be there when she does!) Twisting her mouth free, Arlene commenced into his cheek to whimper her despair, willing he should have his way if only someone, anyone, would listen. She was terrified. She could not explain to herself what had happened. Invitations to parties had stopped, apparently because it embarrassed other kids to be in her presence. It was awful, awful. It drove her crazy to think that what she could not be forgiven was not what she had done but who she was, and gee, whatever could she do about that? Unbuttoning her halter he spread both hands to the bough of her body, shaping them to the satiny completions, fruit tensile and superb beyond her years. (—Say, how'd you like to walk barefoot through an acre of those?") With inhalation hot he bowed his head to try the sweetness thereof from stems pleasure-whetted and roseate. For her mother it was even worse. Little kids called "Halt! Halt!" after her in the street. She had begun to drink; he must not tell a soul, though probably everybody knew; she had loved Johnny so! He knew the job the Town Council had, out of gratitude and commemoration, given her, that of exchanging new light bulbs for burnt-out at the Light and Power office. While she whispered at his cheek, engarrisoned against his hands by sorrow, he loosed her shorts and steadily eased them lower on her hips. Well, yesterday her mother had been drinking and, toward the day's end, rubbed raw by eyes averted and mouths tightened in penalty, had detonated into temper: screaming she hurled bulbs at floor, at walls until Earl Blue, the Town Constable, arrived, taking it for a repetition of the shooting, and somehow got her home. Now isolate, without income, she remained sodden, victimized as was her daughter by the self-derision of an entire village.

—Sewell, no!

This as he attempted forcibly to remove her shorts, accompanied by a hysteric flail of her elbow which caught him at the neck. Fisted, he glared at her in pain and arousal, scouring his anger for speech which would rob her of defense.

An hour earlier he had picked up Morse and Harris Baird and, by design, Arlene, ostensibly to search for the more than twelve thousand dollars the gunmen had cached somewhere in the area. Along this sand road they had careened, State Police and a ragtag posse of American Legionnaires from Thebes armed with shotguns and World War Springfields in pursuit; their dark menace-blue La-Salle sedan had been found out of gasoline; then they themselves were captured in the woods without a shot fired; the

18

whereabouts of the money they had never revealed, claiming it thrown from the sedan window during the chase, and it had since been a summer recreation of young people to treasure-hunt. To date the only prizes were a .38-caliber Hopkins & Allen revolver and, in a woolen sock, steel-jacketed bullets for the weapon. It was a day morose and cloudy, one of those of August in Michigan when summer seems of a mood to regret July the spendthrift, which gave too much too soon of brilliance. The three boys and the girl had driven out Ionian Avenue past that implausible stone exhibit which marked the town's limit on the east. At either side of the state highway towered three columns, one Doric, one Ionic, one Corinthian; standing baseless upon a slab, they supported an architrave triangular in shape, saluting the traveler with this inscription: WELCOME TO THEBES. Quarried in Vermont the shafts, traditionally fluted, were each four feet in diameter, their capitals decorative in the case of the Ionic and Corinthian and simple in that of the Doric; the total width of slab and architrave was twenty feet, the total height twenty-two. This composition's twin stood at the town's western bound where the highway lures level for a mile, but the right-hand set had been toppled some years previously by the battering ram of young Irwin Reichert's automobile, driven head-on into it at great speed and never, as memorial to him and example to teen-age drivers, reërected. Preposterous here, flagrant traffic-stopping mimics of antiquity yet touching somehow in the marble fervor of their homage to an age entombed by centuries and hence serene, the twelve columns had been the gift to Thebes of Grethe Kropf in the 1920's. It was tribute to the Town Council that they were not floodlit by night. Retracing the gunmen's flight the four climbed northward from the floor of the Ionian valley on the way to Smyrna into the fertile corn and wheat lands and turning west again at Delphi Grange Hall onto the sand road, parked beside an orchard and took up the search along the roadside. Presently Sewell had maneuvered Arlene into the back seat of his car, the new Dodge his father had given him that spring, while Morse and Harris continued to explore culvert, ditch and thicket out of sight.

—Lene, damn you, I'll give it to you straight, how long do you think you can let us play with your tits and go up your leg and keep on saying no? After what your father did you don't have a friend left in school except me and Morse and Harris! You just told me about your mother—well, you've made me wait a hell of a long time and if you don't put out now you can cross me off your list, too! I mean it, Lene, he cried, this is your last chance! You've been some-body in this town but you'll be nobody, nobody!

Had he plotted for weeks, had he penciled out the phrases using every lewd resource of his boy's vocabulary, he could not have wrought more immediate and devastating effect. He raped will. He deflowered spirit.

Her eyes blinded themselves. Her hands unclenched at her sides. She sank into the velour, assuming helplessly that posture which admits the ordination of her sex.

Sewell reached. In seconds he had stripped her.

Beauty! He had not known its signification in flesh. He could not speak, so limited is the language of wonder. His eyes burned and watered alternately. Urned symmetry of hips; whited dune of belly; lode triangular and vine-lost from whence the ore of man is taken and to which it must return.

Roughly he disposed her limbs. With crimson difficulty ingress was accomplished.

(—A little oofum-poofum now and then is cherished by the wisest men.)

She moaned once: —Pretend I'm Jane Murninghan.

Upon her he killed the boy and girl they had been.

When he had done he left the car and walked rapidly down the sand road until he found Morse and Harris.

—Forget the money. He came close. —Lene's ready. I knew she was, that's why I picked her up. Go back to the car, one at a time.

—One, two, three, hike, Morse said, already into his cat-stride.

—If she gives you any argument, mention Johnny.

Sewell and Harris waited. Omen of winter, the afternoon grew chill under a low scud of clouds; soon would come the long long autumn, the time of leaf-burning. With cupped hands Harris blew across grass and produced a plaintive, curlew cry. He was fifteen, a year their junior, but so excellent had been his record, so vehement his desire to compete on equal adolescent terms with his brother, that he had been permitted to hurdle eighth grade and enter high school with him.

Morse returned. Harris got to his feet and peered uncertainly through his glasses up and down the road.

—Scared? asked Sewell.

—A little oofum-poofum now and then is cherished by the wisest men, Morse intoned, underlining "wisest."

Deprived of alternative, Harris left them. Morse haunched across from his friend. —You going out for football?

Sewell shook his head. With the coach, who had tried last autumn to make a guard of him when he dreamed only of the backfield, he had quarreled bitterly and dropped himself from the squad; he suckled his rancor; Thebes High, a Class C school, had only one coach, which meant that pride had rendered him ineligible for basketball and track as well.

—You remember up on the Jordan? Morse asked. —We never said it, right out, but this is what we thought, this afternoon happening. And it did.

After a long wait they became restive. —We better go see, Morse suggested, concerned. —He's maybe hung up or something.

They met Harris and Arlene leaving the car like the survivors of an accident, slowly and in shock. Her halter hung loose from her shoulders; he had put on her shorts but in one hand he held balled her panties. She turned into the orchard and tilted against the nearest tree, embracing it as does a child knees, scarring her face to its trunk. —She said to pretend she was Jane Murninghan, Harris blurted. His face was disfigured by effort to dam tears. —It's the worst thing we've ever done, any of us! They stared at Arlene

21

Scripter. A tall girl outcast, ravaged, with long massed hair of a hue called locally "fire-engine red," she made herself daughter to the young tree, her sandals planted flat upon the ground as though to seek the earth's immutability and rescue through its parent roots.

—Listen to me, Lene, Sewell said, you know none of us can ever marry you, don't you? You know that. She was incapable of response. —But we're your friends, we'll make sure you aren't left out of anything. All three of us will take you out in public. Every date we have with Jane we'll have one with you, so you'll be just as popular as she is. That's fair, isn't it? But you have to be fair with us, Lene. If we date you steady you have to put out every time. That's the way it's got to be or you're nobody again, all right? Nobody, remember that. She must have heard, yet so fiercely was she knotted to the tree that sundering her arms taxed the three boys. There fell an evanescent rain as they helped her to the car and drove her back to Thebes.

STROPHE : 1954

The world is inverted: riding a sophist sky below they gaze
upon black earth above, paradoxic and star-pierced. Supine
on plastic rafts the two men drift counterclockwise round
the pool in the patio of the house mountain-set near Phoenix,
Arizona. The pool is underlit; the action of the filter ca-
rousels the rafts along the coping slowly and as, their lower
legs atrail in lambent water, they circumnavigate beneath
the diving board, upon which bottle, ice bucket, and
carafe are stationed, they freshen drinks. The younger man
is Sewell Smith, the older Peckham Hill, his editor, out
from New York by plane this afternoon. This day of May
the temperature has been one hundred but night and water
now are cool; the smooth turf of the patio is spiked in
beds with its antithesis, the cholla, buckhorn, and saguaro
cactus; blue should be the color of the pool but it is chal-
cedony, for its deeper end is filled up with a jetsam of
lawn furniture: aluminum chairs and lounges, a wrought-
iron table and four matching chairs, an outdoor grill, a
sun umbrella and its standard; T-shaped and low, the house
would be imposing except that all the facing wall, win-
dowed from foundation to eave, to frame the whole vast
mural of the light-strewn desert valley, is destroyed, and
plate-glass shards have cut to petals the blossoms of gardenia
and natal plum. For several hours Peckham Hill has sought
the epithet which might abridge the entire scene compre-
hensibly; "bizarre," "supernatural," and "lunatic" he has
run through and is now reduced to adjective defeat.
    —When did she do this?
    —Last night. I went into Scottsdale for something and
when I came back she was gone. She probably flew back to
Vegas.
    —How long have you lived with her?
    —Off and on two years. Mostly on, that's the only time

she was any good. Upright she was stupid and sick, sick. All her brains were in her ass. Besides that she was only nineteen and had problems. A thousand bucks' worth of damage and I suppose I'm liable.

—Whose digs are they?

—Some guy in Kansas City, some shoe-polish tycoon. I ship him six hundred a month.

—She was the girl in *Looking,* wasn't she? Peckham Hill shortens to one word the title, an elision habitually affected by those in publishing. That previous autumn's *Looking for a Location,* the second novel by Sewell Smith, had been a subfictionalized account of the febrile, deviative search for a film location by an independent producing company via chartered plane over much of the western United States; enplaning originally with the producer, director, production manager, the author and a scenarist, the expedition had eventually freighted itself with two stars, the husband of one, the ex-wife of the other, the producer's secretary, the director's mistress, and a starstruck girl native to a small town in New Mexico; with the sexual and creative frenetics of this troupe the book had been entirely concerned.

—That's right. After Vegas we slept around L.A. for a year, first at a beach house at Malibu, a thousand a month, then that place up one of those damn canyons, eight hundred, you know, the place CBS did "Person-to-Person" of me from, with her throwing her butt around as my "secretary," what a crock of crap. Then she took off, like now, and I didn't see her again till this winter, one night on The Strip. She'd become a real pig, but soft-heart, I brought her over here with me. I can't figure it: pro whores never have problems, only amateurs. From the outdoor grill on the pool's bottom an unburnt charcoal briquet is excreted, bobbing to the surface at his elbow; flung haphazardly, it ricochets off the flagstones through the window-gap into the house. —Speaking of money, I'm damn near flat. What am I due?

—Nothing, I'm afraid. You'll have our regular statement next month.

—What's that mean, nothing?

Peckham Hill explains that they have shipped something under thirty thousand of *Looking,* but the novel's apogee on the *Times'* list had been sixth place and now the unsold copies were coming in for credit from retailers. That was the old saw in the book business: gone today, here tomorrow. Unquestionably the reviews had been responsible for the disappointing sales. There would be another paperback payment due the first of the next year, 1955, but he feared hardcover returns would account for most of that.

—Listen, goddammit, the government is on my back. I'm in a real bind on taxes, and don't say who isn't. I know you're supposed to stash enough to cover the year in advance and not touch it, but I didn't, I blew it. My monkey is, I'm a year behind. It wasn't screwing IRS, I just didn't have it, so we made a deal: I make it up in quarterlies this year, four shots plus interest plus penalties, but even then I'm still into them for five thousand, half next month, half in September, and the second tab I don't have. You guys want your tiger in Leavenworth? Jesus, isn't there anything upcoming from anywhere?

About all that could be anticipated, Peckham Hill admits, were odds and ends of foreign monies from *Benison,* but they, as he, Sewell, knew, were very erratic.

Sewell grasps the diving board with such force that his raft is almost overturned. —So you big-time sonabitches get rich again and I take another screwing, just the way I did on *Benison!*

—You may not believe it, Sewell, but without the paperback windfall we'd have lost a packet on *Looking.* At your insistence we overprinted and overbudgeted the advertising. We will have to remainder close to ten thousand copies, and after the impact of the reviews no amount of advertising could have saved the book.

—Nothing personal, Peck. He unhoists himself disgust-

27

edly. —But how in Christ's name a man can make half a million dollars in four years and have nothing to show for it I don't know. Except for what you did to me on taxes. Money. If you've never had it or always had it you don't know what it means; the only way to find out is to come into a lot of it suddenly. I remember one time when I was a kid, my father showing me over a hundred thousand in stock certificates. I thought it was great, sure, but I never understood till lately how it must have hit him, to have that much. It gets a man in the guts. Nobody will ever write the Great American Novel until he opens every safe-deposit box in the country.

Several minutes are required for each revolution of the pool. Arms crossed beneath his head, Sewell reflects while Peckham Hill, attaining the board, refills his glass and drifts along afterward.

—Indians. They've always intrigued me. I know where the Apaches and Navahos were, but what tribes were resident around here in the old days, around Phoenix?

The question is transitional. A man near sixty, he resembles some exotic insect blundered over the coping into the water; his arms and legs are wandlike, the skin pallid; under voluminous swimtrunks he poises on the raft his central bulk, his belly, like an inflated ball easy of puncture, and atop this shell his drink. His face is small and fine-featured and his eyes, pouched and alert, seem not to enjoy but to proofread the stars. Orotund of voice, his enunciation is clipped and British. An editor for thirty years, of these Chief Editor for twelve, and a stockholder in the firm for five, to Sewell he seems at the moment a burnished, cultivated beetle, antecedent of preparatory school and university, a summer place in Maine, dutiful theater-going, the collection of eighteenth-century editions, wide friendships in London, and dry-fly fishing on old Adirondack streams, sticked out now from his hand-tailored hole into a world alien and dangerous. Correspondents by necessity, the two have spent together in New York no more than ten days, most of that in combat over editorial issues posed by the manuscript of *Looking,* and the wariness, the mutual dis-respect crusted over by common business interest with which they parted then have carried over to this afternoon's re-union. In reply to the question Sewell breaks wind raucously.

—Papagos, Pimas, damned if I know. I read somewhere they grew melons and gourds, sort of agricultural shitless wonders, and got the hell kicked out of them by the Apaches every hour on the hour. Peck, let's quit sparring around. You didn't fly out here to check the goddamn aborigines.

—You're very perceptive. He hesitates, indexing to use the language and sequence his mind has stored. —No, my mission is not only distasteful but unprecedented. I ask you a great favor, that you hear me out no matter what reaction intervenes. The fact is, Sewell, we in publishing have had to deal since the war with a phenomenon new to us, what we call the "ancillary writer." He is young, he is coarse, if he has had an education he remains unbenefited by it, the very vulgarity of his writing is its best advertisement, and his material is taken so grossly from his experience that his work is, literally, his life, so that criticism of it constitutes criti-cism of his own character. He has, however, one undeniable talent: he makes money. For himself and for us. Gads, I must diet, between my ribs and hips I have the world's largest wen. Well, the belly has a short memory. It's no longer extraordinary for a new writer to realize—not from hardcover sales although they, too, are sometimes a freakish factor, but from the ancillary rights, serialization, ex-cerpting, television, paperback reprint and motion picture —from a quarter to half a million dollars on a first novel. In these of course we share, so that we're way ahead finan-cially no matter what the novel's literary merits or its luck with the trade. His name national by virtue of his riches, such a writer continues to write; usually his first book has been a war novel, usually his second laments, amid the Hol-lywood or New York or European setting to which the af-fluence from his first book has brought him, the *Reader's-Digest*-fraudulence of commercial success; he continues to work, as I say, the critics continue to assail him, his publisher continues merrily to wholesale the ancillary rights. His own edition, which in the past has been its own end, announcing brilliance and arbitering taste, is now an unimportant, if not apologetic, means. But this is not publishing; it is merchandising; and we know it. We must be businessmen, but we must think of ourselves as something more, we must clutch as to a straw men drowning in money the pretension that we have an obligation both to the reading public and to literature herself. If we don't we are reminded of our function and purpose by the critics. Let us use as an example your case. What— At the shallows his raft collides with his host's knees. Sewell has left his own raft and sits half immersed upon the middle step of the three which descend underwater. —Would you unreef me? Thanks. Beneath Sewell's eyes glides Peckham Hill, averting his to his glass, clattering the ice decisively. —Where were we? Yes, *A Benison on Our Meat.* Despite considerable misgiving we brought the book out almost unedited on the grounds that the very crudeness of its writing would make more natural, more instinctive, the savagery of its indictment of war. Whitman's "barbaric yawp over the roofs of the world," Walt Whitman, the American poet. Incidentally, I wondered often where you found your epigraph, certain you must be unfamiliar with Herrick. Just recently it occurred to me to look under "benison" in Bartlett, and presto. In any event, we were as bowled over by the success of the book as you, otherwise we would certainly have protected you taxwise before publication. Think of it: number one best-seller for a year, book-club selection, finally a motion picture which swept the Academy Awards. To be candid, the firm has netted more from *Benison* than from any other novel we have ever done. This brings me to *Looking.* At the skimmer drain's aperture he puts out a hand to arrest his progress, pausing to examine the weir through which is drawn the surface litter of the pool. —I don't wish to be brutal but you have earned forthrightness. *Looking* is a very bad book, Sewell. Solecisms, failures of syntax, grammatical errors, improprieties in diction; these we expected it would be charged with, but that week of debate with you in New York about them was all we could endure. We let them go. As to the stuff of the book, I have no doubt it's an accurate transcript of the sexual ruckabout in which a film company may indulge, but beyond that and the report of your nightmarish attempts to collaborate on a shooting script with those people, there is absolutely nothing in it, absolutely nothing. To take one instance, your title. *Looking for a Location* was what the company was doing literally; but on a higher, symbolic plane every member of it was looking, every one of us looks, for some location, some place where we may find peace and accomplishment and the sense of participation in man's endless, painful, marvelous caravan. Of this possibility you had never a glimmer. It might have been a fine novel. Dear me, I'm being interminable about this. Well, we surrendered on writing, we surrendered on content, avarice won out over scruples and judgment. Surely the salve of the ancillary rights would heal our wounds, and we did have a fat paperback contract out of it. Then came the reviews. We were braced for mortification, but what we got was murderous. By the way, I approve your decision never to read them. We have no choice. The reviews of *Looking* have been the talk of the trade; the book itself they dismissed with a few sentences as unworthy of serious comment. Instead, it is the firm which has borne the brunt. We should not have published the novel, we should not have published you, in fact, or anyone like you. All the guilt, the treachery to American literature is ours alone.

—We are attacked personally by men of the caliber and reputation of Donald Adams, Edmund Wilson, David Daiches, to name but three. In the history of our house this has never before happened. It places in double jeopardy the critical reception of our fiction lists in the future. It means, in brief, and ironically, that on both moral and financial scores we cannot longer afford either the luxury or the expense of the ancillary writer.

—Get to the point.

The snarl dismays Peckham Hill. With toes prehensile he

31

stays his drift. —We in the firm have been unhappy men of late, Sewell; we have agonized first over our decision and then over who should convey it to you. I volunteered at last because I've been your editor, although in name only, and hence most culpable. It is a cruel delegation, since—

—Get to the point!

—Very well. You'll recall that our *Looking* contract stipulates we are to have first acceptance or rejection of your next book. We waive that stipulation. This has the effect of disassociating us, of making you a free agent in the disposal of your next book. In fine, our relationship, legal as well as literary, is at an end. We regret—

His voice is drowned by the splash. Sewell is over him, seizing him by the throat.

—You New York prick!

Then his ears are stopped with water, his eyes and mouth awash as his raft careens and he is plunged under, throttled, his head banged against the poolside.

Freed as unexpectedly, his feet thud bottom and he heaves up belly-deep to collapse bent over the coping. For a time he remains prostrate, coughing, choking, still terrified by the ferocity of the attack, until outrage strengthens him to turn. Only then is the reason for his deliverance apparent. Sewell Smith sits on the steps looking down at his submerged foot. Red plumes from it, mingling bloodily with the gray of the water. In the thrashing about he has stepped on and splintered the editor's glass. They are long silent. At length Peckham Hill is able to gasp.

—You, you can't take pride in your work or in the way you live. Have you never done anything you can be proud of!

—One thing.

—To be strangled, physically!

—You've let me go.

—We have, we certainly have.

—I've hurt my back again.

—Bully for you! Great Lord!

—I'm sorry.

—Sorry!

—What'll I do?

—Dig ditches! Drive a truck!

—My God, what'll I do.

The editor is anxious to escape the pool but will not approach the steps or his attacker. Grunting at the exertion he clambers over the coping and pads to the far end and seats himself with fundamental sighs upon the diving board. His throat aches, his whole system is aggrieved.

—I like what I've had. I'm used to it. You can't just fly out here and take everything away.

—Oh? And what does "everything" signify? Money? That you seem to have squandered. Your name? The critics have canceled that very effectively. I admit to some slight compassion for you as a creature spawned of greed and exalted by the mass media, but I can't feel the least sympathy for you as a person.

In two hands Peckham Hill grips the board. Are those far-smoldering lights, the wonders of the valley below, the eyes of beasts? Is this upon his skin moisture's rapid evaporation or can it be the hot malevolent breath of night embodied? Only yesterday, he recalls with longing shiver, crossing Park at 50th on his way to luncheon, there was rain upon his cheek, benign and gentlemanly rain. There, in the pool's gray hold, what mad cargo is this, manifest for what psychotic voyage? Why must he engage in colloquy at forty feet with ignorance after the final curtain of relationship has fallen? How came he to this wild and unbecoming place and to this brutish company? Quickly he fills another glass, quickly drinks. Suddenly he is shouted at:

—I'll find somebody else! A hell of a lot of publishers would break their butts to get me!

—A few, doubtless. Not of our stamp and tradition, however. And provided you do produce anything else, which I rather doubt. Your sort generally has one book in him, two at the most, then the pool, artificial to begin with, clutters with rubbish and becomes unfit for use.

—I'll be better, damn you! In the last year I've read the

world's twenty greatest novels, I found a list! And also some books on how to write fiction. I'll quit drinking! Nobody'll ever know my next book is even by me!

Despite himself Peckham Hill is touched. Boisterous, absurd, comic the boasts, hurled not at him but at the entire literary planet, it is not these qualities but their naïveté which moves him, their immaturity by contrast with the squat figure which confronts its fate bowlegged, broadgauged of neck and thigh, martial of jaw: a balding, fatbuttocked pathetic Jove of the paperbacks throwing stones for want of thunderbolts. To smile at pathos, he reflects, is to laugh at tragedy.

—Sewell, I have no axe to grind now. I leave in the morning and very probably we shall never see each other again. I do have some consolation. If you were to stop writing for several years, study the English language, assess the conduct of men with more understanding and magnanimity, all might not be lost.

Sewell Smith reënters the water and stiffly, muffling an exclamation of pain, works himself prone onto the nearest raft. —I can't stop writing. The money's gone and there's nothing else I know but the Army. I'm thirty-three years old.

—By the way, how much water does a pool of this size contain?

—I think about twenty-five thousand gallons. The truth is, I haven't written a word in over a year. You don't have to tell anybody, Hill. I don't have any ideas. If I do have to go on writing, what could I write about?

—Yourself, I suppose, that seems to be fashionable of late: your artistic travail, how you are misunderstood and vilified by the critics, treacherous publishers, so on and so on, together with snippets from earlier, unpublishable work. And how long does it take for all that to be filtered?

—I never needed anything as much in my life. Eight hours. God, God, I have to have an idea.

Downward Peckham Hill considers. Plastic bark and lone

34

passenger float now over the wrought-iron table and its four chairs; astern, as though from some ill-captained ship losing fuel, the delicate blood-plume leeches. —Well, let's take stock, he proceeds sympathetically. —Describing the ancillary writer, I mentioned war and the failure of success as his favorite subjects. The fact is, these and a third have predominated American literature for a generation, the third theme being identity. The novelist returns home to grub sentimentally or Freudianly for his own roots. The archaeology of origins. As a theme it's been horribly debased, but I don't suppose that makes it any less pertinent or worth treating, conditional of course on the integrity the writer brings to it. Wolfe and Marquand come favorably to mind. I recall one item from the biographical sketch you furnished us for the jacket of *Benison:* you hailed from somewhere called Thebes, Michigan. Does it exist or did you read ancient history for a name?

—It's real, a town of two thousand. Forty-one miles north and west of Grand Rapids. I haven't been there in fifteen years, since 1939.

—But the name.

—It's in a valley, of the Ionian River, and in the valley are a lot of towns with names like that: Smyrna, Corinth, Tyre, Sparta, Naxos, Carthage. I don't know why. Head reared he hawks, expels, and ends the pretty foundering of a moth in spittle. —Thebes killed itself trying to be different. They had marble Greek columns at the town limits and the movie was the "Attic" and the weekly paper was the *Argus-Advertiser*. But the whole deal was screwed-up. For example, the River Button runs right under the main street before it joins the Ionian. There used to be a lot of clams, and what they called "button boats" went up and down, scows with rows of lines and hooks dragging bottom and bringing up clams. Then they dried them in big stinking piles and sold the shells for shirt buttons. That's why the name, the River Button. Except that all this was done on the Ionian, somebody just thought Button would be a quaint goddamn name for a river. Typical. Once I wanted to live there all my life. Now I hate it. A small town like that is the bunghole of the country.

—Don't mistake my mention of the theme for a suggestion, Sewell. A subject should force itself upon an author from within; if the imaginative combustion isn't spontaneous nothing good or valid can possibly come of it. No, you'd be better advised to act on my earlier counsel. In any event, I ought to warn you that our decision is irrevocable.

To the metrics of the filter motor beyond the patio wall Peckham Hill fits the word *irrevocable* and listens. This precedent before them, summoning up their nerves and morals, would that other publishers might now reach a hundred like decisions! He is, he knows, a bird too fastidious, too urbane ever to adapt to regions as sere and spiny and 'inhospitable as Arizona; or, metaphorically, ever to accommodate his sensibilities to that desertscape which is contemporary American literature, a dry salt sea citizened with snakes, lizards, scorpions, all manner of repellent creatures: literary businessmen who turn books out with menstrual rhythm, exhibitionists more preoccupied with dust-jacket photography than with their inability to construct a simple plot; paranoiac monsters on the brink of murder; a gamut of deviates and aberrants who session other deviates and aberrants and thus use the whole reading continent for a couch; the women, for the most part plump aged hens a-cluck on roosts of eggs romantic and infertile or clever young mommies who sit their clever children upon toidy-seats and produce catchy titles and bestsellers; circus artists who swing back and forth across the nation on trapezes called TWA and American and United, combing out a scurfy living at the pendular extremes of Broadway and of Hollywood; finally the sophisticates, Connecticut of style but The South, Suh, of inflection, playing with rhetoric and time-schemes and symbols as do baboons with their genitals, ever-promising sex-sly darlings of the academics, so ignorant of, so fearful of facing ebullient, manifold, undiscovered America-here-and-now that they must

flee to Italy or North Africa or the Orient, there backdrop
their works, and from there plane home every five years
luggaged exactly, having weighed and rid themselves of
every overweight ounce of risk, with sixty-six pounds of balls-
lettres. Poetry: masturbated to exhaustion; the drama:
buried alive and cannibal of its own worms; the short story:
*New Yorker*ized; the novel: pimped, cocained, and book-
clubbed into absolute bondage. The Time of the Electric
Typewriter. Of it he has had a bowelful, from it he is almost, lacking four years, free. Ladies? and gentlemen?
thank God! He grew old, he grew old, but he'd be damned
for petrification before he wore his trousers rolled. Another
charcoal briquet sewages up from the pool's intestinal tan-
gle; antidote to nausea, Peckham Hill thinks again of
yesterday's rain and, by memory's kind association, of yesterday's men of letters. As a junior editor raw from college he had been sent for a year to work in England at his
firm's correspondent firm; London, as it had been to Jamie
Boswell, was his beef and mild; like Pepys he kept a diary;
its most precious page recorded a meeting with a great
man. Carrying a letter of introduction from F. N. Doubleday
he had gone into the green and prolix Kentish countryside,
to Bishopsbourne, and there taken tea and talked for two
hours with Joseph Conrad. When he emerged it had been
raining, the most civilized rain of his life. Musing so, fingertips once more scanning the bruised flesh of his throat, he
does not note below him that oath sworn, that invocation breathed over unnatural water:
—Thebes.

STROPHE : 1944

On 1 May 1944 the 11th Infantry Division passed control of its sector to a relieving division and moved back into the dune area near the sea to train for "Operation Buffalo." This was the effort by which the German arch of iron around the Anzio-Nettuno beachhead, unbreakable for more than three months, was at last to be destroyed, enabling the American and British forces to reinforce, perhaps to lead, the general advance of the Fifth Army from Cassino toward Rome, twenty-five miles northward. Keystone of the enemy defensive system about the beachhead was the town of Cisterna, an artillery-rubbled ruin of masonry turned into a fortress; and crucial to the taking of Cisterna was the clearing out of a draw averaging sixty-five feet in width and thirty-five feet in depth which moated the town laterally some one thousand yards to its front. During the three-months' stalemate, night patrolling ascertained, its lower sides had been rat-holed by several companies of the 2nd Panzer Grenadier Regiment, Hermann Goering Division, with tunnels, rifle pits, and machine-gun emplacements. It had been thickly sown with antipersonnel and antitank mines. Its bed was barricaded at intervals with belts of triple-concertina barbed wire. It had been dug originally by Mussolini to drain and reclaim the Pontine Marshes for agriculture. It was designated on maps as Fossa Feminamorta, or "Ditch of Dead Women." The plan of "Operation Buffalo" may be broken into its tactical components as follows: pressure was to be put and maintained on the entire German MLR, or Main Line of Resistance, by all divisions in VI Corps; the 11th Infantry Division was to assault Cisterna frontally, committing all three of its regiments in line, in its center the 13th, responsible among other objectives for the Ditch of Dead Women; and during the period of training the 13th Regiment was to have every assistance of Corps

41

and Division G-2, Intelligence, and G-3, Operations, in devising means to take and clear this most formidable of obstacles before Cisterna. Of the various expedients put forward by the best military brains available, three were adopted. First, in order to render the enemy will more complaisant to attack, it was decided to have, during the general artillery preparation for the breakthrough, a TOT, or Time on Target shoot, along the entire length of the ditch. Employing nine battalions of field artillery, continuous and precise lines of shellfire would fall along both lips of the ravine while the two short sides of the long rectangular "box," composed again of continuous and precise shellfire, would roll inexorably toward one another. The TOT, or box barrage, would be of twenty minutes' duration. Second, a new vehicle called a "scorpion" would precede the infantry advance up the Fossa Feminamorta. This was a medium tank equipped forward with a large rotating flailing device made of chains; although not yet tested in combat, it was believed the scorpion, descending into the ditch down a ramp cut by engineers during the night before the assault, would detonate all mines in its path and, in addition, breach easily the barbed-wire belts. Third, to the problem of moving foot troops up the ditch without cover, subjected as they would be to streams of crossfire from both banks, the Division's Commanding General himself addressed a solution. He had long awaited the opportunity afforded by such a tactical situation to construct and try out in the field an innovation which he called "battle sleds." Narrow steel half-tubes mounted on runners, wide enough to carry one armed infantryman lying down, twelve of these could be harnessed by iron rods behind the scorpion tank and towed; using two other tow tanks behind the lead scorpion, to their consternation the Germans emplaced in the Ditch of Dead Women might then be challenged by three full squads of heavily armed soldiers brought to them in perfect safety and battle-ready. These last small details of "Operation Buffalo" settled, training began at once in an atmosphere of confident resolution. Div Arty gridded and coördinated its TOT shoot. The battle sleds were fashioned and the complement of men to ride them was filled, first by asking for volunteers, and when none stepped forward, simply by cutting cards in Headquarters and eliminating all units but 1st Platoon, Company F, 2nd Battalion, 13th Infantry. Day after day the thirty-six surprised, self-conscious men of this platoon were towed behind the scorpion and two other tanks in file through dummy minefields under the proud supervision of Corps and Divisional commanders. Even the Commanding General, Fifth Army, was flown from Naples to the beachhead to watch one morning's exhibition and afterward expressed himself as highly gratified at the spirit and creativity of the 11th Division. In the night of 21-22 May, while smoke generators blanketed the roads, the 11th Division moved into the lines opposite Cisterna. At 0400 hours began the general artillery preparation for the breakthrough. At 0440 hours commenced the TOT shoot along the Fossa Feminamorta. As the right-hand side of the box closed north the 17th Engineers cut with bulldozers a ramp and at exactly 0500 hours the shelling ceased and the Tank-Battle Sled Team trundled into the Ditch of Dead Women. Thirty-five feet below ground-level the wild anvil of battle above seemed remote and the day's gray blessing was bestowed gently upon the thirty-six men cradled in their steel tubes. Misfortune befell the Team almost immediately. Spring rains had marshed the bed of the ravine, and while the footing was solid enough to pass the scorpion and second tank, the third, keeping to their tracks on order, mired itself inextricably. Since they had not yet reached the enemy area, tank crew and third squad returned on the double for a T-2 recovery vehicle which, incidentally, was not located and could not in any case have been used until night. Scorpion and second tank proceeded meanwhile and entered the mine and wire fields; the scorpion operated admirably, its rotating flails detonating mines every few feet and its treads cutting a fine swath through the concertina. Both tanks snouted into the enemy stretch of the ditch. Instantly a torrent of German automatic weapon and riflefire poured upon them from both sides, screaming off their armor as they responded with machine guns, the way being too narrow to employ their cannon effectively. At this juncture, the drain-bed growing softer, the second tank, maneuvering on the oblique to achieve better traction, struck an antitank mine which blew off one tread, immobilizing it. The twelve men in the sleds lay prone, helmets buried in folded arms, confused, mud-smirched, deafened by the gibbering of bullets, frantically aware their forward progress had been halted for some reason but unwilling, in fact unable, to raise up to see why, to decide what to do, without having heads sheared from their bodies by crossfire. Had the German holes and emplacements been built high enough along the banks to depress aim into the sleds, the squad might have been wiped out with a few bursts; instead, it occurred to the enemy to lob potato-masher grenades over and into the tow-harness. Exploded in air, the fragments tore into the Americans' backs, cleavering off filets from their buttocks; a direct hit filled a sled with bloody, fleshy matter as one might fill a trough with slop for hogs. Within two minutes the twelve tubes became twelve caskets, and it was quite probable no one of the soldiers knew before his own death of the unique slaughter of the other eleven. Thirteenth Infantry Tank-Battle Sled Team was now reduced to the scorpion and the first squad of sledmen. The medium tank continued to roar forward, detonating mines and cutting wire, until it turned, tentatively, an angle. Here the Ditch of Dead Women formed an unobstructed corridor approximately eighty yards long before it angled again, its banks even more heavily bunkered, and here the driver of the tank had through his slit an interesting sight. He gaped straight down the barrel of the most superb of all German weapons: a self-propelled 88mm field gun. Having had four months to provide for the reception of tanks entering the Fossa Feminamorta, the enemy, with habitual foresight, had excavated a cave in the wall of the ditch which faced the corridor, brought down an 88SP

44

and backed it into the cave, camouflaged the aperture with a large green rope net, and trained the protruding muzzle of the gun through the net so that its field of fire was perfect. As the driver stared, the muzzle of the 88 prophesied and the shell pierced the scorpion's turret, its concussion killing the crew instantly. The second shell removed the turret. It will be observed that the extremity of the first sled squad was now similar in every respect to that of the late second squad. Helmet down, helpless, terrified, they lay prone as bands of small-arms fire converged inches above their steel cocoons. After a minute or two it occurred once more to the Germans along the banks to lob grenades over and into the tow-harness. But in the very instant of the idea, in the other instants of ceasing fire and preparing to execute the idea, there intervened one of the human phenomena which make war fascinating. A soldier, impelled by some instinct not yet named but stronger, for the second, than self-preservation, staggered on cramped legs upward from his tube. Able to see what had destroyed the tank, incredibly, inexplicably, he began to run down the Ditch of Dead Women toward the 88SP. He ran slowly, in total silence, weighted with combat pack, ammunition clips, six hand grenades attached to his belt, and carrying a submachine gun. Not until he had covered sixty of the eighty yards to the cave did the Germans react, swinging their weapons and firing at him. Rifle, machine gun and machine pistol bullets spattered the mud under his boots. One round struck his combat pack and sent his mess kit flying from his shoulders. Reaching the muzzle of the 88 he thrust his submachine gun through the aperture in the netting about the barrel and sprayed a full ammunition clip point-blank into the cave, killing two of the three gunners. Then, lifting the netting, he lunged into the cave and encountered a third astonished enemy, whom he clubbed to the ground with such a violent blow of his weapon to the head that its stock was splintered. Just as the American climbed on the track into the bed of the self-propelled gun he met face-to-face a fourth German. This one was un-

45

armed and bareheaded, a man taller and heavier and much older than he, unshaven, who wore, he saw irrelevantly, a gold wrist watch, and who seized him in both arms and bore him backward as they grappled, bending him over the iron side of the vehicle. Like lovers they groaned in each other's faces. Muscles in the American's back gave way under the strain, a current of pain volted down the rear of his left leg, his spine would break if he could not free himself. The German's head was beside his, the German's bared neck bulged against his mouth. He opened wide his jaws, sank his teeth into the neck, closed his jaws and bit so deeply, so desperately that his teeth severed the left carotid artery. Blood spouted in his mouth, in his nose. The German bellowed, released him, sat down stupidly, and stupidly, as might a great child, began to weep. Retching blood, panting with queer animal sounds, the American spun the traverse and elevation wheels, sighted the 88 by squinting down its barrel at one of the hole-mouths in the ditch bank near the blasted scorpion tank, found and tripped the firing mechanism. Recoil slammed him forward on his hands and knees, reverberation cracked his eardrums, but the shell, exploding at the rim of the hole, killed the Germans within and buried them under falling earth. The American reloaded the field gun, aimed and fired at another bunker, this a Spandau machine-gun emplacement, bursting into air the weapon and the bodies of its crew. He fired twice more to the same effect. At this range, no more than eighty yards, even a near-miss served his purpose. There was no firing whatever from the Germans; they withdrew deep into their holes. In another total silence the American shouted at the eleven men still in their battle sleds to come to him. Down the corridor they ran, saved, under the netting, spared, and three of them took over the operation of the 88 while the others placed submachine-gun and riflefire upon the enemy positions. From one hole after another the Germans scurried out with hands high. In a quarter of an hour fifty-eight had surrendered. That area of the Fossa Feminamorta was entirely cleared of enemy by 0530 hours. One of the

46

curious aspects of the first day's struggle for Cisterna became apparent to Division G-3 that night: foot troops of, and armor attached to, the regiments on both the right and left of the 13th Infantry, it developed, had successfully crossed the Ditch of Dead Women, so that the employment of tanks and battle sleds in the center had been wholly unnecessary. During the surrender of the enemy in the corridor the American who had captured and served the self-propelled gun sat hunched forward in the bed of the vehicle, hearing nothing, speaking no word, his face still red-smeared. Beside him lay the big throat-mangled German, long since bled to death, from his wrist the gold watch long since removed. Over and over in his mind the American re-dreamed his role, at once participant in and spectator to his deeds, split-selved, the man-present trying to identify with man-past, twin in him unknown until this day; born out of a circumstantial chemistry and come of age in one sacrificial moment, did he dwell in other men as well, was he lost already, brave shade withdrawn across some Styx of consciousness? Most vivid to him were the total silences while running burdened and before shouting to his squad, absences of sound in which the world was quit of time, so similar to those interregna as Johnny Scripter waited by the curb that afternoon and as they stood triumphant on the dam one night in Thebes.

STROPHE : 1939

Event is innocent, event is witless, and to attribute to it the possession of dark powers, brooding and teleological, is to mistake effect for purpose; yet events by their conjunction may often seem to men to be the fingers of a hand.

Suffering a stroke in February, lingering paralytic for two months, Renis Baird died of a second seizure in April.

His father, Alfred, dead intestate in 1922, had assumed his sons Renis and Charles would together own and operate the Thebes Milling Company.

Own it they might have but Renis ran it. Charles, or "Charlieboy" as Renis called him, fourteen years his junior, was let play clerically in the office, paid an allowance rather than a salary, and permitted to buy, on reasonable terms, each of Renis's year-old Chryslers as he traded them in on new.

Sickly, colorless, introverted, cursed with a childish impediment of speech, Charles had throughout his boyhood been commanded daily by Renis in the presence of an audience to pronounce the word "shirt." Each time, to the listeners' delight, Charlieboy would obey.

—Shit.

Renis Baird left no will, assuming that Charlieboy, unmarried hence heirless, adjudging himself patently unfit to head Thebes Milling, would manage only until Renis's sons, Morse and Harris, could complete their education, at which time he would turn it over to them and revert with relief to his former status.

Inside of ten days of his departure—it was as though he had but driven off, in a cloud of Chryslerian dust, on a selling trip or bound for Chicago for some fun—his wife and brother learned more about the real Renis than they had ever previously known.

With such cavalier disdain for prudence had he lived

51

and spent, Constance Baird found, that the house was heavily mortgaged, he had borrowed to the limit on his life insurance, and what was realizable from his other assets would not keep her and her sons for a year.

To Charlieboy, the books of the company revealed Thebes Milling on the verge of bankruptcy. Pledging plant and equipment, Renis had borrowed in Grand Rapids to speculate in wheat futures and lost with an almost peacock consistency.

Charlieboy succeeded, moreover, not only to the presidency of the mill but to its civic perquisites: he was elected a Director of the Thebes State Bank and appointed to fill out his brother's terms on the Town Council and the School Board.

The rules demanded that he put up or shut up, that overnight, at thirty-six, Charlieboy become Charles Sampter Baird.

Cold but perspiring, tight-mouthed but fidgety, he came one evening to Constance Baird with the facts, papers drawn, and an ultimatum. If she signed, he would try to save the mill, but it would be his mill and that of his issue, should he marry. In addition, he would begin settling Renis's debts, pay off her mortgage, and give her enough yearly to sustain herself so long as she lived. If she did not sign, he would let Thebes Milling go to its creditors and none of them would have either pot or window.

Through widow's tears Constance called his analogy vile and her choice despicable and cruel. She pleaded for the futures, the lives even, of her sons. When he remained adamant she appealed to his memory of Renis, scarce resigned as yet to his grave, whose benevolence had so long sheltered a younger brother from the world's vicissitudes. To this, after he had granted Irony time to clamor the room with laughter and Justice to suffuse her listening cheeks, Charles replied with a single word, pronounced impeccably.

—Shit.

It was April. In May the Vice-President and Cashier of

the Thebes State Bank took his first vacation in fifteen years.

Stricken with influenza, L. V. Smith was ordered to bed by Charles Reason and placed on Dover's powder to reduce his fever. His son Sewell, who had lived alone with him since Catherine Smith's misfortune, cared for him until the fifth day.

On that night he admitted to the house and to his father's bedroom in a group the other six Directors of the bank: Harlan Murninghan, President and Chairman; Charles Baird, Dr. Charles Reason, William Vandevelde, Oram Kropf, and Claude Reichert. They closed the bedroom door. He waited downstairs.

After an hour Claude Reichert came down with his father's request that he leave and spend the night with his friends Morse and Harris. He did so.

The next morning, before he could start for school, he was picked up and driven home by Harlan Murninghan, who accompanied him into the house, asked him to be seated, and informed him then that his father had passed away during the night of lung congestion, frequently a concomitant of influenza.

The body lay now at Vergennes's Funeral Home and the funeral would be on Thursday. Since the house was empty it would be advisable for Sewell to stay with the Bairds until after the services, at which time more permanent arrangements could be made.

It had been his father's dying wish, under the circumstances of his lack of family, except for a married sister living in the Upper Peninsula, that Sewell place his immediate future in the hands of his closest friends, the bank's Directors. This they hoped he would do.

There was one matter more. In his father's absence from the bank there had been a dumbfounding disclosure: for a period of years an illegal mingling of the assets of individual depositors with those of the bank had taken place, followed by the conversion of those assets to the Cashier's personal use. A very considerable sum was involved. It was possible that his father's estate would be liable under the law to make whatever restitution it could, including the house, its effects, his automobile, even Sewell's since he was yet a minor.

He would not speak of the matter at such a tragic time except that there might be rumors, although the Directors were doing everything in their power to keep it secret since it not only impugned the reputation of a man trusted unconditionally by the community but struck at the solvency of the bank itself; in any case, he wanted Sewell to hear of it directly, and he would caution silence no matter what the provocation.

Harlan Murninghan then relocked the house and returned him to the Bairds'.

Event is innocent, event is witless, yet these events by their conjunction seemed to the three young men besieged in the labyrinthine stucco residence of the late Renis Baird to be the finger of a hand merciless and satanic. Told only a week earlier by their mother of the agreement with their uncle she had had no alternative to signing, Morse and Harris had since refused to attend school; now Sewell joined them. For two days they kept indoors, young animals caged by grief and anger, at bay together against a town which, they imagined, exulted in their fall, a town which appeared to spurn, indeed to mock, they imagined, the gift of their lives they would have made to it; by day they slept, by night prowled the icebox for food, drank into Renis's ghostly stocks of beer, and applied talk's poultice to their wounds; Constance Baird they ignored; their class, that of 1939 at Thebes High, would graduate in two weeks and they were resolved not to be present at the ceremony although Harris was valedictorian and Morse, All-State fullback and holder of the state Class C record for the 440-yard dash, a remarkable :50.8, the school's finest athlete since Johnny Scripter, was to receive special recognition for his prowess; in sportsmanlike rotation they had dated Jane Murninghan, Harlan's daughter, through high school, and

54

it was Sewell's turn to take her to the party following Commencement, but now she could not be asked; he and Morse were eighteen, Harris seventeen. Over the hours their multiple tragedy took clear and enormous shape. They were disentitled. To the brothers, lost were father and the reflection of his flamboyance in which, preening themselves, they had learned pride; education at Duke for Morse and Bowdoin for Harris now that funds were unavailable; but theft most appalling, that castle secure for three generations, with rights and latitudes almost baronial in Thebes, the ownership and management of the mill; lost to Sewell were the small, indomitable presence of his only parent, now a myth impeached, a degree from Ann Arbor, the fortune he had seen with his own wide eyes spread out upon a table and those debentures of prospect and help L.V. had pledged, even, perhaps, his home itself, that house of boyish fret and transport, of buried music, of oaks still towering though storm-riven; denied to one of them, which one they could not yet foretell, was Jane Murninghan; and finally, stolen from all three, theirs because they were the sons of their fathers, were those alluvial riches of privilege and decision and social primacy in the quiet stream that was life in Thebes. They were like the right-hand columns at its western limit, Doric and Ionic and Corinthian, based upon immutable marble but toppled in one calamitous minute. So they paced and hit each other's shoulders glancing, idiot blows and talked and sought a focus for their rage, a way to take their world by the nose and tweak it into contrition. Compounding Sewell's frustration was the fact that he could not confide in Morse and Harris as they could in him; any defalcation on his father's part he would die before accepting, and to insist to others, as he must to himself, that his father, rather than failing, had been well on the way to recovery before the Directors' meeting in his room was to hint at the commission of something so heinous that no one, even his friends, would believe him: a crime more ghastly because unintelligible. Between one and two o'clock in the morning of the day L. V. Smith was to be interred his son slipped out of the Baird house and returned half an hour later to announce to Morse and Harris that he had gone home, found entry through an unlatched basement window, packed a suitcase with the few things he wished to keep, and driven back in his car; that he would not attend his father's funeral; that he was leaving Thebes forever; that he would start out at once for Detroit, where he would enlist in the Army.

—Harris, for God's sake, Morse protested, ashamed.

His brother had thrown himself on the bed, a contortion of knobknees and elbows shuddering to repress its sobs. —I can't help it! Sewell leaving town almost the way Johnny had to and the end of everything for us! Don't you remember how it was when we went fishing on the Jordan, that night in the tent and everything we talked about? I do, I've never forgotten, and now it's all wrecked and I don't know why! Jesus to Genoa!

Sewell consented to have a last bottle of beer for the road to Detroit and the Army. Beer loosened tongues, talk turned to retribution, and Sewell implied that somehow, by some black artifice, the bank's Directors were responsible for his father's death; before leaving Thebes there was nothing he'd like better than to telephone them all now, in the midst of the night, and tell them to go to hell, or, even more gratifying, blow the bank the hell up with dynamite. Quite how it was that imprecation settled eventually on Charles Baird alone, piddling, hence more bare-assed brazen, usurper, unless his common culpability in all of their disasters made him an obvious villain; or how there, under the eaves of the house in that cell charged with hatred, beer-fused, adolescent braggartry became threat and threat a practical draft of vengeance, none of them would ever recall with certainty. No matter; they left the Bairds' toward three o'clock and drove in Sewell's car with lights out across Ionian Avenue, parking it behind the old cutter works. On foot then, returning to the main street they began a slow, military advance, stealing from doorway to doorway, avoiding the drowsy bask of the tri-globed, moss-friezed street lights, huddling in shadows to scout up and down. Mute was the marquee of the Attic Theatre, cheerless The Let Live's front; decrepit before Stormy's Garage a solitary car awaited morning's succor; the glow at the rear of the City Hall would be that from the bulb above Earl Blue, the Town Constable, drinking coffee in the jail between rounds of trying locks on doors. They reached the doorway of the State Bank of Thebes and hesitated a final, apprehensive minute. Across the bridged, storeless area loomed the great white frame of the Thebes Milling Company, four-storied, to a small town monument and surety. Under the bridge, channeled to a width of thirty feet between oaken walls, the River Button muscled its green and glassy bulk against twin oaken head gates hung side by side from heavy chains and raised or lowered manually from the catwalk above by means of winches turned with iron rods. To the right, through a flume wood-grated to impede debris, the current's might was directed downward into the basement of the mill, passing through and setting in motion a huge wooden turbine, finding exit out of the turbine box into the millrace. Efficient operation of the system required the maintenance of an eleven-foot head of water, the "head" being the difference in height between the river's level at the gates and at the millrace below the dam. Conspiratorially they moved onto the bridge and vaulting the rail stepped out upon the catwalk, surefooted even in darkness for they had fished for pike from it as children; under them the river spilled beneath the head gates, raised halfway since it was May and the Button ran high. Spoking rods into the winches, Sewell and Morse lowered first the left, then the right-hand gate, until the water ululated only through the flume. A pile of logs and lumber debris, cleared from the flume grate, lay nearby, on the grassed embankment between the dam and the mill, and muttered curses goaded Harris to help in dragging and placing the timbers, the rotting two-by-fours and sixes, against the grate until the flume, too, was sealed. What they had plotted, retaliation more spectacular than

57

the displacement of a privy at Halloween, was to requite Charlieboy Baird through the mill, his now, at the weakest point of its dam structure, the wooden grating at the flume mouth: by clotting it, then increasing the head of water until the grate could no longer bear the pressure, it would give way, they expected, sending a fist of timber smashing through the flume into the turbine box and fouling the blades so completely that only several days' hard labor by millwrights would free them, meanwhile shutting down the mill for lack of power. Only one task more to complete the work. Atop the catwalk, one at each end, were two smaller auxiliary gates, provided against the emergency of flood damage to the main gates; using their combined strength, the three boys tilted these and let them slide at such an angle that the current rammed them solidly athwart and considerably higher than the first gates, raising the river's barricade to eighteen or nineteen feet. Bending, fascinated, they watched the water's level rise as though summoned, rise above the lower gates to breast the extra ramparts until footsteps dropped them crouching, breath-stopped, behind a winch.

On the far side of Ionian Avenue winged Oram Kropf returning home from being read to, hunched and swift, his white cane swinging.

They stood again, sweat-triumphant. They held fast a river by its throat. Suddenly aware of total silence, each of them was captured by a puerile desire to prank that utter somnolence, to bray in chorus so that all the sleeping town might hear: for treachery to our fathers, this turbine; for our privation, this wage of reckoning; wake, you, and see what we have done!

The river spoke. Something more than human, a rumble like that of beginning laughter caused the catwalk to quake, and this was counterpointed by a splash and coursing.

They looked below. They had miscalculated. The Button, past flood stage but still virile with spring's tiding, had risen already to within a foot of the top of the auxiliary gates, and rather than crushing the flume grate relieved itself in streams over the edge of the embankment—insufficient vent, they knew, to ease the awful tonnage of water being measured second by second behind the dam.

Now the river thundered its mirth and the weaving of the catwalk made it difficult to keep their balance, and inches from them, begot in minutes by the Button, a great green god-face was upturned to theirs, boiling with a monstrous amusement.

Terrorized, they rushed along the catwalk, shinnied over the rail, and concrete under them, fled down Ionian Avenue.

Racing, pursued only by themselves, they were shaken, staggered, by a Vulcanian boom which put a period to their youth.

Walls, catwalk, water gates, winches, foundations, flume, turbine, turbine box, all were erupted, swept away. Rafts of the wreckage were borne upon the flood as far as the Button's jointure with the Ionian.

This permanent dam and power system had been engineered by Alfred Baird at the century's change, but since on that very site, in 1838, Carlos Sampter Baird, two pioneer years out from York State, had been aided by his neighbors in constructing the water wheel around which the town had later webbed, the mill was the most venerable, therefore most sacrosanct, institution in Thebes.

STROPHE : 1937

Telephone. Police, Grand Rapids. Robbery minutes ago at Old Kent Savings, the Wealthy Street branch. Three men. Getaway car: LaSalle, 1937, dark blue, four-door, plates KE41018. Seen heading north on M-18 at high speed. If stay on highway should reach Thebes in twelve to fourteen minutes. Time now 3:42. Bandits professionals, weapons pistol, sawed-off shotgun, Thompson sub. Advise not try to intercept but follow, keep in sight. State Police substation at Naxos, further north, radioed and setting up roadblock. He ran out of the jail behind the City Hall and through the rear door of a grocery shouted a bank had been robbed in Grand Rapids and the bandits would be coming through town in minutes and he wanted the clerks to start up their side of the street and order everyone indoors and if they did not obey to make them and then across to the State Bank of Thebes and pounding on the glass doors shouted to L. V. Smith to lock the vault because bank robbers were on the way from Grand Rapids and then next door to a furniture store and shouted to the owner and his employee to start up their side of the street and order everyone indoors and if they did not obey to make them, there might be shooting, then back to the City Hall where two old men nodded, toothless and confused, as he neared on the run shouting to station themselves one on each side of the intersection and halt all traffic, no vehicle was to cross or turn into the street, then ran for the Harley-Davidson and mounted and kicked it roaring blue smoke and turned on the siren and swung round the corner onto Ionian Avenue where his vested and aproned vigilantes had cleared the first block by shouting at pedestrians and ordering people out of parked cars but where the high school having just been dismissed he had to station another man at the next intersection to direct the homebound youngsters to safety before crossing the bridge over the River Button past Thebes Milling to see that the alarm had preceded him for figures darted out of cars and into stores or swayed bewildered as he shouted at them to take cover. His watch read 3:49. Bounding the business area was an intersection cornered by two gas stations, an automobile dealership, and the town Library, the latter occupying the first floor of an old brick house mansard-roofed and corseted with vines and U-turning he found four men gassing cars and waving shotguns and a World War Springfield and wearing American Legion caps who shouted offers of help and he shouted back he wanted none because he would have no one hurt but if they wanted to help for God's sake stand guard at that intersection and the next and prevent any traffic from obstructing the street, at which they nodded fiercely and wheeling east again he caught sight four blocks away of a car pulling into the main street a block beyond his City Hall guards and throttling full out he sped the four blocks and waved the car to the curb and shouted the lady driver out of it and into an ice-cream parlor. It was 3:51. Siren keening, sensing the eyes upon him through every door, every window, he cruised the center-stripe west, patrolling, an Argus sitting the machine statuesquely and trying to impart by posture and slow procession confidence to the town. He reached the Library, circled gracefully and brought the machine alongside the curb, placed one boot for balance on the pavement, eased himself back on the big black-leather saddle, stilled the siren, and tested the hand-grip throttle gradually down to an idle. 3:52.

From this point he could survey Ionian Avenue for a quarter of a mile, to the steeple of the Methodist Church, alone prerogative above the elms, to the high bald bluffs where youngsters feathered down on skis in winter, calling ecstasy in flight. Nothing moved, vehicle, animal, human. It was a scene transfixed, shuttered as though by a camera, by itself developed and printed and by itself suspended in mid-sunshine. He had never before seen it so. As he struck a match a panic scream like that of a woman in labor needled

64

his scalp. Two blocks down, across the street a farmer's wife lumbered awkwardly to a parked car, opened the door and hauled out two small forgotten children and, one under each arm like sacks of grain, lumbered again, not forward, to the near side, but dizzied all the way back to the shelter from which she had burst. The match singed his fingers. He dropped it and lit the cigarette with another. 3:53. The call from Grand Rapids had come in at 3:42 and the estimate had been twelve minutes. The LaSalle should show in one more. He sucked ravenously on the cigarette, then twitched it into the gutter. He unbuttoned his holster. Except for the soft, almost sexual rhythm of the machine between his legs and the puttering of the exhaust behind him the silence was absolute. 3:54.

Peace Officer John Scripter waited astride a glittering, black-and-silver, eighty-cubic-inch, fifty-horsepower Harley-Davidson, the largest motorcycle purchasable in 1937. It would do, he had ascertained, ninety mph, almost as much, though not quite, as that year's LaSalle. He wore a peaked, wide-brimmed hat of good gray felt, a neat gray uniform of whipcord, and his breeches were tailored smartly below the knees into boots of brown polished leather. From his wide belt hung a stubby holster carrying incongruously, not the regular police Smith & Wesson but, at his insistence, his old cavalry .45 caliber automatic.

It was the epoch of the Dillingers, of bank robberies and jailbreaks and radio nets and gun molls and wild, bullet-whipped chases, particularly in the country's middle lands, Ohio and Michigan and Illinois and Wisconsin, and innumerable small towns, not to be outdone by the cities, had in a roosterish excess of public vanity put their aged constables out to grass and hired younger men to defend their health and purse, mounting and accoutering them splendidly. In Thebes, the selection of Johnny Scripter was inevitable: with legend, with color, with derring-do the local imagination coupled his name immediately; more practically, his appointment as "Peace Officer" would eliminate

65

forever the problem of what to do with him. It was the first nakedly emulative, not to say expedient, act in the Town Council's history, and its last.

Until this day, June 2, 1937, Johnny Scripter's duties had appeared to entail patrolling Ionian Avenue for speed violations, checking the locks of business establishments by night, jailing an occasional vagrant only to let him go the following morning after a meal, and one other, of such intrinsic difficulty that no man but he in Thebes might discharge it; merely to station himself hour upon hour astride the huge Harley-Davidson at the curb before the City Hall and there be available to every citizen's gaze, resplendent, calm, in duality of symbol at once guardian of the universal weal and romance's modern emissary, knight fifty-steeded and squireless, troubador with a siren for song.

Johnny wore a cap of curly hair tilted far back on his forehead. He had fair Scandinavian skin and a smile Latin in flash and ebullience. His crane-whoop of greeting twirled your ears and the catcher's mitt of his hand on your back ungummed your teeth. Leaning he stood over six feet and he had been born hipless and his shoulders were made for grappling giants and life to him was a beanstalk into a picaresque sky and he was, he said himself, too damn young to be thirty-nine and it was 3:55 and that LaSalle was overdue and he didn't have an itch of a notion exactly what he'd do when it came but he took up his heart like a horn and blew a long sad sigh out of it and wished he could have for a last minute all the dear good people of Thebes before him unaccustomed though he was to public speaking because if he could have them this was what he'd say:

—Now first base I want to thank everybody here an' the Counsul an' even the taxpayers for appointin' me Peace Officer when this town don't no more need a peace officer than I need some new lies. Jesus t'Genoa, if there's anything we got it's peace! Apologies to you, Rever'nd. My tongue may be polluted but my soul's as pure as the Button in August an' no rain. By the way, that pike I caught when

66

I was a kid in the millrace weighed more nearer seventeen pound than twenty. Yes, friends, Ethel's the best wife an' the best-lookin' a man could stand an' if anything should happen between me an' them bank robbers I hope she'll be took care of. An' my girl Arlene, too, ain't she plannin' to be a beauty, though? I sure do appreciate some of the best boys in town bein' nice to her an' takin' her out, boys like the Bairds an' L.V.'s boy. An' also, if anything should happen, you don't need no peace officer, like I said, all's you need is a constable which you had before, gangsters just ain't going to bother us much in Thebes, an' Earl Blue'd be a good pick. Speakin' of that pike this is prob'ly a right time to tell the whole truth an' nothin' but, as they say in court, so let me get a couple stories straight while I can. That story I tell about down on the Border in '16, well, the part about the cavalry chasin' the Mex'cans in Model T Fords is true, but the way I switch it around for a joke ain't. We just hiked us on shanks' mares home to Texas with our behinds blushin' an' we sure were the laugh of the Rio Grandey. An' that yarn about me an' the Dee-troit Tigers. Well, now, there was a scout, Gander Jones, seen me pitch against the House of David an' nearly shave their beards off with my blue darter fast ball an' he did talk to me afterwards but what he said was, he'd sign me if I could learn better control, an' you know I ain't been a great one for controllin' anything, now have I? Also, I hear some folks have been sayin' for years if I'd of gone to France for the War instead of the Border I'd of smote the Huns hip an' thigh an' got me all kinds of medals. Well, I might of an' I might not. Though I prob'ly would. But how can a man tell what he'll up an' do till his time comes? Now. I sure have asked you to do me a slew of kindnesses but I want to state on oath I won't let you down today when them bank robbers shows up. I guar'-ntee nobody'll get hurt, I'd die before I'd let that happen. You ought to know how I love this town. Jesus t'Genoa, it's beautiful! There ain't a better place to live in Michigan an' maybe the whole world an' I never been away from here but a day before I was so homesick I could of crawled into a hole. An' the good fishin' an' pheasant huntin' an' the way we burn the leaves together, all on one night. I always wished I had me a boy to burn leaves with an' maybe me an' Ethel will yet, them long winter nights makes for powerful cold beds. I've tried to do all I could for this town. I done some few things in athaletics, but Morse Baird, there, he'll be bettern'n I was, you wait an' see. But say, didn' we blister East Grand Rapids that one year, though, didn' we? No, I won't let you down today, on a stack of Bibles I won't. I said you don't need no peace officer, an' you don't, but I see how smart you was. You reckoned there'd come a time like this with gangsters amongst us an' you'd need somebody to look out for you. Well, my dear friends, all the friends I got in the world, you do have somebody an' I hereby swear to make you proud of me. If I never amounted to much before, I will today. I shake hands with every one of you an' thank you.

3:56.

Head swiveled, he saw the dark dot grow. In seconds it passed the Grecian columns at the western limits, the one group standing, the other fallen, and he could identify the car as a blue 1937 LaSalle.

It slackened speed. He guessed thirty mph. He drew down his hat. He heard the hot hiss of tires nearing.

Johnny Scripter throttled up and away from the curb and in less than a hundred feet drew abreast of the sedan on the left.

Beside the driver sat a second man, in the rear seat a third.

He rode tandem with them half a block, then raised his right hand and arm and shouted.

—Halt!

The men in the car did not seem to hear nor did they look at him.

Still another block along Ionian Avenue sedan and motorcycle paraded together, speeds perfectly synchronized. Again he raised his hand and shouted.

—Halt!

The ugly nose of a Thompson submachine gun appeared through the rear window of the heavy car. The muzzle flickered light and chatter.

Johnny Scripter was shot out of the saddle. The motorcycle up-ended into a parked car. The LaSalle accelerated and hurtled swaying out of town.

Men rushed into the stilly street from Reichert's Drugstore. Johnny was dead but they carried him nevertheless upstairs to Charles Reason's office.

He had been hit by eighteen bullets, examination determined. Four had passed completely through him. Slugs had ranged along the bones of his arms and legs, entering, for example, at the thigh and tearing an internal route down to the ankle before emerging. His body was literally tattered.

That the bandits, veering north toward Smyrna and west again at Delphi Grange, pursued by State Police and a posse of Legionnaires, surrendered in the woods near which Sewell Smith and the Baird brothers, two months later, were to drive with Arlene Scripter; that the stolen money was not recovered and lay somewhere free to the finder; that the gunmen were tried and convicted at Tyre, the county seat, of murder in the first degree and sentenced to the life imprisonment obligatory under Michigan law—these were anticlimatic by comparison with the misery and recognition upon which Thebes feasted for a full week. The village told itself that it had reared an authentic, indeed an epic, hero. Alone Johnny Scripter had faced the invaders, alone he had sacrificed himself for his townsmen. So singular had been his gallantry that a short item descriptive of it appeared in practically every Michigan newspaper, even those in Detroit, and so moved by it was his birthplace that in hyperbole of sorrow no measure by which his deed might be honored, his memory enshrined, was overlooked. The schools were dismissed for the day of his interment and when it became obvious the Congregational Church would never bear the weight of mourning, services were transferred to the football field beside the high school. A costly cenotaph of marble for his grave was voted by the Town Council, which in addition assured Johnny's widow lifetime employment in the office of the municipal Light and Power, and in addition to that reëstablished the post of Constable and appointed Earl Blue to it, and in addition to that caused the great Harley-Davidson to be repaired and throned on a pedestal at one end of the Council chamber as perpetual and mechanical relic of that martyrdom, that pure immolation of self which must forever elevate men's spirits. Then Jove, his mood altered to one of Olympian sportiveness, dispatched to Thebes a messenger in the guise of a staff man from the Associated Press bureau in Lansing, who proposed the writing of a story follow-up to catastrophe. Irreverent and impious, even farcical, in the end annihilative, his piece went out by AP wire to every major paper in the nation and was carried by most. Tears in such volume that they raised the local head of water almost to flood stage, imperiling the mill, had been shed, wrote the city coxcomb, for a man who, close inquiry vouchsafed, had not so much as unholstered his pistol, a hick cop, a popinjay, a rube Don Quixote who had hoped to arrest the forces of evil with fustian gesture and pipsqueak, tragicomic "Halt!" Rather than intrepid, the act was one of epic absurdity. Reading the account of Peace Officer John Scripter's promenade, lamblike yet Falstaffian, down Ionian Avenue with the men who slew him, the nation smiled; and reading it also, caught in imbecile allegiance, sensing in its civic viscera the story to be just, the village underwent a second paroxysm, this time of chagrin. In the matter of days idolatry was laid low by derision: the town had given birth, it was clear, not to a Horatius but to an authentic damn fool. Unanimously the Council canceled its expensive monument and voted instead a simple headstone; the Harley-Davidson was removed to a custodial storeroom in City Hall; the appointment of Earl Blue as Constable stood, but he was directed neither to wear a uniform nor to carry a gun. Ridiculed on the streets by small boys cawing

"Halt! Halt!" the widow, she of the voluptuous figure, the pagan and sensual laughter, respected mate of the town's favorite and simultaneously, with lust's odd ambivalence, woman coveted in secret by half its male populace, Ethel Scripter continued to receipt bills and test light bulbs at the Light and Power, but her attitude toward customers was rude in ratio to scorn, her demeanor alcoholic, while her daughter, Arlene, suffered in tender agony the slights of friends, the irreparable damage to her consequence inflicted by a dark blue LaSalle. Opinion's wheel had come full circle; for years the very name of Johnny Scripter would thistle the flesh of Thebes.

STROPHE : 1934

—If you could have your pick, of anybody in town, really anybody, who'd you rather screw?

Of infinite charm and challenge, the subject never failed to engross them, and this question, put without the least diffidence, they considered the more gravely because it diverted thought from the day's central event, one of such thrilling implication that even now, hours later, they were embarrassed to speak of it.

—Jean Harlow, Sewell offered.

—C'mon now, I said in town. A little oofum-poofum now and then, Morse reminded, is cherished by the wisest men.

—I don't know, Sewell said. He did, but to enter her name in such a contest, much less allow it to form upon imagination's lips, would be sacrilege.

—Arlene Scripter, decided Harris. —Gosh, how'd you like to walk barefoot through an acre of those?

—You're both nuts. You know who's prob'ly the most terrific tonk in town?

—Who?

—Who?

—Mrs. Scripter, that's who.

—She's too old, Harris scoffed.

—Old, my butt. Ris, when in hell will you ever learn the score? People do it till they're a hundred if they can. She's about thirty-two, three, young enough to want to and old enough to know how. You take a nonvirgin's word for it, half the men in town would be after that if it weren't for Johnny.

—Nonvirgin, my butt, his brother giggled, impressed despite himself.

They lay close together, each wound like a top in his blankets, and stared back at an older generation of stars aloof in the northern sky. Rival gangs of mosquitoes dared them through the netting at the head end of the pup-tent

75

while a night wind like a bear snuffed along the ground, stirring the bosky fragrances of pine and moss and lichen and birch bark. Morse and Sewell were thirteen, Harris twelve, and in another month they would enter high school. Reference to Johnny was lucky, for it enabled them again to defer voicing what was in their minds, to luxuriate in silent enumeration of his apocrypha: the hauling in of the mightiest pike, a twenty-pounder, ever caught out of the millrace; that Halloween miracle, the tethering of a full-grown Guernsey cow in the steeple of the Methodist Church; his machine-gun arm on the mound, the fast ball which had one-hit the House of David and brought an offer from a big-league scout, and Johnny's immortal conditions, that he'd sign provided he'd never have to go south for spring training and that the Tigers move Navin Field to Thebes; how, a crack-ribbed fullback, he'd accounted for Thebes' only victory over snotty East Grand Rapids, that same year a Zulu center rebounding his team to the state finals in basketball; how, after marriage to Ethel Hoeg, he'd beat the hides off set after set of drums while playing dances up at Delphi Grange with an aggregation celebrated regionally as "McConkle's Nose-Pickers." And the tales he told of his years on the Tex-Mex Border, of señoritas and bandidos and revolutions for your breakfast! Boys in their hearts cast them in mock-Homeric verse, minstreled to popping rifles and the thrum of guitars!

—Johnny ought to have a better job than drawing beer at The Let Live, Harris wished.

—He isn't doing that any more, Sewell said. —They made him quit, Mr. Murninghan and Or'm Kropf. They didn't think it was fit for him.

—Then how'd he get the money to go to the Fair? wondered Morse.

—From your father. Mine, too, I suppose.

Groved in silver birches beside the Jordan River were three tents: theirs, the one in which slept two other boys, and that of Mr. Vandevelde. None of them had ever been as far from home before, none of them had ever fished a stream as noted as the Jordan, nor had Bill Van, the Superintendent of Schools in Thebes; consequently, when Renis Baird concluded his sons were yet too uncultured to appreciate fully the prodigies of the Chicago World's Fair that summer of 1934, including those of Sally Rand, he went himself, with Oram Kropf and Charles Reason and Johnny Scripter, and gladly seconded Bill Van's idea of a fishing jaunt to northern Michigan for Morse and Harris and the three other boys. Supplying most of the equipment, even a canoe rigged atop his car, Mr. Vandevelde had collected twenty-five dollars each from five boys' fathers and chauffeured them two hundred miles north where for a week, ostensibly, he would act as guide, mentor, cook, and disciplinarian. This was the fourth night beside the Jordan, and it had been that afternoon's strange, revelatory episode which kept the three friends, weary though they were, too nerve-taut to sleep.

—He'd have been a hero if they sent him across the big pond 'stead of down on the Border, said Morse. —I bet he'd have won more medals than Sergeant York, even.

—Sure.

—Sure he would.

Thus they paid traditional obeisance to legend. For almost twenty years the good folk of Thebes expiated, with talk and adoration, the one injustice they had done Johnny: vaunting his physical achievements too fulsomely they had neglected to track his intellectual, with the discomfiting result that at nineteen, prepared to graduate from high school, he was persuaded by the School Board in 1916 to enlist in the Army, that body thereby sparing itself the pickle of denying him a diploma on academic grounds. Hence the allegation that those who loved him best had cheated him of later immortality with the A.E.F. by exiling him to service in a forgotten backwash of the war, the Mexican Border Campaign.

—I 'magine there'll be a war for us to go to when we're

77

old enough, Harris said. —There usually is, he added philosophically. —Gosh all hemlock, I hope so! He raised himself, speculative. —Say, if there is, which of us'll be the bravest?

—Me, said Morse.

—No, Harris said. —It might be me.

—You? Sewell punched Morse in the ribs. —You? C'mon, Ris, say "shirt."

—Nope, Sewell'd be the bravest, Harris judged.

—Why him?

—Because of what he did this afternoon.

Then it was out, unboxed, articulated, then they might discuss and analyze its connotations, but first each one, to ready himself for conjecture, to be sure, as a boy must, that the sweetest dreams are made of more than applesauce, reënacted his part in the day's sequence. What had happened was incontrovertibly Mr. Vandevelde's fault. A powerful man nearing forty with eyebrows black and glossy as fur, a whistler, an informal, uncomplicated Dutchman so healthy that he scorned an overcoat in winter, overhearty, of a cheeriness synthetic to youngsters, he had come to Thebes from the Upper Peninsula as principal of one of the two elementary schools in 1928 but had just this June followed the retiring Superintendent of Schools into office. Thinnest of biographies, beyond it the boys had heard only that Bill Van had mounted a bobcat of his own killing and that, aspersion though unintended upon Johnny Scripter, he had fought as a doughboy in France. It took a trip into the north woods, however, they were agreed, to tell what kind of guy you were, and after three days they were vociferous the Superintendent, to borrow Morse Baird's appellation, was a "masterbastard." Waderless, the telescopic rods with which they fished the rivulets near Thebes too short to reach from its banks the Jordan's deeper pools, insect-plagued almost to frenzy, none of them had yet hooked a keeper, while Mr. Vandevelde, declaiming in ministerial basso profundo "And the priests that bore the ark of the covenant of the Lord stood firm on dry ground in the midst of Jordan," each morning portaged his canoe and lunch to the beaver ponds and fished them in comfort, leaving his charges to shift for themselves and admire, at dusk, his limit catch of rainbows. This mid-morning they gave up fishing, and, the day being warm, busied themselves constructing of logs and earth a dam across a tiny tributary of the Jordan which flumed through a culvert under the sand road leading to the camp. In an hour they had their own swimming hole at one end of the culvert, and under noon's bright sun stripped and ottered chattering in and out of the icy water. The calamity was one of heedlessness rather than miscalculation. Shivering, oblivious to all but sensation, they were stunned when the dam gave way and the tributary's head bore the entire culvert twenty feet downstream, washing out the road as well. Mr. Vandevelde had to be summoned. A ponderous inspection made, he handed down judgment as though on tablets of stone: since theirs had been the damage, theirs must be the repair; before his return from fishing they would have the culvert replaced, the road rebuilt. It was the way, quoth the pedagogue, to learn. It was also beyond their powers. Toting sand in pans and bucket they refilled the road, but the culvert, of thick cement and a yard in diameter, the boys could not budge. Hungry, dirty, profane, they exhausted themselves trying until Bill Van portaged his canoe along the road and made pontifical throne upon it to watch. Once more they made the attempt, once more failed.

—Remember, boys, if at first—

—No, goddammit! And goddamn you, Mr. Vandevelde! We won't do any more until you get off your big butt and help!

It was Sewell Smith, hoarse, fisted, who cried out. His language, his hotspur presumption terrified the other boys, and gape-jawed they moved away from him as the Superintendent stood.

—I'll overlook what you said, Sewell. I shall go back to my fishing, and in the meantime—

—The hell you will! Darting to the canoe, Sewell with one wild kick stove a hole in its side, then ran back to his friends. —You don't have the guts to touch me! Not if you want to go on being Superintendent! He scrubbed at the sand and tears on his cheek. —If I tell my father what a bastard you've been on this trip he'll tell his friends, Mr. Baird and Murninghan and Kropf and Doc Reason, and you'll be through! Because that's the School Board, right there!

Hands on hips, man faced boy, and his eyes, sunhatched at the corners, narrowed as though taking aim. —I'll give you a hand, he said.

—No. On another idea, a better but more shocking proof, Sewell gulped breath. —No, you'll do it yourself and we'll watch you for a change.

—Boy, you're going to regret—

Sewell yelled:—You better start, Mr. Vandevelde! My father and his friends hate a poor-sport sonabitch and they run Thebes! And Morse and Harris and me, so will we someday, so get started!

To theirs, to Sewell's own incredulity perhaps, the Superintendent of Schools, his face red-grim, went down into the stream bed and put his shoulder to the culvert. For half an hour he travailed, shoving it with each groaning, Herculean heave only a few inches; he removed his shirt and undershirt; sweat rilled from his chin and sheened his chest; not once did he recognize his audience, not once speak; and not until he sat down heavily, a foot or two scant, and admitted weakly he could not go on without help, it would be dangerous for a man his age to overstrain himself, did Sewell permit his loyal but recreant command to assist in repositioning finally the culvert.

Forget this bull-baiting, this affair of will and honor in its detail they might, but they would remember Sewell's gall, that juggernaut candor, that force, irresistible, imbecile even before seemingly immovable objects, which bespoke a sadism, an iron menace as well as maturity beyond theirs, and above all there would reside in their new bones what he had said. That night, while over them the stars in their hereditary seats presided, the three boys lay embattled in the tent, crucial to one another now, friends indivisible except by death because of what they were and what they would be; lay bacchic after power's first sip; lay enraptured, taking pledges from reality more likely to be kept than those of romance; lay overwhelmed by a syllogism almost epiphanical, the major and minor premises of which they could acknowledge aloud as irrefutable: their fathers did indeed rule Thebes, not by divine right but electively, through faith in them voted; they were indeed the sons of their fathers; hence it must follow, as surrender must ensue to truth's assertion, that they would in their turn succeed to that rule.

—Gosh, we'll be on the School Board! Harris whispered.

—And the Council, said Morse.

—Bank Directors, too, added Sewell.

—Morse and I'll run the mill. I'll be President and he'll be Vice-President in charge of sales.

—The hell you say! I'll be President and you'll be Vice-President in charge of middlings.

—You both better wait and see.

New respect for, deference to him quelled the argument.

—Morse, we've got to look out for Charlieboy, too, the way Dad has.

—Okay, brain. Just you read the books and get me through high school. Say, what'll Sewell do?

— President of the bank, Harris said promptly. —Don't you want to be, huh, Sewell?

—Maybe, maybe not.

—Maybe Pres of the reel comp'ny? Morse hinted slyly.

—I wouldn't mind.

—Listen, you guys. Harris humped up to look down at them. —Let's make a treaty right now about Jane Murninghan. We all want to marry her and one of us will. But let's have rules: take turns dating her till someday she makes up her own mind. If anybody even tries for an extra date, he's a pluperfect masterbastard and the other two really beat him up.

—And nobody tries anything with her either, Morse warned; going up her leg or necking or anything.

—Who would? they demanded.

81

—Okay, let's shake on it, Harris said, and solemnly they complied, gravely entered the lists.

—That means, though, men, Morse reflected, that we got to find us steady tonk elsewhere.

—Ris was right, Sewell said. —Arlene.

—I guess so, Morse agreed thoughtfully. —One of these days Lene'll break down and put out and, men, I want to be there when she does.

Mosquito-hymned, star-convenanted, they might have gallivanted off just then to fish the rivers of fable, where lurk extravagant trout, had they not been rearoused by Harris. —Who wants to be a little frog in a damn big lonesome puddle like Chicago or New York? What have they got that we don't have? Who wouldn't rather be king, even of a small castle? And just think, we'll go to college and someday have kids ourselves and they'll grow up and have just as swell futures as we do! Jesus to Genoa! Substantial pageant, more perfect since more possible than the stuff the dreams of boys are made on, envisioning it they lay close, sleepless, their ark at last firm on dry ground, young men chosen by deity of blood to pass over Jordan, ardent for the trothed land of their lives, trembling to go home to Thebes.

ANTISTROPHE : 1954

Why then should words challenge Eternity,
When greatest men and greatest actions die?

HORACE

Harlan Murninghan

To a cigarette she made love with her mouth, cosseting it wetly, daubing it magenta, and so powerfully, so lewdly did she suck upon it that ravels of tobacco had, after each inhalement, to be spat out with loud plosions of lip and tongue. Her great stained teeth were spaced wide. Her face was goodwife broad and openpored and clamorously rouged and pastured above by hennaed hair cropped short in an Italiante style she had doubtless seen in a movie magazine. Speaking, she perspired; she snuffed now and then her own perfume, liberal and gamy; reminiscent, she scratched a hip, a thigh, a breast. —A knight 'n shinin' armor, that's what Or'm Kropf said he was after the fun'ral to me, but I don't think of him as no knight but jus' a shinin' man, as bright 'n brave yet as he was that day on the street, seventeen years go t'morrow, it was. Now my ol' man was a roothog, holyneck ol' snipe, you know the kinda bird, walks normal but carries their ass ten foot high off the ground. We lived on eighty acres down in the sand, toward Corinth, an' he'd bring Ma an' us kids to town on Sat'day night an' tie us kids to the wagon so's we'd stay pure of the evils of the city. Thebes, min' you, a city! Hughh, hughh. An' I recollect sittin' there with my eyes soul-big at all the 'cetylene lights an' fancy people an' prayin' I'd get older quick so's I could come in ever' day to town to school. Then when I did there was the town sheikhs winkin' at me an' gettin' me out in buggies 'n cars after school an' tellin' me how if a girl wasn't nice, that was, if she didn' let them put the blocks to her, she wouldn' have no dates an' might as well be back on the farm. So I b'lieved it an' let 'em. An' them mongerls followed me aroun' them four years like a bitch dog in heat. How was I to know better, a dumb good-lookin' farm girl with a good build only wanted to be pop'lar an' get asked to all the parties? God, I give away a lot! Hughh, hughh, hughh.

Mrs. Scripter's cough, viscid and harmonious, she allayed with a long impenitent letting-down of beer. From most of her fingernails the scarlet glaze had splayed. —I know jus' how ol' you are. Same age as Lene, thirty-three. To this Sewell made no response; he was already used, in half an hour, to the irrelevancies, the juxtapositions of mood accounted for, at least in part, by her swilling. —They give me this job at the Light an' Power an' I tried to be p'lite to people comin' in ever' day snottier till one day I jus' couldn' take no more. Didn' I bust ever' damn light bulb in the place, though! After that I was no better'n dirt under the feeta this town, but I hel' my head up an' said shit on you brother to ever' man makin' me a indecen' proposition an' I been true to Johnny all this time! Oh God, but my Johnny was a shinin' man! And suddenly, heroine carried away by her own melodrama, Mrs. Scripter cramped shut her small shoat eyes until each one gave forth, pendant below the mascara press, a vintage tear. Undone by grief's accomplishment, she wailed " 'Scuse me!" and rising took her backside inelegantly up the stairs, there to absent herself from felicity awhile.

LIVE BAIT: thus, with a large, ill-lettered sign, the house, which leaned ramshackle at the north edge of Thebes between the street and the River Button, announced a humble commercial hope. Its lower level, actually basement, was cut into the riverbank and entered from the street by an exterior descent of rotted wooden steps. Through gloom repelled only by two fly-stippled light bulbs Sewell, in the absence of his hostess, peered. From its furnishing the basement appeared to serve as living quarters, place of enterprise, and museum: a table was spread with oilcloth, unwashed dishes, dirty cutlery, while nearby were several lop-legged chairs and horsehair davenport; against one wall an old double-doored refrigerator was crowned by a whining unit; a system of iron piping suspended from the ceiling joists let water drop by drop into the two concrete minnow tanks against another wall, the one a-dart with shiners for perch and bass, the other with six-inch chubs for pike;

sheaved overhead between the pipes was an assortment of cane poles and spinning rods for sale; lining a third wall were the flats, moss-filled, of night crawlers; and at one end of the minnow tanks, obscure in a corner, rusted, spider-webbed, Sewell could make out, frowning recognition and dubiety, the shape of an immortal mount: a great black Harley-Davidson motorcycle. He would have risen to examine it had he not followed, above the complaint of the refrigerator and the drip of pipes, the sequence of that woe with which she had closeted herself upstairs: a bladderous stridor in the bowl, the rush of healing waters, then her heavy progress down to him once more.

—Sure you don' wan' a beer? She helped herself to one from the refrigerator, crammed, he could see, not only with bottles but with cartons of night crawlers in lots of fifty and a hundred, uncapped it, cleansed the mouth across the under-flesh of her arm, and took, simultaneously, a chair and a resumptive draught. —Well, well, Sewell Smith come back home rich an' famous. How I knew you was back, Morse Baird tol' me, he works at the reel comp'ny. Ever'body mus' know by now, bigges' damn event aroun' here since you boys blew godlemighty hell outa the dam! Hughh, hughh!

Bone-chilled by the mossy, humid damp of the basement, made more grotto-esque by May's untoward heat and the turgid presence of the Button outside, Sewell stirred. —When you called, you said there was something you had to see me about.

—Jus' to talk, jus' to talk. You was one of the kids looked up to Johnny so much. The obvious equivocation paralyzed her for a moment, bottle and cigarette both halfway to her mouth while she chose between beer, smoke, and garrulity for refuge. —Now this las' book of yours, what's it?

—*Looking for a Location.*

—That's it, about Hollywood 'n all. I ain't much hand to read but I heard it was sexier 'n hell an' I was goin' to but there was a long list of dirty-min's waitin' for it at the Li-barry an' I couldn' keep traipsin' down there, not with Lene livin' upstairs over it. We don' have nothin' to do with each other, Sewell, ain't had for years. Oh God, it's a tragidy, a mother 'n daughter 'stranged! Again she cramped shut her eyes as though to produce appropriate flow but, artful trouper, aware a second miracle might nullify the first's effect, opened them promptly. —This here's a pretty good bus'ness, bait, I mean. There's always boys wants to sell minnas 'n crawlers 'n crickets later on. Take crawlers, I buy 'em two for a penny 'n sell 'em two cents apiece, two dollars a hunderd. Say, if you go for trout while you're back, stop by an' I'll let you have all the crawlers you want, on the house, proud to. She drained the bottle and dropped into it the cigarette butt and barraged in the direction of a minnow tank the last remembrances of tobacco from her mouth. —Bait maybe don't pay the way writin' books does but it keeps a body independen' in a town the same bastids runs it as always did, jus' older 'n more bastidly is all. Except for Claude Reichert an' Renis Baird an' your father. L. V. Smith —she fetched a long, melancholy, abdominal sigh—a man with char'cter. No honester ever come down the road. An' then to have him an' Renis took almos' together that way, an' life givin' you three boys a real rookin', an' you, Sewell, the only one amounted to something, even with your poor mother puttin' on free concerts off the roof—

Steps on the stairs outside, and a man, a customer Sewell did not know, came for a dozen pike minnows. He was on his way, he said, to Murray Lake, and as the proprietress hastened to serve him, as they exchanged technical confidences on the location and extent of the weed beds in Murray Lake, Sewell, bored, went to look through the rear screen door at the River Button, green-black and fat on spring rains. Once he turned his head and, amused, kept it turned. While Mrs. Scripter presided at the tank, bending low to net the minnows and transfer them to his bucket, the customer, practiced fisherman, his hand trolling beneath her skirt, researched for himself the location and extent of her wares. With Sewell's eyes her eyes collided, and when the man had paid and departed it was she who made short shrift of modesty.

88

—You surprised? Well, that's one way to beat the comp'tition. She bunched hands on hips, defiant. —You forget what
a looker I was once, huh, Sewell? Should of been in the
movies, ever'body said so. Why, I had men peckerin' through
the windows 'n under the doors after I was widowed! An' I
still got a goddamn good build!

What Sewell might have said, that in silhouette she resembled a sack of fertilizer on stilts, that she was, in fact, the
most gross, repellent old bag he had seen since the Army,
he did not say; what struck him dumb was not only the ar-
rogance, indomitably female, of her claim but its ghost of
truth. In her early fifties, from shoulder to hip Ethel Scripter was billboard broad, medieval of bosom and belly, but
incongruent, almost ludicrous, was the slimness of her legs,
thigh, calf, ankle, upon which she teetered on feet bound
up in high-strap pumps with spike heels. Visually, the effect
was that of a full-sail ship, once proud but now run by sensual storms onto a rocky coast, any treasures left within the
hulk worth recovery only by desperate natives; or, gustatori-
ally, that of a lavish banquet long ago devoured, from which
a few choice scraps might yet remain for those with appetite to scavenge. —I have to go, he said, disgusted by a salac-
ity which she might still haunt out in him. —I have things
to do.

Her face broke. —Oh, God, no. Real color spurted into
her cheeks, she seemed capable of real tears. —I handled
this mis-rable. Sewell, don't go, I lied. I had a reason to ask
you over but I ain't known how to bring it up, it's too low
an' fearful!

He continued to stand. —What is?

She cocked her head, listening upstairs, stilted past him
to peer out the door, then came close. —Listen. Somethin's
happened, the dirties' goddamn thing ever happened in this
town, worse even than what they done to Johnny after he
died for 'em. I got to have help about it, Sewell, an' right
now you're the most importan' one aroun', why, this town'll
have its pants down as long's you'll stay. Well, it's my girl
Carlie.

—Carlie?

—Carlene, my younges', named after Arlene. A dear sweet little thing, an' Sewell—she's been corruptioned!

—By who?

—Here's how I foun' out. A rill of sweat ran down from the base of her neck to the font formed by her breasts. —She's been spendin' a lot of money, on magazines an' a radio an' clothes an' stuff, money I ain't give 'er. She don' even go into ninth grade till September! Well, I ast 'er where she got it an' she wouldn' tell so I whumped hell outa 'er. Then it all come out, this dirty sonabitch's been screwin' 'er two, three months an' givin' 'er money like my little girl was already a hooker when she don' hardly know where babies comes from! Fourteen years ol', no mor'ls an' no cherry neither! Hughh, hughh, hughh! Oh God, what a cross an' shame to put on a lovin' mother!

—What do you want me to do? Sewell said to keep from grinning.

—I want you to get justus for my Carlie! It's a legal crime, ain't it?

—At fourteen it is, even if she consented. Statutory rape or something.

—Then such a fien' ought to be behin' bars so's other people's daughters'll be safe, oughtn' he?

Her personification of virtue, rampant and outraged, so amused him that he had to chew his lip to prevent guffawing in her face. —All you have to do, Mrs. Scripter, is tell the police.

—The police? Earl Blue, you mean? From a pocket in her dress she snatched a scrap of paper and thrust it at him. —Here! Tell anyone in town this one's gettin' his nookie off a little kid?

Once, twice, thrice Sewell read the name. He went to a chair. He sat down. Level with his stare, across the basement, over the mossy edge of one of the wooden flats, a night crawler, great worm urged to seek escape by some dim annelid foreknowledge of the hook's barb, extended several inches of its slimy length.

—I don't believe it, Sewell said. —He must be seventy.
—Older the buck, her voice intoned, the stiffer the horn.
He heard the match strike, the greedy inspiration.
—Justus, she said softly. —One kin' or another. I'm gone
near-crazy thinkin' what to do. This holyneck—I won' even
mention his name out loud—has got his due comin' a long
time. Body like me'd get laughed outa court, prob'ly, up
agains' him. An' if I was to walk into his offus, a poor weak
woman, an' say me n' Carlie, we'd forget what he's done
for some money, maybe a thousan' dollars, the ol' lecher'd
have my ass'n the street. But if somebody else, a big-shot
writer couldn' be bluffed, say, walks in, he'd shit a hymn-
book. Might even have a couple thousan' dollars up his ol'
bowels, mightn' he? An' split two ways, half for dear little
Carlie's eddication 'n half for the one has guts enough to
get it, why, ever'body'd sleep peaceful, washed in the blood
of my lamb, so to speak. Forgive. An' rich.

In his hand Sewell crushed the paper scrap. To him,
behind him, Ethel Scripter moved, smoking fiercely, with
her usual odors of beer and nicotine osmosed, of bedclothing
groaned and rutted in, of barns where mares were brought
to stallions, cows to bulls for loveless service, with which were
mingled rank, anticipative musk. —Justus, she said.

Most men pay to the place of their birth and sculpture,
once they have gone from it, estovers of remembrance as
necessary as they are figmental. Sewell Smith's exception
perhaps proves the rule. Something there was in his nature,
a quartz of will, a bulldog fixity of purpose gened from his
father, which enabled him to bite on a bone of grudge, bury,
then unearth and gnaw out of it further nourishment, so
that for fifteen years, since the night in 1939 he had run, a
boy kicked, sent howling by concatenation of event, his hatred of Thebes had been rabid. Rather than balm to those
wounds he had expected, success had been salt, and the
reference to Thebes, Michigan, as his starting point on the
jackets of his novels was intended, rather than tribute, to be
insulting credential of how much might derive from how

little. He hated it still. He had returned not by desire but out of real need. He was an author without a publisher and the only way he could get one was to do another book and the only way to produce another book was to get an idea. Any idea would serve, but Peckham Hill's offhand, poolside suggestion Sewell took with the desperation of a hunted beast a hole or a tree. Within a day of the editor's departure he had packed, readied his car, and consolidated his remaining funds. Their total almost unnerved him: for the nearly half a million he had indeed earned in four years, from *Benison* in 1949 and *Looking* in 1953, he had little more than three thousand dollars to show. To cut the hair shorter he must raise between now and September 15th another delinquency payment in addition to that due in June or he would be in even deeper tax trouble. Three thousand dollars and three months to mill out enough manuscript to justify a new firm's advance on it: for a man who had not written a word in more than a year, a man newly habituated to spending three thousand a month, it was a hazardous, fecal margin. Deciding to let his landlord's bill for damages to the glass and patio furniture catch up with him if it could, he drove from Arizona to Thebes in fifty-four hours. Arrived, other than doing what was required to settle himself, he made no attempt to alert the populace, although his car by itself would have been advertisement sufficiently flagrant; under the mud, tar, and stone chips it might be identified as a 1953 Jaguar XK120 roadster of a finish originally white. Upon this vehicle, purchased new during the Malibu days, he had lavished no more care than he did upon his clothing, or any of his owned or rented possessions for that matter: the leather upholstery, once red, was black-veined and grimy, the top, once black, was now gray and rent in several places, the loose canvas flapping loudly at speeds over thirty; on the dashboard the glass face of the tachometer had been shattered; attest to minor accidents, two of the wire wheels had been replaced with discs, the tires conventional in contrast with the two whitewalls, and a section of the right rear fender, bumped out and buffed down to raw metal, had not yet been repainted; the muffler, finally, if not entirely blown was at least pinholed, so that the car, besides the full-throated proclamation of its motor, offered from underneath a bronchial *ora pro nobis.* Worthy of comment the maltreated Jaguar would have been in a city; Thebes had never before been shepherd to such a machine in such a condition.

In any case, Sewell's first human contact with the past, except for the meeting on Mrs. Scripter's premises, had been a telephone call from Harris Baird inviting him to an evening with his old friends at the Creel & Cartridge Club. He accepted, but by the day specified he had half a mind not to appear at all; going to a "party" was one thing, while an "evening with old friends" connoted wet handclasps, cloying reminiscence, embarrassing comparisons, and bumpkin, godawful tedium; and although it would be good to see Harris and Morse again, he hadn't the weirdest notion who in hell else would be there. He compromised: he would go, but he would go late and make an entrance, indicating both disinterest and cognizance of his renown.

A cabin weatherworn and false-faced with logs, in prospect of a small round lake four miles north of Thebes, the Creel & Cartridge had been built in 1923 by a group under the leadership of Oram Kropf and Renis Baird for the purpose, publicly avowed, of affording a headquarters where sportsmen of means, fishers and hunters, might take respite from the strenuosities of field and stream; practically from its founding, however, it was dubbed the "Chip & Cork," and sportsmen of another ilk, their number limited by vocation to poker, had made exclusive use of its facilities. These included little more than two great pine card tables, a polyglot of veteran chairs and davenports, a fireplace over which was mounted a deerhead with Coolidge buttons for eyes and cigar jutting executively from its lips, and a bar behind which, in bottle-sized compartments lettered with their names, prominent among them Smith, Kropf, Reason, Baird, Vandevelde and Scripter, the members stored their paraphernalia.

The invitation had been for nine o'clock; at ten Sewell Smith made his entrance; by 10:10 he had resolved to get stoned and to put on as good a show as possible. In that kaleidoscopic ten minutes he gave up any attempt to defend himself by himself, unallied with liquor, against the ambush of time and inurbanity into which he had swaggered. First, the dramatis personae, his "old friends," consisted of Harris Baird and a wife, Norma, whom he had not known existed but who, conversation developed, had enriched her husband with three children; Morse Baird accompanying Edie Kropf, Oram's daughter and only child, whose name but nothing else he could recall since, being four years older than he, she had graduated from Thebes High just as he entered it; Herbie Teeple, whom he remembered vaguely as being along on the fishing trip to the Jordan, a peripheral friend of boyhood married now to Karen Vergennes, also present and heiress of the local mortician; and Jane Murninghan; eight in all, counting himself. Then the unaccountable absence of Arlene Scripter, who was certainly classifiable as an "old friend." Then Harris Baird, whom he had last seen in headlong flight from their destruction of the mill dam, was and had been long employed at the mill. Then Jane Murninghan, so transubstantiated from his memory of her as to be unrecognizable, her name now Mrs. Charles Reason by virtue of marriage neither to Harris nor Morse but to—yes, by God—Dr. Charles Reason, more than twenty years her elder and compeer of his father. Then they had chipped in to buy, in his honor and for once hang the tremendous expense, a case of champagne, domestic of course, icing it in a tub atop the bar; and since they were eight, someone had calculated the case out to a bottle and a half per guest, but in his absence unable, like children, to wait, none of them probably, Jane Reason excepted, ever having tasted champagne, they had opened one bottle and were sipping timorously, each trying to enjoy it and take care he did not exceed his ration. Then some managerial type had evidently been chosen to deploy the deal, for he was maneuvered onto a barstool and they seated themselves as though on signal

94

around the two card tables opposite where they might, allowed several hours to stare, convince themselves that he was more than optical illusion. Then Norma Baird, clearly selected by lot in advance to tell a funny, poignant, toujours-gay, real-life story which would overture the evening's entertainment, sipped, said something inane about the bubbles tickling her nose, and told the story. Harris, they all knew, she began, was notoriously underpaid by his Uncle Charles. It was spiteful and vicious when you knew all that Harris had done for the mill—but then, she wouldn't go into all that again. Anyway, Harris still had his wonderful sense of humor and this would prove it. Just last Sunday morning he'd been lying in bed while she was getting breakfast, the kids were outdoors, when he called and asked if they were having caviar and champagne for breakfast. She'd hooted, naturally, but he pretended to be mad and ordered her to him from the kitchen in husbandly dudgeon. A champagne and caviar breakfast, he cried, had been one of his lifelong ambitions, and he'd been lying there figuring: she'd been married to him almost seven years, for seven years he'd sacrificed everything for her and the kids, and if she in turn had just put away ten cents a week for that seven years, she'd now have over thirty-six dollars, more than enough to serve him a champagne and caviar breakfast, which was, it seemed to him, the least any loving wife could do for her husband, and why the hell, he roared, hadn't she? And that was the wonderful kind of husband she had. And that was Norma Baird's funny, poignant, toujours-gay, real-life story. It laid a brontosaurian egg. The silence of afterbirth no one knew how to intermit; Sewell thought of breaking wind stereophonically or doing a card trick or dropping his trousers and exhibiting himself; instead, he pulled a bottle from the tub, popped the cork expertly, poured himself a conspicuous tumblerful and drained it. Then there commenced the saddest performance, the most jerkwater, catechetical press conference he had ever undergone; the catch was, he surmised, that they had a Celebrity with a capital C on their hands and were too damn palsied and small-town to be themselves; it

95

had been someone's brainstorm that they should all frame a question or questions to put to the Celebrity and thus pass the time, and this they proceeded to do, for two entire hours, with a sweaty, diffident, yokel monotony. Only Edie Kropf, it seemed, had the guts to get the show on the road, and her question was the wrong one.

—Sewell, why did you come back?

Amid the crossing of legs and repositioning of rears Sewell, brushing her off rather than remark it was none of her goddamn backfence business, inquired if anyone had ever found the robbery money. —You know, the loot they cached up near Delphi Grange after they shot Johnny?

They were relieved to chorus no, no one had, but people winked and wondered whenever a farmer in the area bought a new car.

Herbie Teeple cleared his throat severely enough to do irreparable damage to the trachea. His face was moon, his thin hair oiled, his ear lobes recessed, these attributes producing an effect so spheroid that one felt he might, by inserting thumb and forefinger in the apertures of Herb's ears, roll his head from his shoulders like a bowling ball. His expression, as became the son-in-law of an undertaker, was one of perpetual resignation before a mortality too divine and too lucrative to argue. —Did you come from California, Sewell?

—With a banjo on my knee? No, Arizona.

—Uh. And you're living in your old house? I thought Mrs. Reichert wanted to sell.

—She does. She's been in Florida since Claude died as I get it, and no buyer. So I called her and she was willing to rent.

—Uh. It isn't even furnished, is it?

—Drapes and carpets. I've bought enough to camp out.

—Uh. How long you think you might stay?

—How long you think, 'Erbie?

Karen Teeple came to Herb's rescue, removing his finger from his collar and twittering interest. A small canary-type woman, she seemed to articulate by pecking, as though language were seeds, and "ing" she pronounced "een," a locution Sewell detested. —It must have been thrilleen, Sewell, to be in Hollywood with all those stars and all!

—We call it H-wood.

—I'm simply dyeen to know about Liz Roberts! Did you meet her?

He had not. —Couple times. Busiest pelvis in the world.

—Busiest pel—

—Twenty-seven years old, four husbands, four kids, three miscarriages, one abortion. Action there all the time.

He slid a second bottle from the tub and thumbed the cork.

—Just one thing I want to know, old buddy, Morse said. —We read the papers, sure, but on the level: you really make all that money?

Sewell let them wait while he drank. —Damn well did, half a million. Why, Christ, I took in nearly that from *Ben-'son* in one year.

—How can a book, a book, make that much?

—Should I draw a map? His corroboration of the amount and the tale he next told had the rustics swoggle-jawed and cataleptic; he found himself enjoying himself immensely. —Hear this, he said, tipping his stool aslant the bar. —Now hear this. 1949. *Ben'son*. The novel had been archetypical of the postwar literary period even to the medium of its conveyance: a barracks bag. A sergeant still in the Army and stationed at Camp Patrick Henry, Virginia, one of the many posts garrisoned with middle-aged tanks and fieldpieces, echoing hutments, and a cadre of "career soldiers," so-called, hashmarked anachronisms hermited by war on a darkling plain of peace, Sewell Smith had, on leave, brought his manuscript to New York in a barracks bag. On its fate would rest his election to leave the service or reënlist for another three-year hitch. Presently it reached Peckham Hill's desk. The epigraph from which its title was excerpted had indeed been tracked down in Bartlett's *Familiar Quotations,* and therein to "A Child's Grace" by Herrick: "Here a little child I stand/ Heaving up my either hand/ Cold as pad-

97

docks though they be/ Here I lift them up to Thee/ For a benison to fall/ On our meat, and on us all." The subject of the novel was the soldier as meat, historic product of war's abattoir located and disposed of by the characters, the personnel of a Graves Registration team in France and Germany: fresh carcasses, friend and foe alike; aged carcasses bloated into nursery-rhyme shapes until buttons popped and belts snapped and which, when stepped on to deflate for coffins, emitted doleful, stinking sighs; carcasses decomposed and maggot-sampled; carcasses already butchered by skillful shell and bullet into steaks and chops and roasts; carcasses so hacked and boned and hamburgered as to be unfit for any consumption save that of shovel and basket. Never of their old, their ill, their parasitic, but always of their young, prime, male human life, societies have made free offering to war, deeming it sensibly that resource easiest and most pleasurable to replenish hence cheapest to expend, and the book, though written in a prose guttural and ungrammatic, made such Yahoo, belly-turning contrast between the innocent meat and the national association of flaunt-flag, gold-star, bleeding-heart, home-front cattlemen which sent it tearfully to market, the war-bond infantry, the cost-plus quartermasters, the congressional commandos, the coffee-break tankers, the ration-card rangers, the fallen-arch artillery, that Peckham Hill's house, against its tradition and judgment, contracted to publish and paid an advance. Sgt. Smith was a novelist. —Walked out of there with a check for five thousand, by Christ. Week before that worked all night on my knees won fifty bucks in a crap game. This was for me. *A Benison on Our Meat* was like a knife drawn not across the neck of the American ox but driven fatally into its conscience; in consecutive first place on the *Times* best-seller list for forty-six weeks, it sold over the counter nearly 170,-000 copies, amassing royalties totaling $127,000. —But hardcover income any more is beer money. Anc'llary rights, that's the free ride. For instance, book club took it. Sixty-five G's. Thermal bidding among the paperback firms brought him forty thousand dollars and advances on overseas translations

98

another fifteen. Film rights went, finally, for $225,000. —Okay, buddyroos. Give those figures a bed and see if they like hell sleep. Sounds like a goddamn potful, hey? Forget one thing. Taxes. Truman and Eisenhower crooks, they write a book get special ruling from Internal Revenue, they're not professional writers so they can take capital gains, 25 percent; but a guy name Smith, nobody, still in the Army, writes a book, never had a line in print before, he's a pro, so they sock it to him straight income, the bastards! No provision had been made, of course, in his various contracts for a flash flood of income such as occurred. After running up legal fees of four thousand dollars he was able to obtain a partial spread-back of income over the two years he claimed to have been writing the novel, but it was only partial since those years included full-time soldiering. —Well, to bag it up, goddamn near 70 percent that half million went for taxes. I tell you, in this country you want to make out taxwise speculate peddle poop for armpits incorporate—don't create! Be an artist get the dirty end the stick!

As they sat adding and subtracting, trying to strike an emotional balance between the vast sums he had ticked off and the realities of their own lives, he lifted his tumbler, took a mouthful, and gargled aggrievedly.

Harris whistled. —Jesus to Genoa! He came to the bar and opened a communal bottle, serving the others. —Most of us watched the Academy Awards on television the night *Benison* picked up all the marbles. Were you there, in the theater I mean, or watching yourself, and what did you think?

—Crock crap, you want to know. *Ben'son* should have won and it did. Seven awards one show. Great. But you hear a single one those Israelites, those egos, those mother-sellers, when he walks up the mike speaks his little piece, a single one says thanks, Sewell Smith, making the whole goddamn thing possible writing the book the first place? Christ no. Also working three months the script and no credit. Christ no.

—This is probably a stupid question, Harris said, but I'm curious about the mechanics. What happens, exactly, when you finish a book? What's the procedure?

—The S.O.P., buddyroo, is. I wrap it up send it off to New York.

—No editorial tinkering?

—Book by Sewell Smith? Money in the mattress? Hell no, no changes.

—And you've reached the point where anything you turn out is published?

—Anything. My telephone number on toilet paper they go to press. Hear this. Give you the straight scoop, old friends. Writing's a business now. Field's full guys don't know their ass page eight but they grind organs monkeys take big bills who's going rock boat over comma here semicolon there? Example rigging. Some producer on Coast gets idea for book calls New York publisher says great idea hire someone tear it off I'll buy it x dollars. Publisher calls up some hack some college brain some babe says write this x dollars. She writes can't spell no difference they fix up publish much advertising. Producer on Coast buys two, three thousand copies week in bookstores gets book on best-seller list. Big announcement: book sells studio x dollars big deal anc'llary rights I said.

The question now somewhat academic, Norma Baird nevertheless took her turn. —I'm interested, Sewell, seriously, in the novel as an art form.

—Art shit.

Their determination to forgive the obscenity could not have been more hagiologic had they chosen partners and gone into a square dance.

—*Benison,* Norma went on, two coins of angry color stamped on her cheeks, was autobiographical partly. Then you went to Hollywood to work on the script and flew madly all over with the producer and the others looking for a location and then afterward wrote the second book based on those experiences. So your work is really very autobiographical. Is it too personal if I ask what you may do next?

Sewell made certain his bottle was empty by hoisting it telescopically to an eye. —May open another bottle. Too personal hell yes. Don't let that sweat old friends, though, ask anything, sex life, bowel movements, anything. Ten, twelve books, so many ideas don't know which one, publisher on my back, magazines, TV, everybody wants.

The strain counted now, the effort of the lies, the civility he must maintain under inquisition which pretended to be friendly curiosity. The semicircles about the two card tables reminded him of extras on a set passing time between takes, box-lunch anonymities out of Central Casting who, at once vain and sycophantic, jealous and egalitarian, stationed themselves near the star, daring him not to respond to them and at the same time puke-proud to associate their carbon dioxide with his. Sewell never drank well; and this cheap wine, with its bouquet of skins, stems, and A & P prodigality rather than reducing exacerbated his tension. Already half a bottle beyond his allotment he took a third from the ice. As ship-lost sailors might watch, thirst-crazed, while a brutish captain pigged the last of their water, they watched while he unfoiled the cork, even this a plastic substitute for the real thing.

—We saw the Person-to-Person telecast from your canyon house in Los Angeles. Jane Murninghan Reason was the last country to be heard from.

—Delighted you did. Emplacing the bottle between his knees, aiming it with exaggerated care, he fired a salvo at the deerhead. He was lucky: the cork struck near one of the Coolidge buttons, clattering it to the floor.

—That girl, Jane persisted, the one you introduced as your secretary.

—You're just dyeen know was she one in *Looking*.

—Well, yes.

—You're just dyeen hear whole naughty sinny real-life story.

—Why not?

That, as far as he was concerned, tied it. Very well, by God, if it were not bread but a circus they wanted, if he had to play pimp to their pru, pur, purience, he swore to himself, unable to enunciate because even the tongue of his brain had thickened, if he had to make of his own bed a colosseum and let them herd in to shriek at whatever orgies he might imperially command for the delec, edu, lectation of the dirty-minded, then by God he would, and he would give them their sa, satur, saturnalia double-barrel and three-ring and four-star.

—Aw right okay your servant. He glowered, gulped off half the bottle directly from the bottle, belched suspensefully, and began. —So I lived with this babe. Or she living with me Arizona. She took off last week before I came back here for L.A. or Vegas or somewhere a sick kid nineteen many problems know what she did before she took off? Smash every goddamn window the house threw all lawn furniture in pool thousand dollars' damage. Real pig. But hell in bed. On back a genius. Gave her everything clothes furs bracelet right books to read. Lived with her year L.A. also. How I hooked on with her first place. Aw right okay your servant. Try get picture. Barefoot boy Thebes Mich trying get along in H-wood. Working *Ben'son* scrip thousand a week. So producer wants look for location. Charter plane God knows what cost a day DC-6. Fly all over hell round and round Arizona New Mexco Utah Palm Springs Nevada Vegas Oregon Idaho producer can't make up mind many mental problems work scrip on plane hotels motels more people more people director cameraman other writer stars red carpet welcome. Land. Rent air-condition Cadillacs. All little towns' tongues hang out be location for big pic. Chamber Commerce much business money publicity great thing tourist trade put town on map. So. Bottle high, he poured so much of the wine down his throat that the overflow dribbled over his chin to stain his lapel, his shirt, his necktie. —So. Where the hell's goddamn DC-6? Oh, Caisson, New Mexico. Never heard of it who did. Land Santa Fe drive there. Few hundred people more jackrabbits raise sheep. President Chamber Commerce. Beautiful daughter seventeen Miss Caisson New Mexico tall terrific body bedroom eyes, tan pony-tail hair Christ what body. So out looking for location in rented Cadillac me producer President Chamber Commerce daughter four of us drive all over hell no locations. Caisson shit out of luck also Chamber Commerce him having ruptures lose big-budget pic put town on map. Yells stop car stop car! Unbalanced by an outflung arm he would have crashed to the floor had he not let the bottle fall and stayed himself against the bar. To prevent a recurrence he hunched down on the stool and locked his knees tightly to its legs. —Now get scene. Car stopped middle nowhere. President Chamber Commerce says no location okay but daughter look at her wants be in movies no chance Caisson loaded talent sing dance take her H-wood screen test never have chance like this real producer famous writer let her show you please name of God let her. So there middle nowhere she sings gets out car dances in road nothing much dime dozen on Coast. Producer says thanks don't call us we call you start car. President Chamber Commerce starts cry no screen test his baby daughter says daddy get hell out of car go down road disappear get lost handle this myself. He does. Goes sits on rock cries. Daughter says be a star no matter what going H-wood screen test know what I have to do which one you gents first? Seventeen. Producer yawns, says child, not interested. I by God am. She says okay producer go be nice daddy. Producer friend mine so he goes down road other direction sits on rock. She climbs in back seat. Get picture. Middle nowhere New Mexco up on hills flocks goddamn sheep scene right out of goddamn Bible and Cadillac motor running air-condition sitting on rock one direction President Chamber Commerce crying other direction sitting on rock producer reading *Wall Street Journal* slice Americana go west young man go west get screwed girl wants be movie star!

—But in the book, someone said, it was the producer who—

—Truth stranger fiction.

—You took her with you, you destroyed her!

The accusation was female, but he could scarcely distinguish any voice except his own.

—Destroy her? She goddamn near sprained my balls!

To do something about the horrendous, stentorian hush he felt cataleptically for and found the last bottle in the tub, his fourth, opened it and tried slobbering to drink.

—Hollywood, someone, probably Harris, said. —Even if we hadn't invented it, it would have to exist.

—That, said someone else, identifiable only by the locution, is absolutely the most degradeen, nauseateen story I have ever heard!

—Up your embalm twot, Mrs. Teeple.

—Now just a damn minute, Sewell, there are ladies present—

—Go jump a corpse, 'Erbie!

—The reviews of *Looking* mention his dirty typewriter, someone else, doubtless Edie Kropf, remarked, but they left out his foul mouth.

—Yes, and don't think we didn't read the reviews, too, sniffed Norma Baird, and you may brag about making a lot of money but as to making any contribution to American literature, well—

—Rubes! Jerkwaters! Hayseeds! Clods! Sewell bellowed. He could not distinguish faces, either; he seemed surrounded by leering, Cyclopean, cigar-smoking deerheads. —Minus-minds! Hicks! Autograph hunters! What they heard bellowing, what they saw crouched on the barstool was a man about whom, at thirty-three, there was something repellent and curiously ursiform; heavy-pawed, thick of neck, of shoulders, of thigh, of posterior, his weight had gone not to muscle but to fat and his jaw, stubborn and prognathous, its large-lipped mouth fitted irregularly with teeth, jutted at them as though to grip and rend. His hair, of an innocuous brown and curly, had begun to bald at the crown, and it receded from a forehead high and bulging. His best features were a good, straight nose and eyes which, although imploded and bloodshot, were large and of a blue so pungent that it transfixed. Nothing in his dress or grooming could possibly attract: tailor-made his suit might be but it appeared housing rather than clothing, lived in for months rather than worn; the collar and cuffs of his shirt

were grimy; there was dirt under his fingernails and he
wanted a haircut; the spots of wine-slaver only heightened
the effect of slovenry, of anarchic habit, of the enlisted man
forced against his will into civilian attire. He had subsided
for a moment, addressing them almost soberly. —Hate this
town everybody in it. Tell you what you add up. Nothing.
Nothing you say important nothing you do important. Dead
you are. This town. Only thing ever important happen to
you is—me. Tonight. So tonight great good-all Christ! he
shouted again. —You want show I give you ask everything
no respect famous writer big name jealous brown-nose
bastards! Show you expect free big spenders? You buy
champagne green stamps? Champagne? Piss! Brandishing
the bottle he let the wine spout onto the floor. —There big
spenders! Why hell don't you get class? See world drive
Grand Rapids lots things happen indoor plumbing electricity books music culture get class! Thebes toilet of world
hicks jokes so go home flush yourself small-town turds!
Go—
    Seized by coat-front, he was uplifted, legs dangling, arms
waving insectly, and slammed against the bar. —Goddamn
you, Sewell! someone cried into his face, bending him con-
cavely. —Goddamn you, you've got no cause to act like this
and we don't have to take it! He could not focus on his assailant, but only Morse would possess the strength to do this
to him, to contort him so that the dread, familiar tautening
of the sacroiliac muscles he could not oppose, nor the rubber-
band snap of pain down the rear of his left leg; he was helpless even to obey training's reflex, to bayonet knee terribly
into belly, groin, scrotum. —I ought to beat hell out of you
and make you apologize but you're too stinking drunk. We
used to be your friends and we still are but you sure have
changed, old buddy, and whoever the hell you are we don't
like very much. Now we're going home, like you said. You
stay here and sober up and when you're Sewell again we'll
see you.
    Released, the slide downward, the slow dummy collapse
onto the stool, then to the floor behind it, his legs straddled,

seemed eternal and blessed. He could not see but he could hear them leave: good-byes, clumping of men's shoes, whispers, click of women's heels, the door's circumspection. He was conscious not of abandonment but of dignity reëstablished, stature revived; of the graceful altruism by which he had lent their lives a brief glamour; and of his author's duty now to offer some comment on the universal dullness he had this night conquered. —Here little child I sit heave up my guts, he soliloquized behind the barstool. —Cold buttocks they be lift up to Thee for ben'son fall on show biz on us all. Later, a threnody upon his suffering, his aching back, he sang, in order to do so propping his jaw upon a higher rung. —You're my little true lover little boy blue, he dirged. —But I'm your old Auntie darling can't marry you.

He was maudlin. That all things passed was a cliché, he puled, forcing down more coffee, but it was a low blow that she should be the most altered, in dress and cosmetics and walk closer to a Sunset Strip slutlet than the memory he had cherished for fifteen years. Jane Reason asked how he remembered her. To conceal intent she had driven into Thebes with the others, then returned to the Creel & Cartridge, found him passed out, embracing the legs of the barstool as though they were a mother's; baptism with ice water from the tub relaxed his clutch until she could load him, cursing, into a chair. On a hot plate she made instant coffee, administering it in small dosages, for she had no wish to expedite the sobering process; it was somehow like maturation, and the boy, blurting and tractable, she could learn more from than the man. He wondered aloud what kind of poker his dear dead father played. Close to the belt, he'd bet; wait for the cards, never bluff, but when you got a hand, never fold. She asked again how he remembered her. What about Tony, her older brother? Happily married, two children, an architect living, small world, in Santa Barbara. And did they deal and draw here still, Monday nights before the Council meetings Tuesdays? No. To every game time set a limit. Scarcely the gambling sort, Charles Baird had never taken Renis's seat; her father himself, selectman of God, Irish and Protestant, than whom none were more zealous, clement of human frailty but numbering cards, cigars and drink among perdition's pastimes, attended only to transact town business and read Oram Kropf's cards for him. Those players not dispersed by the years, she concluded, lighting a cigarette, had been changed by them: Oram Kropf's pleasures were now wholly intellectual, while her own husband, the doctor, played other games for higher stakes. As symbol of beauty quintessential she had served at sixteen, seventeen, eighteen, he swore, wrenching at shirt and tie to loosen them; diminutive, fay-smiling, with dimpled cheeks and yellow hair and wind chimes in her laughter, she had been beauty's immanence, hence truth's, which was all infatuate boys might know; therefore they had pacted, he and Morse and Harris, never to desecrate by touch or impure thought their still unravished bride of wet and quiet fancy. Petty theft by one upon her lips, even, would earn a beating from the other two contestants. Impatiently she shook her head. She had come back, she interrupted, to care for him but also to apologize for their behavior. He had been, actually, a little cruel, a little indecent in mixed company, but in justifiable retaliation, she felt, for their questions had all but torn the coat from his back. What, in their extenuation, he must understand was that to his old friends, to herself, he was a celebrity; for years, since the news release from Washington, the town had kept an emotional scrapbook on him, shelved in the place of honor. Morse's laying hands on him was jealousy, raw and simple, that and showing off. Tentatively he stretched, groaned. His back, he complained, his aching GI back, hurt in the war. He knew, didn't he, that she and Morse were divorced?

—Huh?

—Sewell, you must have heard. You knew we eloped the summer after high school. Harris and Arlene Scripter went with us as witnesses, down to Indiana one night.

—No, he snarled, taking the step from a sottish sentimentality to choler in one violent leap. —I'll be a sona-bitch.

—Our little girl was born the next year. Carol. She's four-teen now.

—Why in hell? Why?

—I don't know. I thought I loved him, I was deathly sick of being The Vestal Virgin of Ancient Thebes. And after the mill I was sorry for the three of you. No one could guess what Charles Baird would do about it, and waiting, Morse had begun to drink. I thought marriage would set me free, which was ridiculous. It was a brutal mistake. He went to work for my father and we lived on my money. I saw every change of feature at the Attic. And all this happened a month before I was to leave for college.

He lunged up unsteadily, maddened by an insight. —He got to you! That's how he did it, goddamn him! Had a few drinks and said the hell with it and got your pants off and that was love, to you that was love, wasn't it? Miss Twin-river Reel finally got laid and liked it!

Jane Reason had gone white. —Don't be crude. Didn't it ever occur to any of you I might find it boring, year after year, being a living trophy in some adolescent tournament? That I might want to be a normal girl, a human being?

—Human being hell. Hotbox, you mean. Christ, what ten-buck, B-picture irony—three kids take the Boy Scout oath to keep their hands off a goddamn nympho!

He began to move about the Creel & Cartridge, his control remastered as much by temper as by her ministrations. She observed how ungainly was his walk, which was really a prowl, a hunting with shoulders squared too martially, fore-arms stiff and raised always, cocked as though he were pre-pared to fight. Through a window he scowled at the small lake's round placidity. —So Morse won, he said.

—If you want to put it that way.

The campaign button he had dislodged from the deer-head he kicked into a corner. —So what happened.

—We played the game seven years. He sulked about not moving ahead at the plant, but it wasn't my father's fault;

you can't run a company on good looks. I was bitter at myself mostly. A girl's best years are a high price to pay for a gesture of rebellion and a trip to Indiana. In 1947 we divorced and I married Charles.

—Who was already married.

—As blissfully as I was.

—Met him on the examination table, I suppose.

She pointed. —On that davenport, as a matter of fact.

—God.

—Envious?

He leaned on the bar. —Your timing's sad. Stuck with a horse-and-buggy GP, when if you'd waited till now, till I came back, you might have cashed the big ticket. Mrs. Charles Reason, he jeered. —How old is he? She would not answer. —Goddammit, how old is he?

—Fifty-six.

—Fifty-six! Fatherly with the advice, is he? Creaky in the climax?

—Damn you, Sewell.

—Gets up often at night but not for what you want?

—Damn you.

—Poem: Little Janey Murninghan/ Thought that she had got a man/ But instead of bedtime kicks/ All she got was geriatrics!

When, in tears, her face averted, she had gone, he went behind the bar, opened the compartment lettered Smith and looked within. —Nothing, he said.

A bowl of roses, morning-glories, asters and carnations; amid the pleached blooms yawns, incongruous, serpentine, a howitzer's black muzzle; while over the queer floriculture— come into the garden, Maud, and have your head blown off!—flies in gilt the American Eagle, rampant of pinion, fierce of beak, in his talons quiver of arrows and olive branch. Rectangular, painted on glass, the synthesis uses the lower half of the cherrywood cabinet clock, shielding pendulum and strings and venerable lead weights. From its upper half the glass has been removed, and over the face, its

numerals made indistinct by dust, Oram Kropf's winged
fingers flutter, asking in their passage the hands' position
and relationship, and thus by brief palpation tell the time.
—That education spurned in dissolute youth I strive for,
improbably now, when the labors in its way seem Augean. I
have become, in point of fact, that personage insufferable to
the small town: its historian. From voluptuary to antiquary;
amusing, though not unnatural retrogression when we reflect that the curiosity of the flesh must wane. I importune the
trunk, the attic, the rolltop desk. I send to Lansing, Detroit,
Ann Arbor for books. I pore over them vicariously. I re-
search the early days with as much relish as that with which
I once gluttonized the present. To take a case: Carlos Sampter Baird, our founding miller, Charles's grandfather, got
his surname from an uncle of Spanish blood, an associate
of Aaron Burr's who amassed a fortune importing rum and
slaves. Owner and headmaster of a Latin Academy near
Albany, his soul however tended westward, and so, in 1836,
a year before our statehood, he undertook an hegira. Arriv-
ing, trying to girdle trees and farm a wilderness, weakened
by recurrent bouts of what the settlers called "agur," or ague,
they might have starved, his wife's letters home indicate,
had their fellows not assisted in slapping up a grist mill on
the Button; even then, poor romantic impractical pedagogue, without her divine afflatus he would not have made a
go of it. It was she who bethought herself to open, in an ell
of the structure, a tavern called The Live and Let Live,
forebear and patronymic of our own Mermaid. Moreover—
and this in the tracking down was a delight—if Thebes was
built on beer it may be said that the entire valley of the
Ionian was colonized by fraud. Literally. For how, in the
first place, was our academician persuaded hither? The
agent, it turns out, was one Professor Titus Willow, a scoun-
drel of the most erudite, endearing stock, who met the boat-
loads of emigrants from New York State at the docks of Detroit and fastened for his prey upon just such scholarly,
nincompoop adventurers as Carlos Sampter Baird. The landshark displayed a chart magnificently emblazoned: here was

the storied valley, here the confluence of two noble floods plied already by majestic steamers; there were roads and bridges and fair villages a-building, Thebes and Smyrna, Corinth and Tyre, Sparta and Naxos and Carthage; antiquity transplanted, in the New World the glory of the ancient civilizations relustered! Sign here, O pioneer, and pay to the gods ten dollars an acre! And when they reached idyllic Tempe's Vale—what? Bogs, a few indigent, shell-game savages, and the agur. The lesson is instructive: it is sometimes as prudent to piss on history as to honor it.

Blue-veined, the hands are never still. Plucking at clothing, touching objects, their functions are those of antennae, to investigate and reassure, and the fingers, patrician, tapered to hypersensitivity, seem to seek the click of the world's tumblers. On one of them is a massive diamond ring.

—Do you find Thebes much changed?

—No.

—To the good, to the good. It is a banality of literature that a man must return a stranger to his antecedents. You are fortunate. The disease of small American communities is and always has been glandular, an almost pituitary drive to attract attention and hence to thrive. One exerts itself to stage each year a cherry festival, another a tulip rodeo or onion carnival, another a beauty-queen bacchanal, still another a marine minstrel show or pageant. Growth they equate with prosperity and prosperity with content, forgetting the ills which growth must fetch inevitably in its train. The difference between ambition and aspiration is well-nigh hemispheric; we are not ambitious; we have aspired, rather, at least those of us invested with the power of selection, to remain very much as we are. Horace is our poet, not Eliot, but if we must have a chronicler, let him be Thoreau, not Thucydides. We are, however, hard of head; time we cannot stay, event we cannot ignore, the "Deserted Village" mourned by Goldsmith we neither desire nor expect to recreate. Certain of us have labored all our civic lives to merit and maintain unsullied what we most prize in Thebes: a neighborliness with star and tree and grass; a first-name democracy; a veneration of quiet and a pastoral disdain of pomp and trumpet; a concord of purpose; an atavism which does not cloy; a dignity which few men earn before the grave. That these ends are worthy has been demonstrated in recent years by the great American trampling to the suburbs, the bisonlike stampede to what we here already have and what we intend to keep. Our severest temptation occurred during the period of Grethe's, my wife's, classic madness, but her columns at our limits we do not illuminate at night, one set is fallen and we do not re-ërect it, and the Dionysian theater, still uncompleted, mosses over. At her death the scales of pretension dropped from our eyes, as they did again, for the last time, after the demise of Peace Officer John Scripter. Geography, too, works in our behalf. Thebes is precisely forty and nine-tenths miles from Grand Rapids, officially reckoned at forty-one, and by the grace of that forty-first mile and the proliferation of hutch-housing at its outskirts we have been spared becoming a chancrous adjunct of that city. There have been other factors; the struggle has not been unPyrrhic; so far, though, the field is wholly ours. To put it succinctly, we have, we believe, the twentieth century by the balls. You find your home town recognizable. It is the highest tribute you could pay.

Other than the clock's hasteless tick there is no sound, yet even to the silence, as to the tidal rise and fall of his rhetoric, Oram Kropf appears to listen, head hung gyrally to one side and slightly back; the posture, receptive and critical, might be habitual with a conductor judging on records the balance and tonal qualities of his orchestra. His attire Sewell remembers perfectly, for it has ever been the same: a suit of dark blue, well tailored of the best serge, a white shirt, the collar a size too large, permitting him with hooked finger to feel about the area between cotton and neck, and a somber cravat loosely knotted. The winter suit he wears even in summer. Some cutaneous condition deprives his skin, abnormally white and dry, of moisture's relief.

—I did not ask that you stop by to bear an old man's perorations. Sewell, pardon me. Had you made your mark in

Detroit, say, or Chicago, were your renown primarily local, that would be one thing; but a celebrity in the most national sense we do not know how to treat. Frankly, our knees knock and our tongues are tied. Three different female assemblies have applied to me to apply to you for an appearance before them discussing your work. You do not care to?

—I don't.

—I thought as much. My own request is more modest. I produce each week a column under the heading "Incunabula," which addresses itself to antiquarian or genealogical subjects. Have you any objection to my breaking precedent, in deference to your homecoming, and devoting a column to you?

—Mr. Kropf, if you and the town don't mind, I'd like to be left the hell alone.

—Ah. I understand and sympathize. But I cannot conceive it's being possible.

—Why not?

—Because we have a second hero.

—What's that mean?

—Your Distinguished Service Cross.

—How'd you hear about that?

—Washington took pains that we should, in 1944. Surely you are familiar with the procedure: whenever an award for bravery was granted by one of the services, the Pentagon sent to that serviceman's home-town newspaper a release containing, among other items, the full text of his citation. You must have entered Thebes as your place of residence.

—My God.

—Of course I headlined the story. These were the first tidings we had of your whereabouts or activities in five years. The D.S.C.! We preened ourselves, we basked in the effulgence of your deed. Refresh my memory: what was the name of the place, something grisly and appropriate?

—Fossa Feminamorta.

—The Ditch of Dead Women, yes. And such carnage, such a sanguinary miracle! We were convinced you should have had the Congressional Medal of Honor instead.

—I should have.

—Well, consider, then, the effect of the announcement. Thebes had delivered itself of one hero, you will recall, only to be robbed of him in fetus by a cynicism beyond its control. Johnny Scripter prepared us psychologically, it might be said, for you. Now we had a real champion, his praises heralded officially by the Pentagon. Add to this feat the pyrotechnic of your first novel and our ebullience snapped galluses. To the sword was added laurel; to the cake, icing. Incidentally, Sewell, I have coveted a thousand times the opportunity of saying this to you in person: I read *A Benison on Our Meat* immediately I could obtain copy; the experience was ineffable; the book staked out and set polemical fire to the soul itself; and when I conjectured as to your model, only one man of equal black and hortatory talents came to mind: Juvenal.

White hands sweep the clock. Through a window lowering sun of afternoon sends in a beam to mote the air upon which are suspended, the ear may now define, particles of distant sound, a linotype's jangle, the bump of a flatbed press busy, doubtless, with job printing. Sewell, unwilling to acknowledge commendation from this source, from a threadworn Morris chair inspects the office of the Editor of the *Argus-Advertiser*, published once weekly, on Thursdays. The room is crowded; except for a window and a large framed engraving, its walls from floor to ceiling are tiered with books and shelving; Oram Kropf swivels between two broad tables, and on a low stand at his right, convenient to his gesture, is pedestaled the barefaced cabinet clock. That in the room to which the visitor must soon attend is the framed engraving, which appears to be not print but proof; under close scrutiny it becomes the reproduction, enlarged to dimension in feet, of a magazine advertisement, the flossy paper dulled, even under glass, by age. The illustration is an engraving of an oil circa 1880, the genre that of Adolf Schreyer's school, the scene the vasty Russian steppes in winter across which snowy waste in full careen speeds a single-seater sleigh, or cutter, pulled by a steed muscular and wild, its eyeballs glaring fear, its nostrils snorting frost, while on the seat a noblewoman in attitude of flight grasps the reins with one hand and with her free arm mothers a child, for behind this equipage, gaining fast, fangs dripping, ravens an enormous pack of wolves. A caption in bold type underlines the charming, absurd, romantic depiction: "You're Safe in a Kropf Siberian!"

—Edie informs me your old friends played host to you the other evening. The Chip & Cork has, I fear, fallen into desuetude now that many of its bravest spirits are departed these shores. Renis Baird, Johnny, your father, Claude Reichert—although Claude, abstemious and tight as the paper on the wall, was present but seldom. If style is the man, so is his poker; if, as Pope would have it, mankind's proper study is himself, then an excellent beginning is his demeanor when the chips, so to speak, are down. Many the night I watched L.V. wait hour upon hour for the cards, and when he got them, back them to the hilt; it required real fortitude to stay with him then. But would you believe it? Once a night, consistently, he would steal a pot from under our noses, staying in, drawing one card, at most two, sitting imperturbable as the Grand Canyon and backing his composure until the last of the fainthearts folded and the cards, which he showed willingly, revealed his audacity. He would pull it off only once, but once without fail, and perpetually to our astonishment and chagrin. A man of surprises, your father. I well remember when the Directors appointed him Cashier, in 1924, I believe, and his response: rather than one of elation, it was a request that henceforth, since he detested the names Lucian and Virgil, we call him L.V. It was so voted.

Sewell could not but mark the resemblances between the editor and Peckham Hill. To both senility beckoned; with both the sensations derivable from language bordered on the autoerotic; but most notable, each old party, when it came to the gist of the business at hand, owned a circumlocutory genius; each, having brought himself to water, balked at drinking; each was somehow disinclined either to evacuate or get off the pot. Oram Kropf had raised, successfully and at last, the spirit of L. V. Smith, and having done so would predictably overturn the table and switch on the lights. He settled himself to wait.

—You were too young, during the twenties, to appreciate the series of vicissitudes with which, very like Job, I was tested, and your father, a man private with himself and with the confidences of others would never, I am sure, have mentioned them to you. For ten years the hammer fell again and again. You were noticing just now the proof of the last advertisement of the Kropf Cutter Company which ever appeared; that was 1922. The Kropf Siberian, finest cutter ever custom-made in these United States! Its replica in iron I had wrought for my front lawn: "My name is Ozymandias, king of cutter-manufacturers/ Look on my works, ye Mighty, and despair!" And by 1922 as legendary as the hippogryph, as obsolete as the Conestoga wagon. Attire myself in sackcloth, cover my head with ashes—not I. The fortune my father had acquired I squandered as though, I believe the popular expression goes, there were no tomorrow; animal gratification I rioted in as recklessly as a whore with the clap; for a decade, Ixion in a racoon coat, I revolved on the automobile wheel of my own sins. I was the prime mover in building the Creel & Cartridge; when the four of us helled off to Chicago, Renis and Charles Reason and Johnny and I, all of Johnny's bills I footed. Grethe, bless her indomitable Dutch soul, was long in the dying, but that was finally accomplished. Then, then, woe upon woe, I become conscious, when looking at a light, of a halo about it, an ever-brighter, ever-wider nimbus, I perceive rainbows when it has not rained, there is increasing pressure behind the eyeballs, I am able to apprehend less and less but I put off a visit to Charles Reason. When I do grope my way to him it is too late, and in any event the process, he tells me, would have been irreversible. His verdict: glaucoma. His estimate: six months. Behold Oram Kropf in 1930; behold The Blind Boulevardier, not of the Champs Elysées but of Ionian Avenue; contemplate a relict brought to ruin not by divine experiment but by bereavement, heredity, fornication's golden fleece, and Henry Ford! Nearing seventy, in repose except for the expressive, motile hands, so tall is the editor that even seated one must regard how long are his arms and legs and how spare. His skull is ovoid, and across the white shell's top are placed like bookmarks two combed filaments of hair. He has large ears and a long nose. Among his teeth, most of which he kept, there is much gold craftsmanship. His eyelids repose. —It was 1929. My wife was gone. I was blind. To the crash, due within months, I would be impervious since beyond the house I lived in and a small tumbledown factory personneled with mice I had not a sou. In me worked immortal longings. At precisely which nadir there began the most fecund, in point of fact the only consequential years of my life. I was enabled to buy the *Advertiser*. I learned Braille and how to use a Brailler, although composing I prefer to dictate. I discovered my mind. That education to which I earlier adverted became cerebral rather than testicular. And then, and then, Sewell, a wondrous thing. Braille's resources hinder the scholar, as you may imagine, being a man of letters; Edie wearied eventually of substituting her eyes for mine; I asked a friend to read to me; I asked a second, a third, until I had run the gamut of intimacy; and then one evening at this door I begged a passerby, not for alms but for sight, and he assented. "Reading to Or'm" is now a civic enterprise second only to Theban football, refusal being tantamount to beating one's wife. I keep a list of those I have recruited; we number two thousand souls in Thebes, and in these twenty years well over half, young and old, have become my faculty, some over long periods. This office is become an academy: the operator of a gasoline station I have read from Sir Thomas Browne or *Sartor Resartus;* for a high school halfback I choose *Tom Jones,* the more facile of Browning's monologues, the tone poems of a Pater or a Ruskin; a man of the cloth condescends to regale us with Rabelais; a housewife sharp of tongue sounds from it for the first time the music of a Meredith sonnet; a machinist from the reel company stumbles over *Absalom and Achitophel* or the inci-

117

sive couplets of the *Dunciad;* a feckless husband of indiscriminate libido cannot but ponder his destination midway of a Dantean journey; perusing Gibbon aloud, a counter girl from the five-and-ten must be bemused by the notion that empires flourished before Woolworth, and likewise fell. With the allusions, the contexts, the definitions, I assist; the rest they do themselves. Poetry, fiction, philosophy, drama, criticism, theology, aesthetics—and the upshot? If I tutor them, by their infinite human variety I am made rich beyond Croesus! Every night for me is a matriculation, every reader a course of study, every new voice the ventricle which opens to me a living heart. Out of adversity, then, has come this matchless boon: to know by the ear's instruction the men and women of this town as well as I know its pavements and its sidewalks and its curbstones through a white cane's instincts. It is more than I deserve. Like Job's, my end is more blessed than my beginning. And whose strong back uplifted me, twenty-five long years ago, from the slough of my despond? Whose hand was it led me from the dark wood of my affliction? Sewell, it was your father's.

The bird, wary and sagacious, having soared in ever-narrowing circumspection, comes once more to rest upon its purpose. About one ornamental finger Oram Kropf twists the heavy ring. —There are two pieces of information of which you should be apprised. First, it was I who lent L.V., our new Cashier, sufficient funds to purchase bank shares appropriate to an officer. Second, it was L.V. who came to me, fully aware of my distress, in the summer of 1929, and offered personally to take my note for enough to buy the then *Advertiser*. When I refused, with gratitude, the charity, he offered me in its guise a business proposition: five thousand dollars for the cutter works and the site on which it mildewed. Five thousand for some scrap lumber and a sliver of land not worth together five hundred. I wept —yes, the blind weep—and accepted.

—I don't want to talk about my father.

—But surely, after fifteen years, some palliation—

—Mr. Kropf, how do I get my message over? I don't care to discuss my father period, end of quote, cut.

In the muted room old man and younger take each other's measure by metronome arithmetic. —Very well, Sewell. I am bitterly sorry that the chip you carried away on your shoulder the night of the dam has become a feather. You will, perhaps, permit me one small demurrer. We tried to be, in those hectic few days, gentlemen of elevated motive; when it came to execution, however, we were all thumbs, although in our defense it should be said that none of us had ever been so sorely trammeled; emergency pressed upon emergency; those events I have relieved almost as many times as I have drawn breath. What we would have given—Harlan Murninghan, the two Charles's, Baird and Reason, Bill Vandevelde, Claude Reichert and myself—to recall the runaway, to bring you back by the nape of the neck and talk to you for ten minutes only, but you were vanished as utterly as is flatulence in a windstorm. How could you have known that we were unanimous in resolving to defray every penny of the cost of your education at Ann Arbor? You could not. Our worst ineptitude, probably, was asking Harlan Murninghan to act as tragedy's harbinger, although captaincy in this devolved as naturally upon him as in other affairs. I visualize the scene in horrid detail: our elder Cato, a man of unimpeachable rectitude, our most successful entrepreneur; seated before him, in a house aromatic of catastrophe, a stripling of eighteen; and to this boy, in tones as dispassionate as those with which he might explicate the wisdom of a school bond issue, our senator announces that his father is dead, that his own roof may no longer provide him shelter, and that his father, accounting discloses, is furthermore a thief. Driven as though by Furies, the youth—

—Old man shut your mouth! Sewell is on his feet, his hands slammed down on the table between them. —Do you think I've forgotten? I never have, not for a goddamn day! If you call my father a thief again I'll take your Thesaurus and shove it so far up your ass you'll die of your own vocabulary!

—Sewell, Sewell. The editor's sonority fades to a whisper. —Shall I tell you what the total erosion of the assets of the State Bank of Thebes amounted to in 1939?

—I won't listen.

—Roughly $170,000—more than the institution's entire capital and surplus!

—You lie, lie, lie!

—Sewell, the defalcation had been going on for many years. These are heinous things of which we all hoped you might remain forever ignorant. How, on his salary, do you conceive he put aside five thousand to save me in my hour of need?

—Save you, yes—and then you foul his name! If there was any robbery in that bank, Kropf, it was you and the Directors doing it! You and Murninghan and Reason and Baird and the rest—and you want to know how I know you were the guilty bastards? I have proof, by God, proof! My father had the flu and he was getting well till the night all of you came to see him and went in his bedroom and Reichert came downstairs and asked me to go over to the Bairds'. He was damn near well and the next morning he was dead! Lung congestion, hell! I don't know what you were doing in that bank, the six of you, but whatever it was he found out and to keep him quiet you killed him and Reason certified it natural causes—you dirty thieving smalltown murderers! Oram Kropf's eyelids lie inert except in rare villeinage to emotion; then the muscles in the corners contract, the lids twitch eerily, seem almost capable of rising, as though the dead organs beneath would come to life once more, one dazzling instant more at will's command before the Stygian veil descends. Sewell bends further over the table so that his breathing blasts the old man's visage. —I wish your eyes were open so I could spit in them. I wish you could see how much I hate you and this whole insignificant town. I wish to God I had a way to do to all of you what you did to my father and me. I'm glad you're blind. And the only reason I'm glad you're not deaf too is so you can hear me say good afternoon. Good afternoon.

Of all the holes on Honey Brook this one had been the best loved in Sewell Smith's boyhood: a tiny rivulet three miles west of Thebes, one of several which sourced in springs and peregrinated valleyward through wood and fern to seep demurely into the broad Ionian, small streams leap-wide, Honey Brook ran here snow-cold and dark within a trough of watercress to cavern under a bank of bog. If you tried it from the bank your footstep prenotified the trout. If the sun were at your back, your shadow falling on the water spooked him. To fish the hole giftedly, therefore, you must approach it from above, and Morse Baird watched Sewell bend and lurk through an alder thicket without disturbing a branch, soundlessly extend the telescopic rod to its full eight feet, and standing its length from the stream pay out line so that the night crawler, festooned from the hook's barb in only one place, went writhing naturally with the current free of the watercress and disappeared twenty feet downstream under the bank. Ten seconds passed. Sewell's rod wrist whipped suddenly upward and the taut line backlashed through the branches, spitting leaves. He had missed, but rather than tramping directly to his friend he retraced his tortuous way through the thicket. Getting bait, supplying a rod, and bringing Sewell back to Honey Brook after all these years had been, besides Morse's apology for his physical part in the contretemps at the Creel & Cartridge, his means, almost adolescently hopeless, of restoring not the close consociation of their youth alone but that youth itself.

—Never saw you miss before.

—It's been a long time. I struck too soon. He's there all right, a good one, but he knows we're here now. We'll outstubborn him. My old man was the best brushfisherman I ever knew. If he missed, which was seldom, he would wait, by God, till the trout grew another inch and then take him. He was a sportsman, too, and that's why, thinking back, I was so ticked off at Vandevelde that trip up on the Jordan. We could all brush-fish when we were kids, but we'd never had a crack at a real river, and when we did, he hogged it.

They sat against the sun-warmed bole of an elm. —I'm sorry about bouncing you the other night, old buddy, Morse said.

—I never could drink well. Once, at Fort Meade, Maryland, just before I shipped overseas, some of us took on one hell of a load and then some paratroopers. I always hated paratroopers. The one I had, I picked him up and shoved his head through a pinball machine. He wound up with a partial concussion, half a scalp, and they threw me in the stockade for ninety days. No, you were right. But sober, I'd have killed you.

—Don't I know. Why do you think, all the time in high school, mad as I got at you sometimes, I never offered to fight? I was bigger and in better shape, but something always told me to lie low.

Down toward the Ionian's spring-brown grandeur meadowed a herd of Holsteins; along the damp hummocks by Honey Brook were games of yellow cowslips, or marsh marigolds.

—When did your mother die? Sewell asked.

—During the war. I heard yours did, too.

—Yes. In the happy academy down at Battle Creek where Reason sent her. The word caught up with me about three months later through the Red Cross.

—You have any family left?

—My car. My typewriter. My millions of readers. So you and Jane were married. So you won.

—So I won.

—How?

—Well, after our kid job on the dam, you were gone and Harris and I had to live through two months of pure hell. We graduated, all right, but we didn't know if Uncle Charlieboy would prosecute. He sure could have, about ten years' worth. Anyway, I was new to the bottle and one night on a date with her I said let's tear down to Angola and have some holy matrimony. Harris and Lene Scripter went along as witnesses.

—I still say how.

—You won't believe it.

—Probably.

—The high school hero. You and Harris were on the

bench all along. She loved me, she was just waiting to be asked. Morse grew solemn. —God, I was happy. Making All-State was swell, and the 440 was great, but the biggest thing I ever won was Janey, and I didn't even have to strain. Old buddy, it was the high point of my life. Abashed by confession, Morse pushed at the forelock of blue-black hair as unruly as ever, and the gesture, well-remembered, made possible for Sewell a split-second's conjuring of the friend he had once known: Morse of the Indian good looks, the inviolable brown eyes and heavy lashes and deep-cleft chin, Morse of the leopard reflex and coördination which fairly exploded him through an opponent's backfield and rifled him from the starting-blocks before the gun's report registered on the other runners, Morse incapable of victory by deceit or half-truth. —That trout's ready, he said, taking up the rod. Sewell shook his head. —The hell he isn't. In his turn Sewell followed the caricature Morse Baird had become: jowled, eyes walleted in flesh; there might linger in the full lips, in the white scar-stamp on his forehead, relics of animal attractiveness to women, but all grace was gone, the waist was beer-labeled and the bulk crashed noisily through the alders. Morse wet line too near the hole, let it chute the cavern beneath the bank, retrieved, and let it chute once more before kicking ruefully back to the elm and sitting down with the grunt of defeat.

—What happened to you and Jane?

—Nothing good, except in bed. In his jacket Morse found a cigar, bit off the end and lit it. —Also except our little girl, Carol, who's fourteen now and a princess. I tell you, old buddy, if you're going to knock anyone up, do it on your wedding night in Angola, Indiana: you get a prize in every box. Anyway, if we could have lived in the sack and sent out for meals, we'd still be married. Old Harlan was decent about it, put me to work in the plant. The war came and damn if I didn' turn out to be 4-F. But it saved the company, the war. This was the one field, other than sports, in which Morse could discourse authoritatively, and with directorial jabs of the cigar he explained that while the fishing tackle industry in the U.S. grossed 250 millions annually, it was perhaps the last composed of small, privately owned firms, one of the smallest of which was Twinriver Reels. —We gross around a million and a half a year, but the business is competitive as hell. Originally the company produced casting reels for bass and pike, and automatics for fly-fishing, but since 1950 it had been forced to offer a line of spinning reels. All were expensive, twenty dollars and up, and were stocked only by the more elegant sporting-goods establishments, including Abercrombie & Fitch. —Our big problem's been French and Swedish imports, but we've held our own little slice of the market. I've damn near got down on my knees to old Harlan to advertise, but he still buys a half-column a month in the *Fishing Tackle Trade News,* as he has for twenty years, and always runs the same thing, white space and one line of type: "Twinriver Reels: For Fresh Water, The Finest." You might as well try to shit in a thimble. The company had nearly gone under during the Depression, although Harlan Murninghan's almost religious obduracy, keeping on his sixty-odd employees and turning out an assortment of cheap handsprayers, had hidden it from the community; but the war had resuscitated, indeed brought it to exuberant prosperity. Its labor core, recruited mainly from the considerable percentage of Thebans of Swiss ancestry, watchmakers, as it were, by diathesis, and its reputation for quality control made Twinriver, through subcontracts, a natural supplier for the duration of precision components peculiar to torpedo steering mechanisms and proximity fuses. —To get costs down we're semiautomated now; have to be with the Japanese junk flooding the market, but we've still got the finest product and when you have that you can hang on. Over a hundred on the payroll today.

—What do you do?

—Oh, this and that, trouble-shooter, expediter. On the stogie Morse cudded a vacillatory moment. —No. The hell I am. I won't bull you, old buddy. I'm in shipping. The seven years we were married Murninghan tried me everywhere, purchasing, foreman in stamping, personnel, and I flubbed. The honest-to-john truth is, I don't have it. Ex-father-in-law keeps me on at a hundred a week because I was married to his daughter, a good Samaritan in a Cadillac. But that's another thing I have Charlieboy to thank for: the degree in engineering or bus ad I never got after he stole the mill. And listen to this: he's worth damn near as much as old Harlan now, and who's responsible, who made it for him, who does he give the dirty end of the stick to year in year out on so little salary he can hardly feed his kids? My damn dumb brilliant brother, that's who! Sewell, you can't beat Thebes. And you know who Thebes is, who says fetch or lie down or roll over or beg just as they always did? The Council, the School Board, the bank Directors. The outfits we were going to be on once upon a time, remember? Well, your father's gone and so is mine, so is Claude Reichert, but the rest of the team is still in there calling every play: old Harlan, Charlieboy, Bill Van, that wife-stealing bastard Reason, and Or'm Kropf. God, God, how I hate this town!

—Morse, why don't you take off?

—For where? And do what? I'm not educated for anything. And what would I use for money, old track-meet ribbons? Sewell, give me the straight scoop, how does it feel to be all of a sudden rich?

—Great. Except you get used to it too fast. And you're scared, also, of ever not having it again. You'd do anything not to have that happen.

—But if you've got it, why should you sweat?

—I'm a writer, I'll tell you a story why. In the war, after Anzio, I was in Special Services for the division a while. It was the winter of '44-'45, in the Vosges Mountains, where France and Germany and Switzerland form a triangle. It was cold as a witch's dug and there was a lot of pneumonia and trench foot among the doggies in the lines, so we set up a rest center in Besançon and brought them back by truckloads for showers and dry clothes and hot food and women. We got four whores from Paris and put them in two houses, a pair for officers and a pair for the men. One night in February the house for the men caught fire, gutted all but the walls. I stood in the snow with the two whores and the Mayor and watched it burn. We put the whores in another house and I went there in the morning before the men and took the brunette upstairs. After all, she'd had a night's rest. It was like making love to a dead girl. I remember lying there when I was through, looking out the window and the snowflakes falling into the mouth of a stone gargoyle on the wall next door. The girl lay beside me staring at the ceiling. I asked her what was the problem and she told me. We brought her from Paris in November and this was February. It had been the chance of her life. In four months she and the other one had hauled ten thousand enlisted men's ashes, which came, at five a throw, to fifty thousand dollars, a fortune for them. French girls are thrifty. They had kept all the money in their mattresses and every franc of it had burned. She said a girl has only so much to give to men and she and her friend had given most of it that winter. Nobody would desire them now because no man likes to sleep with tragedy. That's the story. So when the money came, I remembered that girl.

—Okay, okay, Morse said impatiently. But when it piles up, more than you ever knew there was in the world, like with your first book, what do you do with it? For instance?

—For instance. I was in a hotel in New York and that morning I had just opened a bank account with over a hundred thousand in checks and I wanted to go away alone somewhere and think about what had happened to Sewell Smith and me. So I bought a map and put my finger on it and looked. It was Santiago, at the west end of Cuba. So I flew there and drank Hatuey beer and went deep-sea fishing.

—What a life you've lived.

—Only in the last five years. And listen, I hate this town myself, Sewell said, more than you do, but I'd still rather fish this brook than any other piece of water anywhere.

Morse relit. —There's another reason why I stick around, too, old buddy. A little oofum-poofum now and then, you know, is cherished by the wisest men.

The doggerel, repeated out of the universal high school book of lewd, inane verse after fifteen years, stung Sewell, as though by hook, with a sensation alien to him, that of sympathy; in the man beside him a boy yet dwelt, inchoate and pitiful. —Now you give me a for instance, he said lightly.

—Well, I used to run for this town. Now I stand for it. At stud.

—I'm new in these parts. You might give me a number or two.

—I might let you guess a little.

—Arlene Scripter?

—Hell, no, she won't even have a phone. Not that I wouldn't like to, but you'd need an ice pick, not the usual equipment. Something wrong there, old buddy; maybe we got too much mileage out of that in high school.

—Then I give up.

Morse threw the cigar butt as far as he could and remained sitting forward so that Sewell could see only the pannier of his cheek. —You might try my ex-wife. When there was no response he continued. —It's available. And I can recommend it. So can Doc Reason; he got plenty while we were still married. I understand Ray Dickerson, the Cashier at the bank, can also put in a good word for Janey. He's married, three kids, but she can probably wreck that, too. I often think, pal, what pluperfect wetdream fools you and Harris and me were: little gentlemen trying for merit badges with her all those years when she really had round heels. And if you want the facts, I still keep my slice of that market. A little revenge now and then is also cherished by the wisest men. I get it on the old Doc. And he isn't the only one in town, not mentioning any names.

To relieve him, Sewell changed the subject. —I remember once, up on the Jordan, you saying you'd rather put the blocks to Ethel Scripter than anybody else.

Morse grinned, lounging against the elm. —Old live bait? Why, she's been the town whore ever since Johnny got himself shot the hell up. The word I get is, even the kids who bring her night crawlers she pays off in quiff. But once, back when Johnny was alive, or just afterward, I'd still bet that was a piece fit for a king. Morse crossed arms behind his head. —I'm getting old, I guess, living in the past, but you know the best day I ever really had? Not the East game or getting Janey but the one in East Lansing. The 440-yard is the roughest distance. It's like doing the hundred four times plus forty; you go top speed till you fall over dead or finish. But that was the easiest race I ever ran; my wind was good all the way, it felt like I had wings instead of legs; they say that's the way it is when you break a record, it's the only time it's easy. There were eleven of us, I was off the blocks first, and I didn't even hear the others after that. :50.8 That was 1938, old buddy, and after sixteen years it's the only Class C state mark that still stands. It's almost as though what was what Morse Baird was put on earth for: to set that record on that day. And I'm still in damn good shape; I'd lay money I could do it today under :55 flat. He sighed, perplexed by the world's wagging. —So there we were and here we are. I had the body and today it's all I've got except two suits and a year-old car and ten payments yet to go. Harris had the brains and still does, but he's wasted them, thrown them away on this town. Or'm Kropf and the others have sucked him in. He's the only person alive I probably love, but he sure makes it hard for me to. I suppose there are some people who just like to suffer. And you, old buddy, you've picked up all the marbles. Damn if I know what you had, but it must have been something.

Sewell reached for the rod. —I'll show you, he said. His way through the alders was as stealthy as before, his paying out of the line down the current past the watercress and under the bank as skillful. This time, when his rod wrist snapped, the rod boughed and its recoil hurtled the trout out and up and to the right of the stream, and Morse, running, arrived just as Sewell, wetting his hand, from damp ferns lifted the lovely thing, spangled red and purple and gold, disengaged gently the hook, and placed the trout once more, almost with tenderness, in Honey Brook.

—Why in holy hell did you do that? demanded Morse.

What Sewell could not say was that it was not merely a fine brook trout he had set free, but that, more than a supple, iridescent living creature, it was memory's incarnation of young Morse Baird, unvexed and by life as yet unsubjugated, which he willed with all his might to preserve. —So someone else, he said, can teach his son how to fish this stream.

Over the rumble of belting and the squeak and thump of the sifters, four huge polished wooden boxes in line and eight feet square which shook and shimmied rhythmically, sifting flour to another process on a lower floor through billowing cloth teats, Harris shouted statistics at Sewell. From one hundred pounds of wheat, Thebes Milling Company got 72 percent flour, 14 percent bran, and 14 percent middlings. He motioned, and Sewell followed him up a narrow iron staircase to the concrete floor above, the mill's fourth; the climb taxed his legs, for his back, after Morse's assault on him at the Creel & Cartridge, was not yet fully recovered. On this floor were the great old Allis-Chalmers roller mills, or "rolls," as Harris, yelling, termed them, in which the grain was ground, the only real revolution in milling since the use of stone wheels. Ionian County wheat was not suited for bread flour, which had to have a high protein content so that the dough would rise; Michigan soft white wheat, on the other hand, low in protein, was ideal for cookies as it encouraged spreading. That was what had been wrong before. Sewell put hands over his ears to indicate he simply could not hear over the rolls' vociferation and Harris led him to one corner and into a cubicle perhaps four-by-six adorned with a high old-fashioned clerk's table and stool. He closed the door, lowering the din a few decibels.

—This is your office?

—Pray do not asperse the lowly miller. Where Morse's grin was even, Harris's was lopsided, rare and parenthetical to the intense, questioning expression most comfortable to his face. At thirty-two he was still oddly youthful: his frame appeared not to have grown but sprouted, his legs were as long as a stork's, he gangled, he slouched, his wrists and feet and ears were outsize. He was six feet two and could not weigh more than a hundred forty. He wore a denim, flour-dusted miller's cap.

—Morse told me what a screwing you get from Charlie-boy on pay, but a crib for an office while he squats down there in style, God.

—Charles—Harris emphasized the name—is President of the company and my employer. That he happens to be my uncle is irrelevant.

—Meaning what?

—This. Sewell, your father was a silent man and a good one. Mine was an exhibitionist and a fraud. For your information, only his death kept him from ruining this company. God's mill grinds slow but sure, I think that's the exact line, and that was how I found out, slow but damn sure.

—But—

—But was what I said. Let me clue you in. Harris propped an elbow on the high table. —In Dad's day our main product was self-rising flour. He couldn't, or wouldn't, foresee that home baking was on the way out, so he pep-talked all the farmers around here into growing what we call "bastard" wheat to compete with Kansas and Nebraska. It wouldn't rise, it lacked strength, loaf volume was low. Effect: sales of Thebes flour dropped every year and consequently farmers' incomes. Another thing. Across the flutes of Harris's long nose the freckles of his teens, patulous, have spread into a pattern not unlike a trademark. —On cost, a waterpower mill has a slight competitive edge over an electric or Diesel mill provided the system works efficiently. Dad fancied himself a salesman, not an engineer. You remember our system was all wood; well, every time the river flooded the gates had to be raised completely or tear out, so he'd have to switch over to an electric motor, which upped costs. And there you have the worst possible fate for a mill: the wrong wheat, inefficient operation, and a new Chyrsler every year.

—And all this you changed, I suppose, and out of gratitude the company's rewarded you with this luxurious suite of offices.

Harris flushed. —No, Charles did some things, I did others. I persuaded the local farmers to grow Michigan soft white wheat, and between us, Charles and I, we proved to commercial bakers that flour from that wheat would give a maximum spread factor to their cookies. This meant they could use less shortening and sugar, which cut their costs. I also started scientific testing. Come along, let me show you.

And Harris was gone so quickly that Sewell surmised a kind of ruse. When he went out into the deafening grind of the rolls his guide had already opened a door through the wall that seemed to lead into mid-air and nodded Sewell through it. He entered a small room suspended four floors up on the very side of the mill.

Arlene Scripter was there. Harris had already closed the door and said surely they remembered each other, this was the lab and Arlene was the company's technician, she was right now completing an ash test and perhaps Sewell would like to watch, in the meantime he had to go down to the main floor and Sewell could meet him there, no hurry, they must have a lot to talk about being such old friends, well, he'd see them, and he had disappeared.

She was a beautiful woman. She was waiting for a lab oven to cool. She showed him the other equipment, including an actual oven in which she actually baked now and then, measuring height and spread to be sure the flour was consistent in protein. Even in a white uniform she was abundantly beautiful. An ash test was a means of determining the quality of finished flour; the best cookie flour should contain 39-42 percent ash by weight after burning. That hair of fire-engine red, too blatant at sixteen, worn flamboyantly to her shoulders in a page-boy, was now more subdued in hue and pulled back into a severe, massive coil, and in the rust at her temples were vines of gray. What you did was measure out three grams of flour and add three cc of an alcohol solution containing magnesium acetate and ammonium nitrate. Without the inner flush of youth her skin was a stark white. This mixture you placed in a lab oven heated to 850 degrees centigrade; the solution flared off rapidly. This residue had cooled now the requisite half-hour and taking the receptacle from the oven she weighed it on the scales. Arlene congratulated him on his success as a writer and Sewell replied it had been mostly a matter of luck. Her principal routine in the lab was conducting "stream analyses" five or six times daily. The mill's wheat, grown in different soils by different farmers, of course varied, and when it was blown from the silos to the top floor of the mill in four different "streams" to begin processing it was important that the wheat be ground uniformly. When she, in her analyses, discovered variations, she could inform Harris, who could then set his rolls up, more open, or down, tighter. Their mutual constraint, the calisthenics of recall and present judgment inhibited them. The lab's row of windows gave Arlene the finest townscape available, he imagined, to anyone: directly below were the foaming eddies of the millrace where the River Button was manumitted to its T with the Ionian; in the distances both river valleys flung up escarpments, verdant now in May; extended as far as the State Bank of Thebes, the stores on this side of Ionian Avenue seemed staved up on their piles so that the hulls might be debarnacled and calked; on the opposite side of the street-highway the lettering on the marquee of the Attic Theatre was legible, as well as that on the windows of what had once been Reichert's drugstore. Sewell asked where she had been the day Johnny died, if she had seen the shooting; he had. So had she, she said; just out of afternoon classes and on the way home the kids, herself among them, had been halted at the intersection, but most of them a breathless curiosity forced spying round the corner of a building, so that she had seen it all. Full-bosomed, wide-hipped, lips as deep, nostrils as sensitive, tiny mole on one cheekbone decoying as ever, a woman of loveliness annealed, it was incredible to Sewell that she should rouse him no more than stone, but it was true. To the north the Button, wrinkled by wind, divided Thebes, on its left bank, out of sight, Arlene's mother's live-bait emporium, and somewhere on its right, according to legend, Johnny, her father, had been born in the tarpaper hut of her grandfather, old Shack Scripter, one of the last of the Button boatmen. Legend also had it that Shack Scripter was possessed of a fabulously bibulous hound dog into whom, night after night in The Let Live, a full gallon of beer could be induced before he would roll off the table, and that Johnny, who lived a Huck Finn whelphood along the river had been found, by authorities who deemed it proper that at age eleven he should have some schooling, burrowed in a heap of clamshells. For something, anything, else to say, Sewell asked Arlene whimsically if she could point out, from their vantage height, the place along the Button where Johnny had been born and she replied he must know the Button boatmen lived only along the Ionian. She was antithesis: sightly, she was yet unvoluptuous; sensual of hair and face and figure, which she could not help, even her personality disallowed rather than invited. It was as though the sexuality of her high school years, submitted to the oven of his and Morse's and Harris's youthful lusts, had flared off entirely, leaving only an unfeminine ash. Sewell experimented.

—I want to congratulate you, too, Arlene, he said, his hand on the lab door. She faced a window, her back to him. —You're more beautiful than ever.

When, after a full minute, he was assured she would make no answer, he left her to locate Harris. They met on the first floor and walked together out past the one-story frame building which housed the offices of Thebes Milling to Ionian Avenue, onto the bridge, and leaned upon the rail.

—Harris, what in God's name has happened to Lene Scripter?

—Did you notice our new silos? Harris pointed above the mill roof to two enormous concrete cylinders. —They'll store 285,000 bushels. During the harvest period we can buy and test four thousand bushels an hour. He had lit a cigarette now that they were outdoors; it drooped from one corner of his mouth and the smoke, which he forgot to inhale, clouded up under the bill of his cap, drifted, even, behind the lenses of his spectacles. —I wanted to tell you, too, how our power system's been improved. The turbine is steel, for one thing, as are the flume grates, and we now use a three-inch belting impregnated with plastic which wears practically forever. Our main shaft turns a hundred RPM, producing 145 horsepower.

—You mean 145 horsepower will run this whole mill?

—That's right, my good man. When you consider a car engine has to reach thousands of RPM to put out 145 horse, we're achieving tremendous torque from a hundred, real brute force. We almost never have to resort to electric power.

Under them the river attended peacefully to its duty, expressing itself with an almost harmonious roar beneath the gates, its only diversion a sideward purling through the flume grates and thence down to the turbine. —You must be thinking, Harris said, what I am. Except for the other night, this is where we last saw each other, right here, frightened out of our wits at what we'd done, running. Isn't there something about the guilty compulsively returning to the scene of their crimes? We really demolished everything that night, and it must damn near have killed Charles. You see what he did, though: he rebuilt from the bottom up, concrete for head walls and flume, the gates and flume grates and catwalks of iron. It must have cost thousands upon thousands, and to this day I don't know how he raised them. But the point is, he rebuilt permanently, just the way my grandfather Alfred would have wanted it done. After more than a hundred years it's still the Baird mill. Sewell, when I think what I helped do that night, what we almost ruined forever, I can't even recognize the hurt, vindictive, foolish boy I must have been.

—I can. You had pride and guts and when you were kicked you didn't take down your pants and turn the other cheek. That's being a man, not a kid.

Harris was incredulous. —Sewell, you mean after all this time, after all you've achieved, you're still bitter? I don't believe it. There's a line from Herbert: "The mill cannot grind with water that's past."

—Sometimes you sound like Or'm Kropf.

—Well, if you choose a model for diction and quotation, you may as well choose the best.

—The best my ass. The most phony, maybe, the most long-winded. I've listened to him—that's what you do, listen. He belongs in Southern California, not here, conning some cult, wearing goatskins and living on nuts and berries and having weird rituals with young girls—

—Great Lord! someone exclaimed behind them. —You two aren't plotting to do it all over again, I hope!

It was Edie Kropf, and so amused was Harris he clapped her manlike on the shoulder. —Here, Sewell, is the most nubile, common-sensical woman in the county. Edie, I don't think he's seen Blue's yet. Take him to Blue's, buy him some coffee, and he may propose.

—He might, she agreed, but what?

—The All-Bran Ophelia, she began.

—Who?

—Lene.

—Why Ophelia?

—Didn't you feel like ordering her to a nunnery?

—Or a mausoleum.

—And Harris wouldn't answer your question?

—No.

—I know one reason.

—What?

—So do four other people: Lene herself, Morse, Jane Reason, and me.

—Well?

—One more should. You.

—Me?

—I'll tell you on condition you never make it seven. Will you cross your tricky Hollywood heart?

—Done.

—I'm serious.

—So am I.

—When Morse and Jane were married, the night they eloped to Indiana, so were Harris and Lene.

—Married?

—Married.

—How do you know this?

—Because I'm practically the only friend Lene has in the world and she told me.

—What happened?

—To Lene and Harris, nothing. At least in the consummation department. They kept it a secret.

—Harris and Lene. My God. Why?

—You're the author, you have the imagination.

—Then what happened?

—She ran away, just as you did, and to the same place, Detroit. The marriage could be annulled because they'd never lived together, and was. After Harris went into service she moved to Grand Rapids and worked there during the war and afterward. Later, after he'd gone to work in the mill, he found her in Grand Rapids and offered her the job in the lab. She was mad to come home at last. I don't know why she should have been: she might as well be in Grand Rapids, or Mozambique for that matter. She's up in her ivory tower all day, she disappears into an apartment over the Library at night, she goes nowhere, never dates, she has nothing to do with her mother, naturally, Mrs. Live Bait Scripter, I call her The Fisherman's Sadie Thompson—oh, hell. Edie banged mug upon table. —It's not a life for Lene, it's an existence. You men with your war wounds and battle scars and things; psychologically, Lene's at least a paraplegic. And here's the olive of irony in the martini: the girl with the lousy reputation in high school becomes the woman pure as the driven snow, while the virginal little rich girl, not naming anyone, becomes the broad of the back fence.

Blue's belonged to and was operated as a side line by Earl Blue, appointed Town Constable after Johnny Scripter's decease and now risen to the high estate of Deputy County

Sheriff. Businessmen dropped in for coffee in mid-morning and afternoon and came here also for lunch, cribbage, pinochle and poker. Counter and coffee urn were presided over by Earl's wife, a plump matron with upper lip and cheeks hirsute enough to warrant the cognomen "Mrs. Bluebeard." The décor of the place was chastely elegant: linoleum on the floor, oilcoth on the tables, mugs of a size which, though neighborly with stain, made of coffee not a stimulant but a libation, on one wall a 1937 calendar, the month pages torn off to June, the second day circled in black crayon, and behind the counter, placed and framed with conspicuous dignity, the County Health Department's hygienic rating of the establishment: not an A or B but a large scarlet C, one grade above closing on grounds of insalubrity. To these things, however, Sewell gave less attention than to Edith Kropf and to conjecture as to how much more Arlene had revealed to her, how much responsibility for the still-born elopement Edie assigned to him, why, in short, she had determined he should be the sixth in Thebes privy to the precipitate, teen-age blunder. About these matters he was curious, not about Edith Kropf, archetypical of the spinster ingenerate to every small town who, everyone said, must have had numerous opportunities to marry and why, everyone wondered, hadn't she? Her puzzle, easy of solution to Sewell, was one of disproportion; in each physical feature the scales had tipped against her, only slightly, but enough: her dark hair was bobbed a bit too short, her nose and chin were a bit too sharp, her body a bit too angular and wiry; her look was too direct, her clothes too tailored, her grooming too careless, so that her blouse would bunch above her skirt, her make-up too perfunctory, her self-inspection too haphazard, so that she would forget too often to shave her legs.

—Checklist completed?

—Of what?

—Of me.

—Almost.

Edie smiled. —I will for you. I'm thirty-seven. I can fix a

flat tire. I've been proposed to by a football coach, two farmers, a bank teller, and three high school teachers—male, incidentally—and said no in every case, not without some regret. I'm intelligent and a damn good judge of character. I'm a cynic. I can tell, and enjoy hearing, a dirty joke if it's not smutty. If necessary I can handset or run a linotype. I haven't a romantic bone in my body. I work very hard six days a week at the *Arg & Ad,* overseeing the office, the billing, the job work, phoning for social items, making sure the rural correspondents get their stuff in on time, report the Council and School Board meetings, pick up the ads, and on Sunday I wish it were Monday. Lene and I are the charter and only members of The Society of Career Spinsters, Thebes Chapter. I can calculate my matrimonial odds as well as any man, which is why I'm a good businesswoman. At home I cook for my father but he will have no help from me in dressing or in any other respect. I'm reputed to have the sharpest tongue in town and I'm probably the only Democrat. I thought Eisenhower was an amiable five-star poop and still do. For the sake of my health and sanity I have to and can arrange a reasonable sex life. Finally, the only man I date with any regularity is Morse Baird.

She met his stare boldly as he winnowed her last statements.

—Anything else?

—No.

—Sorry, there is. Dad passed on to me the dismal details of his interview with our celebrity the other afternoon. I'm sure he talked too much, but when you're almost seventy and can't see, you talk. It's also one of my congenital failings. He must have bored you silly.

—No apology. He did.

—None offered. And I don't ask any of you, though you did hurt him deeply. I'd just like two minutes of your high-priced time to give you some background on the real-life, wide-screen drama of Oram Kropf. Some things you were too young before to know or realize were even going on. Not to soft-sell you into liking him, but so that you'll at least get some insight into the womb from which was delivered, the crucible out of which was poured this present remarkable man, my father. Or some other damn metaphor. And before Sewell could protest disinterest Edie said that Oram's perpetual lament was that he had been born, only scion of a self-taught mechanic who struck it rich in mid-life by designing and custom-building cutters the equal of any in the country, too early for a raccoon coat and a Stutz Bearcat. By 1908, however, the year of his father's sleighing on to The Great Siberian Beyond, he had everything else: a wild year each at Cornell, Wooster and Albion, which institutions found themselves unequipped to rechannel his genius for riot and venery; sole ownership of the Kropf Cutter Works with a force of workmen whose artisanship made it unnecessary for him to dull his sensibilities with the tedia of management (His favorite tale from that year, told to this day, was of a visit from a young Detroiter who, after a survey of the works, the men, and the superior qualities of the product, offered to join resources in the manufacture of what he called a "horseless carriage," and was of course politely refused. The young man's name had been Henry Ford); and a fortune. From the most formal gardens of Grand Rapids' society Oram plucked one of the choicest roses, Margrethe Rote, for his bride; they made the Grand Tour of Europe; they built their house of brick in Thebes; in 1917 they were blessed with Edith. Then, in the twenties, while the cutter works cobwebbed, while he raced through what remained of his fortune as though bankruptcy were the only experience he yet ravened for, there ensued the series of cataclysms which was to cause his admittedly merited, admittedly untragic fall. —I know all about it, he told me, Sewall interrupted. Undoubtedly, he would have, but let her give him but one example which would show the other face of her father's coin. Grethe, whom Oram had adored yet to whom he had been undeviatingly unfaithful; Grethe, whose fantasy and obsession it had been to produce in Thebes some embolism in tangible stone of ancient glories, to distinguish this village by some extravagant means from its neighbors named also out of antiquity, whose conceit it was that a "Grecian Dramacycle" should be mounted here each summer in an authentic pre-Periclean replica; Grethe, wasting away, for two years, of leukemia; Grethe, from whom her husband had successfully hidden any surmise of that financial mischief nearly fatal now—for her, for his departing wife, Oram had laid out more than thirty thousand dollars so that she might see four sets of columns at the village limits, had plunged a last fifty thousand, scraped together God knew how, into her beloved Theban Theatre, uncompleted, mercifully since it could not have been, before her final dark.

—How am I supposed to react?

—I don't know. Edie seemed spent. Sighing, she tucked in her blouse. —Anyway, that's the kind of man my father is. He loves Thebes. So do I. The trees, the two rivers, the peace, the fine people. A girl has to love a town to be willing to become its old maid.

On a thought she gathered strength, sat bolt upright in her chair. —The other night at the party I asked you why you'd come home and you turned it aside. I ask you again.

—That's none—

—Of my damned business. Unexpectedly, her eyes came alive with a feral, almost paranoiac glitter which belied her no-nonsense hornrims and the composed, dry-skinned façade which was the remainder of her face. —You listen to me, Sewell Smith: I bow to your fame, I genuflect to your riches, but I warn you, don't hurt my town. In any way. I warn you, if you harm us I'll kill you myself.

Each night immediately prior to retiring Harlan Murninghan took a sitz bath. This involved lowering himself into a tub of comfortably hot water to hip level and remaining immersed at least ten minutes. The condition from which he suffered was general among men of his advanced years, prostatic hypertrophy, or hyperplasia, a term coming into increased medical favor, which meant enlargement of the prostate gland. Hearing testimony of painful urination and backache, examining at once for malignance and discovering the enlargement spongy rather than hard, his son-in-law, Charles Reason, had recommended periodic checking, weekly massage, sitz baths, frequent emptying of the bladder whether urgent or not, including the use of a chamber pot at night if getting to the bathroom proved a hindrance to rest, and, since an enlarged prostate is highly susceptible to infection, eventual surgery. The operation Harlan Murninghan had put off for some months; besides the normal human disrelish of hospitals he was prone to that fear of the knife which acuminates with age; but most decisive was his intransigence about surgery until his affairs should be in order, which they assuredly were not.

In the bedroom Carrie Murninghan heard from the tub his groans of easement. —Is it better, dear?

—Much. And I had massage yesterday.

—Did you mention the acreage to Charles?

—No. A prostate massage is not a very opportune time to tell your son-in-law that you don't take his professional advice about an operation because you distrust his personal motives in marrying your daughter in the first place.

With soap and washcloth he began to bathe himself, starting with the pate of his large head, which was somehow made the more noble by being totally bald except for a faint velvet of gray along the sides. At seventy-one the eldest of the five men of Thebes, Michigan, who shared membership on the Town Council, the School Board, and the bank's Board of Directors, Harlan Murninghan was also the most imposing figure; Oram Kropf had likened him to an elder Roman senator, a Cato, and the comparison was not inapt. If in the deliberations of these bodies the others turned to Oram for the why of things, it was to Harlan Murninghan, slow of utterance, sage of counsel, with the gravity of mien and movement which qualifies a man to command, to be the repositor of elective trust, that they turned for the how. He stands several inches over six feet, weighs 240 pounds, and the grandfatherly scope of his abdomen adds to, curiously, rather than detracting from, his stateliness.

—Are you ready for your legs? his wife asked.

—Not yet, my dear.

To a fish The Twinriver Reel Company owed its beginning, to integrity of workmanship its success. Disgruntled by a crude reel which failed him during an engagement with a trophy bass in the year 1909 so that he had to line-haul it to the boat, young Harlan Murninghan, then an employee of Kropf Cutter, a tinkerer steady of hand and knowledgeable with metal, undertook to design his own reel. The result was faultless. A friend wanted one like it, someone else ordered a third; shop was set up in a barn and as, over the next few years, the Swiss-blooded craftsmen at the cutter works were laid off, one by one they were hired by Twinriver Reel, where their natural endowments were ideally suited to less-than-mass manufacture of a small, high-quality product. It was characteristic that the original, causative smallmouth bass, six pounds eight ounces of bronze stick-to-itiveness mounted in 1909 by its captor himself, hung still, fierce-jawed and gill-flared, behind the desk of the company's president.

To marry is to subscribe for life to the most miraculous newspaper in the world: conjugal conversation. Its editions are infinite in number, its coverage is both international and next-door, its headlines never cease to challenge, its features to edify, its comics to amuse, its advertisements to inspire, its editorials to reinforce positions already occupied in alliance for years; and best, perhaps, it divulges not only all the news fit to print but all that is unfit as well. When read each day by husband and wife, then discarded, it is this journal, delivered whatever the weather of love or hate or ennui, published not on paper but on the tissue of mortality itself, which serves as marriage's real wrapping.

—I wrote to Susan today and said they'd better think about coming here for Christmas. I said I was still frightened of flying and old enough not to mind admitting it.

—Christmas is six months away.

—It's well to plan. Tony can afford it, can't he?

—He told me his commissions came to more than twenty thousand last year.

—And it would be good for the children to see snow. And you still give him the thousand a month, don't you?

—Of course.

—Well, then.

Harlan and Carrie Murninghan's custom it was to converse most companionably during their preparations for the night and while in bed, before sleep separated them, and in their forty-nine years of union the major emphases of their talk had been shifted by external, arrogative forces before which, they remarked a thousand times, they seemed helpless as reeds gale-swayed. The last two decades particularly, the late afternoon of life when tranquillity should have been theirs in return for the bread of duty so freely cast upon early waters, had been, instead, tumultuous and inequitable. Anthony, their son, was disinterested in either reels or management; graduated in architecture from the University he joined a firm somewhere in California called Santa Barbara and married someone named Susan to whom the Murninghans were introduced only the day before the wedding, since presenting them by long-distance telephone, as it were, three grandchildren. Then, as inexplicably as though the earth had opened under their feet, Janey had eloped with Morse Baird, depriving herself of the college education planned for her and worse, by an incogitant choice of mate, dooming the marriage at its very inception. High school athletic hero Morse might be, but he was neither Janey's equal intellectually nor, as her father soon ascertained, was he on any level in the plant executive material. Seven connubial years of rancor and misery those had been, cheered only by the birth of little Carol, and they had ended explosively, if not scandalously, in a double divorce and Janey's remarriage to Charles Reason, old enough to be her father and, in fact, about the council table and in the board room, her father's peer! Of these developments the town had been of course briefly apprised by the *Argus-Advertiser,* just as it had been of Harlan Murninghan's many benefactions, such as his gift of an organ to the Congregational Church; the increase of his worldly goods the town could estimate; but the disposition and apportionment of his wealth had been a matter for the Murninghans alone, for Tony and Jane a projection revealed and assented to only in outline, while with Harlan and Carrie it had been over several years that subject on their nightly agenda of paramount and detailed salience. In 1951 an offer to buy Twinriver Reel for $2,100,000 had been made by the Cantlon-Jacob Corporation, a large New Jersey manufacturer of power tools seeking diversification; Cantlon-Jacobs's intentions were to expand, automate fully, and to quantity-produce and market some lines of cheap reels, capitalizing on the reputation of Twinriver; the offer was rejected. Instead, after negotiation with his old friend John Phipps of the Dowagiac Bait and Tackle Company in downstate Cassopolis, Harlan Murninghan had agreed to sell Twinriver to Dowagiac by December 31, 1954, on stipulation that the name, the location, and the types and traditions of production be maintained, for the sum of $1,200,000. The sacrifice to the Murninghan estate amounted therefore to almost one million dollars. The latest of Harlan Murninghan's wills, codiciled and reconciled by attorneys in Grand Rapids, yet still unsigned, finalized the discussions of husband and wife in late May of 1954. Upon his decease the thousand dollars monthly given to Anthony and Jane will cease; each is to receive a single bequest of $25,000. After provision for Federal and state taxes, there will pass to Carrie Murninghan the home, other personal property, and life insurance and securities amounting to approximately $160,000, which she may use and dispose of at her discretion. The bulk of the estate, the $1,200,000 from the sale of Twinriver Reel, is placed in charitable trust administered by the Town Council for the purpose of establishing Murninghan Park, to be situated south of Thebes Milling as far as the Ionian River and adjoining on the west the Button, land now owned by decedent with the exception of six acres, and to consist of a baseball field and stands, softball diamonds, a swimming pool, tennis courts, a picnic grove, a bandshell, and a small auditorium-theater with kitchen facilities. Plans for the park and buildings have been drawn and a contractor-landscaper bid of $800,000 accepted; the income from the residue of

$400,000 is to ensure perpetual maintenance of the park and the employment of a permanent director who will serve as sports instructor for the children of the village (the document names Morse Baird and sets a salary of eight thousand yearly). The terms of this will are unknown to anyone outside the immediate family. The bestowal upon Thebes of Murninghan Park, contemplated by its donor for ten years, is to be announced only after his death. But philanthropy is more often than not made difficult, contradictorily, by self-interest. In the process of acquiring the necessary land, Harlan Murninghan learned to his dismay that a six-acre parcel, that on which stood the old cutter works, in the very center of the site had been purchased in 1948, just before his marriage to Jane, by Charles Reason. A year later the elder man asked his son-in-law to sell and was amazed to be refused. He made two more attempts, each time doubling the offer and each time in vain; then, when he begged Jane to intercede for him with her husband, she stared at him in horror. It was her fault. Awaiting Charles's divorce she had, one night, innocently described to him her father's dream of a park for Thebes and its location; realizing at once that the project would dispossess her, Charles Reason had secretly purchased the six acres, ownership of which, he saw, was crucial. To father and daughter the implication was viciously clear: the doctor had married Jane for the fortune he expected her to inherit. Harlan Murninghan has been unable to this date to buy the vital acreage. Charles Reason makes jest of his efforts, accuses him of knowing a good speculation when he sees one, and the whole sordid business has become, between father and son-in-law, between Charles and Jane Reason themselves, an unbenign internal enlargement, potentially fatal, which only the surgery of candor will reduce, that treatment more excruciating to, more trammeled by, the family relationship than any other. Purgatorially, meanwhile, pends all: the will is unsigned and unrecorded, Murninghan Park exists only on legal parchment, and the end-of-1954 sale deadline of Twinriver Reel to Dowagiac draws within seven months of expiration.

145

—Your plates, dear. Entering the bathroom Carrie held out her hand and obediently Harlan in his sitz bath removed uppers and lowers and gave them to her. These she placed with her own dentures in a single dish of cleansing solution on a shelf, remarking, as she went back to the bedroom: —I'm so tired tonight.

—You don't let Mrs. Ervine do enough.

To herself she acknowledged him right. Forty before she gave up canning, fifty before she allowed Harlan to modernize her kitchen, sixty before he dared hire Mrs. Ervine as full-time household help and then provided she did not "live in," she could never play, despite her husband's seniority of power and affluence, the grande dame of Thebes. At sixty-eight Caroline MacDougald Murninghan, born to frugal farmer parents, who met young Harlan at a grange dance, fell in love and married him immediately, remains fundamentally what she was at eighteen: humble, shy, fearless and devout. She is proud of having, as she puts it, absolutely "no side," and simultaneously ashamed of this claim, for of all the deadly sins the most cardinal to her is pride, and it has been, almost allegorically, her fate and life to be required to wage against it a war as unequal as that between David and Goliath: against pride in her husband's achievement and generosity, in her children, her needlework, the beauty of her home and of the roses in her garden, her position in Theban society, although this has impeded close friendship with others of her own sex, in the fine soprano voice when as a member of the choir she sang duets with Catherine Smith, against pride, even, in the pillars of her faith in God's wisdom and omniscience. This satanic imp which goeth before a fall grigs himself, she has always theorized, upon materialism; the more money, the merrier, the more wanton his terpsichore. Hear how he sounds the horn of her own dear husband's Cadillac! See how he manifests himself in her dear daughter's marital woes, in Charles Reason's perfidy! Her only secret from Harlan is this: that should he predecease her she will sell their home and with the proceeds and the insurance and securities, these so much,

much in excess of her simple needs, live out her time in the doing of good works.

She sat before her dressing table in her nightgown brushing her short white hair, listening to Harlan lift himself heavily from the tub and to his rumbled satisfaction as he toweled. Carrie Murninghan is an extremely small, slight woman with a crooked nose, the result of a tumble from a tree when a child, but the crook of the tip, together with the quick, shy smile which surprises lines and wrinkles out of their accustomed repose, somehow endears rather than uglifying her. Old age she has accepted gracefully, spurning the vanities of tints and waves and creams and lotions. The rue has been what has happened to her body, its wastage, its skeletonizing, its breastlessness; she laughs about it with Harlan, feigning regret that he must share his bed not with a woman but with a little old man.

—Ready for your legs now? she inquired.

—Carrie, will you not come in here for a minute?

Something in his tone alarmed her. —For pity's sake, why not?

—I have something to say to you. If you were looking at me I don't think I could bring myself to say it.

She put down the hairbrush. —All right.

—You must know I have never looked at another woman. I never wished to. Well, I have been unfaithful to you. It doesn't seem possible at my age, but I have been, several times in the past three months. With the Scripter girl.

—Arlene Scripter?

—No, the youngest one, Carlene. That's what makes it even more cursed. She appears older, but I find out she is only fourteen.

She waited at her dressing table for tears to come, but they did not. Somehow she was not unprepared. —Harlan, how did it happen?

She had to strain to hear him. —You remember one night in March I drove to the plant myself, something I had to do? I should have known better, my legs bothered me after the drive down, but I thought I could reach home without having to call Floyd out at that hour. Driving back, they hurt me so that I had to stop by the park across from the church. Someone came by, afoot, and I called and asked if they would drive me home. It was the Scripter girl. She'd never driven a car but I had to have help, and I said I would show her how. We talked a few minutes—I talk to young people very seldom nowadays—and then she drove a while, learning—she seemed to enjoy driving such a big car—for me it was like giving someone a driving lesson. Then, outside of town, she stopped the car and it—I swear she took the initiative, not me. I simply lost my head. Then she drove me home and went on her way. But I arranged to meet her again in the same place, by the park at night. There have been four times since March, the last one three weeks ago. I have given her money. Carrie, I've calculated to tell you every single night, but I've been too afraid and ashamed. That a man my age should be capable of such a thing with a child. I can't even explain it to myself. It so surprised me, that I was physically able, that I even desired to. A man of my years is supposed to want youth more than anything else. For a few minutes with that girl it seemed to me I had it, but since then my conscience has made me glad to be old, glad to know I haven't much time left in which to sin. Harlan Murninghan, a corrupter of children. She heard him lower the toilet lid and sit down. —Well, it's over. No man can ask his wife to forgive him a thing like this. To soil almost fifty years of married life. I pray God, however, Carrie, that you will continue to live with me.

After a moment she blew her nose energetically. —Are you ready for your legs?

—Yes.

—Then I'm coming in. Harlan, before I do, let me say this. Neither of us is to cry. I forgive you. I would forgive anything you could possibly do, I think. Remember, neither of us is to cry.

Carrie Murninghan entered the bathroom. It occurred to her that if she adhered to nightly routine and did his legs first they would face each other, and one, or both, might break down. —I'll oil you first, she said, and taking a plastic bottle of lanolin oil from the medicine cabinet uncapped it and standing over him anointed the bald top of his head, smoothing in the oil with her fingertips so that the scalp would not become desiccated by exposure. —Why did you tell me, dear? You didn't have to.

He said that he would have in any case, he had never kept anything from her; but a terrible shock the preceding day made it imperative. He had been visited in his office by Sewell Smith. Replacing the lanolin Carrie pulled a small stool before her husband, sat down, pushed up his flannel nightshirt and began to rub his legs, kneading gently the muscles and tendons of calves and thighs. Harlan Murninghan had also experienced in the last year or two an infirmity known as intermittent claudication, or hardening of the arteries in his lower extremities; he could no longer walk far or remain standing without pain and the commencement of a limp; indeed, the use of his legs had been sufficiently inhibited to require the services of a Twinriver employee named Floyd as chauffeur and a daily massage by his wife to restore circulation. Young Smith professed to be acting on behalf of Carlene Scripter and Mrs. Scripter. On the verge of hysteria, Carlie had confessed to sexual wrongdoing and named Harlan Murninghan as the one who had led her astray. The girl was fourteen. Harlan Murninghan must be cognizant that under Michigan law no girl, prior to the age of sixteen, might legally give "consent," and that, therefore, any man gaining carnal knowledge of her was guilty of statutory rape, a felony punishable by imprisonment. Mrs. Scripter, said Smith, a mother outraged, wished only that justice be done, that charges be pressed at once and the miscreant requited, but he, Smith, had persuaded her that an effort should first be made to temper justice with lenity, out of this providing for Carlie's future. He brought, then, from the Scripters, a compromise: for a sum payable within two weeks, the matter would be forgotten. And the sum? One hundred thousand dollars. And the alternative? The bringing of formal charges, a trial the defendant would be certain to lose, a prison sentence, plus all the sordid, attendant publicity.

Harlan and Carrie Murninghan gazed at one another, their faces softened, rendered weak, almost infantile by the removal of their dentures. What, Carrie whispered, could he do? He had tried one thing; this afternoon he had been driven to Mrs. Scripter's live bait place on the river, had made his way down the steps, knocked; she would not let him in her house, would not listen to his counteroffer of ten thousand dollars, upbraided him, shouted vituperation until, fearful Floyd might overhear, he had retreated to the car in defeat. He had considered going to Oram Kropf for guidance, but the affair was so personal, so desperate, that he had not dared admit even Oram to his confidence. He was unable as yet to think clearly, but the alternatives seemed to him quite as stark as Sewell Smith had delineated. It was blackmail, of course, but on the other hand he was guilty as charged, his crime was indefensible in or out of court. What they alone knew, she and he, was the effect of either course on their own lives: he could pay the hundred thousand, yes, but by so doing subject himself to further extortion at any time, and each additional bribe of silence would involve redrawing his will, cutting the extent and facilities of the park in order to 'eave enough for her; it was conceivable, should they live long enough, that they could be squeezed dry; yet it was equally probable that if he did not submit, the thing would come to trial, he would go to prison, and how could a man convicted of statutory rape, the whole edifice of his seventy years brought down about him, leave to the town of his birth a park, a bequest, anything bearing his by then obnoxious name?

—Harlan, oh Harlan. Abstractedly she began again his massage. —It's typical of what Ethel Scripter has become, but why would Sewell Smith be a party to it? Why, he used to go with Janey, he was welcome under this roof for years! He's well-to-do, he's famous, what possible reason could he have?

—I don't know.

—Dear, my dear, whatever will we do?

—I don't know.

—Are they better now, your legs?

—Yes, thank you.

—Then will you open the windows while I use the bathroom?

He left her, closing the door behind him, found in a bureau drawer his nightcap and donned it, raised both windows and waited at the bed for her, waited unusually long. When at last she emerged she came to his side.

—I've been thinking as hard as ever I could. We must place our hope and trust where we always have, Harlan. We have two weeks at least. They knelt together beside the bed. —I will tonight, she said. Each took the other's hand. They bowed heads. —Dear, dear Lord, prayed Carrie Murninghan, we have much to ask of Thee this night. Forgive my Harlan. I already have. Surely You and I have grace enough to forgive a single sin in one who has been Thy true disciple for seventy years and my loving helpmate always. We beg, too, that Your Spirit may enter the hearts of those who would harm us and our children and our town. Turn them from malice. Fill them with Thy tenderness, the young man and the woman who transgress against my husband, the girl who tempted him to do evil, and forgive them, too. Finally, our Heavenly Father, we pray Thee to lead Harlan and me out of the wilderness of doubt and misery, show us the way to that peace in which we may complete our days Thy faithful servants. Dear Lord, You must do this. In Your Holy Family's name we ask it. Amen.

She helping him, they rose. She was first into bed, he following after he turned out the lights and stood patriarchal for a moment, awaiting in small sounds and sensations the assurances of his home. They then adjusted to the bed and to each other, lying close according to their need and speaking softly, at intervals, as matters immemorial to their age and conjugation suggested themselves.

—Harlan, people simply aren't the way they used to be. I've decided.

—In what way?

—Sewell Smith, for example. Why he's doing this wicked, wicked thing I'll never understand. L. V. Smith was a fine man, upright in every respect, wasn't he?

—Yes.

—Well, then. People are more complicated today.

He yawned.

She yawned.

—Poor Catherine Smith. Her beautiful voice. I've always blamed myself for not being good Samaritan enough to help her in some way. To prevent her dreadful malady.

—I doubt if you could have.

—I might. One never knows.

—No. I blame myself for not giving you more the last few years, when we've had so much. Indulging you the way Or'm did Grethe.

—I wouldn't have let you, Harlan, you know that. Haven't I told you about the oranges?

She had, in fifty years a hundred times. —I don't believe so.

—If I learned any lesson early, it was that one. I was sixteen, and in those days country people, farmers, never had fruit in the winter except for apples from the cellar. No, I think we had bananas one Christmas. Well, I was sixteen and invited to a party that New Year's at the Rubbins's, they were quite well-off and it was to be a grand occasion. But I let a girl friend, Alice Wright, advise me how to be proud and ladylike and she told me to refuse everything the first time it was offered, to accept only when pressed. Well, during the evening a basket of oranges was passed and I had never tasted one. My mouth watered I wanted one so much, but I was proud and ladylike and said no, thank you, as though we ate them regularly, expecting they'd be passed again. They weren't. I nearly cried. And I never forgot it.

For an appropriate time he seemed to meditate. —Carrie, if anything should happen to me first, I want you to live comfortably. You are amply provided for in the will.

—Whatever made you think I wouldn't?

—I'm not sure. It would be like you to give it all to

charity and stint yourself, which would disturb me very much. I wouldn't rest.

She stirred guiltily. —Folderol, my dear.

He yawned.

She yawned.

—I have to go to the bathroom, he said. —Damn, but it is troublesome.

—Dear, I know it must be. But don't curse and don't walk all the way there and back. Use the commode. That's what it's for and I don't mind.

Fretting thankfully he did so, sliding the chamber pot from beneath the high bed. —Charles keeps after me about operating. He claims I can have no permanent relief until then. Actually, until this Scripter business is settled I don't dare do anything, much less go into a hospital. I have never been so uncertain of myself, never. All my life men have come to me for advice. He let his great weight down beside her once more. —I am not accustomed to being uncertain.

She did not seem to hear. —Dear Alice.

—Who?

—Alice Wright, you remember, the girl friend who told me how to deport myself.

—Oh.

—In her grave these twenty years. The other friends we've had, most of them, your people, mine—Harlan, they're all gone!

He was silent. Rustling, the curtains at the windows stood out with spring; over Harlan and Caroline Murninghan was blown a sign vestigial of winter, connotative by its chill of frozen earth deep-delved; of those beloved dead long lain to rest within it; and of a glacial ice.

—Harlan, I'm cold.

—All right.

Slowly, with patient care each tended to the other, joined, clasped, and held each other close, biding the warmth of fires well-banked.

—Are you cold now?

—No. But her thin arms contracted their embrace. —I'm afraid, she whispered.

—Of what?

—If you went to prison, I'd be alone. There'd be no one to talk to.

—For me, either.

Foreboding made them one, dread fused the slow tolling of worn hearts.

—It would be like dying, Harlan.

—Carrie, we have talked that out. One of us must go before the other.

—But dear, oh my dear, whatever will the one alone do?

—I have prayed that would be the last crisis for us. Now we have another. I don't know, I don't know. I am a confused, ailing old man. And vile.

—You're not old. You have many good years left.

Peril warmed them. In the unknown's face he yawned. She yawned.

—How I wish I knew what to do, she drowsed. —But things are so different today. I'm a helpless old woman.

—No, he soothed, you have many good years ahead. You are not old.

They heard him nibbling somewhere in the house, somewhere in the night perdurable and fearsome, the black and hungry mouse of time to which their fifty years were but a morsel of eternity.

Charles Baird

Having once read an article the subject of which was the creative process and the gist of which was that if one were to be creative he must place himself in a condition of conscious receptivity, whatever the hell that was, and wait for a light to flash or a bell to ring, as in a cartoon, he would say to himself, well, I am conscious, I am bare-assed receptive, I have come home, to the very goddamn roots, and if the article was right, and Peck Hill, the bastard, was right, the bull, the idea, should any time now be coming out of the chute, which it had damn well better, and soon, for the sake of Sewell Smith, world-famous novelist, war hero, virile and colorful figure on the contemporary American Lit scene who, unlike Ernesto Hemingway, pooping around *plazas de toros* and turning buckets of bullshit into money but never having the guts to write about Oak Park, Illinois, has to do it the hard way—unless—unless a certain venerable lecher of this fair village gets the message in the next two weeks that canning the Michigan cherry crop before it is ripe is illegal and decides to unwind the wallet, in which case it may be said that putting the screws on the old is more profitable than screwing the young, or, crime pays better than art, and in which case I will have a cushion, the creative pressure will be off, and the best thing about that kind of loot is that it is nontaxable because you do not declare it. His time he occupied variously. He took inventory of his earthly possessions: two suits, a cashmere sports jacket cigarette-branded on one sleeve, a raincoat, three pairs of shoes, a dressing gown, a scant stock of lesser haberdashery; a portable typewriter; several copy pads, pencils, and some typing paper; three books, a Bartlett, a Thesaurus, and a dictionary; in a blue box, his Distinguished Service Cross; shaving and toilet equipment; two cowhide suitcases; the year-old Jag in which he had vanned these things from Arizona. The dearth did not rankle him; travel light and leave no trace was his motto; and the few furnishings he had bought as cheaply as possible in order to establish residence in the Reichert, once the Smith, house he intended to slough when he took off. He ran over and over in his mind like a formula the raw material with which he must work autobiographically: the war I've used, Hollywood I've used, so that leaves me with a normal childhood and adolescence except for a mother who went off her rocker and a father who was murdered, at least put to death somehow, by six hick types who were covering for something until the time I helped wreck a dam and hauled butt the hell out of here. He drank coffee. He did not write anything. He goldbricked on the rollaway for hours, resting his back and trying to tot up some of the specific sums he had blown in the last two years: during one week he had dropped around $30,000, during another memorable night $12,000, at a crap table in the Sands in Vegas while with the *Location* company; on the morning after an aquabatic three-lay night spent in and out of the Roman bath in his Hollywood house with a starlet called Boobsie, he had taken her into Bev Hills and bought her a chinchilla coat, the tab for which came to damn near $9,000; easy come, you could adage of that deal, easy go; he had experimented for a time with a business manager name of Freednash who had experimented with some speculative land "near" Palm Springs, land which turned out to be thirty miles from nowhere, cost him $21,000, and to which he did not now even have a deed, although Freednash probably did, wherever he was. He slept. He shaved only when going out. He drank much beer. He did not write anything. He had the daily Grand Rapids *Press* delivered. To keep up with the competition in the book industry he read an issue of the *Saturday Review*. Can of beer in hand, for inspiration he roamed the house bottom to top. Here, on a beam over the basement steps, L.V. stored polish and buffer and each morning before going to the bank shined his shoes. Here, in the attached garage, his mother one horrible night redressed a private

157

grievance upon the new Buick his father had that day brought home. A clump of snowball bushes at the far corner of the lawn marked the grave of Powder, spaniel compeer of the elementary grades. The kitchen, once his mother's immaculate reign, he had desecrated with tin cans and bread wrappers. Then the dining room, empty, draped and carpeted, and through French doors the living room, also draped and carpeted sumptuously by a Mrs. Reichert who could afford to be prodigal after Claude's passing, a room long, high-ceilinged, to the eye of the stranger noteworthy only for what seemed in its center to be the camp of a vagrant—rollaway bed, table, opened suitcases, collapsible chair of aluminum and plastic webbing, strew of books, newspapers, clothing—but to Sewell's gaze settled with the furniture of retrospect. Over the Sparton console radio had come nightly for L.V. the drawl and comic crises of Amos 'n Andy until Catherine Smith, in the days of her disorder, had stilled them with a hammer. There, at that end of the room, had stood her huge Chickering grand, unplayed for the ten years it had been her husband's gift except, he was certain, furtively, when she was alone, running from its bench to her chair and to the Bible at the tread of her son home from school, maker of music become mother by some queer, exigent transposition. Through French doors into the entry hall, paneled in walnut, and up the staircase, two-turned, with elaborate walnut balustrade, until the second floor was gained and Sewell could pad through the four bedrooms, empty, carpeted and curtained: the one of the Directors' visitation and his father's dying; his mother's, from whence she reached the porch roof to present herself by night in deranged recital to the town; his own, in which he primped for dates with Jane Murninghan, consecrating himself to her purity, and to which he returned from evenings with Arlene Scripter spent by joyless, automotive ardors; the guest room where, so far as he could recall, no guest had ever dwelt. And each time, the tour done, the almost auto-erotic ransacking of the past completed, standing in one of the rooms rented but possessed by him indubitably, he

158

would quote aloud from Scripture, perhaps from Proverbs: "Put a knife to thy throat, if thou be a man given to appetite."

Or this, from Matthew: "My house shall be called the house of prayer; but ye have made it a den of thieves."

Or this, from Psalms: "Mark the perfect man, and behold the upright."

Or this, perhaps, from Ecclesiastes: "A bird of the air shall carry the voice, and that which hath wings shall tell the matter."

Having intoned, listening, he stood so the first Sunday morning of June when the front door's bell made startling, unliturgical response. He went downstairs. It was Mrs. Scripter and an unexpected escort, Morse Baird. The significance of the pairing, ill-matched and absurd, was nauseously apparent to Sewell: the fourteen-year-old on the Jordan whose highest sexual aspiration was Johnny Scripter's wife, had, after twenty years, attained it. Well, each to his limited triumph. But the couple's contrast in mood he could not account for: subdued, petulant, the widow Scripter sported a right eye swollen almost shut and bruised a vivid green, while Morse was expansive, conferring cigar ash on the carpet as he inspected the living room.

—Say, you didn't bring much with you.

—Travel light and leave no trace. My motto. Sewell offered them the rollaway and both sat down. —What can I do for you church couldn't?

Morse grinned. —Old buddy, I'm surprised at you. Holding out on me.

—Holding out?

—My motto: you can't play the game without a ball. Especially until you know what the game is. Last night Ethel had a little beer and then we had a little conversation. So I know.

—Know what?

—The full deal. About Carlie and ex-father-in-law. And I want in.

—Why?

159

—Simple. Remember in high school you and Harris and me, we were the only guys with our own cars? That car Renis gave me was the only new car I've ever had. Ever since then I've been what you might call a used-car man. The world's full of us. Now I've got a chance to buy me a new one, and what's more, leave this damn town in it and have a stake to start out someplace else.

—There's not much in it, Sewell said carefully. —This is just a nickel-dime favor I'm doing for the lady here, for Johnny's sake.

—Nickel-dime! the lady burst out. —I said to you a couple thousan', for Carlie. Was you going to keep the other ninety-eight?

—How do you know how much I asked?

—Because he come to my place yestiddy, ol' Murninghan, says he won't pay no hunderd thousan' but he might ten. An' I'd of took it, but when he says a hundred thousan' I was so scairt I starts hollerin' at him an' he leaves. So distraught was she still that an unlit cigarette suffered a kind of labial destruction in her mouth. —I never expected to get in deep like this, over my head—it's dang'rous, I tell you! He'll have us in jail before he coughs up any hunderd thousan'!

—Shut up, Ethel, Morse advised. —What did he say when you put it to him?

Sewell sat back more comfortably in the aluminum chair, throwing an exposed leg over the arm and scratching his thigh. Under the monogrammed and crested paisley dressing gown he wore only shorts. —He admitted nothing. I gave him his choice, the money or charges, and two weeks to make up his mind. An offer of ten thousand is as good as a guilty plea. When the hair gets short he'll come through, I'm sure of it now.

—As he damn well should, Morse insisted with righteous mockery. —When an old codger develops hot palms, he ought to pay the price. But listen, Sewell, why we came over. I'm not greedy, just a fair shake's all I want. Call it insurance.

—What's that mean, insurance?

—Well, if it comes to trial, it'll be Harlan Murninghan's word against Carlie's, and in these parts his word they put on stone tablets. My good news is, the first part of it, this isn't the only time our flower girl's been down the garden path. I can testify to that.

—Go on.

—Oh God my little lost baby! groaned the widow, with stubby fingers investigating the state of her eye.

—Ethel here took it pretty hard when I told her last night, Morse said sympathetically, winking. —But the deal is, Carlie's been building herself a reputation all year. They say, down at The Let Live, that they didn't need any sex education in eighth grade this year. Carlie's been teaching her own course, and quite a few boys signed up. That can't be proved, but here's something can. You know reading for Or'm Kropf is a local custom around here. Well, one night in February I was taking my turn and we were talking and I got a clue he was fairly horny—a little oofum-poofum, the wisest men, you know. I was tired so I told him I'd go out and bring him back a reader who might take care of all his problems. It was about ten o'clock. I drove up by the park. Carlie's been seen a lot walking around that park in the evenings lately, getting her exercise, I guess, and there she was this night. I picked her up, no strain, and took her down to the *Arg & Ad* and sent her in and waited. In about ten minutes the light went out in Or'm's office and Carlie didn't.

—You dirty pimp! cried Mrs. Scripter.

—Take it easy, Ethel. Myself, I thought it was more along the line of public service. Helping an elder of the town, you know. And if it was pimping, what does that make your kid?

—Or'm Kropf, said Sewell.

—Or'm Kropf, repeated Morse.

—Oh God if my Johnny was only here!

—And that isn't all, old buddy. Ethel, get ready for a worse one. I mean, a real knee in the crotch. Remember last

161

night when I said I was going upstairs and ask Carlie a few questions—no, you wouldn't, not with the load you had on. Anyway, I did. I asked her had anybody else been educating her about anything besides journalism and the reel business. She took a little convincing, but I finally got the word. Yes, somebody else had. Morse savored the moment. —You ready?

They waited.

—She's also learned one hell of a lot about grinding wheat.

They looked at him.

—That's right, my uncle. Charlieboy and Carliegirl. Three, four times this spring. She's been his little flume and he's been her dear old turbine.

Snatching a handkerchief from her cleavage Mrs. Scripter commenced to snuffle into it a shock genuine, a woe unfeigned, the apparatus of her ducts working, for once, naturally. —Oh my poor sweet baby! she wailed, rocking herself on the rollaway. —Corruptioned in the bud jus' the way I was when I first come to town from the farm, only by ol' lechers not young mongerls. My whole life's been one tragidy after another, goddammit, an' I can't take no more! Hughh, hughh!

In the rubble on his table Sewell located a nail clipper and thoughtfully, lifting one bare foot to the chair edge, began to trim his toenails.

Morse could not contain himself. He lit a fresh cigar. He stood to pace the carpeting, circling them. —I'm sorry about the father-in-law, and Or'm, I guess, even Carlie, though she must be basically hotter than a fiddler's bitch, but my shitheel uncle has finally run fresh out of luck, by God, and I want to help take him to the cleaners. So now you know why I want in, old buddy. I'd do it for free, I really would, but if there's a brass ring on this ride, why shouldn't I have a piece and be able to bust out of here? You've got everything, Sewell, I've got some shirts with the buttons off. Besides, remember, you need at least one witness, and I'm your boy.

He paused for a sign, and there was none. Sewell continued

to trim his toenails. —Also, I may not be executive material but I ain't stupido. Your hands aren't exactly clean. There's a word they use in court for the squeeze you're putting on.

—Blackmail.

—That's right. Well? Am I in or are you out?

—How much, Sewell said, would you say Charles Baird is worth?

—Beats me. A pile, though. Maybe half what Harlan is.

—And Kropf?

—Not much, any more. That paper probably nets him eight, ten thousand a year, though. Why? What are you figuring?

Interested, no longer lachrymose, Mrs. Scripter blew her nose and renestled the soggy handkerchief in her bosom.

—The assessments, Sewell said. He trimmed a last nail and blew the clippings from the chair, then dropped the implement to the table. —Each according to his ability to pay. Murninghan's is set, we'll make Baird's half that, and stick Kropf for a year's income, ten G's.

Morse calculated, and the total caused him to push at his forelock, to sit down again in disbelief. —You'll really try to wring $160,000 out of those old jokers? Christ, they'll never pay that much! Besides, isn't there something in the law about a babe if it can be proved she's laid guys all over the place she's considered a common prostitute and nobody's liable? I've always heard that.

—If she's fourteen years old, she can be the town slot machine and it's still statutory rape.

—I don't know as there's that much money in the world, concurred Mrs. Scripter, nodding at Morse.

—Be reasonable, old buddy. This is Thebes, not New York.

—When a body's short on bait, half a crawler's good as a whole, said the widow.

Sewell shot to his feet, stubbing a forefinger at them as might a drill sergeant. —I've about had it, he rasped. —Now you listen, you gutless small-town wonders. Carlie may be your kid but this is my operation and I'll run it or drop out

163

here and now, and if I do, you haven't got a goddamn prayer. They have the power and the leverage and the brains. Me, they can't touch. I don't need the bucks. All I want is to settle an old count of my own with the three of them, otherwise I wouldn't pick my nose for beer money like this. But when I'm the take-charge guy on anything, my services come high. Fifty percent. However you split the rest, I couldn't care less. Now you decide it's me producing the show for 50 percent or you're on your own and you collect nothing.

—How come, if you don't need it, you take half off the top? Morse asked.

—That is none of your goddamn business.

—Don't blow your stack. Ethel, is this okay with you?

Shoat eyes bewildered, her entire metabolism upset by large sums and vague fears and retributive longings, the widow rubbed her hands together in her lap as though to strike some spark of pith. —Oh God I can't think straight, Morsey. Just about my baby, is all, an' what them ol' bastids done, an' how it'll be the ruination of her.

Morse lowered his head, staring down at the cigar butt between his fingers. A grimace twitched the corners of his mouth. —Old buddy, I remember you out on Honey Brook the other day. I said you must have had something, I didn't know what, and you said "I'll show you." Then you took that trout I'd missed. You knew when and how to slip the hook to him and I didn't. I never have. He raised his head. —So as far as I'm concerned, this is your stream. You can fish it any way you want. What's the next move?

Sewell rigged more surely the sash of his robe. —The next is, you butt out of here, both of you, and don't come back to this house again. We can't afford to be seen together. If we have to meet, we can do it over at her place, at night. Another thing. When is school out? How much longer is Carlie supposed to go?

—This week an' three days next, her mother said.

—Then keep her home. Call the school and tell them she's sick. She won't miss much and the thing is, we don't want anyone to get to her and buy her off.

—I hate to have her get behind any, the widow grumped.
—That kid, Sewell said, is already way ahead. Now you better take off. Tomorrow I'll put the shaft to Baird and Kropf, and give them two weeks also. Another thing, one of these days I'll run over to Tyre and talk to the County Prosecutor. In case we have to tighten the screws a turn, we need to know what the hell is the legal procedure.

—Let's haul, Ethel. Morse gave her a lift up with his hand, then said suddenly, simple-mindedly concerned: Sewell, be honest with me. Will we really luck out on this?

—You can start mentally spending that money.

At the door Mrs. Scripter pulled a compact from her pocket, peered with good eye into its mirror, and from her depths emitted a long sough of disquietude. —That's as may be, she warned, repowdering her bruise. —But you two ain't got no notion what strings them gents can pull. She snapped shut the compact. —Johnny could say, but they buried him.

It happened within minutes after their departure. Receptivity had nothing to do with it. The conception, rather than immaculate, resulted from a series of idle, not unconnected thoughts which, skeined one after another from reverie, were guided onto the loom of his consciousness and there, all at once, stunningly, by some associative process made pattern. After the door closed upon them Sewell brought a can of beer from the kitchen and lolling on the rollaway grinned, first, at recollection of the old Jezebel's parting strut before her mirror. This, second, minded him of his own balding and, third, led him to reflect, metaphorically, that the thirties and forties are the time payments a man makes upon old age. Fourth, old age in the abstract concreted to Harlan Murninghan and Oram Kropf, and then to Charles Baird, not exactly old but meeting his final installments, and then, fifth, to the extreme's opposite, youth, and its relevant embodiment, Carlie Scripter. Sixth, he wondered what she looked like, how she dressed, and where, glandularly, the thing had gone wrong which left her amenable to age's hoary, sage-fingered wenching. He ran off, seventh, in the stag party of imagination, reel after reel of film, scene after erotic scene in which Carlie and the three ancients appeared in various states of undress and various copulative postures. At a kind of subconscious eight-count he was standing, overwhelmed, swaying with the idea, then moving, he knew not on which impulse, through the entry. Here was his book. He was borne up the stairs by it. Time: now. Place: small town. Situation: patriarchs of church, commerce, community involved sexually with young girl. Point: pornography is where you find it. Potential, moneywise: limitless. He had only to tell the story now breaking about him. So sensational was the material that the writing, the structure, the raison d'être would not matter a good goddamn. He could turn it out in three months instead of six. So commercial were its possibilities that half a dozen publishers would light candles at his ass for a contract. One of his stipulations, when he realized what the drug-store turnover might amount to, would be a flat hundred G's for the paperback rights alone. He found himself in one of the bedrooms, the can of beer still in his hand. He pitched it clanking, foaming into a corner. He guaranteed to go on the wagon until this was accomplished. He was wet with sweat. Call him a one-book ejaculation, would they, compare him, as had some of the *Looking* reviews, with the other scaggy olive drab or Marine green pen pals who burst upon the firmament like star shells and thereafter dudded out in ignorance or dementia! He would call the Carlie deal off. His hands shook. The next thing hit him with paratrooper impact. No, not call the Carlie deal off, play it the way L.V. played poker, take the money from Murninghan, Kropf, Baird in return for silence, then avenge yourself on the sons of bitches by publishing the book anyway, change the names, disguise the place a little, any resemblance persons living or dead purely coincidental, but the whole town would know, yes, yes, in its cruddy soul's black bile it would know. To you, Thebes, my last will and testicle! Silence. Screw the identity bit, do a book showing what the hell may be dug up from the puke-bucolic midden that is the small American town. Silence. What was that about it? Where? For your title. Sewell rushed downstairs, into the living room, haunched beside an open suitcase and fumbling through the shirt flaps brought forth the manila folder and opened it to the typewritten pages. His rodomontade across the pool at Peckham Hill that night in Arizona was based on fact: in an attempt at self-education he had indeed read from a list purporting to include the twenty greatest novels ever written, and, chapfallen by his earlier reliance on Bartlett, had copied out of them brief passages which might serve as eventual epigraphs and titles. He located now the lines from George Eliot's *Middlemarch*. Yes, here was the epigraph for the book and yes, by God, here, by excerpting its last five words, was his title: "If we had a keen vision and feeling of all ordinary human life, it would be like hearing the grass grow and the squirrel's heart beat, and we should die of that roar which lies on the other side of silence."

—Eee, eee, eee! mewls Charles Baird.

Remembering the aplomb, the pipsqueak gall with which the man delivered his ultimatum to Renis's widow, Sewell is unprepared, at the confronting's very outset, at the first drop of Carlene Scripter's name, to wrest from Charles Sampter Baird a full confession of guilt and to witness his utter collapse, hands shielding his face effeminately while high violin stridulations escape his fingers. Baird is small of bone and tight of scrotum, one expects, considerably under middle height and smallfooted; the intervention of fifteen years has altered him little except for a cantaloupe belly so rotund that he resembles a figure of fun in a child's tale. His dolly cheeks are sleek and unlined, his mouth cherubic, and his eyes, black colloidal dots in dolly white, are slightly pop. His hair is that sandy hue which seldom grays and when artfully brushed camouflages all attrition. One would fix him at fifty. He nears sixty. Helplessly he hunches in his swivel chair, narrow shoulders convulsed, face covered.

—Eee, eee, what will Lillian do? On one wrist an expensive wrist watch glitters.

Sewell's sadistic meal is one of many courses. It is pleasant to treat with the President of Thebes Milling on such advantageous terms, to behold bank Director, Council and School Board member caitiff by his own conviction, infantile in his remorse. It is pleasant to transfer unto himself, as upward it pulses through the floor into the furniture, into the very walls of the office, the River Button's mighty tribute, the great turbine's revolutionary power. He gluttons on the moment, sips the tears. —Who's Lillian?

—My wife.

—You married? The hell you are. I always figured you for a fag.

—I don't know what that is.

—Fag, queen, homo, fairy.

—I've been married eight years!

—Or if not a fag, a thing with damn strange sex habits. Enticing little kids with candy, that sort of trick. Like Carlie, for instance. Certainly not a normal male.

—Don't you say such things to me!

—Shirt.

Charles Baird fops a silk handkerchief from his pocket and blows, or rather zephyrs, his nose. —We prove our masculinity in different ways. We can't all be war heroes or write smutty books, some of us must do it less spectacularly.

—How's that connect with the price of eggs?

—Dams, not eggs. You left here in such a hurry fifteen years ago, possibly no one has told you what a state my esteemed brother had brought this mill to at his death. The dam you destroyed cost almost a hundred thousand dollars. Peevish for control, for a means of self-aggrandizement which may restore him, Charles Baird pushes from the chair and minces to the window overlooking the dam and flume, presenting his back to his menacer. He moves on short, pigeon steps, brilliant in a plumage of beige beltless slacks, a shirt of lemon, perforated shoes of brown and white. For all practical purposes, he declaims, Thebes Milling had been, that spring of 1939, bankrupt, owing more than the book or resale value of plant and land, both of which Renis had mortgaged to the hilt. Add to that the total loss of the power system, only a fraction of which was covered by insurance, by three thoughtless youths gone berserk, and you had a situation impossible of salvage. But salvage it he had, on his knees, eighteen hours a day, borrowing at usurious rates to rebuild the dam, cutting costs of operation, holding on by his fingernails to their former percentage of the market and screeching for more. —Looking back, I wonder sometimes how I managed it, Renis's little dog doing tricks, fetching and lying down and rolling over until I was thirty-six years old, ill equipped even for living, much less rescuing what my grandfather had begun. But I did, somehow. I gained the respect not only of myself but of the men who've since become my dearest friends, Harlan Murninghan, Oram and the others. And of the town, too, or it would never have elected me to office. Since 1838 this has been the Baird mill. It still is. Equally important, it remains the town's second largest employer, and we have third-generation millhands here. Covertly he dabbed at his eyes. —How I despise myself for crying! I seem to so much lately.

—Am I supposed to be impressed? Sewell asked. —Whatever the business is now, Harris is responsible, and for thanks you give him your garbage.

—As his father did for me!

—That's my point. You get back at the dead through the living, which is what a fruity coward would do. And after stealing the mill from Harris and Morse in the first place.

Charles Baird whirls, hands on hips. —L. V. Smith's son accuse me! How do you dare!

—Baird, I took it from Kropf, I won't from you. Sewell cracks fist into palm. —Any more of that and I'll lay one in your fat gut up to the elbow!

—Are you saying you don't believe me? Charles Baird compresses his mouth so severely that the pout lips disappear. —How on earth, on his salary, could he have acquired a house like that, the cars he owned, even one for you?

—He played the market. He told me.

—And told his friends, too, for years. And did so well at it that some of them asked his advice, and do you know what he said? He said no, because they would speculate, he was investing, and he would never encourage anyone to gamble. Imagine! $170,000!

The coincidence of the amount with that specified by Oram Kropf, rather than unsettling Sewell, infuriates him. —Is that how much the Directors got away with?

—The Directors? Did the Directors have access to those safe-deposit boxes? Could we have known how to slip the hinge-pins?

—Christ, what a concoction.

—Are you afraid to hear how he did it?

—You lying pansy, no, I'm not. Go ahead. But remember, when you're through I'm saving something for you.

Charles Baird resets himself hastily, opens a gold case, drops a cigarette, takes a second and instead of lighting, revolves, fondles it. —You must have seen the old-fashioned lock boxes we used in those days, in the open wooden racks, the locks on the front of each box rather than on the door. All anyone had to do was pull the box from its rack, slip out the hinge-pin at the back—he kept them oiled for the purpose—and raise the lid from the rear. This was a small-town bank. Transactions were very personal. No man in town was considered more principled than your father. People with boxes would sit in his office and as a courtesy he'd step back to the vault and bring their boxes to them. Eventually he would clip the coupons for them himself, put them in the till, and bring back the cash for the customer. Then, about 1925, he began getting into the boxes on his own, removing bearer bonds, selling them to the bank so that they became bank assets, placing them in the bank's bond box, which was kept in the vault, and pocketing the money. An ingenious method, but complicated, because it required him to keep an accurate, running record of the bonds he'd converted, type, serial number, owner's name date of interest due, so forth. Occasionally a customer would ask to clip his own coupon, and then he would have to go into the vault, take the bond from the bond box, transfer it to the right safe-deposit box, and bring the box back to the individual. No one except bank personnel ever went into the vault with him, although the employees were regularly in and out for currency or silver. They would never have presumed to question L. V. Smith. Imagine the records he had to keep! The bonds were usually in denominations of $1000, so that he had to record transactions on at least 170 different bonds! And the sleight-of-hand, much of it at night but some during hours, back and forth from safe-deposit boxes to bond box, then back again! It gives me gooseflesh to think of it! Like acrobats the sentences, high-pitched, exclamatory, tumble and somersault. The little man rejoices in the tattling, both for its own sake and because, embellishing another's guilt, his own, if not expunged, is palliated. —He cashed coupons for the bank, of course, as well as for customers. What to do when someone asked for his coupon and he had already cashed it for the bank's account? Never fear, he had a shift for every contingency. He'd simply put a debit slip in the till, marked "L.V. Smith, $25," remove the money and hand it over to the customer. These slips were called "cash items" because they represented cash, but they were actually his personal I.O.U.'s and their inclusion in bank assets is strictly illegal. Sometimes his debit slips would add up to as much as a thousand dollars, and he'd have to convert another bond from a customer's box to the bank's in order to cover. And there you are. Genius.

—Baird, you should be a writer, you tell a damn good story. The trouble is, none of it holds water. Bank examiners came every goddamn year and sealed the bond box.

—Did you ever know L.V. to be inexpedient? His friends never did. Yes, they sealed the bond box, yes, they checked the bonds individually by number against the "Register," the bank's list of its own bond assets, but when they found some missing, he'd tell them he had several out for purposes of correspondence with a bond house about selling, just a minute and he'd locate them. He'd check his records, remove them from the customers' boxes and bring them to the examiners. Take a vacation? Impossible! Become ill? Un-

171

thinkable! Why, he couldn't be away from that bank and that vault for one full day! One slip, one request in his absence by the wrong customer for his box or his coupon and the game would have been up! What a frightful tight-rope to walk! Charles Baird oscillates his head in horror.
—I dislike intensely being the one to tell you these awful things, but now you have the details you must be able to understand that all men, even the best of us, make mis-takes. To err is human, the poet says, to forgive divine! We long ago forgave your father, we kept his embezzling to ourselves, to this day he stands as high in the town's memory as ever. Have you seen the monument erected on his grave at our expense, the inscription Mrs. Harlan Murninghan herself picked out? Surely, he wheedles, laving lips with tongue, you can do as much for me as the Directors, his friends, did for him. I admit to weakness, I throw myself on your mercy and your tolerance as a man of the world. A thing like this would destroy me. Things aren't going well at home. And there are other reasons I can't tell anyone.

For five minutes Sewell has not moved; Charles Baird's plea appears to beat against a force as stolid, as implacable as the River Button; another minute hums away before he can appraise his failure. The round doll face screws up, his hands unfan across it, he swivels his chair about and once again is pressed to shrill, diaper lament.
—Eee, eee, eee! She made me think of Gloria, her small-ness, her softness, her hair, in the dark I held her on my lap and kissed her and she kissed me! We had a retarded child, Lillian and I, our only child, a little girl, Gloria, she broke our hearts every day but how we loved her, eee, eee! She lived to be six, then the Lord took her from us—but if I closed my eyes I could hold her in my arms again and she was restored, normal, blessed! Eee, I couldn't help myself, I died inside with love and tenderness, I can't help crying, the sorrow, the shame!
—What a crock of crap.
—Insult all that's sacred to me, bully me, but keep my secret for your father's sake! You owe it to me!

—I owe you nothing, I believe nothing coming from a man who did what you've done to an innocent kid. Sewell spoke softly. —No, I'm leaving, you little queer, but before I do, a couple of items. I said I was saving something for you. Here it is. I represent the Scripters, mother and Carlie. You raise fifty thousand dollars and hand it over in the next two weeks or you face a charge of statutory rape. And if it's any consolation, you've got company. Or'm Kropf we've also caught with his degenerate pants down. He sickens me as much as you do, so you can pass the word. I'm giving him two weeks, the same as you, and his tab is ten thousand.

At the door Sewell lingers. —Charlieboy, I'm not surprised you had a retarded kid. You're a retarded man.

He did not call her, she called him, she would be in her car, a convertible, on the Delphi road, then change to his. Following instructions he found her parked and she came at once to the Jaguar saying Charles was wild about sports cars, she indifferent, but this one, with its California plates, its raffish lines, its traumas and dilapidation, reminding her of some coaster of exotic registry and illicit traffic she wanted very much to ride in. She had with her a copy of *Looking for a Location* and a pen and asked him to inscribe it for Carol, her daughter, who was, like all girls in their early teens, swoony about movie stars and anyone associated, however remotely, with movie stars. Opening the book on the car's hood, he wrote, "For Carol, whose mother is still looking," signed it, and gave it to her to read. She thanked him, tore out the page, slid into the Jag and said she knew where to go; he replied he was sure she did.

The day, June's first, was warm and sunny. The leaves were come of age. From marshes frogs referred to summer in speech colloquial and boisterous. They rode with the top down, slowly, the gravel of the road producing against the Jaguar's underside an agreeable tintinnabulation, and the road mounted the hills. Of all blame for their quarrel at the Creel & Cartridge she absolved him; he was drunk, and the disclosure of her marriages, first to Morse, now to

173

Charles Reason, must not have tinctured well the cheap champagne. Her justification for meeting him today was to explain why Charles. They passed the intersecting road down which, he remembered, he and Morse and Harris had transported Lene Scripter for immoral, tenth-grade purposes. With Morse, after their adolescent 440-yard dash to Indiana, she had learned, girl-bride, that sex was not enough, that a mattress was not a magic carpet to the lands she yearned to see, that pity was the arsenic of love, and in desperation to grow, to find out what she might become, to fulfill herself, she had veered to Morse's opposite, a man mature and intelligent and sophisticated, one who could order dinner at the Chambord, gear and corner an Austin-Healey with flair, discuss Camus and Brubeck and Oppenheimer, compose an impeccable vodka Gibson; surely, surely it was possible that the daughter of a small-town manufacturer might find, not only happiness, but glamour and enlightenment with a man twenty years her senior; a marriage it would be, yes, but also a matriculation. She spoke in bursts, as does a machine gun when triggered even slightly, her voice husky. Her whole manner was explosive. She overdramatized. He guessed she would have in Thebes no friend among her own sex. Out of the valley of the Ionian they entered upon a veritable Canaan of homes and barns fat as udders, machinery well kept, cattle rich with pasture, fields where wheat greened and the corn would be much more than knee-high by the Fourth of July. To her Charles had represented, promised, all these things and had, indeed, delivered. Here, she said. He swung the roadster into a grove of maples and braked before a long frame building of two stories and many windows, its concrete porch steps lettered in faded, foot-worn white: Delphi Grange Hall 1902. Rare-coin silver were the sideboards of the Hall for the wood had never known paint. Here, each mid-summer, Grange wives served the famous Delphi Supper: all you could eat for a dollar, all you could gorge of roast chicken, cloved ham, potatoes mashed and scalloped, squash, string beans and limas, carrots, spinach, rad-

174

ishes, celery, corn on the cob, salads of lettuce and tomatoes and apple cubes in whipped cream, homemade bread and rolls and cornbread, pies of pumpkin, mince, cherry, apple, peach, huckleberry, banana cream, raisin, chocolate and lemon meringue, frosted three-layer cakes of yellow, chocolate, spice, angel-food, coffee by the cup or by the gallon; they served a thousand people every year from far and wide and every year a thousand people groaned abdominal vow never to return and they served a thousand people at the Delphi Supper every year. So, she had graduated from Morse Baird High School and enrolled at Charles Reason University and studied a curriculum of philosophy, ethics, taste, literature, values, aesthetics, discrimination, social conscience, only to discover, too late, that her heart could not afford the tuition. Put bluntly, Charles Reason had married her for her money. They left the Jag and finding the Hall door unlocked, entered. The gentleman, the Councilman of breeding, elegance, refinement, had, in reality, damn him, damn him, turned out to be a country general practitioner bled white by Bernice, his divorced wife, a dollar-bill diagnostician, a surgeon-swindler who removed tonsils, adenoids, and, while he was at it, love itself. Swindle him she would if she could, fit him she would if she could with a set of Brooks Brothers horns. On these trestle tables the wives of Delphi hooked rugs, made aprons, quilted blankets; around them Delphi yeomen voted on crop controls; on the walls were hung an American flag and the banners of the 4-H Club and the Future Farmers of America. She leaned against a table. Hers had been a funny function, she said, funny, funny: to be a means to two men's psychic ends: to Morse a chaplet, a laurel, a cup restorative of that pride his bloating athlete's body could never have regained him; to Charles, the man of culture, for his old age an annuity, for the present a credit card affording him a casual, sports-car pomp far in excess of his own wallet's capital. How rich was the jest's cream? How had it all come to pass? Because, funny, funny, a young Ulsterman, a tinkerer, a fisherman had long ago been irked by a reel and

175

resolved to design a better, but before that, even, a century ago, a landshark had sold a bill of fake Arcadian goods to a pedant pioneer. And that, she laughed with shrill, febrile irony, was the story of her life: not dinner at Pavillon but all you could eat for a dollar—not a season at Cap Ferrat but a night in an Indiana motel—not a trophy marlin off the Peruvian coast but a recalcitrant black bass before she was born—just call her a 4-H girl—hooked rugs, husbands, homemade bread and hot pants. Poor Morse! Poor Charles! Poor Jane Murninghan Baird Reason!

Let's go upstairs, he said, in the old days they used to have square dances up there every Saturday night, then later, brawls with music supplied by the Johnny Scripter Orch. No one went up there any more, she said, its use had been prohibited for years, dancing had weakened the joists, but he said let's go anyway. They climbed a creaky stair, opened a creaky door. Into yesterday they stepped. Through dusty windows sunlight cobwebbed a chamber two hundred feet in length, its floor a flawless wooden concavity, the bottom of the bowl sloping gently upward to a joining with the troweled walls; no splintering, no fissures visible, the spine of the old hall had settled, finally and symmetrically, with the weight of a thousand and one Saturday nights. Fancy sets the scene of eld, at nine o'clock the dance is held, fiddler ancient tunes his strings, nasally the caller sings: choose your beaux an' choose your ladies, boy-without-a-gal can go to Hades, form your squares an' everybody bow, this here reel commences now, lift them skirts an' show them legs, careful now don't break no eggs, Adam was weak an' Eve was bad, but criminy the fun they had, stomp that boot an' point that toe, don't give a hoot but do-se-do, what's a little pinch, what's a little smile, give a gal an inch she'll take a mile, allemande left an' allemande right, we country folks can dance all night, but wait: the fiddler slower bows, faltering the do-se-do's, strapping swains are now grown old, berry lips are sere and cold, one by one the partners fade, promenade into the shade, seek a lesson from the dancers, headstones drawl their mournful answers: eternity's tarnation strange, we druther dance at Delphi Grange.

For a while the hall hushed them. Then she said her
father and mother, their golden anniversary nearing, had
first met at a grange dance, Bowne Grange, she thought,
west of here. On his father's first date with his mother, he
said, a square dance in Big Rapids, he had been so poor
he fainted from hunger. She walked to a window, looked out
a moment, then came slowly toward him, letting him see
how, at thirty-three, her blouse had filled, her hips, encased
in pink Capri pants, had learned to harlot, how she could
platinum and feather her hair and self-inflict upon her
mouth a purple wound. She smiled crookedly, lifted hands
prehensile, solicited him to dance. Down the floor's declen-
sion, gingerly, they moved, and reached the nadir.

—Johnny Scripter played here?
—Drums.
—Just think, I have a daughter fourteen.
—Where was the fire?
—Morse wanted to make sure he'd won.
—Doc too old?
—No. He wants to. I won't.
—*Por qué?*
—That's what they do with cows.
—Artificial insemination?
—Yes. To make money.
—You must be very happy.
—What about Arlene Scripter?
—The All-Bran Ophelia.
—Something's wrong and sad and tragic there. I can't
say why or what, but I think I'm to blame.
—You are. Or were.
—Tell me.
—When we were boys, fishing up on the Jordan, we made
a treaty: never to touch you.
—I don't see—
—You were to marry. Lene was to use.
—I still don't—
—We made a deal with her, too, after Johnny went out
like a Keystone Cop. Produce or no dates.
—Oh, no—

—Why not? You were the fiction, someone had to be the fact. You were the princess, someone had to play the slut.
—So when you were—with her—you closed your eyes—
—Pretending it was you. All of us.
She shuddered. —So that's why Harris—
—Married her. I know about that.
—Who told you?
—Edie Kropf. I promised not to pass the word.
—Don't please. Not even Norma knows.
They danced, the sibilance of their shoes on elderly wood like strictures from the past.
—You were darling, though.
—Who?
—The three of you. Like serious, awkward boy-soldiers taking turns standing guard. Belt-back suits and shining ears and slicked-down hair.
—If one of us was sick, the pact was, neither of the other two could substitute.
—I remember. That's why I missed Duke Ellington, Harris had the measles. I cried myself to sleep.
—Morse and I both took Lene, the only time we ever dated her in public, really. Ellington was terrific, Ivy Anderson singing, Cootie Williams on trumpet, and down in front, two string basses.
—Just driving all the way to Grand Rapids for a dance was thrill enough, but that huge Civic Auditorium, the thousands of kids.
—The Big Apple.
—Yes, and the other wonderful bands then. Remember Ted Weems, and Elmo Tanner whistling?
—And Hal Kemp.
—Jimmy Dorsey.
—Chick Webb.
—Benny Goodman.
—Clyde McCoy.
—And Horace Heidt.
—Russ Morgan.
—Father Hines.

—Count Basie.

—Henry Busse.

—You've changed too much.

—So have you.

—You don't need to platinum your hair. Whore up your mouth. Show off your butt.

—Nobody changes. They become what they are. I was a natural-born bitch.

—And I could have had you any time.

—Any time.

—God.

—So have you changed.

—I got smart.

—Your language, your attitudes.

—It's my right. I had a *Time* cover story.

—I memorized it. You've really been practically everywhere?

—Practically.

—I've been to New York once. And you're quite rich?

—Quite.

—Why haven't you married?

—I have.

—Who?

—Myself.

—You loved me once.

—Whoever you were. Whoever I was.

—I suppose you've had every possible sexual experience.

—Several impossible.

—Did you mean what you said at the Creel & Cartridge?

—I said a lot of things.

—That if I'd waited, not married Charles, until you came home, we might have—

—I meant it.

—I hate Thebes. Most of the people I love and respect, my mother and father especially, but the town I despise.

They were not dancing. He had urged her slightly up the floor's incline so that she must lean her weight against him breast to thigh.

—So much I want to see, so many things I want to do. I'm thirty-three. If I could run away.

—If you had the ticket.

—I could never say it when we were young. But you were the one I wanted, not Morse, not Harris, you. If you had only touched me, once.

—I can imagine you in bed.

—I can imagine you.

—You bite.

—Yes.

—You scratch.

—Yes. Yes.

—You use the words.

—Yes, yes, yes.

He mastered her. There, in the hall's old hebetude, so close together as to be coital, the man accepted the resounding of her heart, her breathing's supplicant fevers, as partial reparation for the boy's beguilement, time's swindle of the belt-backed, scrubbed-ear youth. He grasped her by the buttocks, he let her gauge the quantum of his loins' congestion.

—I could take you now.

—Yes. Yes.

—Here. On the floor.

—Yes.

—I won't.

—Damn you.

—Or take you away with me, either.

—Damn you, why not?

—I never buy a package till I try it.

—Try it.

—In bed. All night.

—I can't.

—Then stay in Thebes.

—No.

—All your life. I'll send you postcards.

Against his lower self he fastened, then released, then fastened her again in pagan, oestrual metric.

—Don't. Remember the songs? Don't. Like "True"?
—"Where or When."
—"Pennies from Heaven."
—"Hold Me."
—"Stars Fell on Alabama."
—"Please."
—"I Cried for You."
—"How Deep is the Ocean?"
—"Sophisticated Lady."
—"I've Got You Under my Skin."
—"That Old Feeling."
—"Music, Maestro, Please."
—"Down the Old Ox Road."
—"Too Marvelous for Words."
—Yes. Now. Yes. Now, now, now.

Tremors gripped her. From her throat was torn a cry blasphemous in Delphi Grange. Her head fell on his shoulder.

—Week from tonight, she gasped. —Taking a patient to Ann Arbor, Charles, for tests, staying overnight. A room for us in Grand Rapids, at the Hamlind, get one. I'll be there by nine. "Love in Bloom," "Object of My Affections," "Little Bit Independent."

Ten years of magistracy by the Articles of War and subjection to the proceedings of one court-martial might robe a man for latrine jurisprudence, but civilian law to Sewell was like terrain long held and fortified in depth by an enemy, while to assault it was in his opinion to conduct an infantry operation: train if there was time, but above all, patrol. He went alone the fourteen miles to Tyre, to the county courthouse, and thence to the office of the County Prosecutor, an arid ipso-facto gentleman of middle years named Engelhardt who recognized the author, having read a notice of his temporary residence in Thebes in the papers and would of course, deferential finger tips to finger tips, be glad to describe legal procedures in a hypothetical case. Suppose, said Sewell, this situation. A girl aged fourteen is discovered to have been seduced by several men of prominence in a community. What is the law? What steps does it initiate? What penalties may it impose?

Excuse me, said the Prosecutor, excusing himself bodily from the office. Absent a considerable period, in his stead entered a younger man, giving his name as Collins and introducing himself as the Assistant County Prosecutor. He wore an orange necktie. He took over the Prosecutor's chair, propped his legs comfortably over one corner of the Prosecutor's desk, professed himself honored to meet so renowned a native Ionian, incidentally he'd read *Looking for a Location* and that scene between the movie producer and the girl out in the New Mexico desert, well, wowee, if the expression might be pardoned, but in this racket there was no such thing as a hypothetical case of statutory rape, he knew it, the Prosecutor knew it, and that was why that worthy had been suddenly called to an arraignment or a pissoir or a cup of coffee or something, being a candidate for State Senate in the next election, and if prominent citizens in Thebes had been running around with their flies open it was wiser to let an Assistant Prosecutor take over and explicate the hypothetical law in the hypothetical, ahem, case, okay? Okay.

First, the law. Carnal knowledge of, that was, dipping the wick, in a minor, that was, a girl under sixteen years, was statutory rape whether with her consent or not because a minor could not legally grant consent being assumed to be too young to weigh the consequences which in the case of some kids was a big fat guffaw.

Second, the steps. A charge had to be filed, a complainant had to appear before the Prosecutor, usually the girl's mother or a police officer or a welfare agent. The P.A. talked with the complainant and the girl and if their stories checked out—sometimes an M.D. would be required to attest to defloration—if the P.A. were reasonably convinced of skulduggery, he would authorize a complaint signed before the local Justice of the Peace. The J.P. would then issue a warrant or warrants and turn them over to an officer, a sheriff or deputy, who would serve them. The warrants would specify time and date of examination before the J.P. Men of character and standing, with homes and families and not likely to fly the coop, would not be required to post bond guaranteeing appearance.

Sewell interrupted. Up to this point, would anyone except the principals know what was going on?

No one, Collins said. Only at the actual examination before the J.P. would the story break, and then only if, in the latter's determination, based on reasonable evidence, alleged offense had actually been committed by alleged defendants. This would get it in print, on the back pages of local papers if at all, pages two or three in the Grand Rapids *Press*. The J.P. being convinced, defendants would be allowed bond and arraigned for trial on the next Circuit Court docket, which was public notice. The cat, that was, would be out of the official bag.

Third, the penalty. By Michigan law statutory rape was a felony punishable by any terms of years imprisonment up to and including life.

It would be possible, then, Sewell said, to throw in the cards and withdraw charges at any juncture up to the date and hour of the examination, even though warrants had been served on defendants. No charges, no examination; no examination, no news.

That was right.

And another thing, Sewell asked, how long, after the warrants were served, would examination probably be set?

Probably a week.

From a corner, Collins, the Assistant Prosecuting Attorney, took a yardstick, from a pocket drew a handkerchief, wound it about the end of the yardstick and without lowering his legs from the desk dusted his shoes. He wore pale green socks. It would be not telling tales out of law school, he said, to mention that this particular kind of septic tank stunk up practically every small town in the U.S. every few years. Carrying such a hypothetical case to its ultimate conclusion, trial, sentencing, was a damn shame. Usually, thank

God, reason prevailed and a compromise was reached, a husband found for the girl or some kind of financial provision made for her wear and tear, and no one was the wiser. A stiff prick, so the saying went, had no conscience. Literally, neither did the law. Men did.

So long, Sewell said, and thanks.

Say, Collins said, that *Looking* book, he'd got it out of the Tyre Library, hot-cha-cha, but if he went out and actually bought a copy, the next time the author was in town would he autograph it? His wife would get one hell of a bang out of that.

Yes, Sewell said, he would.

As idiocratic to a family as its name, its population, its health, its climate whether tropic or temperate or polar, its governance whether liege or representative or anarchic, is its odor. For the first hour in the house of Harris and Norma Baird, who had invited him to dinner and the evening, Sewell's sense of smell, bachelor and kithless, was overcome by a bouquet which, although partible by element, utterly defied a final identification. Agglomerate of peeling wallpaper, frankfurters, toothpaste, full diapers, tricycle oil, unmade beds, drying nylons, balding velour furniture, catsup, broken toys, piled newspapers, cigarette butts, overheated television tubes, home permanent chemicals, beans, paperback books, stiffened paint brushes, wax bread wrappers, unflushed toilets, rugs enceinte with dust, rusty roller skates, cat hairs, milk bottles, Vicks Vapo-Rub, burnt toast, badlands of washing to be traversed, licorice, contraceptive jelly, rings around the tub, plastic wood, lost Christmas candy, scorched ironing-board covers—to his nostrils this detrital blend came in time to stand for an effort at living so collectivist, so happy, so almost anthropological that love could be its only label. The Bairds rented a small, paint-poor, tumble-roof house a block from Ionian Avenue and Harris and Sewell waited in a delapidated rattan swing on the front porch from a hole in which protruded a hockey stick and a baseball bat while the children, a boy six and two girls respectively four and two, were fed and wrangled off to bed, after which the adults dined on meat loaf, escalloped potatoes, a molded Jello salad, and a cake which Norma cursed as never equaling the illustration on the box of mix. The pretensions of diction and literary interest she had affected at the Creel & Cartridge salon she now shed with perspiring relief. —Harris, take off that hat. This may not be the Empire Room of the Waldorf-Astoria but you may not eat with your hat on in the presence of the exalted. Short, not yet thirty, she was already stout, with powerful arms and hips, with skin profusely freckled and wisps of innocuous, sparrow-colored hair circling about her ears and languishing down her neck. Not yet thirty she was a little dowdy and knew it and tasteless in dress and knew it and did not give a damn; the daughter of a rural postman she had become, as though born to it, a harassed, small-town matron poultry and protective of her brood. Harris called her "Normie." She called him "Flourhead" with a smile which exposed strong white teeth. While she cleared the dishes Sewell noticed a hitch in her walk, that from the knee down her left leg was spindly —It's not polite to stare, Sewell. Ask. This little girl had polio; one leg atrophied and turned out shorter than the other. I couldn't walk without a brace until I was seventeen. Luckiest thing that ever happened to me, as sexy as I was. That brace preserved my purity until Harris ambled along with brains instead of hot palms. I may not be his peer intellectually—on her way to the kitchen she slapped her husband's hat back on his head —but you have to admit I'm an impeccable housekeeper.

Later, in the living room, Sewell rode sidesaddle an understuffed chair while Harris supined full length on the davenport opposite, his head in Norma's lap. —A fine wife, Sewell, fair, fat and fecund.

She dusted a finger experimentally within his ear's whorl. —I thought so. Flourhead. I know what a coalminer's wife has to contend with. After every delivery I expect Charles Reason to say, "Mrs. Baird, congratulations. You have just given birth to a ten-pound sack of self-rising."

—Black is the hue of vice, my bride, white of virtue. Besides, don't demean the staff of our life.

—Demean it? After three kids I'm terrified of it! And Sewell, about the other night, I was terrified of you, really, so I put up a big, poison-tongue, ladies-literary-club front and I'm sorry. My good looks were I think the only reason Bill Van let me graduate from high school, and there I sat, tapping my dollar-ninety-eight champagne and yakking about your contributions to American Literature, et cetera, et cetera. What I'm trying to say is, an alley cat can look at a king but she has no right to scratch. And I'm sorry.

What they wanted to hear, with a sincerity which disarmed him, was an account of the fifteen years between the night of the dam and the publication of *A Benison on Our Meat,* and somehow, perhaps because he was lonely, perhaps because he had never been in a home as squalid and tribal and loving-fierce as this, perhaps because it was like lying in a pup tent with Harris and Morse and crossing the Jordan of their futures, he talked freely. After Detroit, where he had enlisted, he had taken basic training at Camp Stockton, California, and with more than two years' duty under his belt by Pearl Harbor had been shipped to Fort McClellan, Alabama, made a corporal and served as permanent cadre training infantry replacements for freighting overseas. —I was a bayonet instructor. We used straw dummies in Kraut uniforms. We showed them how to stick it in deep and use one foot to pull it out. Also parry and thrust, and the butt like a club to the side of the head. We ran rookies through a sixteen weeks' course, conditioning and weapons, then loaded them. They really didn't know much but we lied to them and told them they'd get more training before they saw combat and mostly they believed us. They didn't get more, of course, they went the hell into the lines and the life expectancy of a rifleman there was something like minutes. One kid I remember, a fat little Jewish kid from New York, about eighteen, he was supposed to be a prodigy or something on the oboe and even brought it with him to camp. Well, another line of bull we fed them I remember was that if they didn't qualify with the M-1—after all, they were rifle replacements—they'd have to stay at McClellan and go through the whole sixteen weeks again. In other words, until they could shoot a high enough score. This Jewish kid couldn't, so he thought he was a sure bet for Beethoven. He found out. He got his shipping orders like everybody else and the night before they loaded them on trains I located him sitting on one of the cans in the latrine crying and moving his bowels and playing his oboe. I never heard what happened to him. I'd guess he lasted about ten minutes in the lines. That was the way we sent them over, it made no difference if they could shoot or unpin a grenade or tie their shoes. Or play a goddamn oboe.

An altercation with a company commander pried Sewell loose from cadre at McClellan and sent him on to Fort Meade, Maryland, then the drunken brawl which had hospitalized, nearly killed a paratrooper, a court-martial and reduction to private plus six months in the stockade. —By this time it was winter of '44. If there was anything they needed in the ETO it was fresh meat, so they gave us a choice: overseas or stay in stockade. In a month I was with the 11th Division on Anzio. In May we broke out for Rome.

—The Ditch of Dead Women, said Harris. —The D.S.C. Sewell, something's always puzzled me. According to the citation you cleared that ditch practically single-handed. You saved the men in your squad. You killed four Germans yourself and were responsible for capturing fifty-eight. Why not the Congressional Medal of Honor?

—I'll tell you why not: because my coming out of there alive was the dirtiest trick anyone had played on the Army yet. I should have had the Medal, but I should also have had the sense to get killed so it could be posthumous. A live Medal man went back to the States and could talk and be written about and interviewed. Also, in his citation and the effect-of-deed statements they'd have had to tell the truth about the whole operation. The truth was, the Fossa Feminamorta could have been flanked, and was, the Commanding General slaughtered a lot of good guys with those god-

187

damn battle sleds he invented, and finally, the citation would have had to state just how I killed the last Kraut, who damn near broke my back, and the Army thought the American people ought not to know how naughty their little boys could be.

—How did you? It was Norma.

—I bit through an artery in his neck. He bled to death.

—Dear God.

—Well, they had to do something, they couldn't shoot me themselves, so they compromised: they gave me the D.S.C. sort of quietly, kept me out of combat, and assigned me to Division G-1 for the rest of the war. I drove a jeep, I brought in whores from Paris for Rest Centers, I worked with a Graves Registration outfit. I was embarrassing to have around for long. I was sort of a displaced hero.

—And out of the Graves Registration experience, Harris said, came *Benison*.

—Right. Sewell loosened his tie. —After '45 I stayed in the Army, God knows it was all I was good for. I wrote it at Camp Patrick Henry, in longhand. I took it to New York in a barracks bag.

Harris removed his glasses, steel-rimmed and round lensed, the standard G.I. issue, handed them to his wife. He turned his face to Sewell. —I say this honestly. When I read that book I wept. I've been in awe of you ever since. It's odd to be awed by the best friend you've ever had even though you haven't seen or heard from him for years. Sewell, you may not realize what that book represents: it's the last of its kind, the last tortured, maddened scream by a soldier at a civilian world which must have its gladiatorial circuses provided it does not have to participate personally. From now on, it will. Man, woman, and fissionable child, it will. Tell me, out of what did you write the book, hatred or compassion?

—Hatred.

—I hoped it was the other.

—Hatred, hatred, hatred. Reading it, I wanted people to feel my teeth in their neck. I wanted them, by God, to bleed to death.

—Well, whatever your motive, it will live. Long after we're gone. And the irony is, I suppose, that hatred, not pity, set you free. Or did it, I wonder.

—You're damn right it did. You know, Ris, freedom's a funny thing to have handed you, it really scares you. I didn't know what to do with myself for about two years, there was no one to give the orders any more. I spent, I partied, I ran around the country and the world like a, like a—

—Drunken soldier.

Norma went to check the children and bring whatever their thirsts required; Sewell, remarking he was on the cart, settled for coffee.

—And now you've come home again, although Wolfe said you can't. Which is palpably untrue, of course, if you never leave, and I couldn't, even after the dam. As to whether or not he would prosecute, Charles let Morse and me dangle week after week, but I couldn't make the break, emotionally or psychologically. This was home, my bones knew it was, it had been home for a hundred years even though I was only seventeen. Harris described the recurrent nightmare he suffered through in summer sleep that 1939: he dreamt that he had killed his father, symbolic of the dam's destruction, probably, and turning the corpse face up, wakened with a patricidal scream of revelation: the man he had murdered, his real father, was not Renis but Carlos Baird, his great-grandfather. Still he could not flee. He took a job at a gas station, pumping and doing lube work, and remained there even though Morse, by now triumphantly married to Jane Murninghan, demanded that he restore the family scutcheon by taking a desk position under him at Twinriver Reel. He was drafted two weeks before Pearl Harbor, trained by the Quartermaster Corps at Camp Lee, Virginia, shunted from post to post in the States until eventual assignment to 5th Army Supply at Naples. Quickly they dated each other, but Harris had reached Italy in October following the August of 1944 that Sewell had gone to France. At war's end he had been head-quartered in Florence with an overseas point total so lack-luster that he was not shipped home for discharge until

January of 1946. So, he concluded, resquashing his hat and tipping up the brim, his military career had been as superficial as the rest of his life: over four years in uniform and he had never heard a weapon fired in earnest. Sewell began to be annoyed; he was being underplayed; even to costume, faded sports shirt and wash pants, Harris had type-cast himself as the kindly, intelligent, almanac hayseed who would age himself into a town "character." What really aggravated was that it was too ritualized and self-abnegatory: taking poverty's vow the small-town saint donned sackcloth, taking humility's the intellectual ascended into a common, clod-hopping empyrean. It was pure vaudeville; all it needed was a straw stuck between the teeth.

—I'd been home about a month, wondering what to do with myself, when it happened. The phone rang. It was Charles. He spoke to me for the first time in seven years, and to this day I still don't know why. He wanted to know if I wanted to work at the mill. If! Jesus to Genoa!

—No, Joan to the stake, Norma snapped. So irritated was she that Sewell's cup clattered in the saucer as she gave it him. —Sewell, would you like to know what the going rate for Christian martyrs was in those days? Two hundred dollars a month. And what it is today, a wife and three children later? Four hundred. But that isn't the worst. I don't mind eking out an Erskine Caldwell existence, I can even get by without champagne and caviar for breakfast, but Charles Baird has never so much as given our friend here in person or in public one word of credit or thanks when this entire town knows if it hadn't been for him—

—Sewell knows what I've done, I told him.

—Normie, I'm with you. So is Morse.

—Poor relations! she sniffed. —Lillian Baird doesn't even speak to me on the street. If I managed to step into her house she'd have it redecorated.

—This is the family auto-da-fé, Harris grinned, but Normie does the burning, I don't.

—Charlieboy should have cut you into the mill by now, anyway a half, Sewell insisted. —He's no chicken, he's childless, he could sell out any time and leave you holding an empty bag. No, the least he should do is give you back a little of what he stole in the first place.

—I know, Norma began, Confucius say lie still and enjoy it, but your family shouldn't—

—You two, my wife, my friend, let's put one dog to sleep: whatever robbery took place, my own father bears the guilt. Somehow Charles Baird saved the bits and pieces and put them together again. You have to try to understand him. The man made a miracle, really, and in the accomplishment, the miracle made a man of him, a peculiar one, I admit, but a man. I regret his bitterness and misanthropy, I pity him in his greed, but I respect him for the simple fact that the Baird mill still exists so that I can work in it, because that's what I've always wanted to do. And not only do I respect him, so does the town.

—That's what most ticks me off, Sewell said, shaking his head. —To come back and find the same poops running the show in the same way, practically the same Council and School Board—

—Logical. They're the best qualified.

—And get the most loot.

—Not always. Example. And please don't let this go beyond this room. Harris lit a cigarette. —You find you can come home again and recognize the place and people. You're fortunate. If a small town manages that these days it does so only because a few men in power will that it shall, work to that end, sacrifice for it, and trust each other implicitly. His example was two years old. In 1952 a Chicago manufacturer had been amenable to locating a plastics extrusion plant in Thebes provided the town presented it with a site; the plant, employing three hundred, would have enriched the community tremendously through payroll and taxes. Any other town in Michigan would have sold its soul and the bodies of its women to have the new industry. The Council met informally, as usual, at the C & C, and there it turned out that the site desired, a forty-acre tract running south of Thebes Milling as far as the Ionian and adjoining

191

the Button on the west, was owned entirely by Harlan Murninghan, except for one six-acre parcel owned by Charles Reason. Murninghan refused to sell to the town, as did Reason. Charles Baird and Bill Vandevelde accused them of putting their own interests ahead of those of the community; there was considerable heat; the cards went undealt; for the first time a Council division seemed irreducible. Harlan Murninghan asked the others to rely on his judgment, mentioning that he had another project in mind for the acreage, one he did not chose to discuss. The remaining six acres was a matter for settlement between himself and his son-in-law. Mediating, Oram Kropf pointed out what revolutions a new industry would effect in the character and appearance of Thebes, transiliences to which they had previously been unanimous in opposition; he recommended that they now as in the past repose unequivocal faith in the integrity of their own membership. Further discussion elicited the fact that there had been for years an oral compact between Baird and Murninghan stipulating that neither of them, the town's largest employers, would expand his operation so long as he lived. The next night the Council met in chamber and voted negatively on the site proposition. —Result? No new plant. This is still Thebes as we have always known it. I don't think that we appreciate what a courageous, unparalleled thing these men have done for us over the years, and that would include my father and yours, Sewell. They've kept it a small town.

—What's so red-hot about being one-horse? Sewell put it belligerently; the story had bored him, his coffee was cold, weak, instant, and anyway he wanted a drink.

Harris let smoke collect under his hat brim. —There must be something or so many millions wouldn't have tried to recreate it in suburbs. In a world more mass-everything every year, being one-horse is at least being different. I've been to New York and Chicago and Philadelphia and St. Louis on leave from assorted camps, and all I could feel for the inhabitants was sorrow. Note that I use the word *inhabitants*. It seemed to me that they have names but not faces, they wore clothing but it covered nothing, if you suddenly stripped them you'd find not flesh and blood but a sheet of paper with a number on it. Or code perforations. As individuals they were insignificant: they were what they did, in other words, their functions had become their personalities, in other words they were functional rather than human. You can be free in a city if freedom means anonymity. You can be free in a small town, too, but having to govern yourselves so closely you have to be responsible, and of course, the old paradox, the more freedom you have, the less free you are. The best thing about a small town is that people can't be anonymous, they have to operate on a lot of levels, which means they must develop personalities, they must be individuals, and you can know them in all their range and uniqueness. He broke off. —I'm not saying this very coherently. Besides, the ideas aren't mine, they're Or'm Kropf's.

—That bladder of broken wind.

—I think he may be a great man.

—Moses with a white cane.

—I'd compare him to Zeno.

—Who in hell was Zeno?

—The first Stoic. Somewhere around 300 B.C.

—So he's dead. So?

—I'll try to explain. Here's a man who caroused and wasted the first fifty years of his life, trying in the last twenty of it to catch up, to find himself. He's the most omnivorous reader I've ever known. Researching the history of Thebes got him interested in ancient history, which led in turn to classic philosophy. He read Zeno and Epictetus and Marcus Aurelius as though he'd discovered them, he infected everyone with his enthusiasm, but particularly the men who count in town, his friends. I wish to God he'd reached my father in time. He turned the Council and School Board and bank Board and the C & C into his stoa, or school, and he made good Stoics out of Murninghan and Charles Baird and the rest just as Epictetus made better Stoics out of the Romans than the Greeks had ever been.

He's even converted me. For a long time he's directed my reading, but I'll never forget the night he had me read the *Meditations* to him. He must have known I was ready. "Of human life the time is a point," he declaimed, "and the substance is in a flux, and the perception dull, the fabric of the whole body corruptible, and the soul a whirl, and fortune hard to divine, and fame a thing devoid of judgment. And, to say all in a word, everything which belongs to the body is a stream, and what belongs to the soul is a dream and a vapor, and life is a warfare and a stranger's sojourn. What then shall be our guide and escort? One thing, and one only—Philosophy." On the way home I steered by the stars, I walked into trees, I fell up the front steps. Carried away, Harris spoke ever more swiftly; Norma sat beside him, fondly fingered more flour from his ear, moved his class ring, Thebes High, 1939, up his finger and found still more underneath, while he, all unconscious of her maternal pother, crossed and recrossed his legs and semaphored his free arm in the excitement of discourse. —In a nutshell, this is Stoicism. You accept. You tromp hard enough on emotion and appetite to attain peace. But it isn't resignation, either, this is not a passive philosophy but an active one because while you accept your lot, your station in life, you also take on unreservedly the obligations of that lot, that station, whatever it may be. You do your duty to man because all mankind is one, and in doing it, you achieve serenity. It isn't really asceticism, it makes self-discipline a passionate thing, it imposes order on life, which is otherwise chaotic, and which is exactly what art does, impose order on chaos, so that it makes living itself a creative, controlled art.

—Art shit, Sewell said.

Harris gaped. Norma gaped, first at Sewell, then at her husband, shot down in mid-metaphysic flight by the vulgarity, then let her laughter peal. —Oh, Ris, I can't help it, she choked, but that's just what he said at the C & C and I remember our faces! Sewell, you're so sophisticated that you're naïve—you're so crude that you just break me up!

—Well gosh. Hell. Harris reddened, looked as simpleton

and ingenuous as he had again and again when chastened by a bigger, older brother and friend. —I was only trying to explain Stoicism. It's really knocked me out. And I wanted to show how much Or'm Kropf has taught me, not that I'm a disciple or anything like that, but I think it's terrific when you find a group of men in an American small town today who've been inculcated not with Rotarianism or any of that jazz but with an ancient philosophy to such a degree that you can see them working out its precepts not only in their personal lives but in the way they conduct the public affairs of the town they govern.

—Christ on a crutch, Sewell expostulated. —Ris, you still haven't grown up, you still buy a bill of goods like people used to buy the Brooklyn Bridge. I look at these old turds as a club, a small private club that's been running a museum for its own benefit for thirty years.

—The more I know them the more I admire them.

—Then you don't know them enough. What in the pluperfect hell have they ever done for the three of us? I had to leave town. You've stayed and Kropf has conned you into taking a perpetual screwing and liking it. As to Morse—

—I'm sorry about Morse.

—In any case, you don't see them spreading any of the benefits around.

—Well, I can explain that, too. Or'm has a theory to fit everything, and one of them concerns what he calls "stewardship," that is, the winnowing out and preserving the best of the past and present and then the handing down of that responsibility to those most fitted to discharge it in the future. He says the one thing the older generation can never forgive the younger is its youth, that old men give up their perquisites about as gladly as they do their teeth. But in a small town, he claims, the process can be painless and less risky because they have a perfect opportunity to watch and select the right younger men, the new stewards.

—He's winding up again, Norma warned.

—They're opening up the membership, Sewell guessed.

Harris grinned. —Well, yes. This next fall Harlan Murninghan's term's up on the School Board and I'll be nominated. Ditto the year following, when Or'm tells me he won't run again for the Council.

—Stop the presses.

—I'm very honored.

Norma lifted her husband's hat, ran a hand through his hair, already rashed with gray along the sides, and dropped the hat. —Marcus Aurelius Harris, the happy miller.

—The happy steward, Sewell jeered. —On four hundred a month. What a crock of crap. I should write it up for the *Reader's Digest*.

It was the evening's most ill-fated remark, for Norma, conciliatory and seeking another subject, with the best of motives fell upon that of current fiction and Harris, the lines of matrimony already well in hand, took her cue. He had the muleteer manners, indeed, to reveal himself as better read than his guest and as willing, even eager, to be as discursive and tutorial on this topic as he had been on Stoicism; he bandied such names as Sartre and Malraux, unaware that they would be no more familiar to Sewell than Zeno had been, and Epictetus; compensating, perhaps, for his earlier discomfiture, he generalized, in all candor he constructed an involved analogy between recent American literature and very recent, comparing Hemingway and Faulkner and Fitzgerald with wheat of the highest quality, bagging up all younger writers this side the Atlantic, present company excepted, as middlings, feed fit not for human consumption but for that of swine. His performance was like that of a country youth who dares a monster tractor sidehill of a field at full, breakneck speed, showing off and careless that the machine will not much longer, even for him, affront the law of gravity.

—Getting down to cases, Sewell, seriously, what do you think of yourself as a writer?

—I don't.

—No, seriously.

—I don't, I said, goddammit. I think of myself as a businessman with a payroll to meet. My own.

—Of course there's that, the commercial aspect. But I

mean of your stature, where you stand in relation to your contemporaries.

—Put it right: my competition. Well, all right, who are the biggest names in my group, guys my age writing now? Hunched forward, his jaw a-jut from his powerful shoulders like a snapping turtle's head from its shell, Sewell rocked slightly. —Who are they? Smith and Jones and Mailer. The art bastards I don't count, they don't get a fraction of the entertainment dollar. Smith and Jones and Mailer, and as far as I can figure, I've made more money in the last four years than either Jones or Mailer. So I'm ahead and I plan to stay ahead. That's my stature.

—What about literature?

—You know what literature is? It's a guy working at a desk trying to make a living.

—You can't mean that.

—Don't tell me what I can't mean!

—I wouldn't presume to. What I'm trying to introduce is something else entirely. Harris removed his cap himself. —Sewell, you must know we're all for you in Thebes. Practically everybody back here read *Benison*, and I guess shared my feeling of wonder and discovery. Then came *Looking for a Location*, which I read to Oram Kropf and which we discussed an entire evening. I hope you'll take this in the spirit I intend it. But Oram and I felt, and I think it's the general consensus among your friends, that the book was a potboiler. Just raw experience put down for the sake of getting something else in print. And we couldn't understand why the hurry to capitalize on *Benison*. It certainly wasn't money. Example. It was a perfect title, but you failed to exploit it, you never saw that most human beings are figuratively looking for a location, and that by establishing those Hollywood people as symbols and their search for a movie site as the search all of us make, the book might have had meaning on a much more universal level. It might, in fact, have been literature after all. Well, as I say, Oram and I really covered it and you, and what you should do.

If it was plausible Harris should not have sensed the

machine out of control, surely Norma, with the female's premonitory ear should have recognized this as music scarcely calculated to soothe. Either might have observed the red murk rising in Sewell's face.

—You sound like an editor I used to know. And what did you and Or'm decide I should do?

—Wait a long while before you publish again. Four or five years or longer. In the meantime, read and reflect. The travel you've had, but read widely, according to some kind of system, and reflect. Educate yourself. Accept your limitations.

—That ties it.

—Ties it?

With his thick hands Sewell held on to himself by his knees. —Ris, I never beat on you when you were a kid because you'd have fallen apart. Now I won't because you're too goddamn insignificant and fake to work up a sweat over. But I'll give you better advice than Marcus whatever-the-hell his name was or any other dead Greek.

—He was Roman.

—For a switch, take off the goddamn toga and accept your own limitations. You've got no more education or degrees than I have. You're a countrified miller who pulls down four hundred a month and lives in a slum house and kisses his uncle's ass for exercise and in his spare time reads books and knocks his wife up. When you get yourself a name and some money you can be a critic or philosopher or anything else, but in the meantime, kid, you're nobody. From nowhere.

—Sewell, you stop! Norma cried. —He's just as successful as you! In his own way.

—Is he? Then why does he have to put on an act? I had great hopes for him once, but God, those clothes and this Stoic routine—the happy miller—he's happy in a pig's anus!

—So do you put on an act! Norma's distress was ferocious. —You and Jones and Mailer, and your car and drinking and all, like the other night at the Creel & Cartridge—all you were doing was putting on a good show for the local middlebrows!

—Middle, hell!

—All right, low! At least they aren't swelled!

—No, but some of their bellies are, every goddamn nine months! Ris isn't digging his own grave, he's screwing it!

—You don't know what love is!

—Love! That's a laugh. If he was so goddamn much in love with you, how come you were second choice?

—He never really loved Jane Murninghan.

—Didn't he? If it wasn't rebound, how come he married Lene Scripter?

—Don't be ridic—Norma put her hand over her mouth. Harris had been all but forgotten. He slouched white-faced as his wife stared. —Ris, what's he talking about?

—He never told you? Why, this is the Stoic playboy, the marrying miller!

—Harris, I want an answer.

—The night Morse and Jane eloped to Angola, Lene and I went along.

—I know that.

Harris's eyes were closed. He spoke wearily. —After their ceremony, I asked her to marry me and we did.

—I want to know why.

—I felt sorry for her.

—Is that why you married me, too?

—I'll tell you why. Sewell rose, himself exhausted but determined to make his victory gripe. —Because he'd been laying her all through high school. So had Morse. So had I. But this one thought he had to do his duty to his fellow man. Or his fellow piece of tail. You know.

—It never mattered, Harris said. —We never lived together. We had the marriage annulled.

—So don't give me any of that bull again about putting on an act.

—Good night, Sewell. Thank you for coming. Thanks a lot. Norma Baird did not offer her hand, but turned and left the room, the awkwardness of her walk more apparent.

Sewell did not know whether to leave or stay. He examined the table television set in one corner; it was small and cheaply made, undoubtedly purchased on time, and two of the control knobs had been pulled off by the children.

—Ris, you asked for it, he said finally.

—You're not married, you can't realize. This kind of damage takes months or years to repair, if you ever can. Harris opened his eyes. Without glasses, the freckles on his nose made more cicatricial by the pallor of his skin, he looked the way boys do when hospitalized and deathly ill. —Sewell, Sewell, Sewell. This isn't a barracks, it's a home. Normie isn't a paratrooper, she's my wife. The war is over, Sewell. I'm not the enemy. You don't have to bite till you draw blood.

—I'll come directly to the point. I invariably do. I lack a proper bedside manner, perhaps because it's always seemed to me the business of dying should be transacted as unaffectedly as possible. To the point, then. Charles Baird spoke to me yesterday on this matter of the Scripter girl; I've since talked to Or'm Kropf and Harlan Murninghan, to my not inconsiderable shock finding them both involved as well. All three have been explicit, both about their transgressions and your demands. A fine sordid kettle of fish. I must say I was surprised at my father-in-law. I would have bet him physically incapable of coitus, and lost, and incidentally, of this he wasn't guilty until several meetings with her, the girl, had rejuvenated him. Not that it makes any difference, because it would still be contributing to the delinquency of a minor. What's her name?

—Carlene.

—Yes, how poetic. Carlene, The Lily Maid of the Eighth Grade. In any case, during their first two rendezvous, he tells me, she performed fellatio and he cunnilingus. You don't know what these words mean, do you?

—No.

—I thought not, and I shan't inform you, either. Dr. Charles Reason exchanges his white jacket for a camel's-hair sport coat, shoots the French cuffs of his shirt, and seats himself behind the desk. Even for a rural general practitioner his offices are shabby, lacking even the usual framed diplomas, their seals and Latin comforting; this one must double, in fact, for both consultation and examination since against one wall stands a table of brown leatherette, cracked and afflictive. It is early evening. Patients and nurse have departed. The room and its lessee contrast in a manner which must seem to be a patient insolent; on one wall is a calendar upon which, in sanguine color, Norman Rockwell has depicted a dear horse-and-buggy medico bending over the bed of a dear mumpish youngster; the smells are not those of soap and hope and antiseptic but of grubby, lay-it-on-the-line economy and a forlorn, doomed traffic. —Now. I asked you to see me for two reasons. I wish you would drop Charles Baird from the case.

—Why should I?

—Because he has inoperable carcinoma.

—What's that?

—Cancer. He's full of it, or will be. He'll die within six to nine months, a year at most.

—I don't believe it.

—A month ago he came in complaining of a pain, worried about appendicitis. I palpated the mass and intervened surgically at once. It was malignant and already inoperable. I found his liver, for instance, studded with tumor nodules. I sewed him up and told him the truth. No one else knows, not even his wife, whom he intends to spare as long as possible. The pain will be progressive. Shortly he will undergo loss of appetite, weight, nausea, probable obstruction of the bowels. There is absolutely no chance.

—There was for my father.

—L.V.? I don't see the relevance.

—He had flu, not cancer.

—That's right. In those days you put them on Dover's powder, aspirin and opium, to reduce fever, which I did.

—And by the fifth day he was almost well. That night the Directors came. I was asked to sleep at the Baird's. The next morning he was dead. Six men went into his bedroom. I don't know what you did, but he didn't die of lung congestion. Claude Reichert's gone, so I can't touch him, but as long as any of the other five draw breath I won't let them off the hook. Including Charles Baird, much as my heart bleeds for him.

Charles Reason's glasses, modish, glittering, frames molded entirely of aluminum, he takes off, putting a bow tip between his teeth and gnawing on it. The habit has pitted both bows. —We talked about you, too, your purpose in this, Or'm, Harlan, Charles and I. You yourself have most of the embezzlement picture now, I gather. He tilts his chair, rubs the bridge of his nose. —Smith, I've done three things in my life of which I'm ashamed, which I regret profoundly. Two of them I'm willing to relate. The first has nothing to do with your father, but it may astonish you to learn that I'm a moral man and how I came to be that way. 1933. The ethics of medicine concerned me little; if you couldn't treat it or cut it or bill for it, I was uninterested. You remember the night in 1933 when young Irwin Reichert got Claude's car up to at least eighty on the straightaway west of town and rammed head-on into a set of Grethe Kropf's columns, that set the Council has left fallen ever since. It was certainly the most spectacular, one might almost say if he had a sense of humor, the most classic suicide Ionian County had ever enjoyed. I killed him. No one knew it, or yet does, but I did. You wouldn't remember Irwin, but he was seventeen at the time, with an IQ, they found out at the high school, well in the genius range. Six months before graduation and he already had a scholarship in chemistry at Chicago. Outside a lab, however, he was a child. He hit the columns at about 2:00 A.M. At seven the previous evening I'd just left here and gone to my car. He'd been waiting for me, he rushed up in the dark and clutched my arm and poured out this weird story. A week before, he'd had a date with Verna Burleson, a farmer's daughter, and evidently his first tumble in the hay, or in the back seat. He was distraught, almost incoherent, I was tired, I'd seen patients all afternoon and that morning rushed Verna Burleson to Grand Rapids on emergency with a ruptured appendix. I operated, but too late. She died. Young Irwin heard the news at school, in his genius and gullibility connected it with the fun he'd had, and demanded to know if he wasn't responsible, if his getting in there and test-tubing around hadn't produced the rupture. As I say, I was tired, what he didn't know was that the Burleson girl at sixteen had already served as the high school vending machine, sexually, and the whole misconception was so damned amusing and idiotic that, rather than laughing and setting him straight about the resilience and relationship of the female organs, I snarled something about sure, why hell yes, hump a pure virgin like little Verna and you were bound to burst her appendix, whereupon I brushed him off and drove home to have a drink. At two the next morning I was called to the wreck. The irony derives from the fact that Claude was the town's only druggist and pharmacist, did all my work, and here, in my inimitable way, I'd prescribed for his son. Professional courtesy, as it were. Live with a thing like that on your conscience and see how preoccupied you can become with moral considerations. For a time he continues to mouth the aluminum bow. Sewell recalls people saying, years ago, that if another doctor, good, bad, or indifferent, were to set up shop in Thebes, Charles Reason would be unpracticed in two weeks; his manner with patients, while not jocular or perfunctory, has never been intimate, even sympathetic, but more like that of the veterinary than the physician; and there have been other things easy to resent. —Well, I killed your father, too. He waits for reaction. —At least I provided the means. Move the clock ahead, 1939. L.V. Smith, untiring, estimable Vice-President and Cashier, has been bedded down with flu for five days, the first occasion in over twenty years he's been away from his bank more than hour or two. That afternoon the Directors were called in by the Assistant Cashier, himself near collapse. He'd found things in an incredible state, the bank's bond assets were short by thousands, customers' boxes had been entered and the shortage there would amount to God knew how many more thousands, something had to be done at once, he wasn't even sure we were solvent or not. That night we came to your house and held a meeting in L.V.'s room. We put it to him. He hesitated momentarily, calculated, then began at the beginning, methodically, just like him. It was an old story, which I suppose is always new. He wanted money, what money would buy, for himself and for his family. He'd never had anything, nor his people before him, so he devised a system of borrowing funds to invest without hurting anyone. He had monumental confidence in himself. The now-you-see-it-now-you-don't business with customer bonds started as far back as 1926, and by 1928 he was well ahead, principally in Radio, Montgomery Ward, Union Guardian of Detroit, the Shenandoah Trust. Came the crash, and he lost it all. But give up, blow out your brains? Not L.V. Smith, a man of colossal pride. You have another helping of the hair of the dog that's bitten you. By 1937 he was in the clear again, more than a hundred thousand in the clear. The recession of '38 wiped him out a second time. He had us get into one of his suitcoats in the closet; there were all his records in small notebooks; with them we could follow his trail over the entire thirteen years. We pressed him for a rough guess as to what the shortage would total then, and he said calmly he thought about $170,000. You cannot imagine six more naked, stunned men than we, his friends. We knew him as well as we knew ourselves, which meant that each of us was a total stranger to his own soul. I tell you, in that moment we felt the earth revolve. I don't think any of us has ever been quite the same since that night. The State Bank of Thebes was actually, not just on paper, insolvent, and we were opening the doors every day. Then L.V. said he'd just made a decision, not to face trial and the ruin of all he had built, not to recover from the flu, even. "Charles," he said, "I want you to leave me something when you go. I would do as much for you." Everyone looked at me, then lowered his head, which signified a unanimous vote yea. They went out. I had my bag. I put on the table beside the bed four one-grain mor-

204

phine sulphate tablets. Average dosage for alleviation of pain is a quarter-grain. I remember asking him, before I went, how he had the nerve to do it. He thanked me. He seemed to be thinking back over the years the way you replay certain lost poker hands to yourself when the game is over, wondering if you should have drawn to the pair, say, instead of keeping a kicker. He said, "Charles, a man has the guts to do anything he wants." I returned to the house at six in the morning, wrote out the certificate attesting to natural causes, lung congestion, signed it and called Vergennes, the undertaker. Charles Reason waits again for comment, and when there is none, resumes. —And the irony there was that if he hadn't picked up the flu, if he'd been able to hold on another year, with the war coming on and the market rising steadily, he'd have made it at last. He could have closed the books in the black and no one would ever have been the wiser. L.V. was really a remarkable man: he had guts, pride, unbelievable stamina—everything but luck. I said this is one of the things I regret. That's true, but I suppose I would do it again for such a man.

—So you took care of both my parents.

—I hadn't thought of that. In your mother's case I had no choice but to advise committing her. I'm no psychiatrist, even amateur, but don't you see now, Catherine must have known all along what he was up to. For perhaps ten of the thirteen years she had to bottle up the guilt, the conflict between fidelity and honesty, within a personality already introverted. Take gradual withdrawal, add the tensions of the menopause, certainly a contributing factor, and finally she was overwhelmed. Dementia praecox would be my guess, climaxing in the recital from your roof. She had a beautiful voice. And if she couldn't tell, she could sing.

Charles Reason sits suddenly erect. —You're going to write a book about this Scripter thing, aren't you?

—It's an idea. Sewell stirs in his chair, but in no other way do his reflexes betray him.

—You should be good at poker. Well, I try to put the whole perfumed affair together. Your motives I understand

205

perfectly, including that of loyalty to Morse Baird. But I don't get the extortion angle, I can't see why you want the money, too, unless it simply sharpens the blade. I told you I've become a kind of student of morality, and I find this, frankly, the worst, most intricate moral mess in my experience. The deeper you go, the more malignancy. Three elderly men corrupt a young girl, which is immoral. Or she them, also immoral. A charge is pressed by the girl's mother, herself a woman with no morals whatever, not to effect justice but to extort money, legally immoral. She is aided and abetted by a man who is doubtless to share in the proceeds of this legal immorality, but who will doubtless also use the situation for creative purposes, which is a kind of artistic immorality. It seems to me the accusers are as criminal, morally, as the accused. It poses a lovely question: who stinks most, the guilty or the innocent? But then, in this thing, so far as I can biop, there is no innocence. Unless it's in the fundamental flesh we all must wear.

Sewell, who has been slouching, straightens himself preparatory to going. —Theorize all you like, Reason, but in the end there are two cold facts you can't avoid. Carlene Scripter is fourteen. And these are men old enough to know better.

—You won't let Baird off, then.

—Hell, no.

Charles Reason's hands are black with hair. Unaware of himself, with close-clipped nails he scratches hypertensively the back of one hand. —Smith, I have another request, of a more personal nature. You're evidently going to get all you can out of this stopover in Thebes. Does that include my wife?

—It's an idea.

—I followed her the other day. I've become rather expert at it, a regular private eye. I watched the transfer from her car to yours, even the autographing ceremony. By the way, you should take better care of a Jag, a car like that deserves it. Then I tailed the two of you to Delphi Grange. I don't know what transpired, but I repeat my request: let me have my wife.

—Why should I?

—Because I am fifty-six years old and she is all the youth I have.

Sewell is on his feet and buttoning his coat. —Correction. She's all the credit card you need.

—Smith, would you care to hear how I diagnose your case? I liken you to a potential thrombosis. One of the two most popular coronary problems, a blood clot passing through the arteries and eventually reaching the heart, producing occlusion, or stoppage. The sounds of Charles Reasons' scratching are audible. —Yours is emotional rather than organic. Somehow you've survived fifteen years carrying a clot of hatred in your system. We can treat the condition medically with anticoagulants. I can also prescribe for you. Fair exchange is no robbery. My wife for the only preventive which will save you. It's mercy. Simply that. I don't think I could live without Jane and I don't think you can live, taking the verb in its fullest meaning, much longer without administering mercy, not to yourself but to others. Charles Baird would be a good place to begin. If you don't, well, a victim of emotional thrombosis is just as dead as— He looks up from his hands. He addresses an open door.

Romance; by this word, winked out in brilliant lights upon the marquee of her imagination, Lillian Baird self-cast her role in life. If the world were but a stage, which was true, and all the men and women in it merely players, equally demonstrable, she saw herself, all unknown to Charles, as the romantic lead in the road company of a smash success, more ravishingly lovely, more incredibly talented by far than the name star of the New York production who had, she suspected, won the part by going to bed with God, impious bitch, with the result that The Great Producer, as susceptible perhaps to blandishment as any man despite His deity, had cheated her of Broadway's acclaim and exiled her instead to an endless series of subscription audiences in an endless itinerary of tank towns. Her husband, incidentally, she pictured sometimes as a nonentity walk-on, or sometimes, in fonder fancy, as a pitiable stage-door boobus waiting fervidly with flowers for her in the snow.

Heroism; to this fife Charles Baird parades. All unknown to his wife he visualizes himself as the protagonist of an epic scene unballaded and forgot in the vasty theater of the past. In biography he is as well read as anyone in Thebes, even Oram Kropf, although he has specialized in tracing kinship with figures of historic proportions, among them Aeneas, Davy Crockett, Gandhi, Horatius, Danton, Wilson, Garibaldi, Audie Murphy, Wellington, Bismarck, Churchill, Custer, Ney, Earp, Henry V, Villa, Drake, Teddy Roosevelt, Antony, Marlowe, Ty Cobb. Their more widely publicized feats he finds less extraordinary than his own, really, for at least temperament if not destiny had readied and informed this pantheon, while the saving of the mill, the noblest, most audacious gage of his life, had fallen to a younger brother totally unqualified to save anything. It had been like challenging a tubercular Keats rather than a robust Byron to paddle the Hellespont. Span it he had, however, and having to be his own bard in no way detracted, he assured himself, from the enterprise. And even private heroism Fate did not let pass unnoticed: as diadem, grail, conqueror's garland, queen fit to share a secret prince's throne, he had been granted Lillian.

Romance's bower this night was her dressing room, identical with Charles's except for the built-in vanity, with its three-planed full-length mirror and custom-made cabinets for lingerie and sweaters and hosiery and the walk-in closet which held her hundred costumes and her sixty pairs of shoes. Before the mirror she posed in slip and high heels, indecisive: which dress to model for him first? Their bedtime had become stylized: when either had been to Grand Rapids to shop for clothing, and each made a weekly jaunt, she twice usually, he must conceal his purchase until this hour, then model it for the others's approbation. It was their game, their little show, their closet drama. She inhaled gustily, rejoicing in the unbrassièred fettle of her bust, a tall full-bodied brunette of forty-six vain of a bearing she believed regal and imperious. Bending her head, with enameled fingers she sought along the part for gossipy gray roots in the thick hair tinted a romantic, raven black. Finding none, grateful yet vexed because cheated of an immediate trip to the hairdresser's in Grand Rapids, she resolved to go in a day or two anyway for a shampoo and set. She did next a singular thing: slowly she raised her slip over her knees, almost to her hips, slowly turned her image in the masochist mirrors; and as, pestiferously, the blue varicose veins along her flanks and the backs of her legs made claim upon her attention, tears liquified her eyes. Ugly, disfiguring, undeniable, she would have them operated on, tied off, no matter what! How horrid of flesh to give her perfection in all but this! In 1939 she had been Mrs. Lloyd Pope, sister-in-law of Vernon Pope, the Grand Rapids attorney whom Charles Baird had consulted about the take-over of the mill from his deceased brother. A graduate of the University, she met and dated Lloyd in Ann Arbor, taught in the Stockbridge schools until he finished law school, then resurrected herself from the tomb that was rural Stockbridge by marrying him. I could not love thee, dear, so much, lov'd I not Grand Rapids more! It was a city, she had lived there as a girl, friends still remembered her, but dear Lloyd, who executed the physical contract as judiciously as he might the articles of a trust, in 1942 had the temerity to do the unexpected: he died, of a brain tumor. Childless, perishing of tedium, she sat out the war's ensuing three years in widow's weeds, nettled at Eisenhower and MacArthur for prolonging it. By Vernon she was introduced, in 1946, to a small, well-manicured man twelve years her senior who lived in Thebes and turned out to be, not only the silk purse made from a sow's ear, but a single-minded sexual maniac; on their first date he flung himself upon her and kissed her; at dinner, on their second, like a malapert mole his hand delved beneath her skirt during parfait; after the third, having invited himself into her house, he began an assault upon her as mad as it was football; over the furniture, through the rooms, upstairs he blocked and tackled her until finally, worn to a frazzle, her last conscious thought the calculation that Thebes was but forty miles from The Rapids, she succumbed upon her own bed in her own room. They were married, he bought and remodeled the original Baird house, the one in which Renis and Constance had lived—their dressing rooms were before remodeling the single large room occupied by young Morse and Harris—she bore at thirty-nine her first child, a daughter they named Gloria, and in a progressing dumb show of anguish, realized that the committee work of their loins had created not a child but a doll, a blond cuddlesome doll which at age six could neither speak nor feed nor dress itself. When, like a lamb unto His fold Gloria was taken, when they could no longer replenish grief, they withdrew into each other, in a harmless recidivism became themselves more childlike so that in her he might yet have his little girl and she in him her little boy; in a protective mutuality they built out of play-clay, as it were, not love but a spiteful, immature, shout-and-slap affection for each other. They go out seldom in Thebes except as his business and civic activity requires. Lillian is not well liked and cares not a fig; she has no peer socially or financially, unless it would be Caroline Murninghan, too grandmotherly and didactic and herbivorous for her taste. Thus circumscribed, her pleasures are few. With membership in two book clubs she seldom reads the selections. She insists Charles escort her to the concerts of the Grand Rapids Symphony, yet it is she who dozes, not he. She belongs to the A.A.U.W., attending faithfully its luncheons in the city. The Rapids, in fact, not Thebes, she considers her spiritual and cultural home; driving her own car, and badly, so that at least one fender is always dented after a parking mishap, she flees there to spend the entire day, shopping in the morning, lunching at Herpolsheimer's Tea Room, going to the beauty parlor or a movie matinée or shopping again in the afternoon, roaring late and romantically into the double garage, begum of boxes and parcels, czarina of charge accounts. Just as she let fall her slip and dried her eyes with a swoop of Kleenex, she had a hot flash. For an awful, shrieking moment she endured the tennis-racket sensation, every nerve as triced as stringing on the frame of her bones. She was undergoing the last, praise be, phases of the menopause. She flurried into the pink linen dress bought that morning. A size too small?

Heroism's chariot this moment was an Exerbike, a velocipede without wheels in a corner of the bedroom, and mounted on it the President of Thebes Milling, in Jockey shorts and gartered socks and shoes, pumped his nightly and stationary mile. As the pedals revolved and the handlebars trundled up and down he puffed the count, which must reach a thousand. 912, 913, he had to hurry, Lillian would soon be ready to model. The contraption had strengthened his arms and legs, 920, extended his wind, 921, but had not reduced his paunch an iota. Well-preserved at fifty-eight, 924, he! For what? And how many miles? How many miles to Banbury Cross, how long to bring the bad news from Ghent to Aix, how far to carry the mournful message from Charles Reason to García: increasing pain, loss of appetite, weight in any event, nausea, probable obstruction of the bowels. How many miles on the Cancerbike to the big black mill? How sups, boy of Sparta, the fox upon your vitals? 946, 947, 948. His thoughts revolved, trundled. I, Charles Baird, am basically a shy, 951, introspective, 952, responsible, 953, misunderstood, 954, decent, 955, man, 956, and I must tell my wife, 957, now 958, tonight, 959, what I have done, 960, honestly, 961, withholding nothing, 962, but the other, 963, what I have in me, 964, what I will die of soon, 965, I must not mention, 966, for that would be the way of the coward, 967, and above all, 968, you will not cry, 969. He sprinted: 70, 71, 72, 73: it was the last stretch of the Tour de France, the world's greatest velocipedal test, and incredibly, an American fifty-eight years of age, a small paunched cyclist of phenomenal stamina and a valor which surpassed belief would, before multitudes agog, be first across the finish line!

—I'm ready, Charles!

He ceased to pedal and waited while the momentum of the handlebars lifted him erect in the saddle. —All right, my dear.

Lillian swept into the bedroom modeling the new dress, a

sheath of pink linen cut very low and hung from her bare shoulders by two spaghetti straps. —Well? There's a little bolero jacket to match, same material, which they're letting out at the back. Maison Banghart.

—Lillian. Have something dreadful to say to you. He was still winded by his sprint. —Absolutely dreadful.

At the room's far side she twirled, tossing her head hoydenishly, posing in an attitude which had something in it of haute couture, something of cooch. —Perfect for cocktail parties. They never went to cocktail parties. —And only seventy dollars. Well, aren't you going to say you like it? I mean, I think it does a lot for me.

—I'm involved in a despicable situation. Sexually.

—Sexually!

—With the youngest Scripter girl—he gusted the words as rapidly as his lungs would allow—had intimate relations with her and she's only fourteen although I didn't realize it or if I did it seemed impossible because she seems so much more experienced.

She shrunk magniloquently from him until she reached the wall. —Oh. Oh. Oh.

—I'm not the only one, either. Harlan Murninghan and Or'm Kropf are also implicated and her being underage makes it a crime, statutory rape, and now she's told her mother and it's all come to a head. Sewell Smith claims to be acting for them and wants money from us, a lot of it, fifty thousand dollars from me, and if we don't pay they're going to file charges and—

—Despicable! Lillian breathed, seizing his own word as most appropriate but, by accenting the second syllable, mispronouncing it.

Charles gripped the handlebars. —Yes, it is, Lillian, it is, I know it, I should have told you before, but I've been too tortured by shame—

—Oh des*pic*able! she cried.

—Lillian, please, I beg you, don't keep saying that! I have to have help, to decide which way to turn, statuory rape is a felony, I'm told, and we could go to prison for years! Try to imagine what that would—

—You foul little man! You creature! Undone!

Charles hopped down from the Exerbike. —Now Lillian, listen to me, ranting and raving won't—

She crouched, pointing a Medean finger, and stalked. —Poetic justice, Charles Baird! she screeched. —Pure poetic justice! Youth is finally getting back at you! After what you did to the Baird boys, taking their birthright—oh, don't think I don't know about all that—I mean, keeping Harris as a kind of slave all these years, letting him and his babies starve on a mess of pottage while you grew a pot—ha! And now you dare do this to me, make me the laughingstock of the town—Mrs. C. S. Baird, member of the American Association of University Women, wife of a common sex fiend, a raper!

—Rapist, he corrected.

—I mean rapist! she shrieked.

He drew himself up, he quelled a fluttery underlip, he fought with all his main the temptation to hurl at her the flower of his soldiery, that vicious regiment now massed among his tripes, and so save the field in one Napoleonic stroke. —Lillian you hush!

—I will not hush! Her bosom heaved, her eyes blazed, a Juno umbrageous and not to be denied her flibbertigibbet histrionics. —And I'll tell you something, Charles Baird, you —you beast, you poop! To top him she flung wide her arms. —I have a lover!

—A lover?

—And not one like yours, not an infant but a mature man! I've been his mistress for two years! Do you think I fritter away all my time in The Rapids shopping and going to movies? Well, I don't—we have a motel room reserved for us an afternoon every week, so there!

He gasped. The room twanged to her revelation as though to a tuning fork tried by the immortals. So natural to both was that jocund suspension of disbelief with which actors and pubescents, saints and senators are endowed that neither glimpsed the scene's picaresque, Punch-and-Judy melodrama. He faltered to the outsize bed, the buoyant bear garden of their marriage, and slumped upon the damask spread.

He unsnapped a garter, drew off one sock. —I won't ask you who it is.

—You will too! She stamped her foot. —I demand that you ask!

—Very well, Lillian. Who is it?

—Morse Baird!

—Morse Baird?

—Yes, Morse Baird! He loves me and I love him madly and we've talked a lot about my leaving you and our marrying! Now I have ample grounds for divorce after the smutty thing you've done and you'll have to pay a pretty penny!

—Lillian, he doesn't love you.

—He does so!

—He's just using you to hurt me.

—Why shouldn't he have your wife? You have his mill!

He peeled the other buskin, drooped. —It's impossible, Lillian, it's too late, you're too old for him.

—How dare you! I'm no older for him than you were for me!

—And you have varicose veins!

—Oh! Oh! I do not!

—You do! he bawled. —But I love you just the same!

With a lorn keening she flung herself full-length onto the bed, her spasm, her tantrum so hysteric that the flailing of her legs sent her shoes flying from her feet. Her fists pounded, her body writhed, her eyes streamed, but the spectacle of her prostration, somehow innocent in its very theatricality, rather than breaking saved Charles Baird, rather than weakening steeled him. While she moaned he remounted the Exerbike and pedaled dutifully the last few counts of his mile; while she squalled he donned pajamas of aqua silk, entered the bathroom, washed his face, brushed his teeth, including a single bridge, and upon return found her nearly spent, swooning.

—Charles, my life has been so unhappy!

—I know, I know.

—I've been so unlucky with my timing! I mean, losing Lloyd and having Gloria so late and then taking a lover younger than I am and you're right, it is impossible and I do have varicose veins! Hideous!

—Not to me, he comforted, sitting beside her. —My timing's been bad, too. If I'd been born ten years earlier, Renis could never have treated me as he did. There's no harm in telling you now. Do you know that he even set up what he considered a sensible sex life for me? Once a month, for years, he reserved a room for me at the Hamlind in The Rapids and arranged for a prostitute to spend the night with me.

—No—

—Yes. He thought me incapable of handling even that.

Diverted, she blew her nose. —What are they like? Prostitutes, I mean.

—You don't try to remember. Just women who let themselves be used, I guess, pathetic women.

She burrowed again into the spread. —Women like me!

He waited patiently. —Well, he said, we've told each other the truth at last, which is probably the only intelligent thing we've ever done.

—It's true, it is true. She sat up, her cheeks and eyes bloated with misery. —Help me with my dress.

He unzipped her and assisted in struggling the pink linen over her head. —How did it happen with Morse?

She left him, sniffing, and replied from her dressing room. —I met him in The Rapids one day, that was all. What an easy conquest for him, and what a cheap thrill for me, so clandestine and romantic and everything! I was terribly flattered to have a young lover. Remember how I fought you when you first wanted me to make love? Well—I'm so ashamed—I was the seducer this time, really, I suggested the motel and I've even been paying the bill for the room.

—Didn't you even suspect you were his means of hurting me?

—I may have, but didn't even care, tit for tat. He served my purpose, too, to pay you back for what you did to him and his brother when they were boys. I mean, he's nice but he really is a little stupid, and his ego has been so utterly smashed. A failure at everything.

—Not quite. I'm sorry to disillusion you, my dear, but he has quite a reputation as a ladies' man.

—He does? With who?

—I don't keep a list, but it's general knowledge his divorce from Jane Reason may have been final legally but hasn't been physically.

—No!

—Yes.

—Poor Charles Reason!

—Yes. He sat down again. —Were you with him today?

—Who? She did not need to ask.

—Morse.

This she had neither the will nor the strength to affirm.

—My hair's an absolute fright but I'm not going to touch it. Now, be frank about this girl. Coming from a family and an environment like that, I mean a real gutter type, I'm sure you're not the one at fault, and neither are Harlan and Oram. Men are so weak.

—I can't speak for them, but I must bear the onus in my own instance, Lillian. There've been rumors about her all year from the high school, that she's been promiscuous, and one night this winter, I passed her while driving home from Council, walking round the park across from the church. It was a blizzardy night and I offered her a ride. One thing led to another.

—You didn't actually, not actually, have relations with her?

—I did.

His wife emerged in her nightgown, in the light her face flavescent and damnatory with cold cream. —Oh, Charles! I mean, how could you!

It was too much, this tribulation. The doll eyes burned, the cherub mouth formed a soundless O, as of pain, the question cut deep into the cantaloupe belly, and in the narrow cone of his breast his heart melted. —Eee, eee, eee! he wailed, hands sheltering his face. —Because she was so small and helpless, her hair so soft—she made me think of Gloria! I had our little girl again to pet and love!

216

Running to the bed she threw herself between his legs and clasped him as he clasped her and they wobbled and wept, wobbled and wept in a nest silken and chiffon and deliquescent, singing solace to one another in cries almost ornithological.

—Charliedear!

—Lillybaby!

—I forgive you, I forgive you!

—I forgive you!

He was the first to recover. He drew her up beside him. They looked long at each other, inquiring, discovering, each seeing, as though through a stranger's eyes, a stranger's vulnerable, impermanent abode, each meeting, as though they had only then been introduced, a unique, adult human integer. It was between this pair, for a moment man and woman, an encounter tramontane to all their marriage.

—Lillian, we must stop playing at life.

—Yes, we must.

—We are middle-aged and we must act it.

—I'm willing, Charles.

They kissed upon the lips, lightly.

—Lillian, my dearest, I have a proposition to put to you.

—You want to make love-love? she whispered.

—No, I couldn't.

—Why not?

—Because. The difficulty was in being more explicit yet more guarded. —This is too important. It's about business.

—Oh. Then let's be the royal couple! Hastily she turned down the bed, propped the pillows endwise and patted him after her so that the bedroom became a hall of state and, seated side by side, they the king and queen enthroned. She took his hand as though it were orb and scepter. —Now.

—Well, I've been thinking, he began augustly. —It's time I laid Renis's ghost to rest once for all, and the best way to do that, I've decided, is to come to terms with my own conscience about Harris.

—Dear, you can't imagine how long I've waited to hear you say it!

—Here's what I propose. The likelihood is that you will survive me—

—Charliedear!

—Lillian, we have to face the age difference. The company, plant, name and all is worth roughly half a million, give or take a few thousand, and I'm taking close to fifty thousand a year from it before taxes. I have considerable life insurance, you'd have that and the house and cars. I thought I'd go to Vernon, tomorrow perhaps, and have him draw up papers to take effect immediately on our signature. Harris to become equal partner. Upon my death my equity in the mill and income therefrom to pass to you for life. Then, since we have no line, after you're gone, Harris to become sole owner. In other words, to possess the company alone, as I have, and you of course, by redrawing your will, could dispose of your personal property in any way you saw fit. The main object being that it would then remain the Baird mill. How does this sound to you?

—Heavenly! And so traditional! She wriggled with philanthropy. —And how happy poor Norma will be! I mean, they can move out of that wretched little shack! Do you know, I've been so mortified when I met her on the street I couldn't even bring myself to speak?

—Indirectly, too, this arrangement will provide for Morse, he said. —I'm sure Harris will do something for him.

—How intrepid you are, Charliedear, and gallant. He's so pitiful, really. Demure, she smoothed the covers. —So go to Vern, tomorrow, and I'll sign anything you say. And that will take care of everything.

—Not quite. There's the Scripter girl.

—Oh, that, pooh. I don't think anything will come of it, but do you know what I advise? Pay them. How much is it, fifty thousand? Charles, we're rich, pay them and have it over.

He shook his head. —No, Harlan and Or'm and I have agreed to act in concert, as always.

—Oh, disgusting, revolting, I refuse to talk about it any more! She stretched extravagantly, by sovereign proclamation of her muscles, by turn of pillow and descent into percale, banning substances and metaphysics, vices and verdicts, hells, paradises, and all the teeming nuisances which chiggered reality. —Charliedear, do you know what I do want to talk about? Our future. Turn out the light. Snuggle with me. Rolling puppylike in the sudden fearful dark he curled himself into a ball around which she fastened her ample self infatuatedly. —We'll spend more time with each other, she said, anticipating aloud. —I won't go to The Rapids so often and you won't need to go to the mill every day, I mean, not with Harris assuming more responsibility. We'll read the same books and have lovely, stimulating discussions. We'll be man and wife spiritually, we'll grow old gracefully because we'll be truly one. And do let's travel, Charliedear, book cruises to faraway places where they have pagodas and little bells tinkling in the trees and pretty brown girls with their breasts hanging out, wouldn't you like that? He murmured he would, wishing he might murmur, instead, good God, my dear, my sweet, swaddled, middle-aged bride, my change-of-life coquette: my destination at the moment is state's prison in Jackson, the only pagodas guard-towers on its walls, my ticket thanks to a little girl with whom my friends and I have tinkled through a whole archipelago of felony. —I don't know any reason why we shouldn't go on a cruise this next winter. We should make reservations in The Rapids right away—and what fun, Charliedear, looking through the folders and planning our clothes and luggage and things. She yawned. —I'm exhausted, simply exhausted, such a trying day. Hong Kong. Do you like my dress, the new pink? Do you think it's a size too small? He murmured dissent, and gratified, she slackened the web of her arms. —You haven't even seen the other one. Tomorrow night. Dear, dear Charlie. We'll live so happily ever after. Lisbon. Ever, ever after. In his ear the even vows of her sleep were like farewells. She had sailed away from that bleak, pragmatic shingle of recognition upon which they had faced each other minutes ago as vagrantly, as irreversibly, as surely as he must remain, embattled and alone, in his mouth an evil tang, decomposition's foretaste. He wondered.

Did doom come in several flavors, clove, say, wintergreen, butterscotch? Would candy cleanse the gut corrupt, would Life Savers really save? What was the slogan? "They Take Your Breath Away." Indeed! He remembered reading one night to Oram Kropf upon this very topic, from something by some Roman emperor, even the words: "Consider next thy breath. What a trifle ·it is! A little air, and this forever changing: every minute of every hour we are gasping it forth and sucking it in again!" He sucked in a great trifle of fright at another prospect: soon he must meet that brother who had been his keeper, that brother in whose house he dwelt, must in the endless twilight greet that champing Cerberus of a sibling once again! How address him? Gravely? Gladly? Or with a salutation immemorial to Michigan in summer: "Hot enough for you, Renis, you son of a bitch?" He cockled more deeply into the warren of his wife's body. Then, by degrees of pride, he was armored by the grandeur of the deed for once not done, he was thrilled by Roland's horn for once not winded; he had not told her; and it seemed to him the most heroic, Lacedaemonian act a man might perform in this life was to spare his mate as he had this night spared his own the truth. He slept. He dreamed in Latin. *Ave,* Charles Baird, *morituri te salutamus.* Lillian Baird, too, dreamed, of herself voluptuous in a swimsuit before a cabaña at San Remo, say, as young, romantic Latin males trained the terza rima of their stares upon her legs, which were perfect.

Charles Reason

—I no longer qualify as a raconteur, reduced to what might be termed my anecdotage, but one of the most hilarious stories I know is how Johnny Scripter was enticed into matrimony. A regular Restoration comedy of misadventures. Have you never heard it? I presume not, since this was 1919 and Johnny had just returned in sombrero and National Guard uniform from the Mexican Border. She was Ethel Hoeg then, close to graduating from the high school and its unchallenged sexual valedictorian. Oram Kropf moved in his chair. —In any event, Johnny one night rallied to the fallen damsel's cause, rendered her assailants—I believe there were six of them—or ought I say accomplices, hors de combat, and Ethel, in wonderment at the boundlessness of human dupability, forthwith set her cap for young Lochinvar. They went out together. In due course she informed Lister, her father, one of the sandhill cranes south of town and an old skinflint, of an interesting condition. Spewing sulphur and old-time religion, Lister buckboarded in to see me, Harlan Murninghan, and Renis Baird and demanded a .12-gauge solemnization or its equivalent in treasure. Robbing Paul to pay for a peter, as it were. Johnny was never more solvent, of course, than his charm. The town was in stitches, but more than that, concerned, for no one wanted Johnny spliced to such a baggage, so the three of us chipped in two hundred apiece to reduce the lass's shame and swelling. It next developed she was unpregnant after all. To get Johnny she had choused her father, who had in turn plucked us, and there was as much chance of our getting a refund from Lister as of proving Ethel intacta. So we had a hearty laugh at our own expense and rejoiced at Johnny's deliverance. Conceive our chagrin, next, when, anticlimactically, the pair ran off and were married anyway! And when we asked our prodigal why, he responded she was such a four-alarm fire between the sheets he could not live without her! Priceless seventeenth-century bawdy, the whole affair, the teter-totter technique I believe scholars call it, and surely nothing more masterful ever came from Farquhar or Etherege or even Colley Cibber.

—Put your money where your mouth is.

—I beg your pardon?

—Quit beating about the goddamn bush. I didn't ask to see you, Kropf, you invited me. I don't know why. I sent you your bill through Baird, I gave you two weeks to produce or face charges. You have a week left. And that includes the others.

—Sewell, the principals have met on the Scripter matter, and it has fallen to me—

—You're very hot for meetings. What would you call this group—the Council of Aged Cocksmen?

—It's our belief that now, having had time to cool, you must have reconsidered.

—Not a chance.

—You must have concluded that this is a contretemps which we can best solve ourselves, privately, and that your intercession—

—Save your breath. Carlie and her mother alone would have about as much firepower against you as a fart in a foxhole.

—Is there nothing, no word, no consequence, which will dissuade you? Have you thought of the havoc pushing this thing to any legal reckoning will inflict?

—Havoc, hell. I can see one great result: putting behind bars part of the outfit which has run this town like an officers' club for over twenty years. Giving some of the enlisted men a break.

—We are not a cabal, there is nothing jesuitical about the Council and the School Board and the bank's directorship. To the former the voters have elected those they belevied most worthy of confidence; we have never electioneered, never connived for support; and we have evidently exercised our responsibilities to the public satisfaction or we should not have been reëlected time after time. As far as the bank Board is concerned, that is a matter of stock ownership, and while some of us are men of means, I am assuredly not, Bill Vandevelde is not. And I point out that L.V. served with us in these capacities so long as he was able. No, Sewell, justify yourself to yourself in any way you choose, but the inescapable fact remains: these are four honorable men, peccant, it may be, on rare occasion such as this, but in the main temperate and honorable.

Four! It is well for Sewell that the editor cannot see. Four honorable men! Murninghan, Baird, Kropf—and the fourth? Sewell freezes, every nerve-end as espionage-taut as that of an infantry patrol's point man. He clamps upon himself, abjures himself to flank the position, to let the rope of talk uncoil and reveal the unknown fourth.

—It's still a closed corporation, he observes. —Somebody dies off, then somebody else, hand-picked, is allowed to join.

—Not true at all. Although the process of getting the right blood for a transfusion is, I admit, of necessity slow. Men own nothing, remember; they only rent places and objects, in a sense, from time, and the price they pay is their mortality. Certain of us function as caretakers, and the stewardship of a society of human beings, large or small, is not an investiture to be made on a hand of show-down. You have to observe, to inquire, to screen. I don't believe it indiscreet of me to confide that Harris Baird will soon have a seat on the Board, and next year on the Council. We are also keeping an eye on Ray Dickerson, the bank's Cashier. When and if he ceases tomcatting after Jane Reason we're of the opinion he will make an excellent replacement for one of us. Oram Kropf permits himself a small smile, made more oblique by gold. —You seem surprised. Don't be. Her father is fully aware, as is her husband. Thebes is not Brook Farm, and adultery as well as street-paving must legitimately fall within our purview. This is not to say we condone the random condom, we merely recognize its utilitarianism. We accept it as we do bids on asphalt.

—Accept. I got a crawful of that routine from Harris.

—He told me. Between us, Stoicism is best suited to the votary juices of younger men, or, as in the case of the Council, to men unschooled in any of the ancient disciplines. One of my age, whose senses are dulled by the obvious, whose palate is jaded by the amateur and pedestrian, seeks the new, the strange, the exotic—and Sewell, I have found my philosopher! Plato and Aristotle sufficed for a while, but curiosity drew me still further back to the springs from which those rivers burgeoned, to the earlier, dimmer morning of the mind; I read the pre-Socratics, Parmenides, Anaxagoras, Pythagoras, Xenophanes, read, that is, the fragments which survive. Then, around 500 B.C., I found him. Heraclitus of Ephesus, known even then as "The Dark" because of his custom of expressing himself in paradox and aphorism. Prophet, oracle, aristocrat, he offers riddles, couching them in an original, enigmatic style which teases while it illuminates. These snatches, if you will. "The way up and the way down are one and the same." "If you do not expect the unexpected, you will not find it." "It is the opposite which is good for us." "We step and do not step into the same rivers; we are and are not." Baffling? But it is his doctrines of nature and of man which first sent me to the bathroom, my bladder fairly splitting with excitement. Conflict to Heraclitus was the father of everything. Put another way, "That which opposes, fits; different elements make the finest harmony." In the diversity of nature he saw the unity of opposites, day and night, summer and winter, heat and cold, war and peace, life and death. And more, and this is most tantalizing of all, he conceived of man as part and parcel of this general law of the universe, a creature whose whole equilibrium depends on tension, a finite architecture whose consonance is sustained, whose acts are caused, whose very existence is made possible by inimical stresses, reason and appetite, love and vanity, urine and the infinite. The happy man, the balanced man, is he in whom those opposing tensions are best attuned. Do you not apprehend how interesting it may be to study one's self and others according to this principle? To peer through the dark Heraclitan glass at situations which seem on the surface inexplicable, such a one, indeed, as now enmeshes four men full of years, substantial men upon whose roofs the snow has fallen, as the old saw goes, but in whose furnaces, evidently, low fires—

—Four men? Sewell encourages.

—Yes, but even more interesting, yourself. Sewell, I have thought about you. To this whole exigency you alone provide a key—your character, the manner of its forming. I am reminded of the infant Hannibal, brought to the sacrificial altar by Hamilcar, his father, and made to lisp an oath of enmity against the Romans. Under the obligation of this oath he carried arms against Rome all his life, even after the extinction of his native city, dying friendless and in exile by his own hand. Livy is my reference. You, too, appear to have taken a youthful, punitive vow when you left Thebes. Harris and Morse have made peace with enemies supposed; not you. So you have come home, unmollified by success, unappeased by the years. You seize the first opportunity, a brief backslide by four men into concupiscence, seize it to redress old injury. And then—and this is what horns your dilemma—during the very counterstroke itself you discover little by little that the Romans were, after all, estimable men, and that Hamilcar was not! They say that what you don't know doesn't hurt you. On the contrary, it's what a man doesn't know that damages him, and what you have not known about your father has made of you an engine of retaliation. Now you have the truth from the men you would ruin. Harlan Murninghan was too discomposed, too magnanimous to speak, but I had the dismal chore of telling you that L.V. was an embezzler on what, for a small town, was a stunning scale. From Charles Baird you learned how he did it, from Charles Reason the circumstances of that fatal night in your house, the admission—

—Reason!

Sewell almost overturns his chair.

—Reason, by God! The fourth one! This is choice, prime, great!

—I don't follow—

—And you gave it away! Sewell strides about, arms cocked in triumph. —Talk, talk, talk, but finally you say something!

—I thought the girl, surely—

—Carlie'd have named him on the stand, but to have you tell me now is damn kind. Thanks one hell of a lot!

He arrests his own outburst, mind racing. In the office of the *Argus-Advertiser* there is only the padding of his shoes, the clucking of the antique clock, over the unglassed face of which implore the Editor's white hands while the noblewoman sleighs across the wintry wastes and wolves engraved pursue. "You're Safe in a Kropf Siberian!" Oram Kropf sinks back into his chair, self-banished by remorse. —I have given away one of the finest men I know.

—I suppose he got her up in his office. A physical exam, no charge, in the interests of medicine. Well, let's see. I read somewhere doctors average around twenty thousand a year, then tack on another five of the Murninghan money to round it out. You tell Reason what I said: he has one week to pay his bill, like the rest of you, and the price is twenty-five G's.

Oram Kropf brings both palms angrily down on the table-top. —Sewell, there is no categorical imperative of revenge! You must stop! Who do you take up the cudgel for? The girl? She was known to be promiscuous before any of us encountered her, as much sinning as sinned against.

—That'll cut no ice in court, how often or who for she spread her legs. All that has to be proved is she's fourteen. A birth certificate is enough. No, the Scripters have always taken a screwing in this town, and now, for a change, they're going to get a real break. They can even drive a Cadillac like Murninghan.

—Your father, then? You still don't believe him responsible for his own fall?

—He may have been, I'm not saying. But that night it was the six of you, by the good-all Christ, who sat on their fat asses and wallets and decided he should die and let Reason leave him that morphine!

—He would have been convicted on so many counts, the statute of limitations notwithstanding, that he would be in prison to this day.

—Alive, though! When did the Directors get the power of life or death? Prosecution, maybe, but sure as hell not execution!

The Editor inserts a finger between neck and collar, runs it back and forth. —And these ridiculous demands. A hundred thousand dollars from Harlan, fifty from poor Charles Baird, ten from me, now twenty-five from Charles Reason.

—Adds up to more than L.V. took out, doesn't it, and in a lot less time. Sewell reassumes the Morris chair, tilts and plants his heels solidly against the table edge. —But don't give me a production about the traffic not bearing it. I found out four years ago about the heavy money. There's a lot of it around, really, and the ones who have it spend most of their time saying it doesn't exist, convincing the shoe clerks a hundred bucks is a big deal and a thousand is a fortune. I know the score now. None of you is getting hurt. Besides, none of you could have been any kicks for Carlie, she's due something. What'd you give her, a course of lectures?

—I made her a present of a few books. I planned to augment her education.

—Who needs one? Evidently she doesn't.

—Well, a writer for one. It requires an education to know when not to write.

—Thanks. And also to know when not to molest little girls.

—You would break this community's spine, you, the one of whom we were most proud, our most illustrious envoy. You are Scipio, not Hannibal—Scipio who, not content with razing Carthage, sowed its streets with salt. Surely you recognize that what you purpose is extortion, if not blackmail.

—Neither one looks as bad in print as statutory rape.

Momentarily Oram Kropf bows his head, exposing the fibrillar pate. Lifting it, he betrays more: the high forehead glistens with perspiration; even the siccative agent in his skin is overcome by extremity. —We will defend our dignity. We will stand together and obtain counsel and enter a plea of innocent. It will be her word against ours, the word of a child, demonstrably wanton, against that of four respected, elder citizens. No jury in this county will convict on such testimony.

—They will with a witness.

—What do you mean, a witness?

—Hadn't thought of a clincher, had you? Think back, sweat a little. How did you get next to Carlie's small, hot frame in the first place? Somebody brought her to this office one night, sort of a pimp job, didn't they? Sweat some more. She was going to read to you. But suppose that somebody waited outside and saw your lights go out in ten minutes and you didn't leave and neither did she. What do you read in the dark for a whole goddamn hour? "The Dark"— there's a connection! You think any jury will believe you taught her Braille in here that night? Or will they maybe think it was a very old game called Blindman's Buff? You know damn well. No, Kropf, you've had it, you've had it all the way.

—Morse, Morse, what have you done? It is a whisper, incredulous and sorrowing. The tic of eyelids reappears, that desperate vellication which seems about to open the graves of the eyes, and so strong is Sewell's morbid interest in the phenomenon that he lowers his feet, half stands, half crouches at the table, observing as he might an epileptic seizure or another physical disorder, confident that his proximity, his curiosity cannot in turn be observed. —Old men we may be, or middle-aged, or near to death, but we will not give up, we have never given up, declares Oram Kropf.

—We have been good stewards. We have preserved the town in which we live, rescued it from your father's pillage, from the ruffianism and sterility of our time. Suddenly a white cane is taken up, thrust forth, and hooks Sewell's arm. —We will save it again, Sewell, even from you.

Sewell might easily free himself. He is paralyzed, however; the cane is like a finger fleshless, wise, senescent as one of Nestor's might have been, and its touch causes unaccountably, starts achingly in some far, bitter wildwood of his being a thorn of grace, a puberty of tenderness.

The next night Sewell joined Morse and Mrs. Scripter in the latter's live-bait emporium. He first inquired if Carlie had been kept home from school, as he had ordered, and the worthy matron replied yes, she'd called in and said Carlie's been took sick, and today was the last day anyways. Was she upstairs now? No, the poor baby'd got so fidgety from staying to home she'd let her go to the movie tonight. Then where was she now? The first show was out at nine and it was ten. Well, she'd prob'ly stopped for a sodey or something, besides, what was the ruckus? Because, Sewell said, Carlie grew more valuable every day; she had become, in fact, a living, walking gold mine. He told them then. He had talked with Oram Kropf who had, through inadvertence, let slip that Charles Reason had also enjoyed Carlie's apparently all-embracing favors. Mrs. Scripter loosed a calliope of fresh anguish. Morse's jubilation was so intense that he could express it only by opening the screen door and with a mighty heave throwing his empty beer bottle far out over the River Button. Sewell related the further developments. Through the Editor he had sent terms to Reason: twenty-five thousand and one week to pay. The simple sum appeased the widow's woe; addition and division dried her eyes as Sewell continued. Kropf had told him, though, that the four of them were determined to hire an attorney, stand together on their innocence and reputation, and fight; in his opinion this was sheer bluff by old poker players drawing to an inside straight and he was prepared to call it, to throw the fear of God and a royal flush into them. This would be the procedure. Mrs. Scripter would motor with Carlie tomorrow to the courthouse in Tyre, taking the girl's birth certificate, and file a complaint with the Assistant County Prosecutor, a man named Collins, who would ask her questions which she should answer in a demure, truthful manner. If Collins believed her, as he surely must, he would sign a formal complaint before the local Justice of the Peace, who would then issue warrants summoning the four defendants to appear before him at a specified time, probably within a week or two, for examination. This was the real pressure, the genuine turn of the screw. If he were any judge of character, the four would capitulate and pay up, knowing that an official examination which found against them would break the story in the papers. The beauty of the timing was this: according to Collins, with whom he had checked, the warrants would be served secretly on such distinguished personages, so that the four reprobates would have a week to sweat and finally, as the day of their infamy approached, to atone in cash, no checks, please, after which the complaint might be withdrawn, the spoils divided, he himself might hit the road, and the episode be closed. Morse approved highly; he would give anything to see their faces when they were slapped with a warrant; they'd been the law around Thebes so long they wouldn't believe there was law anywhere else and that it didn't scare worth a damn. The wronged mother was timorous of the perils with which a session before the Assistant County Prosecutor might be fraught. She did not know if her old pick-up would make it to Tyre and return. Sewell assured her it would; besides, within two weeks, if all went well and if she wished, she could royal it down Ionian Avenue in a Cadillac. Morse snorted glee at the prospect. What should she have Carlie wear? Costume, Sewell said, would be vital; no make-up, no high heels, she should appear in every aspect modest, virginal, chaste of mind and spirit, yet at the same time martyred and debauched beyond her girlish power to comprehend. Irresolute, fearful,

Mrs. Scripter scratched a hip. —You oughta go with me, Sewell, a plain woman like me don't know what to say. I might lose me my bait license or somethin'. Sewell replied he could not accompany them, it would smell of conspiracy, and she was not to mention his name or Morse's, although she could say she had a witness who had unwittingly procured her daughter on one occasion for what might be presumed to be immoral purposes. For the rest, he advised that she tell the truth, put on the show she had for him the first day he came here, work up a tear or two, demand justice. Honest maternal color made more fraudulent her rouge. —Well. I'll go tomorrow if you say, but I'm havin' more 'n more doubts about it. No, I won't use that money for outhouse paper but I'm jus' as interested in seein' them ol' sex fien's get their comeuppance. An' don't none of us forget who we're really doin' this for—a sweet little thing who come into life as pure's an angel, the way I did! Her ire battened on a thought and she spat vociferously into one of the minnow tanks. —Goddamn men. They run aroun' makin' money an' throwin' it away, writin' books an' lovin' women an' shootin' animals, buildin' up the world and blowin' it to hell, pantin' an' fartin' till they fall down early dead or shrivel up to toothless ol' doddies, but even all that ain't enough, not for men it ain't! You know what they think's the mos' precious thing they got to offer the Almighty an' this green earth? A bunt of their ass, a boom of their heart, an' a spoonful of more men!

Morse begged to drive the Jaguar and Sewell let him with a warning to keep to the side streets, the less they were seen together the better. Oram Kropf had called it accurately: what they were engaged in was itself felonious, and their immunity to prosecution themselves on that count was secured only by the desideratum of their silence on the other. It made for a neat if chancy balance: immovable rape opposed by irresistible extortion. Too enthralled by the car, a toy outlandish and virile, and by this latest divulgence, Morse was unable to appreciate the figure. —I'd almost as soon skip the money to see Doc Reason wearing stripes for tweed. This is the best news yet. Reason! I've won two things in my whole life and never got to keep either. The trophy for the 440 record they put in a glass case up at the high school and Reason put Janey away in a glass split-level. Now, by God, I separate him from her—him and his tailor-made suits and his Austin-Healey she probably paid for. Let him peddle pills to cons for a while. Morse cruised that half of Thebes west of the Button street by street, testing his gearwork, idling for several blocks to listen, troubled obviously by the timing's sprung rhythm and the stertorous hubbub of the muffler, then revving up and cornering to try the car's surefootedness. They passed a modest frame house and Sewell asked if Vandevelde still lived there. —Sure. He's due to retire in a year or two on a fat teaching pension. He hasn't changed. Still goes without an overcoat in winter, still picks up extra bucks giving the same old "Greener Grass" speech at commencements. He's got it made. But this car. Sewell, it's a crime to let a fine piece of machinery like this fall apart when a few hundred would fix it up—valves and rings, new tires and upholstery and top—it'd be good as new. If I had a deluxe bomb like this I'd quit eating, I'd even swear off the ring-dang-doo until I had it in the shape it should be in. Thinking a moment, Sewell made an offer: directly this operation was successful, if Morse would drive him to the Grand Rapids airport in the Jag, he could keep it. —You mean it? Old buddy, you've got a deal! Morse pounded the steering wheel. —Say, you want to hoist a few on me? There's some okay bars between here and The Rapids. Sewell said no, he was strictly a celery-juice man when he had work to do. —Hey, I got an idea. There's a place you should go if you don't mind being a little sneaky. We have to cross Ionian but I'll have you over while Earl Blue's yawning. Morse gunned the roadster across the main street, ignoring the stop sign, and working a circuitous route pulled up to cut the lights and park at the base of one of the two towering storage silos behind Thebes Milling. Into the concrete was set a steel ladder, on one rung of which Morse, leaving the car, laid a hand. —Let's shinny up. Two hundred feet, two hundred steps, nothing on top but some ventilators and the best view in town. C'mon, nobody sure as hell will see us together up there.

Sewell hesitated, then began the ascent, following closely after Morse. He had no fear of height, but within a few steps understood why some psychic apparatus had warned him against the attempt; the narrow rungs forced one to stiffen the spine, to climb erectly, and the effort cost the sacroiliac muscles considerable in support. —Listen, he said, stop once in a while. I have a little back trouble left over from the war.

—The famous G. I. back?

—That's right. Stop now. He relaxed against the cool metal. —This Carlie must be a pistol. She's carried more traffic already than the Panama Canal. What's she like?

—You won't believe it, but I draw a complete damn blank on her. Who notices a kid? Guess I should have, though.

They resumed. Halfway up the great torso they emerged from the mill's placental shadow. —What do you plan to do with your cut? Sewell asked, stopping.

—Well, I told Ethel a third of our half is enough for me. I've already taken a lot in merchandise, you might say. So I should wind up with about thirty thousand. I thought I'd give Ris enough for a decent car, it isn't dignified for him to drive around in junk, and then you know what? I saw this travelogue on Florida in a movie. I've never been there, I've never been anywhere, but it really knocked me out. I'd like to buy me a gas station in some swank place like Palm Beach. You know, one of those ritzy-tit deals with palm trees and grease monkeys in uniforms and carpeted cans. Twenty-five thousand down should swing it. Then the rest of my life I'd eat oranges and give my personal attention to the rich widows coming in with little mechanical problems.

—It's to laugh.

—What is?

—Ris told me. When he pumped gas here before the war
you were bitter about it.

—That's different. He's intelligent. I'm smart.

—Oh.

—Let's go, onwards and upwards.

As they neared the cylinder's crest Sewell insisted they
take another break. —What about you and The Night
Crawler Queen? I remember you predicting once, when
we were just into long pants, that she'd be the greatest loco-
motive invention since the wheel.

—I must have had seeing-eye equipment even at that age.
She was, Johnny thought so and so did everybody else. And
she still is, take my word, allowing a little for handling and
depreciation, and a great old gal, too, heart of gold. C'mon,
over the top.

By the time Sewell clambered gingerly over the edge
Morse had already located under a ventilator hood a spar-
row's nest and torn it from the louvers, after which he con-
ducted his guest seignorially about the rim. There was little view at this hour, actually, even from such an eminence:
in its valley Thebes had bedded down for the night in lavish
fathoms of new summer leaves; one square placid eye, that
of the front of The Let Live, was open, and along Ionian
Avenue the triple globes of the street lights were swarmed
by insects misnamed May flies which, appearing only in
June, lofted from the waters to die in black carouse, brief
and incandescent. Below and to the west Sewell made out
the Library, in front of which Johnny Scripter reined the
Harley-Davidson that day, paladin-in-waiting, while above,
on the upper floor, he glimpsed a vigil light which must
issue from Arlene's apartment and wondered at the coincidence that she should live there, near in space, far in time.
Coincidence or putrescence? Could it be that she, the
All-Bran Ophelia, sickened not of grief at a lover's loss but
of unwholesome congress with a ghost incestuous? Roofing
all other sounds was the monologue of the River Button
underneath its gates out of sight beyond the darkened mill,

talking to itself till morning of fish and floods and freedom. Sewell and Morse sat together against a ventilator, faces whited by refraction from the low and starless tent of night.

—Well, I'm finally on my way, Morse said, putting match to cigar. —Here I sit on top of a hundred thousand bushels of wheat with a fortune and a Jag and a big-shot writer for a friend.

—You come up here often?

—Just at night, this silo or the other. I've never set foot in the mill since we blew the dam, I wouldn't give Charlieboy the satisfaction. It's sort of a kid trick, I suppose, having a hideout. God, I wish I weren't thirty-three. Inside I'm not.

—You'd still rather be in the mill than anywhere, even Florida, wouldn't you?

—Yes, if it was Baird work. Not bagging middlings or anything peon like that. Ris and I could still make a terrific team, me selling and him running the plant.

Sewell weighed confiding what Charles Reason had told him about the impending demise of the President of Thebes Milling, thought better of it. —Do you think Charlieboy will ever do what he should for Ris, give him an interest or make him equal partner or something?

—Hell no. Not even from prison.

—What if he should hit the dirt?

—He never will, he's too cheap. And if he did, Lillian would get it all. She'd go through it in short order, plant, grain, dam, every asset right down to the sweepings. She's a real bird-brain, a dumb middle-aged broad trying to get young again. Morse sat forward. —Hey, somebody's coming.

Below, a car's headlights bored across Ionian Avenue toward the silos, fixed on the parked Jaguar, and the car rattled and braked to a screeching stop. They heard a door slam, then a shout, directed upward.

—Sewell! I know this is your car! Morse! I know you go up there. Come down!

Sewell might have answered had Morse not put a hand on his arm.

—Morse! Sewell! Harris shouted. —Damn you, you come down here!

Morse winked, whispered. —Let him climb it, we had to. They waited until the first tunks of leather vibrated along the ladder, then sat back grinning and allied together against Harris not out of spite or maleficence but because they had always mustered boyhood's plenary advantage of a single year in age, a single grade in school; two against one, they made him run and stumble to catch up with them, extracting the forfeit of poise and self-respect in return for the agate, the slingshot, the kite of equality. Let him climb it; we had to. So Harris climbed, younger brother, younger friend, and it was between Morse and Sewell, for a moment's anachronism, as it had been of yore. They listened as the quick steps slowed. Harris spoke, his voice high-pitched, almost frenzied, cracking off the concrete.

—I know you're up there and I know what you've done, Or'm Kropf told me this afternoon. No wonder you hide! You're at it again, just the way you always were—Sewell has the ideas and Morse, you have the muscle—and what do you do? You humble older men like Bill Van, you take a frightened young girl like Arlene out and use her, you wreck and destroy and smash, people and dams and now a whole town, and I'm supposed to tag along all my life because I'm just Ris! God, what you haven't done!

He was mounting again, nearing them, and in a moment his miller's cap billed over the rim and light flinted from his spectacles. He saw them. —I knew you were here. I'm not coming any further because if I do I'll fight you both! I'd like to throw you both off and watch you fall and die— that's how I feel about you now! Exhausted, he laid his cheek on the cement, holding himself with spare, corded forearms, and the racketing of his breath took on the whinny of repeated sobs. His head came up so sharply that the cap flew off, sailing. —I don't want to be any closer to you than this, ever again, but I've looked and looked for you. I'm in this, too, but for the first time on the other side. When

Or'm told me this afternoon I couldn't even work, I left the mill, I drove all over and didn't even go home for supper— Normie doesn't even know where I am. But I found Carlie Scripter! I saw her coming out of the movie and picked her up and we went out in the country and now I'm just as guilty as Mr. Murninghan and Or'm and Charles Reason and Uncle Charles! So prosecute me, too! If you go through with this godawful thing you'll have to! If you don't file charges against me, too, I'll appear in court and demand to be tried with them and you can send me to jail, too!

—You horse's ass! Morse snapped.

—And if it's money you want, I can raise maybe ten dollars! his brother cried. —But I don't want to see you or be in your presence any more—I don't want you for a brother or friend or even other humans because you're not! I'm going!

He disappeared. Sewell braced himself against the parapet and scolded the descending figure. —Ris, you really are a goddamn fool. You think this'll stop us? Well, it won't. At least the others did it for the right reason, for fun, and that's—

Morse was cursing around his dead cigar. —Everything shot! Money and Florida and everything shot to hell just because my pluperfect, stupid kid brother—

—Now wait a minute, Sewell said. —This changes nothing. I don't intend—

—You'd send Ris up the river?

—It's his trip, not mine.

Morse swung himself onto the ladder. —I'll catch up with him and talk him out of it.

—You can try. Sewell, too, started down. —Myself, I won't be faked out of anything, just remember that.

Harris had already vanished into the gloom massed by the mill and presently Morse was engulfed. Sewell retreated more cautiously down the silo, halting every few rungs to slacken tension in his back. A rattletrap car was started below and pulled away toward Ionian Avenue, flinging pebbles. When Sewell reached the ground Morse waited impatiently beside the Jaguar. —He beat me. Listen, he's probably gone home to tell Norma what a bad boy he's been. If you'll take me over there I can—

—What's the point? He's made his bed.

Morse cast away his cigar butt. —We're not talking about some old codger, this is my brother, remember? It damn sure does change things. I'm not going to be a witness in any case that puts—

—You'll testify if the prosecution calls you whether you want to or not, and if you cover up that's perjury, so you're reamed either way. Sewell eased himself behind the wheel of the roadster. —I'll give Ris this much break. I'll take you back to your girl friend's, you go in and tell the old bag that Carlie is not to mention Ris's name tomorrow in Tyre. Also, tell her to lock that little bitch in a room and keep it locked. Now that's as far as I'll go.

Morse was bewildered. Instead of entering the car he strode aimlessly toward the silo, then reversed direction. —I don't know which end's up. Why in hell would anybody do a lamebrain thing like this? Even him? He stepped on something, stooped and picked up the miller's cap which had fallen from his brother's head. —His cap, he said foolishly. —Ris's cap.

—Let's move, Sewell said. —Onwards and upwards.

Morse poked the cap at him. —I don't know. But when we were fishing and you caught that trout, you let it go. All right, so Ris made a mistake, why do you have to sink the hook in him?

—That was the only trout I ever let go.

—There's such a thing as sportsmanship, old buddy, and friendship—

—Old buddy, I fish for meat.

On certain days *The Other Side of Silence* moved for him, moved by the volition, the independence, the curious kinetic energy with which a novel or story or poem or play sometimes strikes aside the hindrance of a creator and asserts its own self-generative autonomy. For the writer these are fine days: charged properly, the imagination, like the reactor in which a perfectly controlled fission occurs, breeds more fuel than it consumes; the typewriter operates almost unmanually; inanimate objects such as pen and pencil seem to live, to obey a different bidding, to direct his hand, and he is wise to let them. At these times Sewell worked furiously, page after page, so that he had more than a hundred by now, and each one smelt of money. He wrote without regard for the rudiments, much less the amenities; let some nit-picking, grammar-loving editor like Peckham Hill do the coolie labor. The idea's original jolt had carried him through a rough outline for the entire book and this he followed hard-headedly, looking neither to right nor left, neither above plot nor below it. It was a lesson learned in Las Vegas: play the game, not the table or dealer or other players or liquor or noise or need. Besides, holding this raw hand of narrative, the ace of sex and the face card of scatology, you had blackjack, you could not lose.

On a day such as this, however, he was helpless, impotent. He was lonely. The hours tergiversated. He wished he were in New York or the Coast. He worried about how things had gone in Tyre; it was mid-afternoon, they should be back by now, Mrs. Scripter should have called him to report unless she had bollixed matters and was afraid to. He wanted a drink. He would like to get bagged and stay bagged. He had both beer and whiskey on hand but he had taken a goddamn temporary pledge. He had been six weeks now without a woman, he was horny as hell, and it seemed to him the night with Jane Reason at the Hamlind, tomorrow night, would never come. He sat barefooted, costumed as usual in dressing gown over shorts, unshaven, unbathed, shivering. Michigan weather: the body never quite caught up with it. In June heat you perspired, then a breeze tarried and you broke out in gooseflesh; in most arctic winter a perfidious sun warmed the skin. In the midst of languor, an alert, and the converse; the physical equation was always slightly out of whack. Slouched in the collapsible aluminum chair in the center of the long living room, he became conscious of the rubbish of newspapers and crumpled typing paper and the noisome palisades of laundry with which, in addition to opened suitcases, litter of books and magazines, he had gradually, as the weeks passed, walled his encampment; and he regretted having rented a whole house, even if it were his ancestral hall, for he was actually living, aside from minutes in the bathroom and kitchen, in only a few square feet of space. He had entrenched himself as a good infantryman was trained to do, he had taken cover; it had been his invariable practice since leaving Thebes, establishing and in a sense fortifying a small position in a larger sector. On each of the various posts when he had been cadre he had been assigned, alone or with a buck sergeant, a separate room in a barracks housing fifty or more men, and in this he had isolated himself. Overseas he had always scraped his own hole. To one or two rooms, really, of the Hollywood Hills and Arizona houses he had confined himself. Indeed, reflecting, it seemed to him that the tighter the place, the better he liked it. Return to the womb or something. Where, now that he discerned a pattern, had he, during these years, felt more secure, most defensible? It came back to him with truth's disquieting impact: in a narrow steel tube wrought for only one prone, armed man, a battle sled drawn behind a tank, to leave which meant death or horrible maiming, he had been in all his adult life most at home. In his father's house were many mansions. Under a common roof dwelt three covert, undiscovered people. If he had not been an only child. He stopped that. Having trained himself to dig in, to hole up mentally as well as physically, to barricade and wire his mind against the things he did not wish to think about, he could frustrate those patrols of recollection trying to infiltrate the perimeter of his consciousness: his father's damning display of stock certificates upon the table in the Directors' Room, the mad tocsin of his mother to a night-shocked town; if there were other dark subversions crawling, doubts about his future as a writer, invidious comparisons of his stature and talents, those also, by walling his ego with dump heaps, he could deny. Instead of thinking, he listened. He heard, on the other side of the silence, not the grass grow or the squirrel's heart beat but sounds from the far past, strained through the nautilus of memory. He heard the rustle of Catherine Hogg's dress as, in panic flight, she sped from the keys to the Apostles; that contralto voice which, like a bird hushed by the intrusion of a stranger, her son, furled its echoing wings among the nets of drapery. He heard the solemn early-morn procession, not furtive though just audible, of that small indomitable man from his bedroom down the stairs, through entry, dining room, kitchen, down the basement steps to the great furnace drugged with ash, banked against the winter's night, held breath while the small indomitable man put hand to grate handle. Then clang! clang! clang! the grate was wrestled with such vigor that the timbers of the house protested, the tumult so well-remembered that Sewell himself was laid hand on still: not the sun, not the spinning of the planet, but I, Lucian Virgil Smith, have commenced the day, and therefore be it declared that the day is commenced! Sewell stopped his ears and with counterorder of will turned his thoughts to present anxieties. Somewhere along the way, perhaps while outlining, he had seen that *The Other Side of Silence* afforded him a choice of money or of quality. If manufactured as conceived, as speedily and pornographically as possible, it should bring him in a potful in hardcover and paperback contracts, and rumors of the book's inherent sensationalism might effect a movie sale to boot. This was the sure bet, this would get him out of the woods taxwise and livingwise. But he sensed, unfortunately, that there were universals enough in his central situation, opportunities enough to explore character and comment on man's essential predicament so that he might, taking sufficient time and using his share of the Scripter money as a kind of subsidy, make a good book out of it, one which would redeem him with the critics. This was the longshot, however. He was unsure what the universals were, what was man's essential predicament and hence what comment might be made upon it; he was not confident of his power to make the novel good; he was not clear, even, on what he meant by "good." And if he cut the sex and failed in a try for quality, he lost all round, for the road to five-thousand-copy sales was paved with the best creative intentions. He could not chance it, he must stick to his filet-mignon ends and means, but the decision entitled him to sulk for hours at the inequity and nepotism to which the artist was subjected, particularly the artist like himself: the natural genius, the sturdy, plain-spoken yeoman of letters who, springing from the nation's middle soil figuratively as well as geographically, was derided, deprecated, and diddled by his city cousins at either end of the continent, the Japanese-gardener, stocks-and-bonds hornrims on the Coast and the button-down, four martini, you-kiss-my-book-I'll-kiss-your-critical-acumen intelligentsia of Fairfield County. To him these were the Merrill-Lynch-Mafia of fiction, syndicated to protect their own against the gifts of the guileless outlander; to him, in his churlishness, professional America was a freakish female animal with two ill-situated dugs, one under her snout (New York) where she might bite, one under her tail (Hollywood) where she might shit on the interloper, and these were monopolized, suckled dry by a snobbish farrow which, squealing and hogging, doomed the weak, the meek, the youths to Fortune and to Fame unknown, to everlasting runthood. So be it; but Sewell Smith had beaten them before and he would again, Sewell Smith had kicked open the door of The New York, New Haven & Hartford Literary League and in this book he would have an even more invincible battering ram: a four-letter-word, banned-in-Boston, under-the-counter No. 1 best-seller.

—Sewell Smith! he said aloud.

To the name, both threat and incantation, the doorbell responded as defiantly. It was Mrs. Scripter.

—Goddammit, I told you not to come here!

—An' I tol' you you should of gone with me!

—Don't stand out there, come in. Where's Carlie?

—Out 'n the truck.

He bent to reassure himself, but the pick-up was parked

with the driver's side of the cab toward him. —I don't see her.

—She ain't going anywhere. She's had as miser'ble a day as I have.

Sewell slammed the door. —You were supposed to call me. And what took so long?

She ignored him, careening past on feet pitifully bound up once more in high heels. —Hardly a place a body can set down in this pigpen. Heaving her ungainly bulk over a suitcase she reached the aluminum chair and beached herself, coughing and blowing. —Oh God, but I am tucked! Hughh —hughh!

He saw that she had indeed undergone an ordeal. Morse's mark of affection about her right eye had subsided, but her rouge was eroded and her eyes were red with what had evidently been unfeigned, artesian flow. —An' it didn' help none to have Morse come over las' night makin' me swear not to mention his damn sneakin' brother! A girl can't even go to the movie without—

—Take it easy. Let's stick to today and start at the beginning.

—The beginnin', he says. But where's the end of it? The widow extended her legs with such imprudence that the silk skirt of her pink dress slid far above her knees, revealing gartered hose and a white flitch of thigh. —Well, all right, we get to the courthouse an' talk to this man Collins you said to, he's all right but he's no gent. He's got a filthy dirty mind the questions he asks poor Carlie. Anyways, he gets the whole rotten story, Murninghan 'n Baird 'n Reason 'n Or'm Kropf. I'm ready to go but then she has to go in to see Engelhardt, the real Pros'cutin' Attorney, an' I'm not allowed in, she has to go alone! I guess they don't trust me an' here I've even took my bait license along to show I run a legit'mate bus'ness. Two hours she was in there with that withered-up mean ol' bastid—I could hear her cryin' like her little heart was tore out of her. What a mother has to go through! Then they call me in. That Pros'cutor has broke her down an' made her admit to somebody else. Another one—oh

God, why must poor innocent babies be brought into a vale of sin for the pleasure of—

Sewell cut her short. —Never mind that. Who?

She paused for effect. —The man supposed to be an example for the kids of this town, that's who. The one runs the schools—Mister William Vandevelde.

He was truly staggered. He stood rubbing the stubble on his chin, his jaw for once uncontentious. —I don't believe it.

—Well, you better. An' you know where he done it to her? The small eyes squeezed, opened, and presto, under each gleamed a pearl of melancholy. —Caught her passin' a note or something in class an' made her stay after school an' said if she'd be nice to him he'd let her off. So he takes down her precious little pants right there in his office!

—Bill Van. It's too perfect, Sewell said. —All five of them.

—Oh, no, six.

—Six?

—She had to tell about Harris, too.

—Ris? What the hell for? I told you not to!

—Because that Pros'cutor made her, that's why!

—That damn kid can't keep her legs crossed or her mouth shut!

—Don't you dare blame Carlie!

—Blame her? Sewell roared. —She's worse than poison in the town water supply! It would have been easier to find out who she hasn't laid, the little whore!

—You shut your vile mouth! You wan' to be indecen', write it, don't say it! Ethel Scripter's neck and bosom quivered maternal rage. —We're talking about a girl fourteen years old, an' at that age somebody's got to teach you evil, it ain't in you! Well, somebody's taught my Carlie, six of 'em, they all done alike to her, Harris Baird included, so I say let 'em all come to justus, here on earth an' before their Maker!

—All right, don't get your guts in an uproar. Pushing wadded bedding aside, Sewell made a seat on the rollaway. —Where do they go from here, the Prosecutor's office?

—They're havin' warrants issued an' served right away. The examination'll be in a week. At the Justice of the Peace over to Tyre.

—A week. That's fast.

—Yes, an' that Engelhardt, he went on an' on about how I should settle with the six of 'em. He says this ain't the first time a thing like this come up hereabouts, some upstandin' citizens in trouble with a young girl, an' the best thing for everybody an' the town is that the parties should settle it exterjudicial, amongst themselves, that is, an' the charges be dropped. He don't want to know nothin' about it, but he claims that's gen'rally the way it's worked out.

—Oram Kropf told me they'll fight, but I don't think so, Sewell said. —Not now, with the knife out, warrants issued and just a week before it hits the papers. No, my guess is in a day or two they'll fold and be ready to dicker. Listen, Ris Baird hasn't got any money, and Vandevelde is maybe good for a couple thousand, no more. I don't want Harris hurt, he's just a damn fool. Are you agreeable to compromising on the money? Cutting down the total price, say to fifty thousand?

—No.

—A hundred, then?

—No. I want the money, every cent of it.

—But goddammit, the first time you let me in on this and asked me for help you said you wanted justice for Carlie, and you said it again not two minutes ago. Now it's money. Whatever you use for a mind, make it up!

She sniffed. —I don't have to. I'm a woman.

—A woman!

—Yes, I damn well am! she bridled. —An' a human bein', too. You may be another Shakespeare an' a big war hero but you're dumber than a Button-boatman about women. If you have to have it spelled out, why, the reason I want the money is for Morse.

—What for?

Ethel Scripter cast down her eyes, tugged at her skirt with

246

a concern puritan and coquettish. —Morsey an' me are sweet on each other.

—Oh my God.

—You should of noticed that, she continued. —I've had bad luck with Lene an' Carlie, my girls, but I've had worse with men. Nothin's been the same for me since my Johnny was took—you don't have no idee how a town can treat a woman when it's murdered her husban'. Well, poor Morsey's just a overgrown boy yet but he's been awful nice to me, in a female way, an' when we get the money we might jus' run off an' get married an' live somewhere's nice. Missus Morse Baird, it'd—

—I give up, I've heard everything. It was so preposterous that Sewell, unable to laugh, set his face in a caricature of laughter. —I'll put it on the line for you, Ethel. One, you are about a hundred years too late for him. Two, he's been nice in a female way to everything female around here. Three, when he gets the dough he's taking off for Florida, alone, and I know because he said so.

There was something almost of majesty in her ascension from the chair, the hauteur of her pose. —You're a cheap-John liar!

It infuriated him. —Come to the party, for Christ's sake. Morsey! You know what he calls you? The Night Crawler Queen! He wouldn't marry you if you had solid gold teats!

So tragicomic was her gasp of umbrage, so droll, awkward yet splendiferous her buttocking over a suitcase and into the entry that his shouted admonition came after the fact of her departure. —And for the sake of the world, keep that little bitch locked up!

To try once more for a glimpse of Carlie he went a moment later to a window, but the pick-up truck had already vanished behind an egestion oily and infernal.

Once the lights of his car were out he had difficulty adjusting his eyes for it was a night of sickle moon. Gauging by the low pale line of the rail at high-ground level, he moved to-

ward it until there assumed shape before him upon a pedestal midway of the balustered rail the bust of Sophocles. That
of Aeschylus would be to the north, then, for that of Euripi-
des, although commissioned, had not been paid for, hence
not installed upon the pedestal to the south. This much
he remembered; classes in Latin at the high school were
brought here every year and lectured. At the marble-dour
countenance he stopped short in puerile relish: some recent
stripling, his craw full of conjugation, having at hand no
Caesar but two of that deathless triumverate which would
as well represent antiquity, had daubed upon the Sopho-
clean upper lip a mustache of black paint. He reached the
rail and with his foot sent accidentally clanking down the
aisle an empty beer can. She must be here, he was parked
beside her convertible. Telephoning him from downtown
before he was to leave for Grand Rapids, she would not
explain over the phone but said she would meet him at the
theater. When he objected, she replied only that if he wished
to see her at all it had to be there.

—Sewell?

Such were the acoustics that his name was raised to him as
though by pulley, aimed and lucid, and by following the
rope of sonance downward he could see her outlined darkly
against the rail on the amphitheater floor.

—What is this? We had a deal.

—I know. And very practical, too, like taking an appliance
home on trial. I wonder where you'd have taken me. I wonder what you can call home.

Something was wrong. Ordinarily she spoke in hoarse,
explosive bursts; now she checked herself, timed her words
in a manner spurious and premonitive. —Let's cut the goddamn sparring, he demanded. —We've got business in bed.
Now how about it?

Her cigarette burned, dimmed. —Sewell, I asked you to
meet me here so that I could show you something. Look
around you. What do you see?

It was ridiculous. She was as well aware as he that between this place and the silos of Thebes Milling and the

248

lights of Ionian Avenue the night's forbearance hid a thirty-acre wasteland of weeds; these, in their rank turn, cloaked the remains, hoar wood and broken windows, of the Kropf Cutter works and overgrew the tumbledown stands and legendary mound where Johnny Scripter had one-hit the bearded House of David semipros.

—Six, almost seven years ago, my father brought me here one day and told me what he dreamed of doing with this land after he died. He owns all of it now, except for a few acres. If my brother Tony and I were willing to give up most of our inheritance, he intended to sell Twinriver Reel and establish a trust which would build a park for Thebes, Murninghan Park, with income enough to maintain it forever. It was to be his way of repaying the town all he felt he owed it, which was everything. Tony and I said yes, of course.

As she went on, counterfeiting calm, to describe the park's facilities, the baseball fields and tennis courts and swimming pool and picnic grove and auditorium-theater, Sewell, to stifle his frustration, to contain his anger, leaned head-down upon the stone rail, hearing little. She knew; somehow she had learned about her father and Carlie, and there would be for him no night in the Hamlind, no juvenescence of the past, no crime upon a boy's enchantment with a man's iron weaponry of lust: what he could not win then he could not win now, upon the body of this woman he could not befool that old bald cozener, Time. This was what each man would do if he but could, he thought, be later wed to his first love, and neither altered, and in the warm garlands of her limbs replight that troth the years had made impossible. The failure was hers as much as his; more hers, in fact, for she had never lived alone while his had been a futile ranging over empty seas, putting into ports of call where passengers nor cargo waited, anchoring apart, a tramp steamer light of intimacy and tare.

—Even if he is my father, Sewell, isn't that a fine, generous thing to do?

—Morse and I were thirteen and Harris twelve.

—To work for fifty years and then give everything away?

—We were up on the Jordan, fishing, and one night we lay in our tent and planned it all.

—It's almost as though he were making a gift of his life.

The tale, signifying nothing now, he seemed to tell himself. —What we would be in Thebes someday when we grew up.

—And to make that gift after he's gone, so that people's gratitude would not embarrass him or them.

—What we would do. And you were part of it.

—So that they could only thank his memory, isn't that thoughtful and selfless?

—The best part, the most desired.

—How lucky for any little town to have such a park! Where children could play and become strong and their parents rest and renew themselves.

—And each of us would try to win you, fairly and honestly, never taking advantage, never even kissing you.

—And it would always be green and beautiful and perfect.

—So that you'd be perfect for whichever of us won.

—But how awful for Thebes, how cruel to an old man if he could not leave his name behind him!

—We shook hands on it, up there on the Jordan.

—If anyone should shame him from doing this for all those who come after!

—But you let us down—oh God, how you let us down, and nothing's been the same ever since.

—Oh yes, Sewell, I forgot, part of the trust would also be used to finish this theater, to do for Oram's wife what he could never do.

—For me, at least. What you've become I'll never forgive.

—Wouldn't it be awesome and marvelous if it could be finished and we could sit here and be truly taken back in time?

He ceased. He looked about him. The theater, predictably and ironically, was not Theban at all, but Athenian. In 1925, caught up in leukemia's pitiless fantasticality, having already been indulged by her husband to the extent of four sets of marble columns at the village bounds, Margrethe

Kropf, that dowager of do-good calenture, that cartoon matron of civic scrofula, had one last, wayward, premortuary inspiration: to build here, in this ravine on the west bank of the Button near its junction with the Ionian, a theater in which the town might each year produce a "Grecian Dramacycle," attracting from far and wide those who longed to quench their cultural thirsts at ancient, classic founts. That the theater might be authentic even in minutiae, a Professor of Greek, one Dorpfmann, was engaged to design it and oversee construction, and expense, Oram assured him, was to be no object. Dorpfmann's plans were based upon the Theater of Dionysus in Athens in its pre-Periclean period, the fifth century B.C. Out of the ravine was steam-shoveled a semicircular bowl, its river side leveled, and around its slopes were placed thirty-eight rows of curved benches, accommodating 720 spectators. Pedestaled for the three busts, a curved railing ran about the rim of the bowl; two stepped aisles led below to another balustered rail separating auditorium from orchestra and overhanging a water channel for the diversion of rain into an underground conduit and thence into the river. All was of limestone, benches, flooring, water channel, the rail at which Sewell stood, that at which was lit Jane Murninghan Baird Reason's beacon cigarette. Behind her was the orchestra, or dancing area, the area for the chorus, also floored, and behind that, backdropped by lofts of elms at the Button's brink, the foundations for the stage building with its low stage, templed front, wide central door through which a platform might be rolled during a performance, and on its roof a crane, or deus ex machina, for the removal of bodies from the stage or the swift materialization of god-characters. Alas! Orchestra and auditorium were finished, but before the stage building could be realized, in 1926 the wasted frame of its dear patroness was removed from this, its larger stage terrestrial, expunged by machinery not of gods but of cells, a humane intercession, for poor Oram's pockets were picked clean. Dorpfmann was informed; work stopped, the Euripidean pedestal went bare; given to moss and owls, to winds and snows and snakes, to lewd pictographs and lovers and Latin classes was the glory that was Grecian. Now, in dark night, the thin moon's favor lent the scene an air not scatterbrained but charming, faintly elegiac, made of the sequestered vale an ossuary commemorative of fifty thousand dead dollars and of Oram Kropf's bankrupt apologia to his mate, a limestone penance, an acknowledgment of turpitude left to ruin, a lament never concluded for old untruth, for bygone dalliance, and for superannuated whorings. Under Sewell's hands the rail was chill. The theater's abandonment saddened him. In it he perceived his own loss, a symbol unachieved, a relationship which must end unrounded, and, mourning the incompletion, in stone and in his heart, he could not note the practiced yet despairing arc of the woman's cigarette beneath him, could not heed the staccato of the girl's heels as she rushed up the aisle, so that her arrival took him aback.

—What if my mother hadn't called this afternoon, Sewell, what if she hadn't told me! You can't go through with this vicious, senseless thing!

—The hell I can't.

—Even after I've shown you what you'll rob our town of? A beautiful park? she demanded, her speech harsh again and detonative. —How could a man leave anything bearing his name after someone's dragged it in the dust?

—That's up to him.

—Up to him! Don't you realize what this might do to my mother? And that going to prison would surely kill my father? A fine man, generous and public-spirited, a servant of the Lord who's never done anyone harm in his life?

—You can be a character witness.

For a moment Jane Reason turned away. She shuddered. —When I think, if she hadn't called me because she couldn't bear it any longer, alone, if she hadn't, where I'd be now. With you. In a hotel room. You'd have touched me. You'd have made love to me. Sickening, sickening! She swung round. —Only it wouldn't be love, would it, Sewell? That's a thought—you'd have made hate to me, really! How do you make hate to a woman, Sewell? Are there ways you begin and different positions and is the climax death?

—Shut up, he said roughly.

—I won't! You tell, damn you—how do you make hate?

—All right, goddammit, I do hate you! If I'd have liked what you put out, I'd have taken you away from this town just the way you wanted! I planned to screw you until I was tired of you, to use you like a piece of luggage and when you were labeled plain enough, when you showed enough wear, leave you somewhere, in some stinking crib, and go out and get me another! To roar directly in her face, he crouched. —Why shouldn't I? What have you done since I went away to deserve better? You marry my friend, not because you love him but because you've got girlish delusions about being a nympho or something—then you leave him because in your opinion he isn't your equal and old Doc Reason is! But are you even faithful to him? Hell, no! You slip a piece to Morse now and then as consolation—and he isn't the only one, I hear! You stood for something once, to me and Morse and Harris—you still do, but it's something different! I come home and find you married twice and laying both husbands and somebody named Dickerson and Christ knows who else —a real small-time, small-town slut over thirty with perox-ide hair who's read a book and found bed is more educa-tional! Oh, you Murninghans are the answer to the town's problems, by God! The father passes out parks and the daughter hands out tail—well, the only difference between you and Carlie Scripter is that you're older!

Her hands came up hooked as claws, and jewels, catching the quarter-light, gleamed like eyes. —I may be promiscu-ous, I may have intellectual pretensions, I may not be what you once wanted to believe I was. Who ever is to someone else? But we've had time to see what you are now, and if nobody else has the nerve to add you up to yourself, I have. You're a fraud, Sewell, a fraud made out of money and pub-licity. You pretend to be a successful writer when all you are is a cheap product of some kind of New York and Holly-wood assembly line. You couldn't possibly be great because you're ignorant and uneducated—you're a Smith in every way, a Smith—a four-legged thing without a name, without a breed—a dangerous, rabid, mongrel animal!

—What do you call a man who plays with young girls? he shouted. —What's your father? At least I'm no goddamn pervert! And what's your husband? Didn't your mother tell you? You give it to everybody else in town—why didn't you give him enough so he wouldn't have to play with Carlie, too?

When she slapped him, twice, the darkness seemed split, twice, and two dazzling starshells of rage burst.

He hit her with fist, at the side of her face, with force enough to tumble her to the ground.

What surprised him was not that he had hit her or that she had fallen from the blow but that he could be taken so easily from behind, by stealth.

Scarcely had he whirled to the heavy footsteps when something, someone, had him locked in powerful arms and he was wrestled, battered against the limestone railing, an oath and labored breathing hot in his nostrils.

He would have used his knee against whatever, whoever it was but he was bent backward, over the rail, inexorably, bent too far.

It was as though a god-character had been suddenly materialized in a dramacycle of coincidence.

The ground was the bed of a self-propelled 88 gun, the railing was the iron edge, his assailant was the German who would break his spine, and against his lips, bared to his teeth, was the German's throat.

In his lower trunk something crucial to him gave way. He cried aloud in extremity and, letting himself become flexile, yielded the struggle.

For a time, he did not know how long, he was blacked out by agony. He was semiconscious of voices, of a car's motor started, then of a clumsy attempt to lift him from his slump against a baluster.

—Hit her, he muttered.

—I know you did, a man said, winded, and I ain't going to have nobody 'saulting womenfolk around here, in particular a lady like Doc's wife. On your feet now.

—No. I can't.

—What ails you?

—It's Earl Blue, isn't it?

—Dep'ty Sherf Blue.

—Earl.

—And you're young Sew'l. I knew by your car, only one like it in town. In the p'lice bus'ness you got to have your eye peeled for cars.

—It's my back. Hurt in the war.

—I didn't mean to do you no damage. But that was a. and b., 'sault and batt'ry if I ever seen it, or worse. I drive by down here once a night usu'lly, to chase off the neckers and underage drinking, and I heard this racket and snuck up just when you hauled off and swung. That's bad, Sew'l. I ought to lock you up. Town'd prob'ly bust a corset, though, I was to do that.

—You'd be a horse's ass, Earl. This was a private matter.

—I expect. Great spoon, but times has changed. Can you drive?

—I can't even walk.

—How about if I take you to Doc Reason? Can't do that, though, can I?

—I'll be all right after a while.

—I don't know my duty. I'm no chicken and when I grab a man I got to hold on till he hollers. With a grunt the Deputy Sheriff knelt. —Sew'l, I know what you done in It'ly and I got respect for you. Your dad was a dandy, too. I ain't going to lock you up. Tell you what, my car's behind the cutter works, I'll bring it over and you can ride a spell with me till you cool off and can drive your own. That suit you?

Sewell said it would. The pain by now was so acute that he could not care how the next hour was disposed. The sensations in his back and legs were bitterly familiar: from the hips down it was as though he had not been bone and firm tendon ever, but an intricate construction of strings, and these, the knots having been tested first by Morse against the bar at the Creel & Cartridge, then again by scaling the wheat silo, had finally sundered. Until they could be retied, reknotted, and the whole fragile weft of muscle healed once more, he would be, at least figuratively, a man apart. When Earl Blue pulled up, transfixing him for a minute in the patrol car's glare, Sewell had to be assisted physically into the seat.

Earl seemed out of place in a modern prowl car with its two-way radio and antenna and blinker light and siren and the Ionian County Sheriff's insignia on hood and doors, seemed ill-at-ease and under obligation to disparage the vehicle, to disassociate himself from such newfanglement. He directed the car's snout north, through the weed and ruts of the area and onto gravel, past Thebes Milling, then on blacktop across Ionian Avenue and along the street adjacent to the Button. —We don't no more need no prowl car nor no Dep'ty Sherf around here than we need horse troughs. But right after the war the County wanted dep'ties all over, they'd buy the cars and the towns would pay us. So I hardly get one broke in nice and there's a new one out of the taxpayers' hides. He spat out the window with almost municipal righteousness. —Don't even have the radio on much. Like today, a few stole car numbers from The Rapids and a wreck up by Silver Lake, that's all. Been a bad day, though. I have a job to do the meanest ever since I told Mister Baird you and his two nephews tore out his dam and you'd skipped, remember that? P'lice bus'ness, I can't discuss it, but I been putting it off since noon, driving around burning gas and waiting for dark to do it in. That's how come I come to check the old theayter early, for something to do, and heard you and the lady. There was a lessening of pain, now that he could take all tension from his back and legs, and Sewell sat in a kind of stupor remembering, yes, that Earl Blue was reputed to do his law-enforcement with his mouth, sat while the Deputy stopped before a massive house, got out, went to the door, and returned to drive on without breaking the cadence of his discourse. —The wife says you was in one day to my place for coffee, with Miss Kropf. Now there's a hum'rous girl, that Edie, asks me every

256

week for the paper if we're having a crime wave hereabouts. Gray of hair, wearing glasses so lop-fitted that they appeared in peril of slipping over the nub of his nose, Earl was a big man and gross. —Seventeen years on this job and I ain't never had to fire my gun and only pulled it a few times, on drunks. No, we had all our crime in one day, Sew'l. The dashboard's luminousness gave to the contours of his plump, white, pasty cheeks the effect of a filled brassière; the man had become what he had eaten, a synthesis, a digestion of thousands of short-order meals cooked by a hairy wife: hamburgers and French fries, eggs up and over, apple pie, and bearing all before it down the deltas of his kidneys, a turgid Nile of coffee. —You must of seen it in to my place, the calendar for 19 and 37, the month of June still up and my black circle around the second day. Earl stopped the car again, went up on the porch of a small white house, took something from his shirt front and gave it to the man who emerged, a man whose profile seemed familiar to Sewell, then crossed on his way back through the headlights, revealing the livery of his office: khaki pants and frayed white shirt, these braced and spliced by a belt and holster and purple galluses, to one of which was pinned his badge. Sewell asked about the householder. —Why, you know Bill Van. My best hunting partner. Many's the pheasant we knocked down over in the river flats. They had passed the Vergennes Funeral Home, palace of caskets and recorded dirges, nuptial cottage, too, of Herbie and Karen Teeple, and were idling on Ionian now, moving from the west to the east side of Thebes where, about the globes along the sidewalks, Mayflies clotted in assemblage fatal. —Meth'dist Church. I swear I never pass it but I don't think back to the Hall'ween when Johnny someways got that Guernsey cow up in the steeple. Great crawdad, but he was a caution! A third time he stopped the patrol car, left it, and mounted the wooden steps of a house imposing and labyrinthine, one which Sewell identified stabbingly. Suddenly he understood. Even through the remnant of pain, the thwarting, the bitterness, he understood all. The warrants! Three stops—three men—Murninghan—Vandevelde—now Baird. This morning Earl Blue had been summoned to Tyre, there taken receipt of the documents, and, bringing them back to Thebes, concealing them under his shirt, had the entire afternoon and evening, grieving his duty, delayed their service. One week now! But for how many men? Harris, too? Earl Blue had done what the law required of his office and driven another block before Sewell could once more attend his monologue. —This night I'm near the lonesomest man in Thebes. No lonesomer, though, than Johnny was that day. It's a fact, nobody has ever looked at what he done from a p'lice angle. I have, many's the time. Johnny wanted nobody, man nor woman nor child, should get shot. If he'd of blocked off Ionian with cars, bullets would of been thicker than hornets when they seen they was trapped. Same if he'd let them Legionnaires start blazing away like it was the Marne again, or Bully Wood. So what could he do? The cutter of iron was indistinct on the lawn and Earl stood in the porch light taking the paper from his shirt and giving it, head bowed, ashamed, to Oram Kropf. —What could he do but go it alone, get everybody under cover, and try to bluff them killers into figuring him a hick cop, get them to stop and then pull his gun down by the side of that there LaSalle where they couldn't see? That wasn't no grandstand act, that took so much guts nobody but a officer could 'preciate it! Sew'l, I tell you Johnny was as big a hero as you was in what he tried, the only diff'rence being yours worked and his didn't, they tore him to pieces and you're setting here, but you both done it to save others. The patrol car ascended a steep road toward what was called "The Bluffs," a fashionable new residence area high on the hills in back of town where several homes had recently been built by people of means whose published motive was the desire for a valley view. —You wonder what you'd do if you was to hear on the radio they was coming again, in a fast car, with guns, like they done that day on Johnny. I wonder. Seventeen years, though, and the law of aver'ges ain't caught up with me yet. A man don't know what he'd do. This house was new, split-level redwood and glass, and Earl Blue walked along an angled driveway, waited until Charles Reason, clad in sports shirt and Bermuda shorts, emerged. Thinking five now, Murninghan, Vandevelde, Baird, Kropf, Reason, Sewell watched. Would there be a sixth? The Deputy worked himself heavily behind the wheel, seizing upon garrulity again as might some ancient mariner with guest transfixed, held hostage against the law's impersonal cruelty and his own compunction. —No, a man don't know what he'd do. I'm sixty-one come July, Sew'l. Retire in three years on county pension. But if it was to happen, all's I know is I'd die, too, if I had to, for the folks here. Picking his nose with cormorant dedication, Earl let the car roll slowly down the hill against the gears. —There ain't no better gents alive anywheres than them on the Council—no, nor them that's gone on, your dad and Mister Renis Baird, he was a corker. It's gents like them make this as nice a town as there is on earth for a body to live out their days in and sleep peaceful when they lie down to rest. Earl snuffled adenoidally. —I love this here town. Sewell could not much longer endure this bathetic twaddle, this dulcimer folk song; the involuntary rest gave the illusion that he might stand again, walk again, and had it not been for the one final fact as yet unascertained, he would have demanded his release then and there. The patrol car crept. —You can have the cities and the sin, Sew'l, I'll take Thebes. Where does our great men come from anyways? Our corp'ration pres'dents and TV stars and famous writers like yourself? Why, great mud, from small towns, that's where. They were on the valley floor once more, under the leafy aqueducts the lights of the car like lanterns, and their direction was the dreaded one. —I gen'rally catch me a siesty this time of evening, Earl rumbled on, relieving himself of gas on the stomach by means of a long, aeolian effervescence. —Then I take the car and cruise around from 2:00 to 4:00 A.M. Ain't no need for me to be a nighthawk. I asked Or'm Kropf once if I should be on duty all night and he says something I never forgot, recited it from some old-time feller name of Blacksmith or something: "That virtue which requires to be ever guarded is scarce worth the sentinel." I ain't sure of the sense of it but I got a glimmer. Anyways, that hour, two to four, I like best of all. Nobody up much. Doc Reason out on a call, maybe, or maybe Or'm on his way to home from being read to swinging his cane, one gas station open, all the rest sound in their beds and me watching over them. The sent'-nel. I just poke around and around real slow, and come four o'clock and all's well which it always is I go home and crawl in next my wife and sleep like a man earned his day's bread and salt, not the county's Deputy Sherf but the Lord's. The car slowed. Harris, Harris, Harris. Sewell closed his eyes, but too late, for there was the small delapidated house, its porch bearded by misshapen lilac and spiraea bushes, its lawn unkempt, screwed his eyes shut thinking of everything else, anything else, of sex, of how it would have been in bed with Jane, until Earl Blue had the vehicle once more in motion after this, the sixth stop, the sixth disservice, until Earl emitted a costive groan. —Well, I done it, I done my duty, and it's the sorriest day for this town since Johnny—

—Earl, I want out. Goddammit, either lock me up or let me out of this car.

—Keep your shirt on. I will. You can walk now?

—I can walk.

They were proceeding down that block of Ionian which was also a bridge.

—You want to be took to your car?

—No, the Library.

—What for the Library?

—None of your goddamn business.

The patrol car eased to the curb. —Funny you'd want out here, right where Johnny set on his bike waiting for them killers to—

But Sewell had opened the door and monkeylike, with hands gripping the car's top, hauled himself out and upright. His laugh was a rasp. —They might still be around, Earl, the ones who really got him. Maybe he is, too.

—How's that? Come again?

* * *

Across the sidewalk and up the steps of the old brick
house, ivy-cinctured, the first floor of which constituted the
Town Library, his legs sustained him, and for a moment he
rested near a small, lighted window case displaying two
books, two only, which seemed to leap at him with fanged
snigger: *A Benison on Our Meat* and *Looking for a Location.* He spat, and saliva formed on the glass an oystrous
gauntlet. Harris, Harris, Harris. Opening the door he
inched through a dim hall to a flight of stairs and lifting one
dead leg after another ascended perhaps five steps before
an electrocution of suffering cut him down to his knees. He
commenced to crawl upward, step by step, and so racking
was the torture that to distract himself he tried to sing under
his breath a ballad of his mother's he could not have recalled under any circumstance less dire: "On the banks
Allan Water/ When the winter snow fell fast/ Still was seen
miller's daughter/ Chilling blew blast/ But miller's lovely
daughter/ Both from cold and care free/ On banks of
Allan Water/ There corpse lay she." The last mumbled,
mawkish line got him to the second floor, a single door opposite, and here he rested a long while, gathering strength
until, using the knob, with his muscular shoulders and arms
he could hoist himself upright against the door. Again he
waited, trusting the respite from exertion would anneal his
back enough for one final effort. At length, slyly, he knocked.

—Yes?

He dared not reply.

—Who is it?

He knocked a second time. At the instant of crevice he
fell forward, ramming the door open, pushing her backward, and swinging himself round by the door's edge
slammed it shut.

—Sewell!

—Lene, girl.

—What's wrong with you?

The only light was that from another room, probably her
bedroom, and that was indirect so that he could not tell

how she looked, what she wore, even if this were the living room of the apartment, though it must be.

—Sewell, what do you want?

—I told you the other day. More beautiful than ever, you are. Now let's pretend, huh? Make believe it's the old days and I need it and you've got it so let's have it, huh?

—You must be drunk, or crazy. Now please leave, Sewell, please.

—Hell with that. What's the problem, Lene? You never said no before, how come now?

—If you don't leave this minute I'll call for help—I'll call Sheriff Blue!

The reference triggered that fury which, throughout the whole evening's miscarriage, had been compressed in him like powder charges. —Call Johnny you want to! Tell him you're still a Scripter and in this town the Scripter women take care of the men and I need taking care of! He started toward her. —You used to be in heat all the time, you bitch, beautiful bitch, and just because you been spayed—

Terrified, she turned, tried to escape into her bedroom, but his exacerbation enabled him to pursue, to lunge head-long and seize her about the waist so that they crashed together to the floor.

She was sobbing uncontrollably. She wore pajamas, and cursing he tore them away, ripping the cloth from her hips and tearing it in swatches from her shoulders and breasts.

—No, no, no, not again, no, not ever again, no! she keened piteously, hugging her nakedness.

—Why the hell not? he panted. —You should be proud —probably a better piece than she is anyway—

With a convulsive, hysteric leap she burst from him, regaining her feet, but he, still holding one of her arms and rising himself, swung her, hurled her, onto the bed with such ferocity that the fall seemed to deprive her of breath, and she lay on her back utterly subjugated, her eyes blinding themselves, lay in that same sacrificial posture, that same attitude of spirit deflowered, will violated, into which he had bludgeoned her psychically in the back seat of his new car near Delphi Grange when they were sixteen, when Morse and Harris waited down the sand road.

He dragged himself nearer to marvel at the difference the years had wrought, to let sight's stimulus rouse him to struggle out of his coat and trousers and his shorts. The vernal sculpture of the girl was gone; this body was as stately, as classic in its shaft of rib and hip and thigh as a column of Ionic order, the lavish capitals of the breasts as perfect, the belly ornate as the enfabled girdle called Cestus, and even the cornice of reddish hair, marbled delicately with gray and unloosed about her shoulders, imposed upon her beauty not dissonance but harmony.

Lifeless, death-white, embiered, Arlene Scripter might appear, but he had never in his life wanted with such urgency to enter, to possess, to own absolutely and thus from her remembered flesh to cut his pound of meed.

Oblivious even to his own crippling he mounted her, pushed brutally aside her legs, when at the very instant of mastery, poised on all straining, primordial fours, he shouted—not in triumph but in excruciation.

Unmanned, without spine, without physical means of support, eunuch as surely by suffering as he might have been by castration, Sewell collapsed upon her. Strange sounds issued from his lips, terrible, whimpered oaths, he ground his teeth, and for the second time that night he lost consciousness.

Through shock's curtain, later, he understood that she had freed herself of his dead weight, he heard her speak.
—Sewell, what's happened? Are you hurt?
—My back. God, it's gone again, really gone. I can't move.
—What's wrong with it?
—Hurt in the war. Ruptured disc.
—Is there anything I can do? Do you want me to call the doctor?
—No. Know what to do, happens every year or two. Listen, what time is it?

263

—Almost ten.

—Go the drug store, get a roll of three-inch adhesive tape. When do they close?

—At ten. I'll hurry.

He had cognition of her dressing and leaving him but, head on one side staring at the wall, prone, helpless, afraid to move, of little else until Arlene returned, switched on another light, a brighter one, and gasped in revulsion.

—Don't look! he snarled.

—But your hips! Sewell, what's on them?

—Scar tissue. He was hump-hipped; each was deformed, enlarged by ridges of bluish, mottled, hideous flesh. —Don't look, just open the tape and get scissors. I told you, my back goes about once a year. Then I have a choice, stay in bed on it for two or three weeks or get it taped. I tape, because I can move while it's healing and I'm all right in a few days. But the tape draws, the skin blisters underneath and it's hell to take off. That's why the scar tissue, all those blisters about ten times in ten years. Now listen, here's what you have to do. He gave directions: she was to start at one hip and affix a strip across the small of his back, pulling it as taut as she could, and cutting it at the opposite side, applying it strip by strip with all her strength until the swathing reached the end of his spine. Groaning as she bore down, he described the cartilage cushions between the vertebrae called discs, and how a hand-to-hand fight with a German in Italy had herniated, or ruptured, one of his discs so that it exerted pressure on the sciatic nerve down the left leg. For two weeks he could not walk, and for another three only with a limp; ordinarily he would have been hospitalized, shipped home, discharged, but the battalion medic, a doctor humane and aware that his patient was regular Army, that he acknowledged no home but the Army, and was slated either for the Medal of Honor or the D.S.C., reassigned him to Division G-1, allowing him there to convalesce and to do light duty for the remainder of the war.

—I'm hurting you, aren't I?

—You can't help it. The condition had hindered him

264

little since the war; his left leg was slightly atrophied, and the natural favoring of the back made inordinate demands on all the adjacent muscles and tendons and ligaments, so that an incidence of unusual stresses such as he had lately experienced brought on an inevitable recurrence which he preferred to treat himself rather than suffer several weeks' immobilizing. —It damn near kills me when I take off the tape, but I'd rather have that than a fuse operation.

—I'm finished. I'm very sorry—

—I don't like anyone to see me this way. He asked her to do him one more service, to help him on with his undershorts and trousers and then to prop him up on pillows until he should be able to walk again. This she did, after which they must face each other, must each brazen out his embarrassment. —Why did you marry Harris? he blurted.

—Edie said she'd told you.

—That's no answer.

—It wasn't really me you wanted tonight, was it?

—Not at first.

—That's no answer either.

It was as difficult for them to break barriers as it had been that day in the mill's laboratory. In her haste to help him she had thrust a pin or two into her hair, put on slacks and a blouse, and conscious now of her appearance she turned out the brighter fixture, sheltering herself in a corner beyond the cone cast by the lamp beside the bed.

—Why did you?

—Because I was a silly, desperate, frightened girl of eighteen reaching out for what seemed her only chance to escape the Scripter curse—by changing her name to Baird. We'd stood up with Jane and Morse, it was all very exciting and dangerous. Then when Harris asked me, I couldn't resist the temptation. I think it was the most gallant thing I've ever known, his asking me, but as soon as he'd said "I do," I knew my saying yes, my using him, was unfair and cheap and evil. He didn't love me, he was seventeen trying to be a man and a gentleman, and I had taken advantage of him.

—Edie also told me about the annulment and what you

265

did during the war and Harris offering you the job in the mill.

—She's the only friend I have, really. And Harris.

—I've been away so I don't get it. What's this bit about a Scripter curse?

—You wouldn't, Sewell. Your father died a respected man, honored by everyone. You certainly remember how the town turned against mine after the shooting, after that comic piece in the newspapers, how everyone felt he'd made idiots of us all. You remember how my mother started drinking, you know what she became—and still is. In the beginning, though, it wasn't her fault. She was beautiful and she was Johnny's wife, and whatever guilt the town felt about him, later, it took out in revenge on her.

—Guilt?

—Of course. You have to close your eyes for a long, long time to see clearly. Those men who robbed the bank in The Rapids didn't shoot my father. Thebes murdered him.

—I've thought about that myself.

—With kindness. Johnny was always the town's darling, the athletic hero, the story-teller, the shining devil-may-care boy. He must always be protected, never be allowed to grow up or grow old. When the Council decided we needed a guardian with a handsome uniform and something with wings to ride, he had to be the choice. He was the town's youth and daring and strong right arm. Thebes created him, and just as surely, that afternoon, Thebes killed him. When he died, something in the people here died. The way he did it made them ashamed, too, because it was almost like one of the tricks they'd taught him. No one wants to be shamed, so the town could never forgive him. It took out its revenge on his family.

—And replaced him with Earl Blue.

—Yes, because being already middle-aged, Earl could never cheat us. How do you feel now?

—Better. Sewell shifted position. —What I can't figure is, you made a break, why did you come back here?

—Because it's home, Arlene said simply. —Home even

266

though people guessed I'd been promiscuous in high school. Home even in spite of Johnny and the way my mother had turned out. And there were other reasons, things I can't tell you. But I could begin with two real friends, Harris and Edie, who dared to be friends even in public. There was also the job in the lab—Edie calls it my ivory tower—but I love to work up there, high above everything, and there's something so true and pure and basic about the wheat. It's almost as though it cleanses me, makes me grow again inside — She broke off, annoyed with herself. —I'm talking too much because it's so strange to have a listener. Why did you come home?

—Let's see, he said, if I can sit up. He moved his legs sideways, lowered both shoes to the floor, and carefully sat erect. —There. It's working already, the tape. The thing is to take it easy, do it in stages. In a minute I can stand. Listen, Lene, why do you hang around a town that's dead and won't lie down? Do you call this living—alone in a two-by-four apartment over a library? What are you trying to found, your own goddamn convent? With your looks, you could make it big in New York or L.A. I saw you in the original, you know, a while ago, and what a waste of natural resources, what some man is missing. And you can't say you're happy.

—No. But basically these are good people to live among. I may be content in time if I'm honest and turn the other cheek to old slurs, if I hold my head high. And if nothing else happens. And Sewell, I don't think you're happy, either. Woman's intuition.

—Why the hell shouldn't I be? He jerked up the knot of his necktie, so mistied that one end hung six inches below the other. —I've got a name, I've made as much money as any writer in the country the last four years, I've been places and seen things.

—You're also my age, thirty-three, unmarried, with no family, and my guess is that you haven't made friends any more easily than I.

—I can have all the women I want!

—Which isn't the same thing. But can you, really? Evidently not tonight.

—Meaning?

—What it always did. I assume you came here tonight for the same purpose you dated me in high school. Because you couldn't have the one you really wanted.

—Are you still carrying that cross?

—Shouldn't I? Oh, shouldn't I? She came to her feet. —Harris told me once how the three of you, when you were just boys on a fishing trip or something, how you promised each other never to touch Jane Murninghan, but since you had to have sex, you'd get it from me! And you did, too! Have you forgotten that afternoon in your car—you first, then Morse, then poor Harris? But you were the one mostly responsible, Sewell. You killed something in me—I'm not sure what it was—pride, dignity, courage—just the way Thebes destroyed it in my mother when Johnny was gone. I can still remember almost your exact words: "After what your father did you don't have a friend left but us—we can't marry you but every date we have with Jane we'll have one with you, so you'll be just as popular as she is—but you have to put out every time—this is your last chance, Lene—you've been somebody in this town, but if you don't put out now you'll be nobody, nobody!" You remember, oh, you remember! Arlene sat down in an attempt at composure. When she spoke again it was with forbearance. —Sewell, I was only a girl afraid of loneliness, which is the same thing as death when you're sixteen, so I let you have what you wanted then and all through high school, but what you took in exchange was rape as surely as this would have been tonight. Everyone knew you were using me. If I keep to myself now it's because I'm trying to be a little virginal again in my own heart, it's because I'm trying to repair the damage of those awful years—only I can't do it with a bandage. I have to heal myself with time and silence and modesty. You said it yourself tonight: in this town the Scripter women take care of the men. Well, it may be true of my mother and it was once of me, but never again. I don't even know my little sister Carlie—thank God she's only fourteen and too young yet to be in danger—but when she's old enough I'll talk to her and warn her and somehow I'll save her, somehow I will. I have to.

One hand on the bedpost, Sewell began to rise, slowly, and finally stood unaided. With wary steps he moved toward his suitcoat, which he had earlier thrown onto a chair.

—Let me—

—No, he warned sullenly. —I'll do it myself.

It seemed to take minutes for him to don the coat, even longer for him to walk stiffly, robotlike, through the living room of the apartment to the door.

—Listen, he said. —I don't know how to apologize to anybody. I don't know what you say. But I apologize for tonight, what I tried to do. And for that time in the car when we were kids. When I think back, I think maybe it had something to do with your father, too. We'd always thought he was the greatest thing in the world, and then that day on this street he let us down. Maybe we were taking some of our disappointment out on you. There's something else. I might as well go all the way. The other night I was over at Harris's and I blew up at him. He said some pretty childish things about me as a writer and I wanted to hurt him. Norma was there. He opened the door. —So I told her about you and Ris eloping. That she was his second wife. She'd never known. I guess it hit her hard.

—No. No, you couldn't—

—I did, though. I apologize for that, too.

Light from the hall made her face like that of a woman beneath a cowl of darkness, white and graven. He turned from her and rigidly, mechanically, began to descend the stair flight, a squat, portentous figure almost of doom going down, down, down to what no one might conceive; yet at the same time, if you knew, if you had seen his nakedness as she had, this was but a man of tape, a being maintained, held literally together by adhesive.

—Sewell, she said. —Sewell, I want to be sorry for you.

He slipped once, seemed about to fall, but guying himself with one thick paw against the wall, continued.

—Don't be. No one ever has.

Like their three lives, the Reasons' home was built on three levels. Designed to be the talk of Thebes by a young Grand Rapids' architect who particularized in extreme contemporary, it was placed on the far, or precipitous, edge of one of the two-acre lots on The Bluffs, so that more than merely overlooking the décolletage of the valley below, it seemed to leer with a caddish, if not disdainful, obliquity. Slant-roofed, its walls on the brink side were all of glass, the others of California redwood; the heating was gas-fired radiant; the interior paneling and built-ins were of Philippine mahogany; lighting throughout was almost entirely indirect; shocking for Michigan, it had neither basement nor attic. Entering the living room, the central level, abruptly, the visitor stopped abruptly in disbelief: below him, the lower level seemed suspended by a short floating stairway, each step carpeted in a different pastel shade; while the upper, reached by another floating stairway, seemed supported by nothing at all. A trick the structure seemed to be, not really a house in which to live, a feat of levitation, and the multiplicity of color in draperies and décor—chocolate, lime, aqua, black, beige, persimmon, breadfruit—and the myriad planters jungled with exotic vegetation, the furniture twenty-first-century in shapes and materials, imposed upon the home an aspect, a presence which was tom-tom, space-age, Afro-Copenhagen-Oriental; and since the visitor could not know, he could not be disenthralled by the facts that the glass walls tended to frost inch-thick in winter, the radiant heating performed as thought it had gastric acidity, the total cost of the house, including changes, had run over fifty thousand, and that, after Harlan Murninghan had provided the down payment, a twenty-year mortgage in the amount of almost thirty thousand dollars had still to be obtained at 5 percent from the State Bank of Thebes.

For Charles Reason the evening had in only one respect been fortunate: he had had to make no house calls. Jane had gone out early, driving whither he could not imagine but for what purpose he could, and he had put in a mutinous hour with Carol, his stepdaughter, in her room rendering, to the caterwaul of her radio, what assistance he might in the composition of a theme for ninth-grade English, due the next day, entitled "The American Way of Life." The night was warm. Dressed in tennis shirt, shorts and huaraches imported, respectively, from France, J. Press, and Mexico, he sat in a Danish walnut and foam-rubber chair in his study listening, by means of a German hi-fi set concealed behind Philippine mahogany, to a London FF recording of the Ninth Symphony of Shostakovitch. It was an inopportune choice, for the frenetic tempi, the almost jazzy dissidences of the music had not the charm to soothe the savage itching on the backs of his hands and along his bare, hirsute forearms and it was all he could manage to keep himself from himself. After the first side he changed to the more sedative Toscanini interpretation of Saint-Saëns' Third which, in his opinion, was faultless except that he would have preferred the organ of E. Power Biggs to that of George Crook. The strings were superb. The house was still. Carol must be asleep. With whom was Mrs. Charles Reason tonight? He had been too exhausted, too indifferent, for once, to sleuth. Smith? Ray Dickerson? With a not-unattractive wife and two children of his own, Dickerson was a congenital idiot to stallion around with the wife of a bank director, but then, at forty, one had still the right to be an idiot. The house needed oiling; redwood, he recalled someone saying, would go three to five years between oilings; this was four. Morse Baird? That was interesting, to be cuckolded by your wife's former husband. What would be a relevant term for it? Auld lang adultery? He was getting clutch slippage between second and third on his car, the Austin-Healey, and that meant a trip to The Rapids for service and more money. Two coats of redwood oil would run probably five hundred; possibly he could get by with one coat. The Saint-Saëns' third movement soared to its conclusion borne on brasses and kettledrums and he awaited the almost religious exaltation which always uplifted him as the organ, full-pealing, seemed both to buttress and to sanctify the glorious cathedral of sound. The meeting last night: if he read the faces aright, prognosing the extent of fear or submission with a professional's accuracy, the ones he would hedge on would be Vandevelde and young Harris Baird. God damn a God by Whose infinite boneheadedness a man was condemned to begin dying, or worse yet, truckling to his transience, at the instant he began living. In his vexation Charles Reason found the music ended and his fingernails irrepressibly at work from his knuckles to his elbows.

When Jane entered the house and flew up the floating stair he would not have intercepted her, would have missed the livid red stripe on her cheek, had he not been standing to take the record from the turntable.

—What's that? Something new in a beauty mark? He stepped beneath her, looking up in closer examination. —Superficial abrasion, he must have worn a ring. Allow me an adage, my dear: fornication is one thing, but when they start beating you in the bargain, you've hit bottom. Carol's asleep.

She rushed on upstairs, but by the time he had jacketed the Saint-Saëns he was actually scurfing himself. He was not scheduled for another injection until the next day, but deciding he would tear himself to pieces during the night if he delayed, he went into the half-bath and took from the medicine cabinet the vial of ACTH and a hypodermic needle and syringe. For several months Charles Reason had been increasingly troubled by a skin condition which he could diagnose only as a neurodermatitis of some stress sort. Every patient possessed an individual quota of tolerance to stress; that tolerance exceeded, or used up, the symptom in some took the form of heart disease or migraine headaches, in others of an ulcer, in others of a spastic colon, in others, himself for example, on the surface, of a skin disorder, and Lord knew, recent events had made him long ripe for something. Inflammations appeared on the backs of his hands and along both forearms; they itched; he scratched; the more they erupted and multiplied, the more they itched and the more he scratched until the nervous circle of cause-and-effect became insufferable. Rather than seeing a dermatologist in The Rapids, which would involve commuting for x-ray, he resolved to experiment with the new adreno-cortico-trophic-hormone, putting himself on a thrice-weekly dosage of eighty, forty, and twenty units. Each time relief was immediate, his skin had cleared, but within two weeks he was again miserable. This was his last crack at it; he was convinced now that it was some form of planus, perhaps lichen, but he would give the ACTH one more college try. Lowering his shorts he sterilized the needle and withdrew from the vial on impulse a full cc., or eighty instead of forty units, and twisting his body plunged the needle expertly into the fatty tissue of the upper buttock. Replacing the equipment he rezippered his shorts and left the half-bath just as his wife bent over the rail of the stairway.

—What did you mean by "they"? she demanded.

He smiled, slipped off his aluminum glasses, and bit reflectively on one of the bow tips. Charles Reason was considered extraordinarily, perhaps too, handsome for a g.p., and certainly too unravaged by his fifty-six years. With his height, just over six feet, the Tiberian beak of his nose, the firm chin, the straight brown hair which has receded only a little and grayed distinguishingly at the temples, the arrogant guardsman's mustache, the tennis waist and hips, he is the object, except among his intimates on the Council, the School Board, the bank's directorship, and round the table at the Creel & Cartridge, of a wishful, plebeian resentment because he is not what he should, on grounds of wardrobe, tastes, and standard of living, be: a society specialist in a great metropolis. Then, too, there was the victimization of his first wife.

—How could I tell, he countered, which one gave you this

proof of his affection? Dickerson? Or Morse, the ex-champion of the sexual trampoline? Or your latest, our local claim to literary fame? I'm scarcely a statistician, but the fact is I have become quite the hawkshaw. For instance, I trailed you and Smith out to Delphi Grange the other day, where, I assume, you discussed aesthetic theory. Has he promised yet to take you away from all this—to the glitter, say, of Hollywood and Vine?

On her way upstairs again she hurled a parting shot. —At least he wouldn't be marrying me for my money!

He stepped back into his study, to the wall of glass, and musing over the few sporadic twinklings in the village below, wondered if the men and women there gazed upward now and then in jealousy, and seeing lights above, wondered what transpired within the Reason domicile. They could not be sure, they could only guess. Well, let them wonder what transpired upon the height, curse the wine and caviar to pass; and Dr. Reason one calm summer night, stayed home and stuck a needle in his ass. —At least he wouldn't be marrying me for my money! Touché, Jane Murninghan Baird my beloved Reason. All I owe, I owe to our sainted Twinriver Reel, and I am not even a fisherman but a punster, an aphorist, a paraphraser, and a barefoot boy who has taken fifty-six years to travel from New Ulm, Minnesota, to Thebes, Michigan. When he considered that journey, a peregrination, as it were, from nowhere to nowhere, he was reminded of the occasion when, reading to Oram Kropf from Bulfinch's *Age of Fable,* he had come upon Virgil's description of the infernal regions, and therein, an account of the damnation of Sisyphus, whose eternal torture it was to roll a huge stone to a hilltop only to have it roll down again; and it seemed to him, standing before his window on The Bluffs, that his own endeavors, every frigging one, had indeed, in their retributive futility, been Sisyphean. In youth willing enough to practice medicine, like his father, he was however unwilling to become, as had his father, a small-town g.p.; as an undergrad at Minnesota his monomania was to specialize, take his boards in gyn or derm or path or something, anything which would get him into a city and high income bracket. Logically, toward the end of his first year in med school at Michigan, his father passed on; logically, the insurance was insufficient to graduate him. Crisis wed him to Bernice Hansen, an R.N. twenty-eight years old to his twenty-three with whom he had frequently and unjoyously slept. She continued to work; the twain borrowed; he finished internship and at twenty-seven, burdened with debt, took the best offer he could locate, signing papers to legalize a 60-40 percent proposition to share and gradually assume ownership of the offices and practice of one James Kemper, a man then in his sixties and the only doctor in Thebes, Michigan, a hamlet somewhere up near Grand Rapids. What began as expediency ended in quicksand. Logically, Dr. Kemper died; logically, his widow continued to collect. After five years Charles Reason was out of debt, owned a monopoly practice, an equity in a decent home, and had become exactly and logically what he had guaranteed himself with all youth's trenchancy never to be: a small-town general practitioner. At the bottom of life's hill his stone then reposed.

With the Fates, during the 1930's and 1940's, he made comparative peace. His maladroit contribution to the suicide of Claude Reichert's son endowed him with a quality of mercy which would never again, he believed, be strained. In his soul he took a hypocritic oath to count his blessings, to love his wife, to roust gladly out in the middle of the night, if need be, for a case of constipation. Poker helped, as did his partners at the C & C, Renis Baird, Oram Kropf, Harlan Murninghan, Bill Van, L. V. Smith, and the inimitable Johnny Scripter; the science of local government interested him, he discovered, as much if not more than that of chirurgery. The midge in the ointment of his new self-possession, however, his new maturity, was Bernice. An epitome of her faults would have required volumes; to list but a few, she was jealous of him, as his nurse she handled his statements with the altruism of an usurer, she would have no children, she would not hear of his enlisting during

275

the war, her hatred of F.D.R. was Fascist in its virulence, she was prone to a waspish martyrdom over her part in helping him through med school, she was penurious, shrewing incessantly about his appreciation of records, books, cars, clothes, travel, and upon the act of marriage she conferred the same scientific objectivity with which she disposed of a stool specimen.

Then, in 1947, he fell in love with Jane Baird and she with him. He could scarcely believe his luck; he was forty-nine, she was twenty-six, beautiful, passionate, and she would come into a fortune. Bernice's asking price for a divorce was astronomical: house, car, insurance, and alimony of a thousand monthly. He paid, for Jane's thousand a month from Harlan Murninghan would cover the alimony and on the net from his practice of sixteen thousand a year they could live adequately until such time as the paternal melon could be cut. Thebes might spit and sputter, but with his stone Charles Reason had at last reached the summit.

Its immediate downward plunge was hence the more hellish. Conceive his dismay, the enema of all his hopes, when, in 1948, but weeks before the nuptials, he was apprised by his bride-to-be of that posthumous park bequest of her father's which would to all practical effect disinherit her! Dry-throated, close-mouthed, he went the following day and bought on a note for seven thousand dollars from Claude Reichert, who had in turn salvaged it for a song from the assets sold by court order from the L. V. Smith estate, the six-acre site of the old cutter works, shrewd enough to foresee that his ownership would effectively block any fruition of Harlan Murninghan's philanthropy. At this impasse affairs have remained, despite the schizoid botch it has made of their matrimony, for almost eight years.

—Charles, said L. V. Smith that night, a man has the guts to do anything he wants. Truth? And truth ne'er hurts the teller? Ah, but morphine sulphate may!

At the wall of glass surmounting the valley Charles Reason meditated yet, his stone unbudged, his thoughts ambagious and out of joint. Movement overhead; that would be his wife, in her bathroom. I am fifty-six, this is 1954, therefore I do not belong to this century. I should be near old Kemper's situation now, shored up by stocks and bonds and annuities and ready to indenture some young stethoscopic slave full of beans and hot to heal, even in the midst of night. I have no regrets about taking her from Morse Baird, no remorse about Morse; then he may have been a marvelous muscular conveyance, but today a bodkin of fat, a cod for every piece in Thebes. Jane a trophy he could never keep. What preoccupies the others now, this moment? Does Charlie Baird, hasting himself to some unmalignant cloud, speed the last mad miles upon his Exerbike? Does that old Diocletian, my father-in-law, revel in his sitz bath? Who reads to Oram Kropf at this hour? Bill Van and Dorth, no doubt, together undergo the faery hypnosis of their television. At his feet no lights glimmered now but those along Ionian Avenue, those at the street corners, and those pathing the way for a single automobile. When you think of it, only three of us matter at night in Thebes, really matter— Oram, Earl Blue, and I. No, let us have stress rather than sentimentality, ACTH before unction. But if I have never been close to my patients I could not help it, being what I am, a man not apathetic but cankered by his own incompetence, not bloodless but wrathful because they expected so much from me and I could accomplish so bitterly little. In the end all I could ever do was gain them a flyspeck more of time, delay them a few moments before their touristry to the infernal regions, grant them imaginings so slender, so paltry, and so dear before the long, long dream not theirs but His, and that was all that I could ever do. Accept, you Stoic bastard. Physician, if you cannot heal, at least accept thyself.

—Charles, will you come up here, please?

When he climbed to her level she had changed to shorts and halter and sat in the center of the Swedish davenport. Arrayed on the glass Noguchi coffee table were the magazines to which they subscribed, *Time, The New Yorker,*

Saturday Review, Harper's, Holiday, and on the latest issues of these Jane arched her bare feet.

—I wish you'd sit down and we could talk for a while as though we were strangers who happened to meet. She indicated her cheek. —I intended to treat this some way, then I thought no, I want a scar.

She was remarkably calm, recounting the arrangements she had made to spend the night with Sewell Smith at the Hamlind, the tacit understanding, on her part at least, that if both were satisfied, she would eventually leave Thebes with him. Then, just this afternoon, her mother called and told her about the Carlene Scripter thing and Sewell's role in it. She hated to use the word "salvation," it sounded so fake, but that's what Carrie's call had been. She met Sewell instead at the old theater, they quarreled, he called her a small-town slut, which was true, a nymphomaniac, which was not, she assessed his merits and reputation as a writer with equal candor, he then said something which caused her to slap him, and he in retaliation hit her, knocking her down. Thus her face.

He watched her. —I'm sorry you had to find out about your father. Incidentally, I know something about stress. If you want to let go, Jane, let go.

—No. We're strangers, I said. What I want is to have you ask me what made me slap him.

—Consider yourself asked.

—He said that you're just as involved with Carlene Scripter as my father.

—He's a swine and a liar.

—It isn't true, then?

—After eight years I'd expect you'd credit my appetites as being somewhat more gourmet. The double note of the chimes interrupted him. —I'll get it. He went to the door, switched on the entry light, and stepping outside closed the door behind him.

I will not let go, she thought waiting, I won't be shrill or hysteric or anything, but damn, damn, damn, I wish I could. I think what we say to each other the next few minutes will probably be the most important things we've ever said to each other or ever will.

—Well, he said, returning.

—Who was it?

—Earl Blue.

Standing, almost smiling, in one of his hands he held a folded document which he tapped smartly across the palm of the other hand. —Well, well. He sat down. He unfolded the document, scanned it quickly folded it again.

—What's that?

Her husband removed his glasses, extended his legs, and lying back as far as the cocoanut-shell chair would allow him, closed his eyes. —Well. And I was just prescribing release.

—Charles, what's wrong?

—Nothing. Except that among the swine and liars you may now number Charles Reason, M.D. That paper is a warrant served upon me by the Deputy Sheriff of Ionian County. Earl is serving five others tonight, upon your father, Charlie Baird, Bill Van, Oram Kropf, and Harris Baird. The warrants call for our appearance in Justice Court in Tyre next week for examination on a charge of statutory rape against us filed with the County Prosecutor by Mrs. John Scripter on behalf of her minor daughter Carlene. I can't seem to stop talking. I don't know how much your mother could tell you, in her state, especially since she knows only about Harlan, but I can fill in all the picturesque details. The girl, Carlie, is fourteen. Statutory rape is a felony calling for, in Michigan, a prison term up to life. Harris Baird had her the other night deliberately, to associate himself with us, an act splendid or feeble-minded, depending on your point of view. Sexually, the girl herself is a kind of female Automat, but even with her consent, intimate knowledge of her viands is rape. Forgive me, I'm not being very coherent. She should have a legend embroidered on her panties: "Abandon hope, all ye who enter here." I'll warrant you, it takes something special for a man to be amusing about such a story.

—Charles, Charles—

—No soap opera, please, he gestured, eyes yet closed. —Just strangers, remember? In any event, Smith is the prime mover in the enterprise. He's set a different blackmail figure for the five of us; to each according to his sins, from each according to his ability to pay. Charlie Baird gave me the word on her one day in the office, that her custom was to take the air of an evening near the Congregational Church, a kind of carnal constitutional, and lo, one night when you went out, so did I. Several, in fact. My fine, incidentally, is twenty-five thousand. I've considered selling the Healey, putting a second mortgage on the house, cutting down on magazines and records—now I'm not being funny. None of us knew about the others until our celebrity arrived in town and found, evidently, that the live-bait business might be more lucrative than art. So there we are: an eighth-grade Penelope and her five suitors. We've had several meetings on the subject, naturally, and only last night decided, being old hands at poker, that Smith's deadline for payment was pure bluff and we would call it. For once we were dead wrong. He has the cards and Earl Blue is showing them. Charles Reason rubbed his eyes, sat up, put on his glasses. —What it has cost me to tell you this you will never know.

The cumbersome silence was indeed like that which falls between chance travelers. They did not look at one another.

—Are you sure Carol's asleep? Jane asked at length.

—She must be, I don't hear her radio. He glanced in exasperation about the room. —Christ, Christ, Christ, what I've done.

—I want to cry for you, she said, and for my father and mother and I can't even do that. I think you have to earn the right to tears, and I haven't.

He extracted himself from the chair. —Anyone for tennis? Shall we get stoned?

—No.

—Shall we change the subject?

—Yes, let's.

He moved to the glass wall of the living room, stared out, turned back and sat on the second step of the floating stair leading to the bedroom level.

—We can't change it, she said. —What have all of you decided to do?

—As of last night, to stand together, deny everything. It's the girl's word against ours, legally, and we're gambling again that no local magistrate, knowing what our lives add up to collectively, will accept hers and bind us over. We've even talked Harris, the eager candidate for the stake, into joining the game for the town's sake. On our own side we can offer character witnesses till the good J.P. considers canonizing us. And any scrutiny of the character of the Scripters, the mother, Carlie, the elder damsel Arlene, must work in our favor. If Johnny—may he have a heavenly audience always—if Johnny were still here, none of this would have transpired.

—I wish Arlene could be kept out of it.

—Why?

—Because whatever she did, years ago, was my fault indirectly. She explained.

—That damned pimply triumvirate again. I'm sorry. Well, I see no point in raking over her career; testimony of mother and Carlie will be what's at issue, really. He made a hasty, instinctive determination to avoid any reference to Morse Baird's threatened appearance as a witness and its obvious motivations. —I think we have a fair chance of "beating the rap," to use the parlance, but if we lose, if we are arraigned for trial in Circuit Court, then we emblazon every newspaper in the state, and regardless of outcome, we still lose. Absently he scratched the back of one hand.

—Aye, there's the rub.

—Your hand.

—Oh. I'm tired.

—What Carrie can't comprehend, or I either, is why my father would be tempted in the first place. He's an old man, and not well.

—It's no phenomenon. We don't know why, but in old

gents with prostate trouble, no matter how moral they may be, the psychic desire for young girls increases. It's another of life's sneaky tricks on the elderly.

—I see. But you're not elderly.

—So why should Charles Reason trifle? A better question: why Charles Reason? He assumed a posture almost boyish, drawing up his sharp knees and resting his chin on them. —Retribution, I expect. An eye for an eye, Carlie Scripter for Ray Dickerson, if you could gambol down the garden path, so could I. He gnawed reflectively on an aluminum bow tip. Fifty-six is over the hill sexually, but it was gratifying to find, too, that although I might no longer be physically desirable to you, I seemed to be to her, to a mere girl half your age. He raised his eyebrows. —This may be useful after all, being impersonal, doing a little clinical analysis. We never have.

—You were wrong about not being physically desirable to me.

His look was steady. —Oh? And Morse? Ray? Smith?

—The acreage. You'd married my inheritance, not me. What else could I believe after my father told me you'd bought the six acres and wouldn't sell to him?

—I married you because I loved you.

—But I gave away his secret, about the park, trusting you, and you took advantage.

He pulled at his mustache in irritation. —My God, all these years, infants, both of us! I knew you knew and you knew I knew you knew and round and round the mulberry bush we've gone. Jane, you think I'm strong. I am despicably weak. You think I'm wise, witty, cultured. I am stupid. Listen, this is what I thought was my dilemma. You have never heard anything more imbecile, more putrid, in your life, including statutory rape, but it's true, I presume it's behind my stress problem, in fact. I thought myself too old to hold you without money. Bernice took everything I had and would continue to. If I sold to Harlan, you would never inherit and you'd leave me for someone like Smith. If I didn't, if I played a vicious waiting game until Harlan died, while you might be unfaithful for the present, afterward I could divert you with travel, et cetera, and over the long haul keep you. And if I still couldn't, if you filed for divorce, I could bring countersuit on grounds of adultery and collect my share. The stress, the pressure, have been unspeakable. What I am accused of committing under the law with the girl is a bagatelle compared to what I've committed against you and your father. So. Weak, asinine, and deadliest of all, mercenary as hell. He put on his glasses. —In any event, it's over. Now that it's too late, I did last night what I should have done long ago. I unbastardized myself slightly. I gave Harlan a deed to the six acres.

—Oh. Oh. She put her head down. —Oh damn, damn, I'm so glad. What did he say?

—Nothing. He put his arms around me.

—I want to myself.

—No.

He abrades himself as much inwardly as out, she thought; I know less of him now than I did seven years ago. She kept her head down. —Then let me do something else. Let me tell you what I've been, what—

She could not go on, and seeing this, he came to her rescue. —I was noticing our magazines. We subscribe to all but the one we've evidently needed: *True Confessions.*

She smiled, eyes glistening. —They say it's great for the soul.

—And for the skin, I hope.

—Let me tell you, though, please.

—You have beautiful feet, Mrs. Reason.

—Sewell said tonight the only difference between me and Carlie Scripter is that I'm older. I'm not, really, I'm just as immature as she must be. Dissatisfied with everything, the way I act, even the way I look—thirty-three trying to appear twenty-three, hair, nails, color of lipstick, being burlesque, practically, when I walk—dissatisfied with Thebes, wanting to run away from it, away from home the way an adolescent does. When, if I were mature, the way you are, I'd have recognized by now that all I need, basically, to be happy, to live a full life, is right here.

—You mean, as Bill Van so originally puts it in com-

mencement addresses, that the grass is not greener elsewhere?

—Sometimes the cornier things sound, the truer they are.
Immature, selfish, bored, restless—do you know who I'm a
new model of? Lillian Baird.

—You want a cigarette, don't you, Janey?

—Dying for one. But that's how childish I am. I knew
how important this talk would be to us and I thought not
smoking would be a sign of solemnity. Or something.

He smiled, stood, and started down the stair. —I'll fetch
you one.

—Thanks. Keep listening though, Charles, please. I said
what I need to be happy is right here. The first thing was
proof that you loved me for myself, not my father's money,
which I have now. The way I love you for yourself.

—And not my Austin-Healey? He came back with a cigarette and lit it for her.

She inhaled and blew serious smoke at him. —The second
thing is just plain damn grow up and be a woman. To see,
as you once did, that the challenge is here, now, wherever
you happen to be. To make the best of things as they are.

He had gone to the glass wall. —Accept, accept, he murmured, but not to her. —I've been racking my imagination
for an analogy for our predicament. Suitably solemn.

—So have I. Marriage can be like a miniature prison,
with only two cells and two prisoners— Charles, I'm sorry!

—It's very apt. Go on.

—Well, each prisoner has the key to the other's cell and
they only need to exchange and both would be free. She
stubbed her cigarette. —Have we?

—Yes, my girl, my dear grown-up girl, we have. But the
turn of the screw again is that I think we shall have little
chance to use them.

—Why not?

He turned. —Because I doubt that the six of us will stand
together. Being unanimously honorable, I doubt that we
can lie unanimously. One or more of us will admit everything at the examination and our case will collapse. We will

be arraigned and at the trial plead guilty, throwing ourselves upon the mercy of the court. The judge will show
lenience, taking into consideration our years and records:
we will get something approximating two-to-four-year terms.
A doctor convicted of a felony has his license to practice
revoked by the State Medical Board. He seemed to study
his forearms as though they were a patient's, not his own.
—I wish with all my heart I could promise we should walk
together hand-in-hand into the golden, mature sunset of the
last reel, but I can't. And the good deal about your being
grown-up finally is that I don't have to. Five days, he said,
five cursed days till the examination. I wish it were tomorrow. He sighed. —Janey, I'm whipped. To bed, to bed.
We've had a high-calory emotional meal. Let sleep knit up
the ravell'd digestive processes.

—Won't you even kiss me?

—No. Which should indicate how much I, in my turn,
in my strange, profound, perverted turn, love you.

She did not contend, but climbed the floating stair,
checked on Carol, and went to her room. Locking the door,
switching out the lights, he followed, disappearing into his.
They had separate baths as well as bedrooms.

Jane Reason brushed her teeth, disinterested, for once, in
her mirror's presentation. A man of that age and character,
a man like him, she thought, is the most complex, fascinating, mysterious, wonderful, weak, intricate, noble living
thing on earth. The hell with putting up my hair.

Charles Reason brushed his teeth. Ah, the female of the
species, he thought; during the transition period, when she
is no longer girl and not yet wholly woman, she is the most
inscrutable, awesome, delightful, nitwitted, logical, captivat-
ing, marvelous, unparalleled of all the living organisms. The
hell with pajamas, summer's here.

After opening his window and getting naked into bed,
however, he did put on his gloves, ordinary white cotton
work gloves, and pulled down about their wristlets broad
rubber bands so that he could not remove the gloves in his
sleep and scarify himself awake. Darkening the room he

recited to himself his nightly invocation: Now I lay me down to itch, a poor benighted son of a bitch; and if you die before your season, Old Scratch will have your soul, Charles Reason.

She came to him suddenly, on vagary's propulsion, wearing only a hip-length summer nightgown, and rushing into his bed, twining him in her arms, whispered that she would no longer listen, as she had in the past, to arguments about his age, cogent and contraceptive though they might be; there came a time when the heart's deductions must prevail; in short, no matter what each had done, no matter what dire augury ahead, she loved him dearly, madly, utterly, and she wanted his child. He teased her, inquiring if she desired a son named Felonious after his father, but she kissed him, kissed him well, and he, silenced, touched to that quick beyond fatigue, made exorable by gratitude, and roused, conquered by the dialectic of her lips, her warmth, her quicksilver youth, did sturdily as she wished, did gladly as his sympathy for her enjoined, so that there, in the expectant night, each locked the other into the vaster prison which is love.

With a parting kiss she left him for the other bed, saying she would sleep with him henceforth. She would not let him pull on his gloves again, but extending her arm took his hand in hers, promising to keep it fast till morning and thus prevent his torment.

When the even pulse of her breathing assured him that she slept, he pressed her hand, wondering at the paradoxes of its strength and pliancy, its firmness and resilience. This stuff, he thought, this living stuff, our skin: my wife's, a precious husk which holds my hostage now to the hereafter; my own, the scabbed, hairy, sensitive livery wherein I must fop out my alloted years; this living stuff, our skin: this envelope, so often misaddressed, so often dispatched into the world with insufficient postage; this enchanting gullet of ambrosial zephyrs and bad breath; this tender blossom, pistil and stamen, a casket of beauty prepared for us at birth; this Darwinian mucilage binding bone to spirit, divinity to bowels, exigeant vice to exigeant virtue; this costly wrapping in which, like finest Havana leaf, we puff ourselves away to perfect ash; this tactile boundary of our small cellular selves, puny, two-legged nations vociferous of our rights to life, liberty, and the pursuit of antibiotics, crying peace but strife-ridden ever, waging within our territories civil and corpuscular wars, putting down riots of the adrenals, having to choose eventually between anginal boom, thrombotic bust, and a riffraff host of kindred catastrophies or lento, cackling, geriatric decline and fall; this coat of mail impervious to jousting's lance yet blooded by the proboscis of a mosquito; this wind-sock according to which, during solo hours, we direct the tricky private craft of our consciences into landings sometimes lethal; this miracle fabric, Skinlon, by which our charms and monstrosities equally are girt, but which, advertisement to the contrary, wrinkles, takes much pressing, and attracts more mundane lint than we had known existed; this prose of flesh, a vulgate language all may speak but few may comprehend (the best way to explore the universe is to look through a telescope into someone's navel); this living stuff, a mortal, multicolored rind which, when removed at last, the fruit thereof we give the earth to eat. Lord, he prayed, if Thou art hungry, as indeed Thou damned well art, bless this food to Thy use, Amen.

Sewell and Morse rankle me not. I pity them.

Bernice, too.

I love my wife, and her daughter, and the child my wife and I may have this night conceived.

And my friends, those present, those unaccounted for.

I love men better than myself.

With this recognizance, delayed five decades, Charles Reason surprised himself into sleep.

William Vandevelde

Morse Baird was killed, or took his own life, the following night.

When Mrs. Scripter telephoned it was almost eleven, and Sewell would have ordered her to sober up and sack it off had not a single bell of cast-iron alarm sounded over the wire and clanged through her slurred speech: Morse was there, at her place, plaster'd, and threat'ning not to go through with it, not to show up as a witnuss, and worse, to run to the p'lice and tell the score and she didn' know what to do and he, Sew'l, had better get his tokus over. He did; only four days remained before the examination in Tyre and he could not chance at this late date any abortion by beer of his plans. They were down in the basement of the tabescent house on the Button, and his impression of the pair was that this place provided for them a perfectly natural habitat: trussed up in a wrapper featuring a pattern of Polynesian blooms splashed in wild Gauguin hues, the sprightly dame was ensconced at one end of the table on which empty beer bottles were arrayed like chessmen, while Morse, at the other end, was done out in blue jeans and a T-shirt flared at the belly, and sweat-stained, panting in the humid dankness and the drip of water from the system of pipes, they seemed rather like bait themselves, a brace of plump frogs succulent for pike. Sewell surmised that their evening's program had run on the order, roughly, of sex-fight-truce-beer-sex-fight-truce-beer, and that it was in the latter respite that they awaited his arrival. His first concern, however, was not for them.

—Where's Carlie?

—Upstairs. 'Ner room.

—Locked in?

—Yup.

—Can she hear us?

—Got 'er radio on.

—Now what the hell's the trouble?

—Ol' buddy, I'm not about to testify 'gainst Ris. Be the firs' admit it, prob'ly wouldn' even got through school without his brains, prob'ly wouldn' got where I am without Ris, the pluperfec' goddamn fool. But he's my brother, ol' buddy, an' I'm not about send 'im up the river. Morse swigged defiantly and pouched the cool glass under his T-shirt.

—Then don't. So you don't like money. I told you, it makes no difference whether you go on the stand or not. In this case it all boils down to whether the J.P. takes Carlie's word or theirs, and I'm betting on hers. At least enough to bind them for trial. That's what counts and they know it.

—Her word, shit.

—You shut your nasty mouth, there's ladies present, quoth the widow.

Morse glowered. —Not only won't testify, you go through with this an' I'll have a talk with the cops 'bout blackmail.

—Be a horse's ass, cut your own throat in the bargain, it still won't matter. The six of them will stand trial on rape charges unless they produce before then. Why don't you go home and sleep it off? This is the hard time for us, the next four days, waiting, but we have to sweat it out. C'mon, how about it, old buddy?

Checkmated, bewildered, Morse tugged at his forelock, lunged up, banged down the bottle and swaying across behind a minnow tank pawed away a cairn of cobwebs and wheeled the great black-and-rust Harley-Davidson into the open, reared a leg over the moldy saddle and yawed aboard.

—Halt! He threw up a hand and belched historically.

—Sewell, my ol' man still alive an' kicking an' L.V., too, everything'd be okay. They'd know move to make. Hell that is, Renis'd prob'ly got his nookie off Carlie himself, he was sure the type. He heeled the starter of the motorcycle, slapped in frustration at one of the handgrips. —This pile junk. Halt! Cause everything. I tell you, but for this pile junk an' the dumb, big-mouth, show-off rode it—

—Ooooo! cried the beldam. —Johnny was a shinin' man

an' you pups looked up to 'im like he was Chris' Almighty an' Dizzy Dean an' Robin Hood an', an U-lyssis, an' you had cause to jus' like I did!

—Aw right, aw right, Morse subsided. —Ol' buddy, bring me 'nother brew, ol' bag here won't.

—One more. On condition you go home then and sack out.

—Deal.

Sewell uncapped a bottle and handed it to him. Morse wiped the top with a grimy palm and drank. For a time he straddled the bike, blinking first at Sewell, then at the widow. —Lissen, team. He drank again. —Lissen. Blood's thickern 'n money. I got to save Ris an' don't know no other way. Got a prop'sition. Be the bes' way out for Carlie'n all of us. Figured it out myself, I can be pretty sharp I have to. What Carlie needs is get married some decen' guy. Then she's happy, respec'ble married woman an' we drop charges an' everything's hunky-dory. So I got jus' the guy marry 'er. Big break for the kid. Me. Miz Morse Baird. How 'bout that? Scripter get name of Baird, big name 'n this town.

Sewell was too surprised to say anything, but the proposition's effect on Ethel Scripter, even in her condition, could not have been more telling had Morse got down on one knee and asked formally for her daughter's hand. She gaped; fires started up in her broad cheeks; her eyelids fluttered, and when it seemed she might give the intensity of her feelings away, might allay vanity's hunger with a shower of genuine manna, she undredged herself hastily from her seat, treated herself to more refreshment from the whining refrigerator, lowered her backside once more and stared.

—You marry my girl.

—Sure. How gen'rous can a guy be? Carlie gets good name, you get son-in-law aroun' the house. Nice 'rangement, huh?

Sewell's assessment of this development was that he should stay out of it unless intercession were crucial; this was between them, a private rupture; what he had told her about Morse's intention to take off for Florida alone after the pay-off had evidently gone in one feminine ear and out the other, so that her shock, her betrayal now was femininely authentic. Warily he sat down on the edge of one of the concrete minnow tanks.

—You marry my baby.

—Why not?

—You're too old for 'er.

—Hell. Twenty years diff'rence is all, shy a year. What the hell, you're twenty years older'n me.

Mrs. Scripter lit a cigarette and spat tobacco. —I'll tell you the real reason, Morse Baird. You ain't good enough for my Carlie.

—What? For that lil' tramp? Ha! But good 'nough for you, huh? You jealous your own kid, Ethel? Baird not good 'nough for a Scripter? Lissen, she'd be lucky. I'd be the one get the shaft aroun' town, marryin' 'er. You think she's cherry or something? You think she took a goddamn corr's-pondence course 'n screwin'? They laughed when she sat down the back seat, but when she began play—ha!

—You shut up!

—Hell I will. She learned aw right, but right 'n 'er own home from two damn good teachers—her own ma an' 'er older sister! You raise a kid 'n a whorehouse she's gonna be a whore! I'm the one takin' short end this deal, I'm the boy tearin' down good name 'n rep'tation to save a damnfool kid brother!

She sucked on her cigarette, marshaling a termagancy which would summon the tide of insult to her favor. —She'd be lucky t' marry you.

—She sure would.

—An' get the Baird name.

—Oldes' name aroun' here, Ethel, ol' girl. Started this goddamn town with a goddamn mill.

—An' what's it come to? High-collar t'shirtsleeves 'n about four gen'rations. Your ol' man Renis was a heller 'n nearly went bust. Now your brother bags wheat 'n raises brats an you, you got a big whang 'n that's all. My girl Lene works there an' you dassent even go in the mill, you have to sneak up on one of them silos at night an' hide out like some cry-baby with 'is sugar teat took away! An' ol' Harlan Murning-han, he jus' keeps you on a payrool 'cause he's the soul of char'ty. I s'pose you told Sew'l here you're a big shot at the reel comp'ny—you know what he does, Sew'l? Packs reels in a box for seventy'five a week—that's what this Baird's amounted to!

Sewell's sentiments might lie, for friendship's sake, with Morse, beleaguered on the motorcycle, but he could also sympathize with the furious, kingfisher swoop of a woman, even an Ethel Scripter, scorned. He would remain aloof, would let them tire themselves with invective until he might step in as arbiter. In the depths of the tank fat shiners darted and rolled, their undersides gleaming; their subterranean, insensate relationships he would no more attempt to fathom or pass judgment on than that which roiled the murky air of the basement.

—An' you got the brass-ass gall t'talk about my Johnny! The diff'rence is, you brag an' he did!

—Sure, got himself full of bullets!

—Defendin' this town! An' he fought a war, too!

—Sure, in Texas!

—Well, he wasn't no 4-F slacker! What the hell you ever done or won, I'd jus' like t'know?

—Jane Murninghan, that's what! Beat everybody out!

—An' couldn' keep 'er! Give 'er up to Doc Reason, some-body with some class! Well, that's what Carlie'll have when we get the money, somebody with class! I wouldn' let you have 'er if you was to knock 'er up!

Flayed beyond his own pride's enduring, Morse slung his empty bottle against the side of a tank, shattering glass.

—You ol' town pump, I'll tell you what else! I ran the 440 in :50.8 sixteen years ago an' the high school's got the cup t'prove it an' that record's still on the books, oldes' record'n Class C comp'tition!

—Bein' the town pump's better'n bein' the handle! Class C's about your speed! Look at you—couldn't even keep in shape—all butt'n blubber—why, you couldn' run to the can if you was drownin' in your own piss!

293

—I could still do it!

—Shit you could!

—I could do it in 55 flat anyway!

—Flat's right! Flat on your gut!

—I'll show you! Morse bellowed, pitching himself off the Harley-Davidson so clumsily that the machine crashed over on its side. —55 flat! C'mon outside, time me!

—Morse, for Christ's sake, Sewell interjected. —Knock it off. You couldn't run a hundred in 55 and you know it. Now let's cut this comedy—

—Put up or shut up, both you! Morse staggered across the basement and stumbled up the stairs. —C'mon you ol' bitch!

—I will, so help me, I will! And Ethel Scripter followed him, slapping Sewell's restraining hand aside. —Only way t'show 'im up, Sew'l, so's he'll forget this crap about marryin' Carlie an' settle down t'bus'ness!

To Sewell, halfway up the outside stair behind her waddle, the thing made, suddenly, a kind of sense: let Morse fall on his face and disabuse himself of illusion and the crackpot scheme of wedding Carlie; let his aging queen have her triumph; then let the twain minister to hangovers for a day or two until the defendants-to-be capitulated, after which, so far as he was concerned, they might drink themselves into the stuporous bliss they so richly deserved. But if this methodology made sense, what ensued on street level did not. Confronted by his boast, neighbor now to the reality of the street and of his flesh, his lungs, his heavy legs, Morse posed objections almost fearful. —Well, how'n hell we going measure quarter mile? An' I got no startin' blocks, cost me two, three seconds anyways right there! Who's gonna time? Not that ol' witch! There was much commotion and pounding on fenders before matters could be settled. A city block measured roughly a hundred yards plus; Morse must run four of them, starting at the nearest corner, in fifty-five seconds. Sewell would send him by a horn blast, would then follow in his car with the widow and serve both as timer and driver. Mrs. Scripter, it was next ascertained, was physically unsuited to the Jaguar. Essaying entry, she became wedged between door hinge and windshield and combined efforts were required to free her from the roadster. They repaired to Morse's car. He could not locate his ignition key. They repaired to the widow's pick-up, which Sewell could not start. She took the wheel finally, and finally maledicted it to life. One headlight was out, but the other fixed upon Morse with a single bleary, inauspicious eye as the athlete staggered to the corner, knelt with fundament high, and nearly toppled to the pavement, inducing from his lady a harridan guffaw. Once again he knelt. Sewell removed his wrist watch and held the dial near the dashboard. As the sweep second hand neared the top of its arc he was puzzled by a sensation of regret. He sent Morse with the horn. He got away with surprising grace. Up the darkened street along the River Button, past doors and windows comatose and uncaring, swept the weird Olympiad, a race against time already expended, against thirty-three years already victor. Even under the impediment of blue jeans and sneakers, Morse ran the first block in a fine fourteen seconds, a white moth beneath the street light, a ghost flying from dark to dark as though to resolve the dilemma of its homelessness, the slamming of his rubber soles and the detonations of his breath audible over the archaic pick-up's coughing at his heels. Midway of the second hundred the runner dropped as though struck by a bullet. The vehicle might have run him down had Sewell not spun the steering wheel.

—What's matter'th him? asked Ethel Scripter.

—I don't know. He could be dead.

—Oh God.

—I've seen men fall that way.

Driver and timer sat motionless. —I had nothing to do with this, Sewell said carefully. —It was between you and him. He left the truck and squatting in its stare turned Morse over. Impact with blacktop had ribboned the Indian forelock with skin scrapings and fresh blood welled from lacerations of the chin and nose, yet the expression of the face was that of a boyish serenity, a repose between games. Saying nothing to the woman, Sewell walked to the nearest house, pounded patiently on the door until he was admitted, and asked that Dr. Reason be called, there'd been an accident. This done, he returned to the pick-up. —He's dead. Reason's on the way. When he gets here, let me do the talking.

—There was no wail of grief from Ethel Scripter, no sodden protest against loss. —Do I have to get out? I look a sight.

—No, stay inside. Turn off the engine.

She complied. —Don' I have the shittenes' luck with my men, though? He done it a-purpose so's he wouldn' have t'go t'court.

—What makes you think that?

—Why, he's had heart trouble. Kep' 'im out of the war. Couple times, when we was jus' finished with our fun, you know, lately, I seen 'im sort of pass out.

Sewell reached into the cab and pulled her head out the window as though it were an overripe Tahitian flower on a stem. —Goddamn you, he said slowly. —He was my friend. If you knew about his heart, why in hell did you let him run?

—I didn' know he'd die! she bawled laryngeally. Oh God, you think I'd kill the little I got lef'? And while Sewell waited on the running board she lapsed into inebriate maundering. —I was too ol' for 'im, he was right. He'd never of married me or took me to Floridey. I never ought to of come into Thebes off the farm, jus' stayed out there an' lived a wholesome, natur'l life. He was too ol' for Carlie, too. Poor Morsey, he didn't know what t'be but a Baird, an' he couldn', so he couldn' be nobody. Better for 'im this way. But I do have pee-poor luck with men. One damn tragidy after 'nother. Oh God, we need rain. I'm almos' out of crawlers.

Charles Reason arrived in Austin-Healey and sports attire, examined Morse, pronounced him dead, told the householder whom Sewell had roused to telephone Vergennes and have them come over for the body, then brusquely inquired the circumstances. Sewell was as terse as possible.

—Running the quarter-mile? That was intelligent. The

doctor tossed his bag into the car and took place beside it.
—Great God.
—He wanted to, Sewell said.
—Of course he did. With a ten-year history of atherosclerosis, hardening of the smaller arteries, chest pains, weakness, cold sweats, warnings from me—of course he wanted to. I'll certify natural causes, but I put it bluntly to you, Smith: you couldn't have been more effective with a rifle.

As he drove off, Sewell shouted after him. —Or with morphine sulphate!

When the Vergennes hearse had taken away the body, while the pick-up rattled them unfunereally back to her place, Ethel Scripter was rendered sober by a parallel so close as to seem consanguine. —Oh God, Sew'l, when he went down so sudden, like he was shot, who'd it make you think of? Who was you reminded of went down jus' that way? she gasped. —You know!

The race against time was run on Friday right. Services for Morse Baird were announced for the afternoon of the Monday following, two days before the examination in Tyre of those summoned by warrant.

Every command of instinct and training obliged Sewell to go more deeply into hiding, to take better cover, to look upon the rented house as an emplacement which must be held for four days against attacks sure to come: Other than sloppy appeals to dissuade him from his course similar to that made by Jane Reason, what form they might assume he could not guess, but from the edges of a situation where so much pressure had been now applied upon so many lives, where the time grew so short, something strange, perhaps violent, was bound to suppurate. It was like affixing adhesive tape tightly to flesh: thus artificially you could transfer stress from muscle to skin, itself a more delicate medium, but if the retransfer were not accomplished soon enough, the tape removed before blistering began, the effect he had learned could be more cruel, more grim, than the original cause.

297

He went downtown to stock up on enough groceries to last the seige. Outwardly Thebes seemed quiet, dinky, picturesque but wearisome as ever, but there was no way to hear what tumult hallooed on the other side of the tedium.

Saturday and Sunday he passed safely. He slept undisturbed. He went without shaving. Among his belongings was a packet of laudatory reviews of *Benison,* and these he reread with satisfaction.

He found himself able to write more than ten pages of the new book each day.

He planned. If, as he expected, the phone rang at any minute and it was Oram Kropf with a surrender offer from the six, a compromise, he would accept anything down to a hundred thousand, pay the old harpy, murderess, whatever she was, her half and decamp the hell out of Thebes forever. With fifty G's he could travel again, first class, to Europe perhaps—Paris or Zurich or Lisbon were quick choices—he could make of the novel a thing as fine as *Benison,* confounding the critics and reminting his name. If they did not fold, which was inconceivable, he would leave town the morning of the examination, Wednesday, head for New York with 150 pages of manuscript and see what could be swung in the way of a contract advance from some publisher, after which he would grind out the goddamn book there or on the Coast. The call, however, must certainly be made. He saw his position as impregnable, the case for the plaintiff, Carlene Scripter, as weakened only a little by the loss of Morse Baird's testimony.

For those two hermetic days he very successfully sealed himself off from any emotion more powerful than regret at Morse's passing and annoyance at its manner and untimeliness. He told himself that it had either been an accident, in which event there was no point to inculpating anyone or anything except the law of averages, or a pratfall, grandstand gesture of oblation, the handing over of self on a tarnished silver platter to Ris, in which event it capped meaninglessly a life without meaning. Rather than eclectic, Sewell's knowledge of other men, based as it had been on the asocial name-rank-and-serial-number herding of the barracks and the commercial come-and-go of his successful years, was as meager, as stunted as his knowledge of himself, but one axiom of conduct in human relationships he had made standard operating procedure: if you let yourself become involved in the concerns of others, if you accepted responsibility for their deeds or interests, you got your ass inevitably in a sling. In short, never volunteer. There was always vivid to his recollection the example of the Fossa Feminamorta. Volunteers to ride in the battle sleds had been called for, and not a goddamn dogface had been stupid enough to step forward, so someone cut cards and the poor bastards in 1st Platoon, Company F, had won and in the winning got themselves slaughtered. The moral was, when you sensed in advance that society, that great mindless paramilitary organization, had scheduled a sodomy for someone, why the hell bend over?

By Monday the self-imposed stockading got to him. He could not write. He roamed the house ill-temperedly, peering through the windows. There were but forty-eight hours to bear now before the examination, and if the old man, L. V., could wait thirteen years for the gun to go off, if that were true, he could stick two days. He went through his things, deciding what to take with him when he pulled out of Thebes and what to leave. The discovery of a single clean shirt gave him the idea of attending Morse's funeral, and this, dividing itself amoeba-like, produced a counterpart, that of using the race against time and the services as material for his book, making sure the reader got his money's worth in suicide, murder, tragedy, etc., as well as sex. Harris would be in church, of course, although the five elderly principals would be unlikely to mourn in person the elimination of a prosecution witness, but word would get around, and his public appearance, wholly confident, implacable, would be a sign to the five that they could neither outgut or outstay him, hence they had goddamn well better come to terms fast.

A half-hour before services he was shaved and dressed in the less rumpled of his two suits and pacing the downstairs when he answered the doorbell and admitted Arlene Scripter. She wore her white uniform, she had just walked out of the mill lab and, since she could not go to her mother, had come directly to him. The last block she had practically run. —This house, she said. —I've never been in it before. In high school no one would invite me into a house like this. Sewell gestured toward the living room but she refused, she preferred to stand there in the entry, her back against the door. —And just the other night, when you came to my apartment, I said, my little sister, I didn't even know her but I was glad she was only fourteen and too young to be in danger because soon I could talk to her and save her, didn't I? She was bewildered and distraught, and her irrelevance, the loss of that cool beauty of which events had dispossessed her, made him curiously sullen and edgy. She knew, she said. Edie Kropf had come to the lab this morning and told her everything, having just learned from Oram, her father, about Carlie and the men and Harris and her mother and Morse and him. She had been unable to work, even to think. She had arranged to go to the funeral but now, after this, she could not, it would be sacrilege for a Scripter to be there. All she could do was come to him and find out why, why.

The question, unintentionally melodramatic, irritated him. —You said it yourself. You were never invited here, you can't even go to the funeral of an old friend. Lene, in a couple days your mother and Carlie can buy the goddamn church. He recounted her mother's first appeal to him for justice on his return to Thebes, explaining that as the thing had spread, as more people had been indicted, he had seen a way to settle all kinds of old scores for her family: Johnny's sentencing to death by the town, if that was what it was, its maltreatment of his widow and daughter, and now the corruption of the last Scripter. —So it's simple. There's nothing in it for me but pleasure, pure lead-pipe pleasure. As for the town, whatever it gets it deserves.

—And the innocent, the families of these men?

—They didn't consider them, why in hell should I? Sewell

flared. —Don't give me a bad time, Lene. I haven't raped a fourteen-year-old kid.

—No, she laughed strangely, I was sixteen that day. You remember, in your car, with Morse and Harris. Sixteen! To his amazement she asked him to stop, to drop the charges or to persuade her mother to drop them. He owed her this debt. This was how he could repay her for what he had committed when she was a girl, friendless and bearing the brunt of the town's scorn. —Sewell, don't you understand that if you don't do this, it will be just as awful for my mother and sister and me as it was after Johnny? I can't live in Thebes, no one would ever forgive me, I can't be what I've been trying so desperately to be again all these years, I'll have to leave, and where will I go, what will I do? Sewell, I'm not asking a favor, I'm begging you for my life.

He sat down rigidly on a stairstep, jabbing a finger with each point. He advised her to get some things straight. One, it was out of his hands, it was a matter between six men and a statute. Two, in his opinion, her calling what she lived now in Thebes a life was a laugh. Having to leave would be the best break she ever had. Third, he had learned long ago, the hard way, to look out for himself, to leave people the hell alone because there was nothing you could do for them.

She closed her eyes, leaning more heavily against the door, and shook her head. No, it wasn't true, you could do everything, you could in fact give what she asked him for, a life, and as evidence she would tell him something no one in Thebes had ever guessed. During the war, after the annulment of her marriage to Harris, she had lived in Grand Rapids, working in a furniture plant converted to the mass production of transport gliders. There she had met Charles Baird, then a bachelor, a pathetic little popinjay of forty trying to break free of the image and servility imposed upon him by his dead brother Renis, to emerge into a character and manhood of his own. She sympathized with his struggle, she went out with him. He assaulted her, comically and in vain, for she was stronger than he. He later wept and explained; his only adult sexual experience had been arranged by Renis, who had supplied him periodically with a room in the Hamlind Hotel and a prostitute. With this absurd, hop-o'-my-thumb Casanova she had entered into and carried out an agreement: she became and remained his mistress for the two years of the war's duration, after which Charles Baird, true to his word, offered his nephew Harris employment at Thebes Milling. To this day Harris did not fathom his uncle's change of heart, did not realize that someone, she, had made it possible for him to be what he most wished, a miller, and to this day she was both ashamed and proud of what she had done. She had made so many mistakes. To herself she seemed sometimes like a girl taken away and used by enemy troops in wartime, used brutally, then released and forced to walk, head shaven, down the streets of a small and infernal world. —And it isn't over, I hoped and believed it was, but it isn't. What you started you've come back to repeat, in a more terrible way than before. Sewell, I don't really care about my mother and sister now, it's too late for them, but I care deeply about these men and their families even though they don't about me. All I have to offer is myself. You wanted me once, and the other night, too—very well, if you'll have the charges dropped I'll go away with you, anywhere, as long as you like, and sleep with you, and when you're tired of me I'll leave. And Sewell, I'll even tell you I love you. If that will make it easier for you, I'll say I love you as often as you want to hear it—

—Even! Love me! His roar forced open her eyes. —What the hell you think you are? What the good-all Christ have you got under your skirt that's so valuable—the crown jewels? Well you haven't—I've been there, remember, and I know!

His outburst astonished her. It was that of a man hurt profoundly, and furious at the revelation that he could be hurt. He had risen, backing up the steps, his face red, and he crouched, might have sprung at her had he not seemed leashed by the tie and collar constricting his thick neck.

—You put me on the same level as a small-town queer like Charlieboy Baird? This is Sewell Smith you're talking to, a bigger name than you've ever met in person or ever will again! No Scripter peddles her quiff to somebody like me—she gives it away!

His rage distracted and perplexed her. She studied him curiously. —I hurt you. I didn't mean to. How? By saying I'd lie about love? When what you need and can't have is the real thing?

—I don't need anyone or anything! he shouted.

—Sewell, Sewell. You said the other night no one has ever felt sorry for you. I do now. Not angry, but sorrier for you than for myself or my mother or sister. It must be like being dead in the midst of life, needing love and pity and being unable to create them in anyone except in books. Behind her back Arlene turned the doorknob and drew the door ajar. —I won't ask anything of you. I'll see my mother and try—

—You do that! You finally made it into this house and you've slutted it up long enough—now get the hell across the river where you belong—into the whorehouse with the other two bims!

The mendicant Jaguar begs and flaps along Ionian Avenue. On the wheel his palms perspire. His sensations are those of shock verging into fear at a vulnerability within himself which Arlene Scripter has exposed. As though unruddered, driverless, the roadster passes a small park. Innocent and elm-dight, its suggestions are of swinging, jacks, and jump rope, of childrens' joyances and laughter rather than of sins and old men's heats and a child's noctambulations. The car stops before the Congregational Church, white and modest. He enters. He is early. He is ushered to a seat. There is an embarrassment of flowers about the casket. On only one other occasion, he recalls, has Thebes raised to its defense such fragrant, legionary force. The church fills. Harris and Norma Baird and their children appear and are seated in a front pew. The organ, a long-ago gift of Harlan Murninghan, chords. He sits head-down. On either side people press against him. He curses his coming. A diffident

303

choir's requiem commences, the soprano not Carrie Murninghan's, the contralto not Catherine Smith's, the song a
simple hymn rather than a bedlam litany from a rooftop. A
minister takes the pulpit, a young man he does not know,
undistinguished of voice and feature, and prays. He announces then an obvious text, a secular theme for his remarks, the poem by A. E. Housman beginning "The lads in
their hundreds." Not a seat remains. Doors have been opened
so that the throng in the entry may hear. The minister in-
tones the poem's first stanza: "The lads in their hundreds
to Ludlow come in for the fair / There's men from the
barn and the forge and the mill and the fold / The lads for
the girls and the lads for the liquor are there / And there
with the rest are the lads that will never be old." From his
lips the anapaests blunder. Each of the remaining twelve
lines he pauses after, drudging out an explication of its
pertinence to the life of the deceased, so that in Sewell's
brain, the alternation of lines and contiguities with his own
espials and demurrers and remembrances becomes a wild,
threnodic recitative. "There's chaps from the town and the
field and the till and the cart." He sees the Murninghans,
doddering, majestic Harlan and his tiny, shriveled mate,
who would have to show for an ex-son-in-law. The town
stud is dead. Have you raised the hundred thousand yet,
old libertine? In the Theban pantheon, Morse is ranged
by the reverend beside another hero fleet of foot and renowned of exploit. "And many to count are the stalwart,
and many the brave." Think of Johnny, not of Morse. Jane
Reason is there, and her husband, Charles, physician and
student of morality, the means of murder, man's avarice,
and the tender pudenda of young girls. What said she when
you told your wife, physician? "And many the handsome of
face and the handsome of heart." The oaken pew is hard to
his spine. The tales Johnny told! Boys in their hearts cast
them in mock-Homeric verse, one especially, minstreled to
popping rifles and the thrumming of guitars! "And few that
will carry their looks or their truth to the grave." Nothing
about a beer belly. It was 1917, and Johnny, a sergeant in

charge of a God-forgot checkpoint along the Texas-Mexican border, had word that one of Villa's outlaw bands had raided nearby Big Spring, shot up the town fancy and done a lot of looting before tarantelling south again. "I wish one could know them, I wish there were tokens to tell." A little oofum-poofum now and then is cherished by the wisest men. Under these circumstances his orders were to pursue, capture, and return for trial, but his command amounted only to a dozen dumb-rah-rah-eastern-college-boy-National-Guard-cavalrymen who'd fed their horses wet hay and ballooned them up with colic. Nothing about winning Janey Murninghan, then losing her. "The fortunate fellows that now you can never discern." Why have they come, the Bairds, Charlieboy and Lillian? Veiled and tearful is the lady, becoming her black; grave and cancerous her natty little knave late of hotel rooms and orgasms balled by an elder brother. So, in lieu of animals, Johnny rounded up three Model T Fords in town and with much cranking and cursing and cheering and saber-brandishing, off they all bounced and rattled and honked across the border down into Chihuahua. Nothing about being robbed of his birthright and wrecking a goddamn avuncular dam. "And then one could talk with them friendly and wish them farewell." True: the oldest Class C track record extant is the :50.8 quarter-mile of Morse Baird for Thebes High set at the state meet in 1938. Not true: that he would have run it the other night in less than fifty-five seconds had he not encountered ticker trouble. Well, they Sheridaned the Mexican's trail and that night, after numerous stops for repairs to the Fords, caught up with the varmints at a rancho near Exquisita. Nothing about his packing reels in boxes in the Shipping Department at Twinriver Reel, subsisting on the crumbs of an old bass fisherman's commiseration. "And watch them depart on the way that they will not return." Nothing about a frightened boy of thirty-three hiding on a grain silo from the umbrae of his blood, the spooks of Carlos Sampter, Alfred, and Renis Baird. Leaving the cars and attacking the rancho on foot in pitch-dark, blasting Springfields in all directions, they had a grand old Fourth-of-July melee, without casualties, but dawn's early light disclosed the gol-darndest thing you could never guess: although they had captured the Mexicans' mounts, the outlaws themselves were vamoosed and so were the Model T's! Lo, the Vande-veldes, Bill and Dorth, bear of a man, cheerful elk of a woman, why in the name of God should they pass over Jordan where the grass is greener to bewail the quietus of the prosecution's only witness? "But now you may stare as you like and there's nothing to scan." He goggles. It is she, bawdy Diana, goddess of the hops, Pasiphaë to a Harley-Davidson, mammary Helen to the town's two heroes; podded out in purple silk, the legendary Ethel Scripter dares display a public grief, sniffs, snuffs, turns on the waterworks. Shame-faced, drag-tailed, Johnny's expedition rode for Texas on the exhausted nags, but lo, those dustdevils behind them, swirl-ing nigh! Nothing about a tragic fall from great sexual heights, from the virgin, honeyed embraces of an heiress to buttocky clipping in a basement. I am not responsible. "And brushing your elbow unguessed-at and not to be told." Finally, Edie Kropf and her father, Oram. It is too much. Blind Boulevardier of Ionian Avenue, you have fewer than forty-eight hours to unstoic thyself and thy disciples, to get them off their autocratic asses and to the State Bank of Thebes or slug the statutory hemlock! To their everlasting flabber-gastment it was the Mexicans a-chase in the flivvers, honking and shooting and cheering *"Vivan los automoviles! Vivan los productos mechanicos d'Estados Unidos!"* The tape has hands. They grip his hips. His flesh crawls. His back throbs. I am not responsible. "They carry back bright to the coiner the mintage of man." For you the lie of love will do. It must be like being dead in the midst of life. Only because the Fords one by one foundered with lame axles and boiled-out radiators were the Americans able to reach Big Spring safely, and only because Sergeant Scripter failed to report the inci-dent was the first wholly mechanized cavalry operation in history to this day unrecorded and unhallowed. Jesus to Genoa, Johnny, what a story! Halt! Was it true? On a stack of Bibles, before the green and springtime souls of three boys, will you swear it, Johnny? I am not responsible! "The lads that will die in their glory and never be old." He groans aloud. He seizes the top of the pew before him and hauls himself to his feet. He trips over the knees of other mourners. He stumbles down the aisle. The nave murmurs. The service waits. He churls into the entry, shouldering a rude, apostate way through the press and out the door. Reaching his car he drops heavily into it, starts the engine, backs from the curb, pulls ahead, stops in the street, and there beside the church, beside the park, in the pious hush of afternoon floorboards the accelerator. Sirening higher and higher, ripping into the elm leaves, invading profanely the sanctuary, the sound of the Jaguar drills, becoming, not as he intends, a blasphemous hurrah for the hero, a gage of warning to the town, but that of a demented woman's screaming. Men with wrathy faces run from the church toward him, and seeing them he engages gears and careens the roadster away as though in a race, tires eructing smoke.

Had he been able to sleep he would still have heard the attempt to gain entrance to the house, so like the incautious scurryings of a squirrel were the footsteps on the front porch, so brash the trying of the door, and being fully wakened, even grimly diverted by the ineptitude of the thing, he waited until whoever it was left the porch and going to the window watched whoever it was move round the house to the side door and then he was no longer diverted. The figure trying this door was female; in one hand a gun glinted. Unsuccessful at the second door she vanished just as he remembered he had not locked the garage. His heart valved. He was alarmed not by the weapon but by the clumsiness, the noisy signs of aberration which certified she would use it. The garage door clicked. She could enter now by the kitchen. He reached for the telephone book and on bare feet slipped into a corner of the entry hall, pulling the French door in front of him as cover. Whoever it was crossed the kitchen, the dining room, stalking him, then passed, and on a three-count he lobbed the telephone book across the entry to thud against walnut paneling. It was a trick you learned in house-to-house fighting. Whoever it was started, wheeled, and in reflex fired at the sound, and in the gun flash and report and splinter of walnut he was upon her from behind, her arms vised in his. Doubling her hand back upon its wrist had to be done quickly, for her strength was inordinate and he could not long trust his back, but she gasped in pain and let go and he shoved her headlong, retrieved the weapon and switched on the chandelier. It was Edie Kropf. The gun was an old .45 Army automatic.

He sat on the stairs, ejected the clip from the butt, lobbed the gun back so that it struck her leg, and swore at her for a moment with a calm maleficence until he saw that she could not hear. He would not have believed Edie Kropf, the spinster who by her own confession could run a linotype, change a flat, business-manage a newspaper, and arrange a rational sex life, capable of hysteria. She sprawled on the carpet, her angular body writhing, her sharp face an ugly cosmetic smear, her hornrims pushed up on her forehead, and with birdlike shrillings and dry sobs she mixed a kind of manic chant, snatches of which were intelligible and interesting enough to cause him to listen carefully. Where was Arlene? Dear, dumb, haunted Morse dead. What had happened to her friend? Could anyone imagine what it was like to love a man for eleven years and never to sleep with him and then to lose him to an unjust law? The gun. She had warned him that if he hurt her town she would kill him herself. Her father had told her this morning. Not to confide in someone had been impossible. Arlene had not returned to the lab, was not in her apartment, either. About himself and Carlene Scripter and Charles Reason and Harlan Murninghan and Charles Baird and Harris and Bill, her own Bill Van. She had not even known where to find a gun, driving the hills for hours, then recalling Bill kept a World War I pistol in his locker at the Creel & Cartridge. By killing him she could have saved them all, saved Thebes itself. He was fifty, she twenty-six. This was in 1943, when they had fallen inexplicably in love and had not known what to do. It was decided, after some months, that he should divorce Dorth. What had he done to Arlene? How much more could that poor creature be expected to bear because she was a Scripter? She had gone to her father, Oram, and he, concerned more for the public weal than for his own flesh and blood, had not only refused consent but threatened retribution. To him the town's placidity meant more than the happiness of a middle-aged Superintendent of Schools and his old-maid paramour. How sickening at the church, when he had rushed out and with Hollywood gall desecrated his friend's last rites! Should they marry, the School Board would have Bill's job, and see, moreover, that he did not obtain another easily. What had become of Arlene? So, for eleven years they had kissed only, an incredible feat, had shared a kind of mental marriage in which each sacrificed himself for the other. How many more besides Morse, her father, her best friend, herself, would he pull down into darkness with him? Why should she not tell now, when nothing mattered, with the examination only hours away, when all the abnegation and control and denial had been turned into an empty joke flung from a foul mouth?

—Why don't you shave your legs?

He thought with this query to sting her to lucidity. He was tired, and so hackneyed and rural was her story of star-crossed, loin-clogged, back-road passions that it bored him. Turn over any rotten log in a small town, it seemed, and something trivial and slimy crawled out. He could conceive of no way to use it in *Silence* except as a kind of footnote in futility. She continued to weep.

He tried again. —Morse would lay anything.

When this, too, was ineffective, he stepped over, held her up by one shoulder, and cuffed her with the flat of his hand as one might a drunk or a froward child. The blow sent her hornrims flying. She blinked at him and fumbled in a pocket of her skirt.

—Now pick up your toys and go home, Edie.

She blew her nose. —Where's Arlene?

—How should I know? She was here before the funeral, she gave me a song-and-dance, she took off.

Edie Kropf squinted, located her glasses, and the act of putting them on seemed to furnish, as though out of a compact, that gloss of asperity with which she ordinarily coated herself. —I heard you. About my legs and Morse. She looked into the living room. —Let me see what lives here. My Lord, look at this. Some kind of animal that dirties its own nest. Ugh. Returning, she shook her head. —Once I saw Earl Blue shoot a mad dog which had to be put out of its misery before it bit someone. Pardon my language, but you pathetic, inhuman son of a bitch. I wish I could have done as much for you.

—Sure, I'm a real masterbastard. Except that I don't break and enter in the night. I don't try to kill anyone. I don't wreck happy homes. And I don't rape kids in the eighth grade.

She bit her lip. —I'm not going to cry again, not good old Edie Kropf, town cynic and Democrat. I wanted very much to shoot you—you need it, and your life isn't worth the little finger of any one of these men you're close to destroying. She stooped and picked up the automatic. —The slowest draw in town, but the fastest tongue. Very well. I want to hurt you some way before I go. I'm not sure it's possible, but even a brute will bleed if you beat it hard enough. Just because my father and the others have, I see no reason to protect you any longer. I said you were pathetic. There must be a lot more to the heredity thing than I realized. In your case, I blamed it on environment, but now I think you can't help being what you are. Not the son of a father like yours.

Edie Kropf could not expect, not having been present, that this reference to his father would produce in Sewell a reaction as pervading as that worked upon by him by Arlene's tender of a lie of love, but where that had been one of fury, this new display was one of agitation, of unhinging, almost of terror. Again, as before, he backed up the stairs.

—You don't know anything. I don't care what they say. And they told me they'd never said anything.

—What are you talking about?

—Nothing's been proved! He's dead and it's just their word. They had something to hide!

She stared at him blankly as he barked at her, in dirty T-shirt and undershorts, bare and bandy-legged, more ludicrous than menacing. —I do know, she said, sensing a triumph. —Everyone in town my age or older knew, including your mother. What do you suppose drove her out of her mind—the weather or her time of life? Edie Kropf came to the foot of the stairs, causing him to retreat beyond the lower landing. —Why, you really don't know, do you? No one's ever had the nerve to give you the word, have they? Oh, this is great, this is perfect! She paused to savor the sight of him hunched above her, peering through the balustrade like a youngster about to be punished. With his fingers he seemed to be shucking the unfired cartridges from the pistol clip.

—You leave me alone! he ordered.

—Gladly, gladly! But before I do, you hear this, celebrity, war hero, pathetic son of a bitch! After Johnny Scripter was gone, who did all the men in town put up for first prize in the sexual raffle? You remember, his widow of course! The immortal Ethel! But who had the brass to buy all the tickets? Who won? Who set her up in the bait business? Who took her to bed practically in plain sight of the world for over a year? You guessed it! That paragon, that pillar, member of the Council, the School Board, Vice-President of the bank—your little masterlover of a father!

Her voice grated through the house. She waited for response from him but there was none, and so shielded by the balustrade was he that she could not see his face. She waved the sterile weapon happily at him. —I didn't shoot you and I'm glad. This was so much better. Now, friend, I'll leave you more alone than you've ever been in your life.

After she had gone he sat a long time on the stairs, clutching the loose cartridges as might a schoolboy a handful of stones or marbles. He did not yet believe, he would not yet accept the literality of Edie Kropf's impeachment. To love-lorn ravings, to the sour spilt milk of spinsterhood, to any frontal assault he was in fact impervious as the massive door of a vault. What she had achieved was flanking, more subtle, the subliminal opening at the rear of that box in which the past was deposited for safety from the embezzling conscious, so that now, sitting there almost in hiding from himself, he could, by studying its contents, identify his mother's deed and assign it import. L.V. had that spring evening driven home without any pre-announcement a new 1937 Buick sedan. During the night Sewell was wakened by his father, who was dressed, and told to come downstairs. He had called Stormy at his house, and asked him as a favor to open up the repair shop so that he might bring the car in at once, at four in the morning, before anyone on the street could witness its condition. Father and son walked round the automobile. Catherine Hogg, that stranger with whom they dwelt, had evidently labored half the night with chisel, chipping down through new finish to raw metal to inscribe upon the four door panels of the gleaming blue sedan four fierce verses, one each from Proverbs, Matthew, Psalms, and Ecclesiastes. These were to this night, sixteen years later, etched in the raw metal of her son's nature, but only at this moment, as he crouched behind the rail, was he capable of their exegesis. She had known. Charles Reason had surmised correctly. She had lived long with theft's dagger at her breast. "Charles, a man has the guts to do anything he wants." She had also known, or had just learned, about Ethel Scripter. "The three most important organs of a man's body are his mind, his penis, and his pocketbook." Slowly he pulled himself erect and let himself down the stairs. By means of the light cast into the living room from the chandelier there appeared upon the pane of one of the three wide windows an ectype not of himself but of that man who, gambling his genes and begetting a son, must now, with truth's terrible iteration, undergo at his hands a different death. "Put a knife to thy throat," Sewell said, "if thou be a man given to appetite," and taking a single cartridge he hurled it at the pane with all his might. As the image vanished in shatter, as he moved further into the room and another took shape, he threw a second time, saying loudly: "My house shall be called the house of prayer; but ye have made it a den of thieves." At the third window, at the instant of impact, his quotation was that which she had hand-lettered upon the right rear door of the car: "Mark the perfect man, and behold the upright!" Stumbling over the trashy strong-point no longer defensible he rose to find a final adumbration in the window of the dining room and shouting hoarsely sprayed the remainder of his ammunition: "A bird of the air shall carry the voice, and that which hath wings shall tell the matter!" And with this parricide in glass, so like the taxings graven on steel tablets by his mother, reduplicating too the ruin by which a wretched girl in Arizona had signified deliverance from him, Sewell Smith believed himself at last enfranchised of his father. He was not; he had but entered upon a new and vaster tendance as steward to other men.

For dinner they had baked ham and in culinary paean to summer their first potato salad and corn on the cob, besides hot rolls and a salad of fruit. Dorth had also made a fresh rhubarb pie, but this they renounced, she because she worried about her weight, and Bill, although he never put on a pound, because his abstinence made hers easier to suffer. Then, while they were having coffee, facing each other across the kitchen table, two hefty, healthy, unperjured people, Bill Van, without exordium of any kind, told his wife almost everything. He had put it off because he was so blasted ashamed and in order to spare her as long as possible; and now that he had got the hook out of his eye he was going outdoors for a while, he could not bear to look at her, and besides, it would be nonsensical of them not to collect their thoughts before they spoke of it again. Oh, yes, she had never baked a better ham and in twenty-five years of marriage he had never loved her more.

So saying, Bill Van went outdoors, wheeled the hand mower from the garage and commenced to mow his lawn. It was not quite seven o'clock and there was ample light even though the back yard of the small white-shingled house was dusked by pines so princely that he could cut beneath them without bending. Up and down he strode, his swaths geometric, congratulating himself on the absence of crab grass and theorizing it must have something to do with the drought. He stopped to sniff the air: the woodsman in him prognosticated rain, and when it rained and Parnell Creek up by Cannonsburg was coffee-colored he would get bait at the Widow Scripter's and have a crack at the German Browns, using a spinner. Then he remembered noting the daubed sign at the Widow's, "No Crawlers," and remembered, too, that he could not go there and he sighed, a long Daedalian sigh out of an artless man.

Time has treated the Superintendent of Schools handsomely. At sixty-one, due to retire at sixty-two to an outdoor life and the highest regard of the taxpayers, he was yet a prime specimen, broad-shouldered, waist dependable as a rifle stock, eyes crow-sharp, his short hair a pelt of the best gray, a handshake like a trap, and so sanguine was his temperament and metabolism that he still walked the mile to his office daily, even in blizzards, sans overcoat. Fortune has used him as cheerfully. Graduated from Ypsilanti Normal in 1914, he taught two years, enlisted in the Marines, stalked and slew a young Hun in Belleau Wood (discovering in himself a rapture in killing which he has never revealed, even to Dorth), sailed home to become Principal at L'Anse in the Upper Peninsula, where he bagged deer, bear, and the bobcat couchant on his mantel, in 1928 came to Thebes as Principal and was made Superintendent in 1935, when Adam Wingeier retired. If he has faced a few crises professionally, he has had for twenty years a Board of friends tried and true behind him; if not a big winner at cards, he has been philosophical about his small losses and been dubbed by Oram Kropf "The Henry David Thoreau of Draw Poker." If married late, he married lucky. If comparatively inarticulate, he is nevertheless a past President of the State Superintendents Association and has lobbied successfully in Lansing.

If he has never outgrown an antipathy to the Republican Party, thanks to a flyer on margin just prior to the crash, he has been able, thanks to the Australian ballot, to vote straight Democratic in every subsequent election (another secret he has not shared with Dorth), to keep his apostasy, except for one confidant of similar persuasion, to himself. If he has not kept up over the years the reading, cultural or academic, expected of a public school administrator, no one is the wiser but he and Dorth and the television antenna sovereign as an oil rig on their rooftop. If his only commencement address, entitled "The Greener Grass" and plagiarized honestly from that old chestnut called "Acres of Diamonds," has been yawned through by almost every graduating class in eighteen counties for eighteen years, repetition has not dulled sincerity. If, when he was fifty, a flower budded in his Netherland soil and has there bloomed ever since, gentling the hunter, confusing the husband, father and citizen, it has been both a surprise of beauty and a fardel of which the years, by themselves, have gradually relieved him. He ceased to mow. He stood for a moment, sturdy in T-shirt and Army suntans and moccasins and muscles, reflecting. If nothing was as good for the bowels as a thorough purging, it followed that nothing would be as good for the spirit. Reflecting so, willing soldier still, Bill Van marched dutifully into the kitchen.

Let them, he said to Dorth, have the rhubarb pie after all, and another cup of coffee. And while she served them and they ate he told her about himself and Edith Kropf, omitting nothing, shaking his head at what must seem as unbelievable to her as it did to him, but which he would swear to: that an eleven-year relationship had never gone, physically, beyond a kiss and an embrace. The pie was summer in the mouth. And here was another singular thing: it was this very continence, crazy, he supposed, but also laudable and somehow like a poem, which had kept the candle flickering for a decade, he saw now, because after the Scripter girl, after the dikes of frustration were washed away in a salt flood of sin, he had stopped loving Edie Kropf, had not loved her for months, and pitying her, had yet found no way to tell her so. He lit his pipe. Could she, Dorth, understand how this could be? But before she could do more than nod dumbly, embarrassment and shame propelled Bill once more from the table and out the door.

His wife remained at table a while, her pie untasted, at fifty-five a strapping, apple-cheeked, slap-you-on-the-back Rotary-Ann with moon face, smile inlaid with silver, straight gray hair molded to her head like a helmet, and not until a single tear's loud plop into her coffee smote her ears could she rouse herself to do the dishes. She moved about in a kitchen suddenly become a world she had never made, leaving the dishes, returning to them, doing odd chores which did not need doing.

Dorth dotes on risqué jokes, bangs a rag-time piano, and is the life of a party.

She watered the ivy twining from a wine bottle on her window sill.

Dorothy Ritzema graduated from Kalamazoo College, taught Phys Ed and Domestic Science at Naxos High, fretted she would never marry, then just bemoaning thirty met William Vandevelde at a district Michigan Education Association meeting. On their wedding night in June twenty-five years ago, in an old resort hotel in Benton Harbor, on the Lake Michigan shore, the most uproarious episode of their life occurred.

She watched him steam up and down the back yard behind the mower as virtuously as a canal boat, piping smoke, and watching, not thinking, scraped her wedge of pie down the disposer.

They discovered forthwith that their sex life would be fine and ardent and gymnastic, and in that first glad grappling, a happy hurly-burly like two untrained bears a-dance, so heedless and fettlesome was their last Elysian lunge that it burst the bed from its legs and hurtled springs, mattress and newlyweds to the wooden floor with such a bombination as to bring guests, staff and management running, while even Lake Michigan foamed up the beach in skittish tides.

Dorth removed the lint-catcher from her automatic washer and removed the lint from the lint-catcher. Upon her husband and their son, Ronnie, a graduate of Michigan State, a radarman serving at the Anacostia Naval Air Station near Washington, upon his wife and their new baby as upon her appliances she lavishes a love as opulent as her bosom. It is as difficult for her to comprehend the fact of grandmotherhood as the fact of statutory rape. She claims never to have had a sick day, she thrives on the out-of-doors, she can skin game, clean fish, and the best time of each year to her is that week in November when she accompanies Bill and three of his pals north to a cabin near L'Anse for deer-hunting.

With cleanser Dorth scours and rescours a pristine sink.

There she cooks for them and keeps the cabin clean and strays the snow-pranked woods in red wool and at night plays cards with them and then beds down under fur, sealing her smelly, bearded mate to her warmth as does a cast-iron stove a soapstone.

Overwhelmed, woebegone, no longer a creature of infinite and matchless risibility, Dorth glanced up in dread. Here Bill came again! *God zij met ons,* what now?

He had, he said, getting a molar grip on his pipe, one last thing to avow, and while it was something of which he was proud rather than ashamed, its effects would settle heavily on them. The six involved had all along been of one mind not to compound felony by turning over funds to young Smith or the girl's mother, but this afternoon, at their last meeting, he had divulged his intention to tell the truth, to admit under oath to being guilty of relations with the girl and to accept, as a good stoic should, the consequences. This of course broke their ranks and made mincemeat of any possible defense, but it seemed to him that lying was also compounding evil, and the superintendent of a school system could not be a liar. He told them he was sorry, but his old friends, bless them, had neither reproached nor sought to dissuade him even though they knew full well his option meant prison for them all, as he hoped she would not, and there, that was everything.

—I meant to tell you before, Dorth said. —I knew a long time ago about Edith and you. Seven years, I guess it's been.

—You did? Holy Toledo.

—Yes. And you'd never imagine who told me. Poor thing, she had no friends here, and still doesn't, but can you believe it, trying to make one by telling a woman her husband was seeing another woman? I never said anything, I just waited. Poor, flighty, unhappy thing. Lillian Baird.

—Oh, he said. —Is the movie at nine?

—Yes, nine.

—Then I've got time before dark to water. It's thunderation dry.

—Shall I make popcorn?

He nodded absently on his way out, thinking as he wheeled away the mower and pulled the sprinkler to a corner of the lawn and turned it on, I've handled this badly, like a kid caught in the cookie jar, piling one thing on top of another, and I should know by now she adapts slowly, bit by bit, and she was just now coming to terms with herself about Edie and me so that pleading guilty at the examination day after tomorrow and prison and all that nasty business went right over her head. It will knock her off her pins later, and I damn well better be ready to help. He stood at parade rest under a pine as twilight stepped in dainty and shy as a doe and her fawn to drink. Dorth was a magnificent girl. He did not deserve her. To know about himself and Edie for seven years and not to say a word. He moved the sprinkler. The fan of water played with dulcet infallibility back and forth, back and forth, a comfort to his senses. I don't feel sixty-one. Dorth was his rock, his right arm, his rib. It was dark. Whistling "The Dutch company is the best company, that ever came over from old Germany," he turned off the sprinkler and entered the house.

After the felicity of their years together in Thebes, their son, their grandson, their friends, their health, the greatest boon life had bestowed upon Bill and Dorth Vandevelde was television. They were among the first to buy a set and to install the towering antenna necessary for reception of the

318

Grand Rapids channels; they watched several hours of programming nightly, attending to quiz shows and situation comedies and variety shows with equal concentration, their only appeasement either of conscience or public opinion the drawing of the living-room window shades. Their favorite viewing was the old movie sponsored twice weekly by a jolly Grand Rapids used-car dealer whose sales pseudonym was "The Good Patroon," and to this Dorth, having drawn the shades and seated herself on the davenport with a large bowl of popcorn, had already tuned in when Bill joined her, removed his moccasins with a grunt, put his feet up on the hassock, and reached into the bowl. This evening's stellar, first-run presentation was "Man Against the Bad Men," starring Johnny Mack Brown.

—I don't care what happens in court, Dorth said. —No one will ever make me believe it was any of your doing.

Bill understood that her reference was to Carlene Scripter, not to Edie, that she was considering his disclosures in their original sequence, point by point, and in this feminine, self-rising manner attempting to regain a tranquillity recollected in emotion.

—It was and it wasn't. A teacher, an administrator, over the years has lots of temptations. You know, girls in trouble of one kind or another, and they come to you hoping you'll get them out of it and hinting if you will they'll be nice to you. Mostly they're not serious, but Dorth, I've never walked into a buzzsaw like this. She was caught passing a note to an older boy, a senior, and sent to me. It was this last February, late in the afternoon, everyone gone, in my office. I've never read such a piece of filth as that note. She'd evidently tripped the light fantastic with the boy and was proposing more. I intended to call her mother and suspend her for a week or two. Bill crunched in abhorrence on an unpopped kernel. —I shouldn't tell you what she did. It's too disgusting, and it doesn't excuse me, not one whit.

—What?

—It's not fit to hear.

—Bill, you tell me!

319

—Well, I was standing beside my desk, and she came close to me and rubbed herself against me. And then—it was terrible—she opened my fly and put her hand inside. It happened so quickly, I didn't know what I was doing. She was so nervy and cheap-John, well, it excited me. And Dorth, that isn't all. I was weak, I arranged for her to come to the office late two other times. No fool like an old fool.

—I've been thinking. Bill, I'm to blame, really, for Edie and the girl. I've had it on my mind for so long, you just have to listen to me, Dorth implored. —I've been a millstone around your neck, I've tied you down to Thebes, I've kept you in a rut of TV and cribbage and hunting and fishing and not reading or improving yourself, when if I'd encouraged you and improved my own mind and made you get your Master's summers and maybe even your Doctor's you'd be head of a big-city system by now, a famous educator, and none of this would have happened.

—My dear, my dear.

—No, it's true, she insisted stoutly, I haven't been the wife I should. A vegetable, a turnip, playing the piano and getting fat, and the more I realized I was holding you back, the more I ate, and the more I ate, the fatter and lazier I got, and you never put on a pound. All this time I've reckoned why Edie Kropf appealed to you and the other way, because she's an intellectual and you were starved for intellectual discussion —and of course she found the same thing in you, a mind that only needed whetting, which she could do. Oh, you were perfectly matched—no wonder you loved her!

—Dorth, poop. Do you know why nothing ever came of Edie and me? Or'm threatened to have my job when she told him about us, if we got married, but that wasn't the real reason. If we'd wanted to enough, that wouldn't have stopped us.

—Then why? I'd have done anything you wanted.

—Because. In the first place, I was too old for her, we both had to face that. You forget, old lady, I'm a grandfather, I do too sometimes. Second, because I think Edie saw, after a time, that I was just the opposite of what she wanted to believe me—no intellectual or scholar, not ambitious at all, but a simple gink, a shoes-off man of pretty narrow interests who never cared a tinker's damn to be anything more than what he was. A small-town superintendent. And content to be so. Third, my dear, if I loved Edie at first, and I admit honestly I had an itch or something, what I had for you all along was much more strong and permanent and substantial. Something a lot better than love. Something to live with. And she must have guessed that also. No, Edie's the one we should feel sorry for, not ourselves.

—Oh. I am, too. Poor lonely thing, she hasn't anyone and I have.

The Good Patroon was extolling the merits of a low-mileage 1953 Mercury.

—Let's take a bladder break, Bill said.

—Shall I make another popper?

—Why not? At the hall door he turned. —And you are not too fat, woman. Holy Toledo. You're just right. He turned again. —And I like TV a damn sight better than the *MEA Journal* and from now on we aren't going to pull the shades.

He was seated again before she had buttered the new popperful and he thought well, so far, so good, she has absorbed two of the three bumps I've given her tonight, the Scripter thing and Edie, without much damage, but she isn't indestructible, no one is, and soon the last one, the .12-gauge, is going to hit her. I wonder if there isn't some way I can get her ready for it.

Dorth brought in the fresh bowl and "Man Against the Bad Men" had resumed.

—I was wondering, Bill said, the other day, why a rotten thing like this should happen to the five of us so late in life, just when we're so close to sitting back and picking the fruits. It's wages for sin, I expect, with the girl, and rightful, but as far as I know it's the only one we've committed. And it's pretty rotten to have your reputation and good works go down the drain because of one misstep.

321

—And not really your fault either, Dorth seconded loyally. —Not with a girl as smutty as that. I'd like to get her over my knee, I tell you, I'd hot her pants up for her.

—Then I thought, no, it isn't her at all, it's what we've been in Thebes, Harlan and I and Or'm and the two Charles's, and before us Renis and L.V. and Claude. Do you know what we've been? An oligarchy.

—A what?

—I was sure there was a word for it, so I looked it up in the dictionary. "Oligarchy: a form of government in which the power is vested in a few," he quoted with satisfaction. —Well, a few of us have had the power here for a long time, and maybe it was wrong. The town's best interests we've always put before our own, but still, maybe we should have served our terms and bowed out long ago.

Dorth looked him square in the eye. —Don't you say that, Bill Vandevelde. Who'd have done a better job? Name somebody. Who'd have been fairer and squarer and worked harder? Doughtily she thrust a handful of popcorn at him. —You've been upright, wonderful servants, all of you, and Thebes wouldn't be what it is today if it hadn't been for you. If everybody didn't know that, would they have voted for you time after time?

The Good Patroon was selling a 1949 Olds station wagon at no money down and thirty-six months to pay.

—I'll step outside a minute, Bill said, and doing so, standing on the porch in his stocking feet thought there, it worked, she has her hackles up and I pray to God she will forget about day after tomorrow until at least tomorrow. He sniffed at the stars and again, despite the butter and salt rimming his nostrils, intuited rain.

It was not, however, to be. Dorth, dear Dorth, seemed not to watch the film at all: her look was glued above the set where, upon the mantel, skulked that taxidermic symbol of nature's indifference to man's fortunes, Bill's mangy bobcat, its ruff and stubby tail rampant, its baleful, vitreous eye fixing hers. Hers, not his, fell. Her cheeks ripened.

—Bill, do you have to tell the truth?

—Dorth, I do. You know I do. And so will the others when their time comes, they can't help it.

—And will you really go to prison?

—I'm afraid so.

Her lip quivered. —Then I'll be alone, won't I, and what will I do? Oh, Bill, Bill!

They held each other close on the davenport, overturning the popcorn bowl, swaying together in consolatory exercise. About them dire winds galed and tall pines seemed to topple. She asked how long his sentence might be, and his guess was four years, which, with time off for the behavior to be expected of a public school superintendent, might shorten itself to two. What should she do? Sell the house and leave Thebes? By no means, this was their home, she must stay and care for it against his return, she could hire a boy to mow and tend the lawn. Loneliness assailed her, and over his shoulder, as she blinked aghast through tears, there seemed to take place upon the screen a devilish denouement to "Man Against the Bad Men." Would she have any friends? Of course she would; all the families would be in the same boat; they could be company to one another, she and Carrie Murninghan and Edie and Jane Reason and Lillian and Norma Baird. He had thought it through carefully; living alone, her expenses would be less and she would be financially secure. His salary would end, of course, but they owned the house free and clear, he would convert his life insurance so that it began to pay monthly at sixty-two. He had called the State Retirement Board in Lansing, and the commission of a felony would not nullify his right to a pension of two hundred a month, again beginning next year. Moreover, they had a savings account and twenty-two thousand in school bonds, which would bring her close to nine hundred a year tax-free. And over the long haul they were in grand shape, because at sixty-five a little Social Security would commence. Dorth heard him not. In the last scene of the film, goodness perished and evil triumphed in a mad theodicy, a topsy-turvification of character and formula as The Good Patroon corporealized smiling over the hood of a 1951 Chevy.

Dorth burst from the cradle endlessly rocking of her husband's big arms and snapped off the set as though it were tuned to hell's channel itself and seizing the bowl bent to clear the floor of popcorn. On hands and knees they worked together. When finished, Bill suggested they hit the hay. She asked if he were hungry and he, pondering, replied he could eat a bite. They went silently into the kitchen and Dorth made them sandwiches of the baked ham and her own bread and cups of instant coffee and they sat across the small table from each other masticating silently.

—Dorth.

—Yes.

—I voted for Roosevelt in 1932 and I've voted Democratic in every national election since. And from now on I'm going to admit it.

—Oh. All right.

Through the screened window came the dry tremolo scraping from the trees of the season's first cicadas.

—And Dorth. In the war, when we were fighting in Belleau Wood, I shot a German boy who couldn't have been more than eighteen. This was what I was supposed to do, kill the Huns, and he would have shot me if I hadn't seen him first, I know that, but one thing has pestered me ever since. Maybe I should have been sorry, the way soldiers always are in the movies, afterward, but I wasn't. The bad thing is, as I remember, it gave me a kind of thrill, what you feel when you get your deer. Do you think there's something the matter with me?

—No. What was that word again?

—Oligarchy. Dorth.

—Oligarchy. Bill, please, I can't take any more tonight.

—This is the last, I promise. All my life I've thought the best thing a man could be was a good sportsman. I've tried to be, I obey the laws, I put out my fires, but once, a long time ago, 1934 I think it was, I took some boys fishing up on the Jordan. You remember, the Baird brothers and young Smith and a couple others. Well, I had a canoe along and used it myself on the beaver ponds and got my limit every day. But the poor boys, they had short rods and no waders and couldn't reach the deep pools and got skunked and eaten alive by mosquitoes. It was no fun for them, I guess, the trip, and it was mighty small and mean of me, but I'd never fished a famous stream like the Jordan before and I just didn't think what a trick I was pulling on them. I suppose they've never forgiven me and I don't blame them. I can't abide a poor sport myself.

He waited, studying his plate, then looked up at a sound similar to, yet more human than that of the cicadas. It was Dorth, crying and trying not to, her body quaking, her head bowed to hide from him her face.

—I can't go hunting with you! was her sudden sob and apperception. —No cooking, no cabin to clean or woods to walk in! I can't go north without you or anywhere, I can't do anything, I can't live without you for two years!

So stricken was he that he could not move. —Dorth, you'll be all right, he stammered. Holy Toledo, you'll have Ronnie and the baby and the house and TV and everything.

—I won't have you! she cried. —We're just little people and all we have is each other and I'm afraid!

It was this word, from the mouth of a Dorth to whom fear was unknown, which caused Bill Van's stout heart to start with anguish and acknowledgment as does a golden pheasant at the instant of its slaying, start, then fold its wings and plummet earthward, caused him to rise and fall beside his wife and put his arms about her bounteous hips and buss her neck and cheeks and nose and forehead as she wept. —My dear, good, brave little girl, he crooned, my dear, good, brave little girl.

Oram Kropf

Upon the valleys of the Button and Ionian, upon Thebes began to close an implacable door of dark cloud and the static air was charged with electricity; sullen flowed the rivers beneath the door's mass; old men foresightful of bone stepped from The Let Live to wager on rain and soothsay hail; housewives of sibylline gift hung out their wash with flimsy confidence; the hills frowned; it was Tuesday, the day before an examination in Tyre. Of these carking presages Sewell was too much conscious as he went downtown in the morning, withdrew at the bank the balance of his account, bought a cashier's check for twenty-five hundred dollars, which he mailed at the post office to Internal Revenue in Los Angeles, and counted the remainder, something under three hundred, enough to get him to New York but little more, and even with what he had in pocket a smaller, bitterer nut than he had had at any time since lugging the MS. of *Benison* out of Camp Patrick Henry in a barracks bag. He filled the Jag's tank and plagued himself with the contingency that the machine might never make it to New York. He drove back to the house. He was unable to write. He skimmed the 150 pages of *Silence* and, allowing for his mood, judged the stuff about as cruddy as anything he had ever turned out and he could hear with what sucks and cluckings a literary faggot like Peckham Hill would dislocate himself from it, but: it was also, as a piece of pornography, about as white-hot as Carlie Scripter must be a piece of tail, and as such, worth at least a five-G advance from some printer with more cupidity than scruples, of which there must be beaucoup around. Himself, just dipping into it damn near got him an erection. Publish under a nom de plume he might, but the money he had to have, and between him and Christ-knew-what these pages were all that stood. In the afternoon the black door of the sky was slammed shut upon Thebes by thunder which rolled through the broken windows of the downstairs; detonations sent him striding from dim room to dim room and plucked at nerves already harp-taut. Yet it did not rain, neither was there lightning. It was as though, he thought, some titanic, constipated, Poe-type raven had spread its feathery, sable butt over the world but never more could crap. He wanted a drink. He wanted to haul out of Thebes as much as any place he had ever been in his life, with the possible exception of Thebes the first time and later the Ditch of Dead Women. He should pack and load the car, he would be taking off early in the morning if not tonight, but the state of the living room, now nearly impassable at its center, incapacitated him; it had become, in these short yet protracted six weeks a garbage dump, a compost heap, an Augean stable dunged with the exuviations of his stay; what indeed, to use Edie Kropf's question, had lived here? There was his second-hand furniture, rollaway bed tangled with snotty sheets and a blanket, collapsible chair with split plastic webbing, table warped under the burden of newspapers, spine-sprung books, typing paper, magazines, and portable typewriter; about all this had been thrown up high, malodorous, unsteady muniments based upon his opened suitcases and constructed of dirty shirts and socks and underwear, neckties, beer cans, stubble blown from an overstuffed electric razor, empty cardboard boxes, soft drink bottles, tin cans from which he had eaten beans and fruit, crumpled paper, orts of old sandwiches, finger and toenail clips, wadded facial tissues, filthy towels, all the parings, shavings, and redundance of his person, all the scurf of his rented, vengeful, insular days in Thebes. The poverty, the stink, the task, daunted him. He would leave the house as it was. He would leave it now but for the off-chance that the phone would still ring, it was not too late for them to compromise and cough up, they had until ten o'clock in the morning to save their skins. Were they too tight, too recalcitrant, too doddery not to recognize they were screwed, blued, and tattooed? It was piss-plain they were not going to call. Something had gone wrong, he could not imagine what. From room to room the sky's artillery tracked him. Around four o'clock he telephoned Collins, the Assistant Prosecutor, in Tyre, Collins of the orange tie and green socks, identified himself, and asked if the examination were still on for 10:00 A.M. the next day. It was. What were the odds on getting it rescheduled a day or two later? No cigar, unless the J.P., who by the way was a crochety old rip, had affidavit, for instance, from an M.D. that plaintiff or witnesses or defendants were physically unable to appear, in which event he might grant a stay. Could M.D. be one of the defendants? Hell, no. Suppose he, Smith, decided to have the charges dropped entirely? That would be dandy but for one item: it was legally none of his, Smith's, business, except maybe as an inquisitive author; complaint could be withdrawn only in writing by complainant, in this case the estimable, charming, wronged mother who had filed on behalf of her darling, deflowered daughter, a minor, to wit, Ethel Scripter. That the only way? The only way, pal, barring atomic war, act of God, or the J.P. keeling over of congenital cantankerousness, pretty good, eh? If written withdrawal of complaint reached him, Collins, or the J.P., at any time before 10:00 A.M., exam could be called off? Sure, he assumed; say, what went on over there? Say, he'd done what he said, gone out and actually paid cash over to The Rapids for a copy of *Looking for a Location,* hot-cha-cha, telling his wife Smith had promised to autograph it, and if he was coming over tomorrow or soon, would he? Yes, Sewell said, cutting the connection, he would. His distemper of spirit mounted as the barrage rumbled overhead into evening. For some kind of ultimate Time on Target shoot, he believed, he had been made the objective. For him some Line of Departure had been reached. Then, abruptly, the cannonading ceased, and he stood, breathing hard, in total, terrible silence. Under the clutch of the adhesive across his back and hips he could feel the blistering, the distension of the pus sacs, and realized he had delayed too long: his back was healed, but he would be personally unable to remove the bandaging. He could no longer bear to be alone and immured. He must venture outside himself. He left the house.

*　*　*

Aware of a flicker of curtain he knocked repeatedly at the door without answer until at length Harris came out apologizing that he could not invite him in, Norma would not allow him to set foot in her house, he was sorry, but surely Sewell understood her feelings, and Sewell explained that was why he had come himself, to apologize to both of them for having put the needle unnecessarily in Norma about the elopement, his and Arlene's. Water over the dam now, Harris dismissed it, unimportant water.

—Ris, I'm leaving town, I've got to talk to somebody, will you just sit with me a minute, out here?

Harris hesitated, then said all right, he would, but the swing was grounded now, all he could offer was the porch steps, and when they were seated before the paint-poor, tumble-roof house the grass loomed up at such height about them that they could scarcely see as far as the street and Sewell's car. That was a local joke, he added: the younger Bairds didn't dare mow their lawn for fear of turning up another kid.

—Ris, I'm not to blame for Morse, honest to God I'm not.

—I believe you, though probably not for your reasons. Morse died twice, long ago, first when he couldn't go into the mill, then again when Jane divorced him. I think this was his way of removing what was left, the physical entity which was still capable, just by existing, of harming me or anyone else.

—You really mean that?

The heat oppressed, borne down upon them both by the night and the incubus of low cloud with which it was mingled; the air, however, had changed; dry and surcharged earlier, it was humid, almost mammary with promise, and candied to the nose came the scent from the banked, misshapen spiraea bushes of their minuscule white flowers.

—We'll have rain, Harris said. —I should have cut the lawn. The old codgers at The Let Live say we'll have a cloudburst.

—You really mean it, about my not being responsible?

330

—Sewell, how does it feel to destroy a town? Harris asked nonpertinently. —You must have seen them blown to rubble in Europe, you must have participated yourself, but what sensations do you have when you do it single-handed, just by passing through, when you wreck one from within, disembowel it, as it were?

Sewell insisted he had not done any such goddamn thing. Presumably he meant the six of them; so the examination was tomorrow morning, so they had nothing to sweat, he had figured it out, if they stuck together it would be Carlie's and her mother's word against theirs, there was no witness now, she wasn't knocked up, and on that basis no J.P. hereabouts would bind them over for trial. They were pillars, solid citizens, so forth.

—No, Harris said. —That was the original plan. Now it's all over. At our last meeting, yesterday, Bill Van told us he will admit everything, and of course, if he does, we all will. These men have the habit of truth. No, Sewell, you've accomplished what you set out to: we will stand trial, plead guilty, and take our sentences. You have us in the palm of your hand, not that we are much prize.

Just because they were going to be old-fashioned horses' asses, Sewell demanded, did he, Harris, have to be? And why in holy hell had he sought out Carlie and incriminated himself in the first place?

—Because, in one respect, I was exactly that, an old-fashioned if juvenile horse's ass, Harris acknowledged. —Something out of the past, when we were boys together, assured me that if I were involved, what we had in common would prevent you from injuring me, and so I could save the others by nailing myself to their cross. I was wrong. Sewell, you move in a straight line from one point to another; ideas, associations, emotions, deviate you not an inch. His tone was patient. —And something else, too. According to legend, Thebes was founded by six men—Cadmus, son of Agenor, King of Phoenicia, and five companions. You know how I feel about Harlan Murninghan and Or'm and the two Charles's and Bill Van. Well, if Or'm is not Cadmus and the other four were not the founders of this town, they have been its stewards. I've made them my models, I was proud to be taken into their company, brash as I am, because they're committed to Thebes, to the same ends and means, to the same kind of life I wished to live, and therefore I was committed to whatever overtook them. I wanted to share their lot. This, I suppose, is all Greek to you. To me it was merely Grecian.

—Models! Sewell spat out the word, and in the same breath gave away, to justify himself, the secret with which Arlene had trusted him: how Charles Baird had bartered with her during the war, leasing her body for a promise to employ his nephew.

—Oh, no, Harris protested. —Oh God, she didn't.

Hell, yes, some hops in a hotel room had pulled the trick, not kinship or generosity. Furthermore, Charlieboy was dying of cancer, and was he too stupid to see that in a few months, when his uncle was gone, the mill would probably change ownership, and he would have the ground cut out from under him?

—I wonder what you'll make of this, Harris said. —He told me this morning about his cancer. And that wasn't all. He's changed his will and had other papers drawn. I am now equal partner in the mill, and when Lillian passes on, I become sole owner. The bite of the timing, thanks to you, is razor-sharp. I shall rejoice, the best guess is, from two to four years. But how do you operate a mill from prison? And should we change the name to Thebes Felony Company?

Sewell said nothing, and Harris gathered himself, rose, pushed up his glasses, then took a few aimless steps down the walk. A distant street light did not soften the lines and angles of his long frame, his spindleshanks, the pinch of his cheeks, the jug handles of his ears. —The happy miller, he said. Then, suddenly, he stooped, unspeared a blade of grass, and with a motion well-remembered cupped it in his hands, placed them over his mouth and blew the plaintive, curlew cry of yesteryear.

—Ris, Sewell said thickly.

—What?

—I found out about my father. He stole money from the bank. For a long time. Almost two hundred thousand.

—So? I found out about mine, too.

—He was a thief.

—Renis was a phony.

—The night I came to your house to sleep. Before the dam. He was dead in the morning, but not from flu. They'd found out, the Directors, and came to see him. He asked them to leave him something, and Reason did. An overdose of morphine sulphate.

—They would do that for him. He was one of them. And they kept it to themselves, didn't they?

—That isn't all.

—Don't tell me any more.

On the walk, a few feet away, Harris squatted and once again blew the reed of grass, the sound poignant and intolerable.

—Don't, Sewell said. —Don't do that any more.

—If you wish. I must say I'm surprised to find you vulnerable. Sewell Smith, the famous stranger in our midst. Harris tilted the grass blade between his teeth. —It's unreal, sitting here with you, talking, when what you've started in motion will soon sweep away everything I have, not to speak of the pride and dignity and good names of the men I most admire. Norma in the house, watching us through a curtain, I imagine. The kids asleep. Sewell, I've considered killing you. I was desperate enough at first. Time took care of that, thank God. Then I consoled myself by despising you. But now, old friend, I can't even do that. The fact is, all I feel about you is curiosity. I've thought about you a great deal, remembering all the way back to when we went fishing on the Jordan and you, thirteen years old, made a grown man, a school superintendent, bend to your will in front of youngsters. I suppose Bill Van has never forgotten. Then there was Arlene up in the hills that day, you knowing somehow it was the right time to rape her because Johnny was just gone. And that's what it was, a more criminal assault than what we're to be charged with and punished for by the state. Then the mill dam—that, too, was your idea. Sewell, do I finally make out pattern? Hasn't there always been in you an innate menace—I lack the word—a potential violence? I remember always being a little afraid of you, in awe of you, just as I was of your father. So was Morse, he told me so, he was much bigger and stronger than you but he never dared fight with you. If I do find an archetype, it isn't that of the soldier—most of us have been soldiers—but of the warrior. You wage war. It's your nature to war endlessly. One of the results of war is that each makes the next, though it is more awful, more endurable. The brutalizing effect is cumulative, and our, and your, tolerance to horror greater. Well, then, the warrior. Truce, amity, reason, these you cannot know. To your mill, all wheat is foul and full of weeds. Over your sights, all men are enemies. Even *Benison,* your protest against war, was motivated, you admitted yourself, by hate. For peace you are untrained, and the heroics of peace you can neither comprehend nor even recognize. What you describe Arlene as doing for me with my uncle, his passing the Baird mill on to me, my brother's unselfishness for my sake, your father's friends granting him the most fundamental right on earth, the right to leave it and be remembered with respect—these acts would baffle you if you could take notice of them. But they are bright, active verbs in a language the mercenary is never taught. And it was Cadmus, incidentally, who is supposed to have introduced the alphabet into Greece. And also, and not incidentally, most of these ideas about you aren't mine, I've talked about you with Oram Kropf, who knows men as well as anyone can. The only piece we can't find a place for in the puzzle is the Distinguished Service Cross. That simply doesn't jibe, to me. Harris paused to shift the blade of grass from one side of his mouth to the other. —Well, the warrior must go on fighting, even if only his friends. He can't help himself. Sewell, I'm sorry to say it, but I feel nothing for you now, not anger or pity or an ache for old times. Nothing. Should I condemn or judge a weapon, a rifle or pistol or machine gun, because its function is to take life? No. I merely forgive you. I forgive the undistinguished service you've done the place where we were born. Something is overtaking you. I watched you rush out of church, I heard the terrible yell which came out of you more than it did out of your car. Now you tell me about your father, a whistle of grass brings you pain. The six of us have our examination tomorrow. Yours, apparently, is tonight. Levering himself by his knees, Harris stood. —Sewell, good night and God help you, because even though you've won, as I said to you before, the war is over.

He flinched, almost in alarm, as Sewell came at him out of the darkness. —Damn you, Ris, you didn't hear what I said!

—About what?

—About my father! And there's more I've found out about him! He and— His tongue refused the toxicant of her name.

—Keep it, Harris said, as booty.

—I'm in trouble myself, with the government, tax trouble. And my back. I had to have the money!

—Jesus to Genoa, Harris whispered, shaking his head as he brushed past and started up the steps, but Sewell reached for him, took the belt of his blue jeans and held him fast until he whirled about, pulling down his glasses in bewilderment.

—Ris, wait a minute for God's sake! I talked to the Prosecutor this afternoon, in Tyre. He can't put off the exam, but here's what, he can call it off if the complaint's withdrawn, yes, he can, in writing, any time before ten tomorrow! So I'm going right now to find her, old buddy! Harris heard him rush down the walk, his car door open and slam, his hoarse reassurance out the window. —Mrs. Scripter, she does anything I tell her! You call the others and say it's going to be all right, called off, they're safe! I'll find her and get her to drop the goddamn charges, old buddy! Honest to Christ, I will!

LIVE BAIT; down the shimmying wooden stairway of the house beside the Button; from the screen door a glare, and through the glare was stamped upon his sight a print hideous because it seemed predestined, distorted as only truth distorts. The grot of the basement. Naked light bulbs. Flats of moss. Two fishermen, heavy men with pike faces, one examining the huge talismanic Harley-Davidson athwart a wall. Arlene Scripter, found. Arlene, her coil of auburn hair loose and tangled, her white lab uniform stained, unbuttoned down the front, bending over a minnow tank to net and transfer shiners to a bucket. A second customer, the same practiced fisherman served by the mother on Sewell's first visit to the basement, inclined now with the daughter, his hand spooning inside the bosom of her uniform, enjoying, having transposed daughter and mother, the same pilferage of flesh. Sewell tore open the screen door. —Leave her alone, you sonabitch! What the hell you think this is, a whorehouse? Get out of here! Rubber-booted, the two men edged shoulder to shoulder, big men, one grunting who was he, no skin off his butt, right to buy bait. —I said take off, you bastards! Licking lips, the other, calculating, said bowlegs here wasn't so big, didn't look so tough, two of them to his one, he wanted his clock cleaned they might just could do that for him. He glanced about, searching, spied something overhead between the iron pipes, reached and hauled down an eight-foot spinning rod of pliant fiberglas. His knuckles whitened around the cork grip, and raising the rod he began to snap its length as one might a snake by its tail. —You see this? I said go. I'll show you what I can do with this, you sonabitches. His arm circled. The whip of the rod, swifter than the eye, sang about the basement. One slash severed a light cord and the bulb exploded on concrete. Another sent moss shredding from a flat. —I'll cut your god-damn heads off with this! I'll pick out your eyes! Sewell yelled. —I said you bastards take off! The fishermen backed away, staring, apprehending he would do what he threatened, this stalking, muscular half-man, half-animal with shirt collar open and sleeves bunched over flailing arm, lips pulled back over irregular teeth, and when the scythe of the rod came close to their heads they ducked and trampled swearing out the rear door. Like a lance Sewell cast the rod clattering after them, spun about to find Arlene slumped at the table, face buried in her arms. —Lene, my God, what goes on here?

Her response, spasmodic and exhausted, was that this was where she belonged, the town had always thought so, after tomorrow morning she could not return to the lab, no decent home in Thebes would open its door to her, what else could she do but return here at last and apprentice herself to her mother so that she might, in her turn, instruct Carlie?

—Whores, he said. He seemed to hear her but to relate her meaning to himself. —Had lots of whores. You do in the Army. And afterward, everywhere, even though one I paid off in chinchilla. Bev Hills. But I was good to them. I can be good to people. Once, Lene, I was walking in Soho. Full of accordion stores and whores. Rhymes. He sat down on the edge of a minnow tank. —Anyway, I picked up this girl, went to her room and wiped off her lipstick and rouge and mascara and she was just a country girl not long up to London. I made her wash her face and put a ribbon in her hair and gave her two pounds and didn't touch her and told her to go out that way and she'd have better luck. Ooo, she said, aren't ee a queer 'un. You don't have to be a whore, Lene. You're too beautiful. My father was a thief. He took two hundred thousand out of the bank.

She lifted her head and put her chin in her hands, looking through him from gray eyes void of expression. —I was wondering, she said. —Wondering if anyone I ever knew, besides myself, was ever as lonely as you. And needed to be loved as much. And not being loved, even with a lie, needed to hurt the world so much.

—My father and your mother. After Johnny. He put a palm under the drip from a pipe until it filled, then splashed water across his sweaty face. —When we were young. Did you know about them?

—Yes.

—Did everybody?

—I think so, yes.

—Everybody but me. He sat erect, stretching, testing, grimacing with a distress almost sensual.

—Sewell, I'm in love with Harris. I've always been.

—It's the truth about them?

—Near Delphi Grange that day, in your car, first you and then Morse.

337

—About the men tomorrow. From his hand he dribbled water down the collar of his shirt. —I had to have the money, that was why. I owe the government.

—But Harris didn't. Sewell, he cried.

—My mother knew. Drove her crazy.

—I can't leave Thebes, ever again, but I can't stay.

—Ris says I'm a warrior.

—I remember your father, his being here.

—You should have seen what she did to his car.

—A warrior.

—I remember Johnny, too. But on the street.

—She had a beautiful voice.

—I don't want to be. Lene. Listen to me. After I got rich and famous, I couldn't stay in one place, I kept moving the way you do in the service, transferring myself, writing my own orders like I was my own CP. I really traveled, but without any plan. I'd go somewhere and get on a boat, or to an airport and take a seat on the first plane out, I'd close my eyes and put my finger on a map and then open them and pack. It was crazy, where I'd go. Once I ended up in Georgetown, British Guiana, and I was sitting in a park by a pond and looking at me, with their heads out of the water chewing weeds, were three sea cows. I've taken a freighter from Mazatlán to Skagway, from Port Vendres, in France, to Bizerte, and one from Bari, Italy, to a port called Split, in Yugoslavia. Also I used to like the feeder airlines, the lost ones you don't hear about with old DC-3's for equipment, ones like Apache and North Central and Allegheny. There's one out west called Bonanza, and I've made the whole route, coming in at night to little towns like Indio and Prescott and Santa Ana and El Centro and Yuma and Apple Valley and Kingman and Flagstaff and Riverside. I like that, sort of going round and round over deserts and mountains and ending up nowhere and alone and in the middle of night. You never knew quite where you were or where you'd come from. Another time, I remember, I got off Bonanza at Blythe, California, around two in the morning, and looked in the phone book for the number of somebody named Smith, and I called him and said we were probably related, and asked what he was doing with his life, I was the famous writer but I'd like to be friends with him. He said I was drunk but I was sober. I've called people named Smith in the middle of night all over the country. Lene, listen. I want the war to be over, I have no children or family or even friends, not even an agent, and I'm tired and my back hurts like hell, the tape you put on. When you came to the house you said if I'd have the charges against these men dropped you'd go away with me and say you loved me as often as I wanted to hear it. That really hurt, I was surprised. Well, that's why I'm here, to fix up about tomorrow. I've promised Ris there'll be no exam tomorrow. If I do this, will you do what you said, go away with me?

During this, with a diffidence almost comical, he had busied himself with the water, but now he crossed to the table. Her head was once more down, her cheek pressed to the oilcloth in a young girl's attitude. —Lene. That's why I came here, to see your mother. All she has to do is withdraw the complaint in writing. Where is she?

—At the cemetery.

—The cemetery?

—That's where they get night crawlers. She said it would rain.

—Will you go away with me? You don't even have to lie, you don't have to love me, I won't touch you, not once, just be with me. You are so beautiful. And I have to have somebody to talk to sometimes. With cautious finger he made contact with the skin of her arm. —Lene, I have to have somebody.

She did not move. —You'll do this even if I don't go with you?

—Yes. I will.

—Then I will. I don't know what else to do.

—God, that's great! Lene, God, I'm glad! Listen, I'll find your mother now and come right back and you be ready and we'll get my stuff and take off. In a burst of excitement he paced round the table. —We'll stop in Tyre and leave the paper with the Prosecutor—I have to autograph a book for

him, too—then be on our way to New York or L.A. or somewhere, it doesn't matter now. Lene, this is so damn, damn
nice of you. God, but I'm grateful! From behind, he reached
down and lifted her face. —God, just let me kiss your forehead because I'm so grateful. He kissed her. He swung open
the screen door. —I'll be right back. Somebody to talk to,
and have I got a lot to say! You wouldn't believe what a bastard I am!

The old men erred. Weather has its own wisdom. After
noisy labor the heavens over Thebes brought forth neither
hail nor torrent but in clement stillness a mist, a fragmenta-
tion of rain through which, its windshield blades inoperative,
the Jaguar prowled along narrow lanes of sand, beast unbecoming a necropolis, growling under oaks and maples and
hunting slowly with its headbeams among the slabs and pillars, tablets and memoria. She must be here; far out among
the gravestones winked a diablerie of flashlights as several
boys hunted, too, picking from the wet grass the harvest of the
marble orchard, dropping it in coffee cans. He came up suddenly behind the parked pick-up, left the car and went to the
Widow Scripter. She lolled under a maple upon the plinth of
a high monument, a pail between the knees of her slacks, a
petunia limp in the lapel of her jacket, a beer bottle queenly
in one hand.
    —Sew'l, she greeted him. —Set down. Ain't going to pay,
are they? Old skinflints. They're so tight I bet they let their
farts in paper bags an' save 'em. I figured they wouldn', damn
'em, so when I see it'd rain I got me a crew of boys an' come
out. You know I ain't had no crawlers 'n two weeks? Bad for
bus'ness. Tomorrow come mornin' they'll get their comeuppance, though, when me an' my kiddie gets on the stand. You
heard anything?
    —Yes. That's why I was looking for you. They're going to
plead guilty, all of them, and take their sentences.
    —Well, three cheers. Serve 'em right. I hope they get shut
up for life, what they got left of it. We'll see who laughs last.

Say, my boys is doin' fine. This's the time for crawlers, y'know, rain after a long dry. They come out t'screw. I might jus' go home with eight, nine hundred, penny apiece to the kids, sell 'em two cents apiece. My hair-do's going t'hell'n this soup an' I got the catarrha bad. Hughh, hughh! Say, you want t'see Morsey's grave? I stole me a flow'r from it. Woman's got t'have a lil' purtyness in 'er life.

Sewell sat beside her on the slab. —Ethel, why I've come, I've changed my mind. If we can't get money out of them, we might as well give it up as a bad job. Their rotting in prison won't help Carlie. You've taken my advice right along, and here's what I think now. The examination tomorrow can be called off if you just put in writing that you withdraw your complaint. You'd better do it, and I'll take it over to Tyre tonight.

—Up your tokus! An' let them ol' sex fien's corruption all the other girlies in town? In malty grouch the lady drained her bottle and tossed it over her shoulder so that it rolled clanking against a marker. —Nossir, if there ain't no money in it, I'm goin' t'have me some pers-nal dues! Hughh, hughh!

—For what?

—For Johnny, that's what! An' for Morse!

—And for my father?

She peered at him. —Who tol' you?

—Edie Kropf.

—That one, if she had more tit 'n less tongue she'd be happier.

—My father and you. It's true, isn't it?

One of her minions approached, his container full, and as the worthy matron, pleased at the interruption, held her own flashlight and counted, the youngster let slide, one by one, a hundred night crawlers into the pail between her knees. —See here, Sew'l, she said when the boy had disappeared, and directed the beam downward. The pail was half full of great worms, a whitish, gelid, sinuous mass alive and octopal about the cylinder of a bottle. —Damn good way t'keep beer cold! She slipped the bottle from the invertebrate muck, dried its slime on her slacks, opened it, refreshed herself, lit a cigarette, and rid her lips of tobacco by loud expectoration. —Where was we? Oh. Sew'l, what'd you think of your ol' man? When he was alive, I mean?

—I don't know any more.

—Sew'l, I loved 'im. Not like Johnny, a differ'nt way, but oh, God, I did. L.V. was the bes' thing could of happen'd t'me after Johnny. You recollect how the whole town turned on me an' mine. You was a Scripter an' you was dirt. Nobody t'talk to or warm your feet on. Well, that lil' L.V., what a buster he was, gave me more support 'n a girdle, bought me the house, set me up in bus'ness, an' was my tower an' bower. He was strong, too, like a midget rassler dressed up in preacher's clothes, with 'is shoes an' mustache so black an' shiny an' him so sober an' sly. But when it come to the bed, I tell you he was a Samson! Say— Snapping on her light, she focused it on the grass, capturing in its circle two night crawlers imparadised in love's fine frenzy, transport extending their lengths to seven or eight inches, and as the viscous coupling proceeded apace, she stripped them up together and dropped them hedonistic in the pail, once more dousing her light. —He was gen'rous, too, like Johnny, an' brave, both their hearts was big as bass drums, but the diff'rence was, Johnny was a shinin' man an' L.V. was secret. She paused, saying reverential beads, drank, puffed. —F'rinstance, your daddy'd come up from nothin', off a farm like I was, an' made money an' run the town with the others, but the other side, what half the worl' takes off its pants for, why, he didn't know his nether parts from a cattle morgidge. Sex? Why, him an' me might of been Adam 'n Eve 'n The Garden of Grunt! An' afterwards he'd strut aroun' an' aroun' the bed like a banty rooster, poundin' his chest an' crowin'! He—

—That's enough, Sewell interjected. —I don't want to hear any more about him.

—Why not?

—Because he was a thief. He embezzled from the bank for thirteen years. That's where your house came from.

—Shit he did.

—He did.

342

—I s'pose they tol' you an' you b'lieved it! Now you lissen. If anybody bezzled, it was them ol' corncobs, them buggers of Directors. That night he called me on the phone from your house. You was over to the Baird boys an' he was alone. He tol' me he loved me an' said good-bye. Nex' mornin' he was gone, sudden, jus' like Johnny, an' I knew they'd done 'im in some way—

—No, he did it himself. They'd discovered the shortage and he couldn't stand the disgrace and everything, so he asked Reason to leave him something, a drug, and he did. It was a favor. And they've never told anyone until me.

The Widow Scripter smoked and pondered, finished the beer, threw away the bottle, scratched and cogitated, fondled the limp memento mori of her flower. On chill stone they sat apart, enveloped in moisture. It was as though the night were a great ripe plum from which the juice was coaxed interminably.

—So, concluded she, they killed my men, all three. Johnny by braggin' on 'im too much, L.V. by givin' 'im poison, an' Morsey by not lettin' 'im in the Baird mill. I hope they can't sleep this night, that they're lyin' there awake with their ol' livers an' mis'ries an' sins.

—No. No, they didn't, not really. Ethel, they aren't bad men. So they made a mistake with Carlie, they know it, they're sorry, and it was probably her fault as much as theirs. They gave my father a way out and we can do as much for them. I promised Harris, who's my friend, just a few minutes ago, that I'd see you and get you to withdraw the complaint. All you have to do is put it down on paper. I want you to do it.

—Won't.

—Ethel, you have to.

—Shit I do. Talk up a storm, you want to, but they still laid dirty rapin' han's on my baby, a fourteen-year-ol' bride of the Lord!

—Goddammit, if you won't do it for them you've got to for me! Sewell sprang up, looking to be certain he was not overheard. Ghoulish flashlights flickered on and off as boys unburied treasure among the graves. —You asked me to help you, Ethel, when I first came back, and goddammit I have, all I could, and now it's over. This means one hell of a lot to me, more than you know, and you've got to!

—Help? What help you been? she challenged. —You traipse me up an' down an' over to Tyre an' called my Carlie a lil' bitch an' what've I got out of it but sorrow an' soakin' wet? An' you ain't been kind, neither, you ain't once treated me like a woman an' a human bein'! I tol' you you may be another Shakespeare an' a big war hero but you don't know beans about women an' people an' you ain't got no feelin's! What'd you do back in high school to my girl Lene, huh? She ain't never said but I can guess—took advantage of 'er the way them town sheikhs did of me when I come in off the farm—an' there wasn't no shinin' Johnny to save 'er like there was for me! So I won't write out nothin'!—you can go t'hell an' them doddy ol' snarks t' prison! Hey!

His hands were round her throat, his voice was guttural. —I could choke it out of you, Ethel.

—You wouldn', Sew'l. She urged her body, the plump stem of her throat toward him rather than away. —You couldn', Sew'l. Ain't that sof' skin, though? Her broad face was close to his, her natural scents, piscine and toothsome, plucked at the hairs in his nose, diddled impurely through him to his groin. —Life in the ol' girl yet, huh, Sew'l?

He sickened. —Now I know where hell is, he muttered. —It's between your legs.

He fell away from her and cleansed his hands in the grass as she began to snuffle righteously. —No, they're goin' t' pay in the mornin', that's what. You go on. I'll stay here with my sweeties, my three darlin's. They're all here an' still takin' care of me even if you nor nobody else will. She belched. —Say, that's a good one—still takin' care of me—they feed the crawlers an' the crawlers feeds me!

—What's that mean, they're all here?

—You don' know? Don't you look where you set your fat rump? Well, look!

She lurched from the base of the monument and raising her flashlight upward transfixed in its ray, fully twelve feet above the base, an ornamental urn of burnished red granite, partially draped, then swept the light down an imposing column to the plinth which had served them as seat and along its inscription: "Lucian Virgil Smith—1889-1939—HIS WORK IS DONE." Her catarrhal laugh bayed after him as Sewell with a groan fled from the sight, slipped, fell, and stumbled toward the car. —Hughh, hughh! His work's done—hell it is—not till tomorrow! Justus!

Now is Thebes rain-shrouded. From forested elms is let down rain modest as charity, empirical as prayer. Herbie Teeple, he of the recessed ear lobes, Karen's husband, likes to walk in the rain and think, as befits a prospective mortician, long thoughts. Before the ancient brick Grand Rapids-Gothic home of Oram Kropf he halts. Someone hammers at the door, shouts, but the house is dark. Hounded, someone departs on the run, crashes into that renowned equipage which crowns the lawn, that rheum-encrusted incarnation of the past: a full-size replica in iron of the Kropf Siberian Cutter. Someone clings, battered, to a runner. Dutifully Herbie Teeple nears, intending condolence. It is Sewell Smith. He is pleased to encounter Sewell because Karen, he explains, wishes to apologize for her remarks at the party at the Creel & Cartridge, after all, who is she to insult a famous author? Where is Oram Kropf, where is Oram Kropf, moans Sewell. Herbie inquires his difficulty. It has something unintelligible to do with a festering of flesh across his back and hips. Karen wishes further to extend an invitation to dinner some night so that they may discuss books and literature. Where is Oram Kropf, Sewell yells at him. Well, seems to him he did see Or'm a bit ago, down on Ionian, yes, letting himself into the bank, but he does hope Sewell will accept his wife's humble apology and come to dinner some night and discuss books and literature. He addresses rain, for Sewell is gone as though pursued by Furies.

345

Before the State Bank of Thebes the car of Coventry bearing California plates, scarred, alien, and ill-used machine, meets an ignoble end. Aimed in desperation rather than steered, it careens on shimmering pavement against the high curb; a front tire bursts, the wire spokes snap like strings, the wheel crumples, the Jaguar sags to its axle. Heedless, he leaves the car, beats a tattoo on the double door until, after long wait, a shade is raised and there appears, behind the glass, a death's-head, a skull ghostly and blank-lidded. The door opens.

—It's Sewell, isn't it?

—Yes. How did you know?

—We must know more than we see.

The only light on the bank's floor is the small lamp on the desk behind the spindled rail which illuminates a name plate black on bronze: Raymond Dickerson, Vice-President and Cashier.

—I've come from the cemetery. Who put up the monument?

—Let me draw the shade. I have a key, all the Directors do, but my concerns here tonight are more personal than official.

—There wasn't any money for a monument, even a funeral. Who paid for it?

—We did, his friends. You are correct, the bonding company had first claim upon everything in his estate, but we felt it our obligation to furnish a suitable marker, just as we did to make provision for your education. The choice of an epitaph we left to Carrie Murninghan, a woman unexceptionably pious. Any irony, I can assure you, was inadvertent.

Hanging his white cane in the crook of an arm, Oram Kropf withdraws to one of the oaken customers' tables, in his blue suit merging with the floor's gloom. On the table paper rustles as his spidery hands trifle with deposit pads; there is in his demeanor a tentativeness, an irresolution curious and new.

—A strange day, a strange rain.

—Why I went to the cemetery tonight, Harris told me

346

you're going to plead guilty in the morning. I went to see Mrs. Scripter, to get her to withdraw the complaint. She won't.

—I suppose not.

—I did everything I could. She says if she can't have the money she wants justice.

—For Peace Officer John Scripter, I presume. And I am not sure but that her claim is valid. We do indeed, Renis and I and your father and Charles Reason, bear partial responsibility for the manner of his death in this street. Rear someone to manhood in perfect innocence and he is bound to expect, when the chips are down, that the simple apposition of good to evil will carry the field.

—The night Earl Blue served the warrants, I was with him. He thinks the way Johnny planned it was sound, from a police angle.

—It may have been. Regrettably, however, this is not the age of martyrdom, but of the Associated Press. I expect, too, that Ethel is not a little embittered by a more recent deprivation, that of a young lover. I refer to poor Morse.

—She mentioned him. Also my father.

—Ah. Now there is not much more for you to learn, is there? Your father. A remarkable individual. Covetous. Liberal. Intransigent. Vain. Fearless. Unscrupulous. Loyal. Vulgar. Steadfast. Furtive. Precise. Weak. Arrogant. Servile. Amicable. Dangerous. Idealistic. Damned. In short, every mote of flesh, every ligature of spirit, a man.

The adjectival rise to ceiling, the caesuras, the fall of words again to parquetry and ear awake in Sewell a bygone echo, troubling and acoustic. The moment's awkwardness is magnified by a formality, an affectation in the older man which is almost pitiable. —I shouldn't have come here, but I wanted to tell you what I tried to do and how sorry I am, how really sorry I am it didn't work. I should have realized, I'm about the last person you'd want to see, the whole thing is my fault, and I've sort of gone crazy tonight trying to fix—

—No, on the contrary, no. Oram Kropf is close to being addled. He assures his guest he is welcome, his shift in par-

347

tisanship and his attempt to alter the course of event are most cheering. —The fact is, though, Sewell, that you do arrive inopportunely. Tomorrow it's to be, then. This means that none of us has much time to put his affairs in order, and I had come to the bank to dispose of one last tag-end. Matter. Leftover. The fact is, I am embarrassed. I have been deliberating if I should make you privy to my task. Let me think. Yes. Another test, though somewhat belated, of whether or not Sewell Smith is educable. Yes, by all means. Will you come with me, Sewell, downstairs?

Swiftly he sets off, The Blind Boulevardier with cane alate, past the tellers' cages, through a door, past the vault, down a hall, then descends a flight of steps into the bank's basement, Sewell following. The basement is small and littered; set into one wall of brick is an incinerator door; there is an odor of smoke; against another wall lists on three legs a fusty wooden rack of antiquated safe-deposit boxes, tin and lock-fronted. With his cane the Editor gestures.

—Here they are. We have modernized the institution to the extent of a new vault and boxes, of course, but this one set I asked be retained as a mnemonic device. Would you care to see how he did it? From one tier he slides a box, holds it before Sewell, turns it endwise. —It is locked. With tapered finger tip he pushes out the hinge-pin at the back and easily lifts the lid. —Lo. One flogs his brain for the lines most apt. "No mask like open truth to cover lies/ As to go naked is the best disguise." Congreve. Or this, from *Paradise Lost:* "Open, ye heavens, your living doors; let in/ The great Creator from his work return'd/ Magnificent, his six days' work, a world." And when one keeps the pins well oiled, the trick is expedited. But I digress. For the garrulous man, quotation is the thief of time. He returns the empty box to its pigeonhole. —Sewell, what mean and base do you know of me?

—You helled around a lot when you were young.

—Guilty.

—You were unfaithful to your wife.

—Guilty.

348

He hesitates uneasily. —You wouldn't let Edie and Bill Van get married.

—Ah. To cover his confusion Oram Kropf runs his finger round the collar of his shirt, plucks at his tie. —Guilty again. And you believe it hard of me to assume prepotency for ten years, to deny the pair their wedded sport? "Yes, my darling daughter/ Hang your clothes on a hickory limb/ But don't go near the water"? Guilty, perhaps, but not of selfishness. I based my objections on a regard for the general eudemonia. Had I let them marry, two of the triangle would have been happy, or so they fancied; only Dorth would suffer; not true; Bill is simply not Edie's match intellectually; she understands this now, although she will not admit it to herself; so must he; the entire trio, therefore, would have been wretched. My only consideration was the greatest happiness for the greatest number, and in this instance one agony, my Edie's, was better than three. He stands for a moment, immutable and tall as an obelisk, head cocked, confirming his own casuistry, then steps again to the rack of boxes. —Well, to return to our subject. These things are the worst you know of me. Would that they were. It has been my lifelong misfortune to be demonized by my glands. I have worshiped, I fear, the Priapean gods. His tone grows harsh, masochist. —I have been, to put it plainly, randy as hell. The world, I thought, was a pair of thighs, and it was my masculine embassy to part them. It was also my misfortune to lose my sight, to grow old, and hence to want opportunity. From the street corners of your sixties, you will one day find, few Carlene Scripters beckon. And to revert to my cryptographer, Heraclitus, The Dark, "The way up and the way down are one and the same." In any event, my dark, my depravity, my onanism, if you will, has driven me over the past several years to put together as fine a cumulation of erotica for the blind male as may exist. Here. Removing a large flat box from the rack he opens it from the rear and passes it on to Sewell. —Sex for the sightless. Voyeurism is of course not possible; you have only hearing and touch. Queasy, nonplused, Sewell examines the contents. There are massive books in Braille: Henry Miller, *The Memoirs of Fanny Hill,* de Sade, *The Thousand Nights and a Night,* Apollinaire; there are recordings with Spanish labels of what he gathers to be the sounds of coitus in all its audible, aphrodisiac spectrum; there are terra cotta statuettes of the female form and smaller delineations of its integrants to be stroked, petted, manipulated: breasts haughty and languid, buttocks dimpled with youth and indigent with age, mouths kiss-stung, mouths adder-tongued, mouths carnivorous and vaginal; finally, there are mounts of Venus in rubber and plastic and wood, of all sizes, hues and subspecies, each one christened roguishly, in raised letters—introduction to the imagination—with a feminine name: Kitty, Hilde, Gina, Marlene, Rosita, Elise, Chloe, Doll, Corinne, Daisy. —A cloacal proclivity, and a costly one. The records, for example, come from Buenos Aires, and the Braille volumes from Helsinki. These boxes I call my reliquaries. I had burned the curios in two when you knocked. You can conceive my discomfiture, thinking I had everything in order, then realizing in panic just tonight that I had not disposed of this hoard, which, should I not survive a sentence, would surely be unearthed and credited to my memory. And then you appeared and I was caught black-handed. If you are done, Sewell, will you assist me by stoking the fiery furnace?

Sewell complies, emptying a second, third, and fourth box into the incinerator as they are passed him unerringly, clangs shut the door.

Oram Kropf dusts his hands in relief. —Good riddance to bad rubbish. This was a legacy I had no wish to leave. Thank you. Now, like the phoenix, let us ascend reborn from our own ashes. He leads the way, climbing. On a riser edge worn smooth the sole of one oxford glissades. His leg goes out from under him and the long, brittle figure crashes sprawling on its side, the cane clattering below. He lies helpless until Sewell's arm rights him, brings him to a sitting position.

—Are you all right?

—I am sixty-eight. I have a bad hip.

—Is there anything I can do?

—I never fall. Let me rest. I pride myself on it. Never. The

sough of his breath is like that of wind against tattered sails.
—Sewell, who will read to me in prison? What will I do if
there is no one to read to me?
   —I'll get your cane.
   —You know the worst. Do you despise me?
   —No.
   —Then you may be redeemed.
   —Harris says I'm a warrior.
   —Perhaps. To the warrior, one is either friend or foe.
   —Here's your cane.
   —But all men, Sewell, like all cats in the dark, are gray.
   —You don't know the worst of me.
   —Reason and appetite, love and vanity, urine and the in-
finite.
   —Mr. Kropf—
   —Let us go upstairs.
   —Yes.
   —Sewell, I have a wondrous thing to tell! And vivified by
the prospect, rejecting aid, he levers himself up and attains
the bank's main floor, limping down the hall to the Directors'
Room, locating without difficulty a light and dropping into
one of the eight armchairs. —Sit near me. His cane he brings
down across the long table before him as though it were a
gavel, cutting short, from somewhere distant, a clock's eu-
phonious petition. —What time was that?
   —Ten, I think.
   —Exactly twelve hours, then.
   A weary Sewell braces himself erectly with his elbows in order to avoid contact between his back and the oak of his chair.
—Earlier tonight I called the Assistant Prosecutor in Tyre to
see if I couldn't get the exam put off some way. It couldn't be.
   —No. Nor do I think it should. Shall we begin by accepting
turpitude on the part of all five of us? Harris's impulse was
more misdemeanor than felony. Have you been in this room
before?
   —Once. He brought me in here one night and showed me
a box full of stock certificates. He spread them out on the
table, more than a hundred thousand dollars' worth. I thought

we were rich and he'd done it himself. I really respected him.
—But you have finally accepted the fact of his dishonesty.
—Yes. It took a long time.
—Well and good. And interesting. Forgive me if I bring out the harness before I have the horse. Interesting, I repeat, because here you have someone returning after long absence, the prodigal carrying with him an equipment of memory and bias; the stone of his illusions is struck not by drops of water but by a round of iron and devastating blows: his father stole what he could and copulated where he dared; simultaneously he discovers that those he has believed reprehensible have instead done on his father's behalf all that men under like circumstances may do for one another; and simultaneously, he discovers how imperfect, if not criminal, are these very Samaritans; one of them takes him down into a private gutter and reveals a moral squalor literally international in scope. What is he to think? How is he to act? Rather than a catharsis of hate, he knows only cramp. The scales of his esteem, his values, almost of his sanity, rather than balancing depend now on one side, now on the other, seemingly beyond his power to adjudicate or comprehend. Oram Kropf leans forward, shoots his cuffs. —Let me unbalance them still further, Sewell. Hear me carefully. In our vault there were two hundred safe-deposit boxes. Over the thirteen years, how many do you think he entered?
—I don't know.
—Almost all. And by whom were they rented?
—I don't know.
—By the well-to-do, of course, but also by others, by retired farmers, by widows for their mites, by church and social groups, by the Council— Sewell, the lifeblood of a good part of Thebes was sealed within those boxes and L.V., that small, amazing surgeon, had bathed his arms in it up to the elbows! But at long, long last I may finish the story for someone! Let us go back to that night.

Stagewright's instinct or twinge of recollection causes the Editor to bow his head, to wait as Sewell waits.—Ten o'clock? Twelve hours. Against the dry skin along his cheekbone his fingers rasp.—It was ten o'clock when we left your father's room. Charles Reason, as you now know, stayed behind a moment, then joined us outside. L.V. had admitted everything, the full, catastrophic extent. We stood there in the darkness on your lawn, the six of us, like drunken men hanging on each other for support, like dead men almost. I remember the bulwark of Harlan Murninghan's shoulder. Besides the arrogation of life and death we had just claimed, what now fell upon us like these hills was that the State Bank of Thebes, of which we were custodians in quiddity as well as in law, was as of that moment insolvent. It had no legal right to open its doors on the morrow. Except to us and to the town it was, and still is, a pygmy institution; capital and surplus amounted only to sixty thousand dollars, but your father had confessed to the conversion of $170,000! What, in the name of God, to do? Telephone the State Banking Department in Lansing, have them lock and post the doors, let the newspapers lick their chops over L.V.'s ingenuity as they had over Johnny's moonheadedness, but even worse, impoverish the aged, make destitute the retired, dry the commercial stream, bankrupt the various organizations, the town government itself—commit, in other words, a civic murder? We came down to meet in this very room, Sewell, around this table. Claude Reichert, as I recall, was alone capable of figures. We took off our coats. We waited. This was what, Claude said eventually, we fronted. L.V. was bonded for $25,000; add to that our capital and surplus, subtract from $170,000, and we had a deficit of $85,000. There would be realizable, he estimated, from your father's estate, his holdings, the house, furnishings, car, so forth, after the bonding company had satisfied itself, another twenty-five, which brought the shortage down to $60,000. If this were somehow raised, our capital, without which under state law we could not function, would be replaced, and every bond asset of every boxholder converted by your father to his private use made good. $60,000. A negligible sum by your standards, Sewell, and today's, but this was June of 1939. The country had never really recovered from depression. By any criterion, these were not rich men. Harlan Murninghan called the meeting to order and himself offered a motion that we, the stockholders, vote two 100 percent levies upon ourselves, each in the amount of $30,000, the first to compensate in full all box-holders at loss, the second to replenish our capital and hence, by complying with the legal requirement, to open our doors the next day as though nothing untoward had transpired. This meant a levy by each man upon himself of ten thousand. There was no second to this motion. Sewell, try to see this room as I could not, try to peer into these faces! Harlan's, mine, Claude's, the two Charles's, Bill Van's. Watch them as they struggle, each with his interior dragon to slay, and three of them actually standing to gain financially should the motion fail of passage since their own notes at this bank, if it closes, can be compromised in receivership! Here is Harlan, who has weathered the thirties and kept his people on at Twinriver by swallowing his pride and making sprayers and borrowing all the law allows from this bank and in Grand Rapids as well—does he dare stretch his credit to the breaking point? Bill Van has nothing but his house and life insurance—will he put them on the block and chance losing the little a schoolmaster may hope to accumulate? Then Charles Baird, fighting to salvage what his brother has nearly scuttled, already in pawn up to his ears both to this institution and others—has he the courage to cast dice so patently loaded against his point? Will Oram Kropf put up as collateral a weekly paper which two-bit though it be, constitutes his only means of livelihood? Can Claude Rei-chert, penny-wise pillroller, he of the alum rectum, can Claude, still shriveled by grief at the tragic encounter be-tween his brilliant boy Irwin and a set of our columns, pre-scribe for himself a liberality which goes against the very grain of his nature? How may Charles Reason, milked dry by old Kemper and Kemper's widow and Bernice and his own expensive tastes, scrape up ten thousand dollars ex-cept by applying to a usurer or doing abortions in a back room? Around this table, Sewell, they sit, the motion before them still unseconded. Time spares, time reproaches them.

Which will it be: their perishable hides or the public good? A second is heard. The question is called for. The motion carries unanimously, as ever! In the morning, there being enough cash on hand to provide for anything barring a run, the State Bank of Thebes opened its doors as usual while the six of us drove to The Rapids, borrowed fifty thousand dollars temporarily from the Old Kent Savings and, still unnerved by our own daring, brought it back here in a valise. In a valise! To this day, no one who was not present here except you is aware that this wondrous thing came to pass. And what does the story signify? Sewell, simply this: that the topography of the human soul is as varied as that of the earth itself. This is but to platitudinize that you must try to see men whole, to judge them wholly, to take into account not only their low swamps and deserts but their steep sierras and arable lands as well. With mortals, as with cards, play the percentages; you may draw successfully to a straight of vice, but more frequently a full house of virtue will take the pot. Five of the six who sat here fifteen years ago, who tomorrow morning bow before your avenging staff, have sinned irrefutably. But have they not atoned for a Carlene Scripter in other ways and in full measure? They owe her much, I grant, not the least of which is the fallacy of youth recaptured —in decaying trees the sap may still run high! Yet now, for one sonnet by these ancient poetasters, for one ode to lost and perfect loveliness cracked out by these old urns, must they endure absolute denigration? Must a whole town stand with them in the stocks? Think what they have done for Thebes! If I could will but one law, it would direct that the statutory rape of our countryside in certain places cease, that certain small towns, for the sake of abundance and diversity in our national character, remain small, that in them time bide, and that in those villages so designated the best, the wisest stewards be appointed to watch over them. And how interesting the contrast, yet the similarity, between you and Peace Officer John Scripter, who, as I theorized earlier, was convinced that evil, when confronted by good, must inevitably be vanquished. While you, with a simplicity or obtuseness curiously tantamount to his, reach the opposite conclusion: that the good represented by these six men must, when challenged by you with a single evil instance, act the utter coward. Neither of course can be true. Where was I? I ramble. I am tired. I am afraid. I plead for myself, which I will not do.

—I didn't know all this. About the bank.

—We must know more than we see.

Oram Kropf's inertness, the unseasonal convention of his attire, remind Sewell of that quaint landmark on his lawn, the cutter rusting and archaic.

—Sewell, I should think I might inquire now, since this is doubtless the last time we shall talk. You have been in Thebes six brief weeks, your animosity, your vindictiveness at work among us like a plague. Why? Why did you come home?

—If you want to know the truth, maybe to get material for a book. I was fresh out of ideas.

The Editor's smile is fleeting; golden inlays gleam and are gone. —Are you serious?

—Yes. I'd done a war book and the Hollywood thing and a friend of mine said I should try the homecoming bit. You know, dig up the roots.

—But this is bearded, Sewell! And deliberately to reënact the stereotype—it is melodrama of the most blatant sort. Why, the theme has been done to death!

—Not by me. For an instant Sewell's jaw obtrudes with its former truculence. —You forget, you have a big enough name and anything sells. Hell, in the last four years I've made twice what he stole!

—Ah. How revealing. To outcompete your own chromosomes. Flesh and the checkbook. But suppose we assume you have won in every contest with him. Now you should seek a new experience.

—What?

—Begging your indulgence, I would like to defer that topic. Oram Kropf's hands, lapidary, never still, take up his white cane, extension of himself; with its curl he reaches, finds, puts pressure against Sewell's forearm. —Turnabout is fair play. I am going to be cruel. Sewell, you are not a writer.

—I said, downstairs, you didn't know the worst of me.

—Which is?

—My publisher's taken me off his list. I don't even have a publisher. Not only that, I'm broke and behind on taxes. I've spent everything. I came home because I had to scrounge another idea to get back in business. Then the Carlie deal opened up and I needed money.

—And we would not pay.

—No. I was boxed. But I thought of writing a book about Carlie and the rest of you, a real sex manual. Somebody'd be sure to merchandise it. I was going to double-cross you even if you paid. I've got over a hundred pages done, at the house.

—I surmised something like this. So did Charles Reason, who is very astute.

—You don't have to be sharp to recognize a bastard. And I am. God, I am.

The cane is removed. The Editor relaxes, muses. —I am grateful you told me. Do not be too hard on yourself. You are not entirely at fault. I watch the trends in publishing with keen interest. If you are not a writer, in the most meaningful sense of the term, who is today? Few there are. No, you are the product of an era in which a Gresham's Law of literature seems operative: bad writing drives out good. We are embarked upon a period, I gather, of printers who are not publishers, of novels which are not fiction, of merchandise which is not books, of rapid scanning which is not reading, and of scribblers who are neither literate nor cultured nor knowledgeable enough of their fellows to be more than entertainers —certainly not men of letters. Today's coefficient of success appears to be column inches of newsprint or television exposure, and your example is but one of the phenomena with which we shall have to cope. There is a curious inversion: you, the writer, do not create for the films, for the page, for the TV screen, for the stage; by these media you are created. And the tragedy is that the mass arts can provide someone like you with a name, with equipment, with a routine, with subjects, with an organization almost corporate—with everything, in short, except talent. Or take the contrary hocus-pocus, the man who succeeds by scarcely creating at all. That is to say, he publishes one fairish book, a short story or two, then pulls in his antennae and withdraws from the world. Before his refusal to lay his ability on the line again, the critics genuflect; on his silence they dote; now they are free to hypothecate, to cult up around his few, flickering candles, to transmogrify him into living legend. Who shall cry them wrong? If you cannot prove homicide without a corpse, you cannot disprove genius without a corpus of work. Well, it is a time of shoddy, of gaseosity bound in buckram. It is a time of writers who have much to say, but alas, only about themselves, and in the upshot they are not worth the listening to. There are exceptions, but the modern authoress seems to compose not in ink but in a sort of diaphragmatic jelly, while the male hack unzips his trousers and taps his automatic Scripto on the keys of an electric typewriter. Faugh! I become gross. And bitter. A shoemaker should give no opinion beyond the shoes, and my point is, if you are not a writer, do not write. But I am tired and afraid. I pity myself. I wonder who will read to me. I dread tomorrow. And not so much for myself as for the others. It will be bad enough for young Harris, but the rest—what the disgrace, the ignominy will do to them and to those they love, incarceration aside, is unspeakable. Charles Reason, our physician and student of morality; Bill Van, soon to retire and be freed once more into the green second boyhood of field and stream; Charles Baird, who saved his forebears' mill, who carries even now in his entrails a sentence more dire than a court may mete out; grand Harlan, our elder statesman, God bless him—oh, Sewell, these are good men, they must not be brought down tomorrow for a single frailty, a winter's misstep— "In Adam's fall we sinned all!" The great globe of skull turns, the visage is averted. —Pardon me, I had promised myself not to give way to emotion.

—Mr. Kropf, I want to help them! Sewell shoved his chair, forgetting in sympathy with the old man's grief his back, his own eyes closing as wood scarified his mid-section. —But they can't put it off and she won't drop the charges. I've tried everything—my God, what else can I do?

—I don't know myself, I don't know. But Sewell, there is always something. Let me think. Wait. There is another question I have wanted to put to you since you arrived. How shall I ask? It is very personal. I have brooded over your citation for the award of the Distinguished Service Cross in Italy. Fossa Feminamorta, the Ditch of Dead Women—how marvelously macabre an appellation. And your performance there—a deed intrepid by any definition, of the highest human magnitude. There you were, trapped with your squad in those battle sleds, all twelve faced with annihilation; you, Sewell, take the bit in your teeth—my language is not very military—you do the impossible, you turn defeat into victory. To ask if the salvation of your comrades impelled you to this act would be inane, but may I make some deduction of this kind?

—I never thought about it. I guess so.

—It must have been. Surely one can draw no suicidal inference. And when it was over, how did you feel?

—Somebody asked me, not long ago, if I'd ever done anything in my life I was proud of. I said yes, one thing.

—You had every right. You have it still. Now. Does it square? Fingers at the gray runes of hair across his head, Oram Kropf absorbs himself in lucubration. At a window, blandished by light, a moth with its wings prays entrance. The Directors' Room is unpretentious, its walls smoked, and the air is mellow with nostalgia, cured with an omnium-gatherum of buggy leather, normalcy, humble dividends declared, gobboon brass, fossil motions made and seconded, plug tobacco, the greenback epistemology of several generations of simple men in shirtsleeves. —It does, indeed it does, and it is brilliant and pertinent and exciting. It takes my breath away. Oram Kropf sits forward, speaks with his old sonority. —Sewell, there are some thoughts I have never put into words because I could not, a concept or two I have not yet framed. Let me try. I must try, for what I say may be the very pulse of our situation tonight. Now. Of all my curiosities, the one most

359

constant has been that about the absolutes. Courage, deity, love, death, power, cowardice, beauty, evil. These are the planets toward which man beams the impulse of his queries, hoping for, waiting till, signals, answers, rebound to him across the silences. Courage. I have long held the theory that to assign predominance to the instinct of self-preservation is to number men among the beasts; there must be something else, an x-factor, some other mainspring of action, or how explain gallantry in battle, how account for the innumerable small sainthoods of civilian life? No, there must be another thing in us, whatever our degree or estate, an urge sacrificial, stronger by far than any other, which from time to time strips us of self, armors us against a crippling world, drives us at last to lofty deeds, transforms us all, for minutes or for hours, into heroes. For lack of a better term, let us call it the instinct to magnificence. I believe it lies deep in us. I believe it is a lode the riches of which we have never exploited. I believe that in order to educe it, in order to use its glorious and incalculable potential, we must first achieve in ourselves that attunement of opposing tensions, we must then arrange in our daily life that conjoining of circumstances which will force upon us conduct in relation to other men equal in selflessness to that of those we honor in war. Do you follow me? What is required is that we discern or create in our affairs the conditions in which the instinct to magnificence must demonstrate itself. And Sewell, they are here, all about us! They were present on the night I have just described to you, that night of hinge events—to them must be ascribed the decision of those men who sat at this table—this room was their Fossa! They are here even now, fifteen years later, they cry out for the resolution of yet another human dilemma! What will the warrior do—for these are friends, not foes, and trapped as surely as were his comrades in actual arms? Do you understand me, Sewell? Do you understand me?

A solemn concourse of notes, eleven in sum, proceeds from a clock down the hall, intrudes upon them, passes. Above the white cane on the table Sewell's blunt paws suspend.

—It is a divining rod. Take it.

—I'm not sure. No, I don't understand, I don't have the mind. Mr. Kropf, all I can think about is tomorrow and the five of you and Harris and what I've started that I can't finish. And I want to finish it but I don't know how. I'd do anything, God I would, but what?

—Take it.

Sewell accedes, grasps the white cane as though from its marrow to wring strength, from its purpose to foreknow direction.

—One man may not tell another what he must do. Such things, Sewell, fall within the jurisdiction of the heart. I have little wisdom. I have come to only a few conclusions. Good cancels evil. Proof of the existence of God would disappoint rather than exalt me, for it would vitiate the drama of our lives. Man is a miracle. His miracle is that in spite of the delicate and ticklish equipoise between civilization and apehood he is yet able on occasion to will himself to noble measures. For this humanity we must forgive him all else. And because of it, we must have faith in him. I am incorrigibly optimistic of man's future, give or take a few eons: not only will he survive, I am convinced, but he will triumph. Unique, awesome antling, I believe him unconquerable, even by his own gods. Then, the hinge event. Once, when I was young, I heard a roué, rapscallion friend of my father, observe that you travel not to see the world but to find out who you are. I thought this profound; it was arrant nonsense, and a fraud, moreover, by which millions have been eternally deceived. Discovery of self is attained neither by movement nor introspection but by deed, sometimes by total offertory of self; it may be slow and accretive or instantaneous and radiant, ending in a moment of sublime truth. When all is done, though, what cuts the mustard is not who one may be but what. He pauses, his voice hushes. —So, Sewell, you have come home. Lines occur to me but I cannot attribute them. "To an open house in the evening/ Home shall men come/ To an older place than Eden/ And a taller town than Rome." You return to Thebes, perhaps unknown even to yourself, to find out who you are, to seek the anchorage for which all men yearn, and I, rather

361

than bidding you stay, must speed you onward. Yet I have a word which may ease your journey. Sewell— The ague of his lids begins, the passionate rejuvenation of nerve which, it seems, will bare the tombs of the eyes.

—Sewell, every man has three fathers. The one he must own, the one he might have preferred, and finally, most mysterious parent, the one who would have wished to be his sire. If L.V. was in fact your father, Johnny surely was in fancy. And the third? Sewell, having none of my own, I long ago adopted in my dreams a son. He had been sorely beset, he was alone, and I would do for him whatever was in my power, for he was dear to me. Sewell, my son, to you my house is open.

Tortured beyond enduring, Sewell dares not beg to have the bandages stripped from him, is as unwilling to entrust the task to blindness as he is to expose the raw flesh of his emotions to a sightlessness which is omniscient. —Mr. Kropf, I can't take much more, I can't take any more! bursts from him. Head lowered to the tabletop, he crushes his stubbled cheek against the fascis of the white cane. The trial of old familial hand upon his shoulder is like a vesturing.

—Sewell, Sewell, lost son. To greatness summoned once before, across the sea. Upon whom now I serve a final warrant.

In the house among the lightning-riven oaks, shatter-windowed, open to the night and to the rudimentary rain, he stands before his bivouac. He must leave. He must pack. He tugs at the corner of a suitcase protruding from a cairn of soiled clothing, stops.

He has no car. His car is downtown, disabled against a curb. Did he walk here, then, from the bank? There used to be a bus to Grand Rapids every morning. He cannot escape till morning.

He clears his throat, breaks into words and flat, atonal self-abuse: "Flee, big-assed bird, to your mountain/ Thou who art weary of sin/ Go to the clear-flowing—"

He joggles at steps on the front porch and a light, unhurried beating on the door. He steps warily to open it.

—Hey. It's me. Carlie.

—Carlie? My God.

—Hey, you gonna invite me in?

—You're supposed to be locked up.

She sidles past him. —For life? That's a hot one. I have been, for two weeks, and I've about gone nuts. What a drag. What am I, a bomb or something? Ethel's out with some kids getting crawlers and Lene left so I made it out a window. I didn't know where else to go. They roll up the sidewalks in this jerky town after dark. She glances about the entry hall, trying to be both casual and circumspect. —I've never been in this house. It's okay. She wears blue jeans, scuffed ballet slippers, and a boy's shirt with sleeves rolled to the elbows and tails tied round her waist in a large knot. She walks into the living room. —What a hole! It's as stinky as my room after two weeks. She kicks her way into the center of his encampment, toys disinterestedly with some of the accumulation on the table, strikes a typewriter key, then takes from her shirt pocket a cigarette and lights it. Opening her mouth to show a small bombburst of smoke, she inhales deeply with an ah-sound and the ball of smoke disappears down her throat.

—You're too young to smoke.

—Don't be square.

—And you have to go home.

—You got a radio, Sewell?

—No.

—How about a beer?

—For you?

—Don't have a hernia. Sure, it's always on ice and Ethel never keeps count. Hey, Sewell, what's the scoop? I mean about tomorrow. Are we rich?

—No.

—Too bad, how sad.

He scowls at her as, diminutive even for her fourteen years, she lounges, almost poses, on the rollaway, scattering petulant ash. Her face is still chubby with baby fat, her nose is pug, her mouth is a lollypop of purple, her teeth need braces, her eyes are jejune and close-set, her eyebrows have been tweezed into

363

cheap crescents, and her hair, dust-brown, is coarse and cut short. She is slovenly. She wants soap and water. She is ill-at-ease despite the insouciance of her sprawl, for between drags at the cigarette she puts stubby fingers to her mouth, not to suck but to bite at her nails with little clicks. She is not even precociously developed; her hips are scrawny and, rather than young breasts pouting at inattention, from her dampened shirt-front poke two tiny knobs fit only for turning. This is Carlene Scripter. She is not seductive, only available. He cannot believe that she should have debauched either man or boy, much less aroused them sufficiently to debauch her. And suddenly there skyrockets in him the hope that it has all been, this story of the Scripters, mother and daughter, a monstrous lavatory fable written in their own sulphuric and unlucky blood.

—Carlie, I want to hear it from you. Was what you told the Prosecutor in Tyre that day the God's truth, about you and those men?

—A brew and I'll tell you.

—No.

—Then shove. You want to hear the dirt you can produce.

—All right. Then you're going the hell home. And I don't have any cold.

When he brings the beer she tastes it as though rinsing her mouth. —Ugh. Hey, isn't it real mad, us being on the same team, sort of, all this time and never even talking to each other?

—Let's go.

—Okay, okay. Don't be so stuck up. And she begins the recital of her adventures, gay and slangy, a kind of "Carlie in Lewdland"; enjoying the spotlight she shocks her listener into the shadows beyond the periphery of his belongings by stringing together like flawed pearls a whole lexicography of four-letter words; she regales him with a compendium of spicy particulars: what the men had enticed her to, the noises they made during love's rickety old labors, how much money and what trinkets they had lavished upon their darling. She was explicit; the bestridings of senility amused her; she prided herself on her skill at getting the most out of her ancient steeds, slapping bald heads and spurring bare behinds to a gallop. Unwittingly she gave herself away. Like Tantalus they had moiled to assuage desire, but her indifference to sex, her whorishness, her essential frigidity must have denied them ever. And for a curtain line she described Oram Kropf's employment of a silver vacuum-pump device obtainable only from Paris which, when put into operation by her at the proper juncture, could effect erection in the elderly, otherwise impotent male. —A real little pump it was, no kidding, she laughs, with a little handle, and old Kropf, he'd call me his pretty fire girlie and say he was burning up and it was time to run out the pumper, don't spare the horses—

—That's enough! he lashes out. —God, it is true.

—Thanks! And don't be so nasty-nice. You like to hear about it. Men do, they've got dirty minds. Hey, you want to hear the dirtiest joke in the world? This kid says to his sister, you're a better piece than Mom, she says yeah, that's what Pop says.

—It's stopped raining.

—What a square you are. I want another beer.

—No.

She bounces upon a wadded pillow. —All right, you talk to me. Hey, Sewell, I know what, tell me about Hollywood and how you get in pictures. You have to screw to be a star, that's what I heard. She waits, then sits up in surprise to watch him as he wanders absently the far end of the room, chinking out of window frames the remaining shards of glass, singing in monotone to himself: "You're my little true lover/ You're my little boy blue/ But I'm your old Auntie, darling/ And I cannot marry you."

She giggles. —What a cornball song. That'll never make the top ten.

—Carlie, they're going to plead guilty in the morning, all of them. They'll go to prison. Do you want to see them in prison, those old men?

—Too bad, how sad.

—You're a pig, aren't you, a baby pig? he cries furiously. —And someday you'll be a real grown-up pig!

—Sticks and stones. I want a beer.

—All right, goddammit, I'll give you one, then you're going
to do me a favor. He bangs about in the kitchen, returns with
a bottle and plows through a midden of laundry and suitcases
to hand it to her. —There. Now here's what I want you to do.
You're just a kid and you don't know the score. Tomorrow,
when you testify, I want you to swear it was all a lie, no matter
what your mother says, tell the J.P. nobody laid a hand on
you.

—I hate warm beer.

A breeze glides through the room, eddying papers from the
table to the floor.

—Did you hear me?

—Pardon my burp. Yes, I heard you and you must be mad,
mad. I won't do it.

—You have to.

Drinking, she gurgles a laugh. —No, because I cannot tell
a lie, ha-ha. So palpable is his menace that she rushes into
explanation, biting her nails. —Now don't have a hernia.
Sewell, you should of seen me over at Tyre that day, in a
white dress, a real Sunday School angel, and cryin' and all,
did I ever put on a terrific act! Well, I wanna get out of this
draggy, one-horse, stupid town. I really wanna be an actress,
that's my ambition. And I was thinkin', this time, with a real
trial, there'll be reporters and pictures of me and everything
and what a chance to be in the papers! Get the message?

—Sorry. In a case like this they keep the girl's name out of
it. No pictures, nothing.

—They do? Damn. She sulks, empties the bottle. —Hey,
warm beer's not bad.

—All right, that's settled. Then will you do what I ask,
Carlie? Say you lied before?

—Won't.

—My God, what's there to lose?

She gnaws the purple of her underlip; she is sorry for herself. —Shit on everybody.

Bending over her he takes her hands in his. —Carlie, I
want you to understand, it's so important you understand.
None of this is your fault, I see that. You're what you are,

366

and the way you've been brought up you can't help it. But tomorrow is not going to happen, we mustn't let it, these men haven't done anything bad enough to deserve going to prison. They're old and tired and they've done too much for Thebes to pay through the nose for one mistake. I'll do anything to keep the exam from being held tomorrow, anything.

Her smile is arch, muzzy. —Tell me more, daddy-o, I like it.

—Carlie, I've got an idea. How about if we go away together, right now, just pull out and go to some state where a girl your age can get married, and we get married? How'd you like that? In Arkansas, I think you can. Mrs. Sewell Smith, the famous writer's wife. Then you wouldn't have to testify tomorrow and you really would get your picture in the papers.

—Sew'lie, this is so sudden! She sways up, slithers an arm about him. —You're a doll, she breathes, you really are. Hey, what's on your back?

He recoils at her touch. —Don't. That's tape, it's blistered underneath. It's been on too long.

—Blistered? Want me to take it off?

—No.

But she is solicitous, claiming to be expert at peeling sunburn and pinching blackheads and stuff like that. —So how about it? Let me, huh, let me?

—It should come off. But if you're not careful you could damn near kill me.

She promises to be, it will be like a game, she the nurse, he the patient, and Sewell, weakening at the prospect of relief, allows her to position him at the nearest wall, against which he leans with both hands while she removes his shirt. The swollen web of bandage makes her gasp. —Gee. What kicks! Here we go! And before he can prevent her, she takes an edge of tape and with a cheer of eighth-grade glee rips it from one hump-hip to another. He yells. Pain paralyzes him. He sags against the wall as though flogged, arms outstretched, incapable of stopping her, aware only, through a film of sensation, of her excitement, of her sadism as she tears loose a second adhesive swath. This punctures the massive blisters

367

which have for days grown and festered beneath. Pus spurts. She unbuckles his trousers, pulls them down, and his shorts, and squealing her pleasure strips the third, fourth, and last bands free. Balling his shirt she swabs roughly at the raw meat of his back, drying the terrible lesions. What she has accomplished, reducing malehood to impotence, mastering another human being her senior and superior, in some perverted way elates and kindles her. She rids herself of blue jeans and panties, reaches between his legs, grasps him. —Gee, that was terrific, wow! An' look what I found! she exclaims, copycatting passion. —Root of all evil! Hey, Sew'lie, we can't get married but we can sure ditty-boo, can't we? C'mon, Carlie's been outa circulation two weeks an' needs a good fucking —c'mon daddy-o, you wanna fuck your lil' girl? A dumb animal tricked, tortured, stricken, convulsively he moves his head from side to side. —What a party-pooper. Hell with you, then. She leaves him in disgust and after a time, wearing only her shirt, brings another beer from the kitchen and lights a cigarette. —How you doin', Sew'lie?

He is seated on the floor. Unguent to his lacerated skin, a wind gusts through the room.

—Put on your clothes.

—Won't.

—You said. Why can't we get married?

—'Cause you're too ol'. She giggles, salutes his years with the bottle. —An' too ugly. An' too broke. An' don' tell me you're not. I heard Morse 'n Ethel talkin' one day an' they figured you mus' be broke or you wouldn' try so hard to shake down my dear ol' daddy-os. Right?

—Why can't we?

She frowns. —Don't be a dope. Making her ah-sound she swallows a ball of smoke. —You haven' heard the lates' hit 'n the top ten? She does a crude dance, vocalizing and grinding her hips. "You're my lil' true lover/ You're my lil' boy blue/ But I'm your lil' sis Carlie/ So I can' marry you." She climaxes with a pelvic bump. —Hey, how's that? Have I got talen'? She stares into his stare. —What's your problem? Didn' you dig me? Okay, here's a po-em. "A lil' inces' now 'n then is cherish' by the wises' men." Her crescent eyebrows wrinkle. —An' you're too damn stupid! Don' you know brother 'n sister can' get married?

He rises, rolling back and forth on thick thighs and calves. He understands. Sweat beads his bulging forehead, glistens about the imploded eyes. His jaw hinges in and out.

—Didn't know. And you'd have let me. You'd have done it. Worse than I am, you are. Sick baby pig.

He takes one lunging, ursiform step toward her, his foot plunges through the top of a cardboard box and he collapses on all fours in a crash and tumble of tin cans and clothing and bottles.

—Who's a pig? Carlie snorts. —Don't be so shook up. We're jus' half, so what's the dif? Ethel got real stoned once an' tol' me. I guess after Johnny got shot she an' your ol' man screwed up a real storm an' after he died he left 'er a lil' souv'nir—me. You mean you never knew before? Nobody tol' you? Hey, where you goin'?

He has crawled away from her, crawled ᴖ hands and knees through his own offal out of sight.

She sniffs. —Okay, pig, go eat garbage. Be stuck up with your own half-sister. She stretches out on the rollaway, a tipsy, dimestore odalisque. —Also you're too beat up for me. What's matter 'th your back?

—Carlie. He speaks quietly, traumatically, from the far end of the room.

—Hey, big-shot writer 'n hero 'n brother, tell me 'bout Hol-wood.

—Carlie, would you like to go to the Coast and have a screen test?

She clicks suspiciously at a fingernail. —You could get me one? How?

—Connections.

—Oh. Musing, she picks her nose. —When'd we start?

—Tonight.

—An' you'd get free ditty-boo from me all the way, I s'pose.

—No.

—A real screen tes'?

—Real.

—What's in it for you, broth?

—You wouldn't testify tomorrow. You wouldn't be here.

—Oh, 'Sthat all? She butts her cigarette on the top of his typewriter. —Okay, it's a deal. We'll have kicks! She wriggles ecstatically. —Hey, Sew'lie, clue me on what it's like out there!

—In a minute. First I have to do some things. I'll bring you another beer. In a moment he appears, smiling, covers her nakedness with a sheet and puts the bottle to her mouth as he might to that of an infant. —There. You be a good girl and I'll be right back.

From the table he gathers up a pile of manuscript weighted by the blue box containing his D.S.C. and carrying it with him into the kitchen locates a bottle of whiskey in a cupboard. This he uncaps but from it does not drink. As he moves through the dining room and entry hall he sings quite loudly another song, martial and tuneless: "And while the glorious battle raged/ It lightened freedom's will/ For, boy, the God of freedom bless'd/ The Sword of Bunker Hill."

Carlie laughs. —Where'd you latch on t' those cornball songs?

—From my mother.

He climbs the stairs, turns on a hall fixture, and going to a back bedroom spreads the manuscript page by page on the floor to make a white trail leading from one room into another. There are enough sheets to take him into all rooms and down the full length of the hall. Then, retracing the path, with exaggerated care he lets whiskey splash upon each page. In one bedroom he pauses long enough to raise a window, put out his head and whistle shrilly in the direction of the snowball bushes under which the spaniel of his boyhood is buried. —Here, Powder, you little bastard! When the spoor of manuscript has been soaked to its end he returns a second time to its beginning, strikes a folder match and drops it upon his title page. Hurrying now, he descends to the living room, en-

370

ters his stronghold, eases the bottle from the girl's fingers, and lying down upon the sheet beside her pillows her head gently on his arm. She is quite drunk. She smiles blissfully. —We almost did one hell of an awful thing, Carlie. You should have told me about us sooner. It's good to find out I have a family, though, even a half-sister. Somebody to talk to, you know. You couldn't remember Johnny because he was killed before you were born, but he was swell to talk to. He told great stories. I promised to tell you about the Coast, didn't I? Well, Los Angeles is the biggest, craziest city you've ever seen, spread out all over hell's half-acre, and so are the movie studios, MGM down in Culver City, which is part of L.A., Warner's way up in Burbank, another part. Oram Kropf talked to me tonight. Most of what he said I didn't understand, but some of it I did. Columbia is sort of in the center, in what you'd call Hollywood, where the TV and radio studios are and the Sunset Strip and the corner of Hollywood and Vine. You couldn't remember our father, either, of course. I do. You know what I remember best about him? The way we used to burn the leaves together every fall. Everybody did it the same night. The boys would rake them up in big piles after school and that night after supper the fathers and sons would burn them. It was really something, really beautiful. You were right, Carlie. I am too old and ugly and beat up. I'm also too goddam dumb. That's why I'm not a very hot writer even though I've made a lot of money. When I was a boy, all I wanted was to be somebody important and respected right here in Thebes, and never go away. I'd rather have been that, even, than what I have been. The truth about me is, I'm not a writer at all, and I'm not going to pretend I am from now on. Her eyes beer-glazed, she yawns a protest. —Oh, about the Coast, sure. Well, the best part of L.A., I think, is the Hollywood Hills just above Sunset Boulevard. They're bare and cut up with canyons and golden in the sunshine and the houses are built right out over the canyons. They just seem to hang in the air. A lot of film people live there. I had a house there once. Carlie, you're going to be in the papers after all. Most people in Thebes won't understand tomorrow what we did, they'll think we deserved what happened, but a few will and they'll be grateful and that's how they'll remember us. I suppose you never read my books. The first one was called *A Benison on Our Meat,* which was out of a poem. "Here a little child I stand," is the way it starts. Well, that's how I feel now, like a little kid, as young as you. "Heaving up my either hand." That's to pray, to say grace. "Cold as paddocks though they be—" Paddocks are frogs or toads and you know how cold they are. "Here I lift them up to Thee." God. "For a benison to fall on our meat and on us all." Benison means blessing. Sewell hears a roaring in the night, a vast ah-sound which is not the wind. He turns the girl to him, binding her childish body in his arms to make them one, compassing her as though they shared a tube of steel. He whispers tenderly. —You poor, homely, sick little girl. Born without anything, really, and trying to be somebody the best way you could, any way, like me. That's what we're going to do tonight, Carlie, bless a lot of people. I don't know you and you don't know me, really, but the two of us are taking off and there can't be any examination tomorrow, not without you. Urine and the infinite. That's one of Oram Kropf's sayings. It's a long, long way to the Coast. The way up and the way down are the same. I don't know how else to do it. You're almost asleep now, aren't you? In a few minutes, though, you'll be awake and frightened, but I'll be with you and you must not think of what's happening but of how you and I are making up for everything we've done. Please don't fight it too hard. I can hold you, but I want you to accept it, and yourself, as I will. The most beautiful sight out there is looking out from the Hollywood Hills at night over all of Los Angeles, with millions of colored lights sparkling. Out there they call it "The Jewelbox." If you're somebody, you nearly believe it all belongs to you. And you will be somebody soon, I promise. You'll be a star. Carlie, this is a fine little town, though, Thebes.

ABOUT THE AUTHOR

GLENDON SWARTHOUT was born in Pinckney, Michigan, and is a graduate both of the University of Michigan and Michigan State University. During the war he served with the infantry in Europe. His novel, *They Came to Cordura,* a tragedy, was filmed by Columbia Pictures and featured the late Gary Cooper in his last outdoor role; *Where the Boys Are,* a comedy produced by Metro-Goldwyn-Maycr, may have been in part responsible for the recent, well-publicized rites of spring-vacationing college students in Fort Lauderdale, Florida. With *Welcome to Thebes* he essays not only a third style but a third genre, that of the modern melodrama.

Mr. Swarthout, his wife and son live in Scottsdale, Arizona.